DESTRUCTION OF CHAOS

THE BOOKS OF THE CUARI
BOOK 3

MARIE ANDREAS

Other Books by Marie Andreas

THE LOST ANCIENTS
Book One: The Glass Gargoyle
Book Two: The Obsidian Chimera
Book Three: The Emerald Dragon
Book Four: The Sapphire Manticore
Book Five: The Golden Basilisk
Book Six: The Diamond Sphinx

THE LOST ANCIENTS: DRAGON'S BLOOD
Book One: The Seeker's Chest
Book Two: The Finder's Crown
Book Three: The Hunter's Chalice

THE ASARLAÍ WARS TRILOGY
Book One: Warrior Wench
Book Two: Victorious Dead
Book Three: Defiant Ruin

THE CODE OF THE KEEPER
Book One: Traitor's Folly
Book Two: Destroyer's Curse

THE ADVENTURES OF SMITH AND JONES
A Curious Invasion
The Mayhem of Mermaids
An Intrigue of Pharaohs

BROKEN VEIL
Book One: The Girl with the Iron Wing
Book Two: An Uncommon Truth of Dying
Book Three: Through a Veil Darkly

BOOKS OF THE CUARI
Book One: Essence of Chaos
Book Two: Division of Chaos
Book Three: Destruction of Chaos

**MAGIC AND SORCERY
CHRONICLES TRILOGY**
A Touch of Magic
A Slice of Sorcery
A Dash of Devilry

ACKNOWLEDGMENTS

Writing is easy—take a bunch of weird ideas and mush them together. And then lie about how easy it is. Writing is hard, I love it, but it's hard. It would be impossible without a lot of other folks.

I'd like to thank everyone who has ever supported me, read chapters, edited, let me cry on their shoulder, read my books, given nice reviews, and/or bought me soothing beverages. I could never have done this without ALL of you. I can't list you all here, but you mean the world to me.

My awesome round of editors/beta/proofreaders: Lisa Andreas, Patti Huber, Lynne Mayfield, and Laura Schilling. Any errors or mistakes that remain are completely mine.

And to the two extremely talented artists of Joolz & Jarling (Julie Nicholls and Uwe Jarling) thank you for a gorgeous cover!

Thank you to The Killion Group for interior print formatting.

To all my readers—thank you for coming along for the ride!

CHAPTER ONE

———

JENNA SWORE AS THE CARRIAGE they'd bought—the third one since they left Strann—shuddered as its left front wheel wobbled dramatically.

Their prior carriage lost its right wheel after a few days. This one only lasted a day.

"And again, why is it that we need a carriage instead of riding our horses? They were fine for the way in." Jenna would be the first to admit the carriage was less jarring than hours and days of being in the saddle, but this way was slower. Even without constantly stopping for repairs or replacements.

She knew that Storm, Keanin, and Edgar would probably make it to Irundail before them, regardless. Unless there was more fighting in the north than they'd heard or problems at sea. But she still wanted to rejoin them as soon as possible.

Lithunane had fallen.

That news was unbelievable and terrifying.

Someone murdered Prince Resstlin before he was crowned as king. More of the royal family weren't killed in the attack because they weren't present when Lithunane fell. Most remained in Irundail in the north.

Last week, she'd been happy for stopping Ravenhearst and slowing down Qhazborh's followers, but that joy was short-lived as they received news of Lithunane's fall.

Information on the fall had been sporadic since then. Even with taran wands, few details were known. It could take weeks for those fleeing Lithunane to get to the safety of Irundail to the far north of the country. As far as they knew, Rachael and Tor Ranshal were traveling with Armsmaster Garlan and as many of the guards as they could gather.

Most of the guards and citizens were slaughtered before they knew the capital was under attack.

Garlan and Rachael each had a taran wand, but there was some magical interference limiting their usage. A few days ago, Rachael said she thought it was getting better the further they got from the remains of Lithunane, but they hadn't been able to reach her or Garlan since then.

Storm, Keanin, Edgar, and their new traveling companions were at sea—something that interfered with the taran wands as well. The last update they received was that all of them were alive and on their way to Irundail but no one had heard from them in a few days.

Jenna was contemplating freeing her horse from the ones following the carriage and racing directly for Irundail alone.

"Because there could be people looking for us." Ghortin had a hood pulled low over his head as he drove and stayed hunched over like an old man. At over three thousand years old, he was old—but it wasn't noticeable normally. This was his attempt at a disguise.

Carabella snorted from her seat in the back. "We could outrun them. You and Jenna can still use magic. Crell is extremely talented at firing arrows from horseback. This *thing* is slowing us." She flexed her long, delicate fingers toward her son, Ghortin.

Carabella was a full cuari, one of a mystical band of one hundred immortals charged with protecting the other races.

At the moment, she was the only one of the hundred still on this plane. The enemy had captured the other ninety-nine to hinder the defenses of this world. They'd been imprisoned while using magic, and so Carabella, one of the most magically powerful beings in the world—couldn't cast even the simplest of spells without the risk that she would be taken as well.

Jenna didn't blame her for being annoyed. Not only was Jenna concerned about saving this new home world of hers, but she'd been told that failing to save *this* world would doom others. Including good old Earth and her former home of Los Angeles. Jenna was offered a chance to go back to L.A., but too much of her heart was here now. For good or ill, this was now her home. But she didn't want Earth to be destroyed either.

The carriage continued to wobble and then lurched to a stop and tilted to the side. The wheel was broken.

"This isn't working," Crell said. She was riding as guard alongside the carriage, but stopped and glared at the broken wheel. Crell was a derawri. Like most of her people, she was less than four feet high but fierce. She had long deep red hair and a sweet face. Unless she was facing you with a weapon—then sweet was probably the last word anyone would use. She'd been a family protector for the kelar royal family of Traanafaeren for years as the children grew up. She had also most likely trained many of the guards who were killed in Lithunane.

Jenna was surprised Crell hadn't raced off to Irundail already.

"I think you're outvoted. Let's abandon this thing and continue on horseback. We can keep the extra horse to carry our packs." Carabella was already getting out of the carriage when the first arrow struck the side of it.

"Stand down, Strann scum! You'll die here or go back to where you came from."

Crell spun and fired an arrow back. "We're not from Strann and watch who you insult."

Jenna hadn't heard a scream at Crell's arrow. Most likely it, like the one that hit the carriage, was a warning shot.

"Crell?" A dark-clad kelar stepped out of the trees. His

clothing was the mottled combination of greens and browns that Crell's rangers wore to stay hidden in the woods.

"Filian! Damn man, you are a sight for sore eyes." Crell swung off her horse and clasped the man's arm. "How'd you get up here so fast? Who's with you?"

Like many full-blooded kelar, he was tall, slender, and had sharply pointed ears, and wide-set tilted eyes. But that height difference didn't interfere with Crell at all.

Two groups of fighters answered to Crell—her rangers were people she selected from all three races. They traveled Traanafaeren protecting people in a less formal way than the soldiers and guards. The second group was from her family ties in the kingdom of Derawri. She held the status of Ki', a powerful commander. She could control a group of deathsworn; hardened derawri warriors who would fight until death.

She preferred her rangers. When she'd left Lithunane a few weeks ago to travel with Jenna, Ghortin, and Carabella, she'd sent her deathsworn back to Derawri. The rangers she'd asked to stay and protect Lithunane.

Ten more brown and green-clad people—three kelar, five humans, and two derawri came out of the trees. All looked to be in rough shape but were able to walk.

"We were spelled here. Well, not here exactly, but a few days' run south of here." Filian shook his head but noticeably didn't put away his bow. "The palace mages were trying to get as many people out of Lithunane as possible when the attack came—whether or not we wanted it." His scowl indicated they hadn't chosen to be magicked anywhere. "Somehow we got caught up in a spell and ended up here."

Crell sighed. "I note there aren't any of our mages with you. Good intentions by those magic users or not, it would have been better had you been able to escort some of the refugees." She nodded to the rest of the rangers.

"But it is good to see you. Why were you heading toward Strann?"

"That was my idea, sorry, Crell." A derawri woman stepped forward. Her dark hair was cut short, and she had a long scar on the side of her face. Her smile discounted her words. "I knew where you were heading and thought you might need help. Since we were stuck up here, anyway."

"You're a troublemaker, Sorcha." Crell clasped the woman's arm fondly. "Might have been a good idea, but we're on our way to Irundail. After we dump this carriage." She shot a glare toward Ghortin.

Jenna glared also. Ghortin might have been considering abandoning his carriage and his disguise that went with it before this, but anything new could change that.

But he held up his hands in surrender. "We'll dump it." He nodded to the rangers. "We might need some help to get it off the road. Make it look like an accident, too."

"Don't embellish. You always make lies too detailed." Carabella climbed out of the carriage and nodded to the rangers. "Nice of you to come to help us out. No horses?"

Sorcha shrugged. "We weren't given the option to get them. But have no fear, we can keep up. And it's not as if we don't know where you're going."

The brawniest of the rangers moved the offending carriage into the woods, ignoring Ghortin as he made it look like an accident.

Jenna adjusted her pack on her horse as Ghortin continued fussing. "I seriously doubt anyone is going to even see it, let alone figure out it was us, after two other carriage changes."

"A job worth doing is worth doing right." Ghortin dusted himself off, gathered his things, and mounted his horse.

"It wasn't worth doing." Carabella had Ghortin disguise her ears and eyes to look more human and less cuari when they'd approached the human kingdom of Strann. She tugged the fabric that covered the tips of her ears. "Do I look correct? Are your spells still holding?"

Normal cuari pupils were slitted, like a cat's. Carabella's dark green eyes currently looked extremely human.

"You look perfectly human," Jenna responded when Ghortin didn't.

Ghortin shrugged.

"Thank you, my dear." Carabella gave a haughty sniff and continued down the trail.

Crell quickly mounted her horse to follow, with Jenna not far behind. They gave the carriage horse to a ranger who'd twisted his ankle when they'd been magically flung to the north.

He'd fought against riding until Crell gave him a narrow-eyed glare.

Ghortin motioned for the injured ranger and his horse to go before him. The rest of the rangers jogged along the trail.

"Now, isn't this much better?" Carabella held up her hands to point out how lovely things were. And that no horse would dare to need guidance from her.

Crell spoke in low tones to Filian and Sorcha, frowning at the things they told her. These were the first eyewitness accounts of what had happened in Lithunane. Taran wand communication had become so sporadic that details were impossible to get.

The rest of the rangers jogged along the edges of the road, sending off single runners from time to time to scout.

Jenna opened her mouth to tell them that no one had approached them, or even been seen on this road, for the entire week. Then shook her head and shut her mouth. Crell wouldn't have accepted that, and neither would her people. They needed the searches for peace of mind if nothing else.

"Excuse me for being so bold, but you're Prince Corin's fiancée, yes?" The older derawri woman running nearest to her asked politely. In some strange way, she reminded Jenna of Rachael. If Rachael hadn't been a kelar.

"Not really. Let me guess, you saw the farewell outside the palace?" She smiled in case any of her lingering annoyance at the stunt Storm pulled hung to her words.

When Storm, Keanin, and Edgar left Lithunane over a month ago, he'd implied that they were engaged. He didn't want her out on the road in such troubling times and rightly guessed that his brother Resstlin wouldn't let a royal fiancée go anywhere.

"I did, actually we all did. They stationed our group right outside the palace. How do you 'not really' become engaged?"

Jenna briefly filled her in on the important parts. No reason for the entire story.

"That sounds like him. Crell used to tell us stories of the wild prince when he was growing up."

"Crell had her rangers that long?"

"I was one of her deathsworn. The first ranger, so to speak. My name is Calle, by the way."

Jenna nodded. "I'm Jenna, which I'm sure you already know." She laughed. "It's nice to meet you."

"It's nice to meet you as well."

"Attack!" The rangers who'd been scouting in the forest raced back as arrows flew around them.

CHAPTER TWO

—◆—

STORM SWORE AS THEIR SHIP finally moved forward to dock. The town of Erlinda was swarming with activity, but little of it pertained to getting ships into dock. Mostly it was simply people panicking and running about.

News of the death of Prince Resstlin, and of the fall of Lithunane, had spread quickly. Erlinda was part of Traanafaeren at the extreme northern end. If an attack came from outside, they would be one of the next to fall. And the citizens of the town knew it.

Considering what he and his companions had faced in Craelyn, he didn't blame them.

Talia yelled to the few dock hands still working and helped them secure the lines to their ship. Her brother, Diath, watched with a grin. He was still injured, there hadn't been a way to heal him on the open sea. But he looked grateful to be alive. And amused at his guard captain sister handling his ship.

Few people faced a demonspawn and lived to talk about it. Let alone facing two. Diath hadn't said much about his fight and spent most of the week's sea travel resting.

Under Talia's orders.

The trip from Craelyn to Erlinda normally took a few days. But they'd barely escaped the town and hadn't used regular sea channels to do so. Not to mention, not knowing who or what might be after them meant going far from the coast and taking a longer route down.

Keanin tried to push them harder, using his own depleted magics to fill the sails when he could. There was a ship with demonspawn ahead of them. Those on board included odd creations that had tapped into Keanin's genetic and magical self and found a way to reproduce demonspawn hybrids. They needed to be destroyed before they gave birth to the abominations they carried.

His focus changed when they got the notification from Garlan that Lithunane had fallen. Keanin was raised with the royal family, and while he wasn't any fonder of Resstlin than Storm was, his loss, and that of so many others in the palace, hit him hard.

He stopped pushing the sails after the second day unless asked.

He'd mostly recovered from massively overusing his magic in Craelyn, but Storm was concerned at the way Edgar, also a magic user, watched him carefully. Even now, while they were all on deck and mundanely securing the ship.

Storm shook his head. That was another item on a growing list of things that would have to wait until they got to Irundail. He turned to Talia. "You all might want to ride with us to Irundail. I don't know how long it will take King Philia of Khelaran to recover his strength, nor how many of his soldiers he lost. He might not have much control over the traitors still in his midst. If our enemies come down from there, this town will be a primary target."

"I need to stay and defend Erlinda." Talia looked more like a city guard than a pirate now—her more recent look. "But I think Diath, Hon, and Flini should go with you. You need to get to the new capital." She knew who Storm and his friends really were.

"I'm not leaving you. Or this town." Diath shook his head and turned to Storm. "Thank you for helping to rescue me, but I'll defend this place."

Talia narrowed her eyes and crossed her arms. "You're injured."

"Not having this argument." Diath walked down the plank empty-handed. Any of his belongings were long gone.

Hon and Flini shrugged.

"Sorry, but we're staying too. The guards can't be the only ones defending this place." Hon tipped his head to Storm, Keanin, and Edgar, and followed his friends to the dock.

"I would stay to help you." Keanin's beautiful golden eyes appeared conflicted. He'd fallen hard for Talia, but Storm was like a brother to him. Not to mention the rest of the royal family.

The tall blonde woman smiled and took his arms. "I believe you would. But while we will have our own battles here, the larger ones will come to Irundail. It is a powerful refuge, or so I've heard, but nothing is unbreakable. When it falls, they'll need you." She looked up at Storm and Edgar. "All of you."

Storm lifted his pack as the rest of them left the ship. "I also wish we could stay. But you're right about the threat. Lithunane was never as secure as Irundail, but it had impressive hidden defenses. That it fell so suddenly is terrifying."

Edgar watched the dock—and the ships leaving. "They don't care where they're going. I thought the ships heading south could only leave at night." Long-lost magic users had changed the coast along Erlinda in the distant past. Getting in and out was difficult except during specific times.

Judging by the ships leaving, they were willing to take their chances as long as it got them away from Erlinda.

"None of them are going north. Why would they think Khelaran would be a threat?" Keanin joined his friends watching the surrounding ships. "There wasn't any proof of who led the attack against Lithunane, was there? No one here would know what happened in Craelyn, right?"

Keanin and Edgar had cleared out a group of demon-spawn poised to take over the Khelaran capital. Or rather, exposed them for what they were, which made them weaker and easier to kill.

Craelyn had gone through hard times long ago—hence the controlled waterway access—and also a nearly impassable land access along the coast. Had anyone come down from Craelyn with news of an attack within the past week, they would have faced the same issues Storm and his companions did.

"That's a good question." Talia nodded to the two guards as they left the dock. "But feelings about Khelaran have always been tense here. Many felt there should have been a stronger presence from Lithunane here in the north. Irundail is only a few days' ride, but we never see people coming from there to check on any of us along the northern coast."

Storm nodded. "I don't disagree. And right now, I truly wish that there had been a royal presence here. We'll still need to travel incognito, thank you for keeping our secrets. I'd like to get out of town before night falls. Edgar? Can you get us horses? Cost is no limit. I'd hoped to be in Irundail days ago, but let's get there as quickly as possible."

Edgar nodded and shook hands with Talia, Diath, Hon, and Flini. Then he vanished into the crowd.

"I'd like to speak to Talia alone?" Keanin gave her a serious look.

"Come this way. We can secure food for your travels. Even a few days of travel are better with something in your stomach." Talia led him down toward the food vendors and the crowds swarming around them.

Storm nodded to the remaining three. "Guard each other well, and if the chance arises, come to Irundail.

Mention my name and give the guards this coin. They'll escort you all to me." He handed them what looked like a normal coin, but it flashed even though there was no sun hitting it.

"I finally meet royalty and it's not a beautiful princess." Diath laughed, took the coin, and shook Storm's hand. "But thank you for helping rescue me."

"I'm glad we got to you in time." Storm put his eye-patch back on. Thanks to the type of dye Edgar had used on his face, he still had the facial markings of a Crailian sell-sword. Might as well take advantage of the disguise. It was more important than before that no one knew Prince Corin was roaming the countryside.

"Just remember, if things get bad, get your sister and your friends, and all of you come to Irundail." Storm shook his head. If he could, he'd bring this entire town to Irundail. But they didn't have time to convince them all to leave. Ships were fleeing, but more came in with supplies. The ones staying were settling in for a siege. "I'll have Prince Res—Justlantin send over troops to help support your efforts." That slip hurt. Storm and his brother Resstlin, late heir to the throne, had never been close. But it was still hard to think of him as gone. Especially so soon after losing their father.

Diath clasped Storm's shoulder. "Thank you." He nodded behind Storm, where Edgar came up with six horses loaded with expensive looking full tack. "Your friend is exceedingly quick."

"There looks to be only three of us." Storm raised an eyebrow toward the extra horses.

Edgar shrugged. "Aye, but the one selling these wanted to sell them all together. So, I figured, since coin was no object, might as well." His grin lit his dark face. "Not to mention that we can rotate the horses as we ride. You're not the only one who wants to get to Irundail quickly." His smile vanished.

Anyone who'd lived in the palace in Lithunane had lost people in the slaughter. No one knew how many friends they'd lost as communications, even with the taran wands, were jumbled.

"I'm an idiot." Edgar shook his head and handed the cord with the line of horses to Storm.

"It wasn't a bad idea." Storm continued focusing on the surrounding crowds.

"No, we need to find a place to reach out to our friends with the wands. Or at least try. I don't think all the communication disturbance we hit was just from the ocean."

Hon and Flini said their goodbyes and vanished into the crowd.

Diath watched Edgar, then nodded. "Your tricky stick thing. I can find an alley that shouldn't be occupied. And will allow for your herd." He laughed as he walked past Edgar's horses.

Edgar held the taran wand but kept it out of sight as he, Storm, and their horses followed Diath.

Edgar knew horses and he'd done well. All six were in excellent shape and followed without question. Storm kept an eye out for Keanin as they walked.

He knew his friend was having a seriously difficult time leaving Talia, but she was a guardswoman and took her duty seriously. Keanin had duties as well, some he didn't even know about. The issue of him being a missing Khelaran royal was something best dealt with when they were safe.

And when they had a place to lock Keanin up if he tried to run when he was informed of it. Keanin's parents were killed in the Markare when he was a baby—they were scientists investigating the area around the closed portal. Keanin was the only survivor.

While he'd been raised by the royal family of Traana-faeren, he might not be happy to find out he had a connection to the Khelaran royals. And that his parents hadn't been who he'd been told they were.

The alley was as Diath said, and he moved to the far end to give Edgar and Storm privacy. Everyone on the ship knew of the taran wand, but as it didn't work on the water well, they hadn't seen it work often.

"I wish we'd been able to give one to my mother. Or someone else in Irundail," Storm said. "I don't know that anyone from Lithunane has made it there yet." The ride between the two cities was normally a few weeks. A single rider with spare horses could make it in a week, but they would be hard-pressed to do so.

Hopefully, some of the far-speaking mages living in Lithunane survived the attack and got the word to the Queen and the rest of the royals in Irundail.

"True and true. Shall I try Ghortin first?" Edgar's smile said he knew what Storm was suppressing since they fled to the ocean.

The woman he loved, Jenna, was somewhere outside of Strann. They'd found out that she and the others survived, escaped, and had the third cuari book they'd needed, but no further communication could be made.

"Yes. Please." He didn't hold out his hand, but it was twitching.

Edgar grinned and called Ghortin on the wand.

CHAPTER THREE

"ATTACK!" ANOTHER RANGER YELLED AS he came running back from the other direction. There were a lot of arrows, but so far, the hits were minimal.

Jenna looked over and saw Ghortin grimacing in pain. An arrow struck him in the thigh, but the pain appeared to be coming from holding up the spell shield he was supporting over everyone—or as many as he could reach.

"Crell, grab him. He's going to fall. Carabella, don't even think of reaching for magic," Jenna yelled as she reached into the chaotic realm and pulled enough Power to support Ghortin's spell.

A few arrows were still getting through, and she fought to protect them all. Two rangers further out were down, but she couldn't see how badly injured they were.

Fear, anger, and frustration from the past few weeks fueled her spell and she not only tightened the shield, but she magically returned the arrows to their senders. The rangers stepped out from under the shield to fire as well, then quickly returned inside.

Jenna hadn't done a spell like that before, but hopefully, the screams she heard were the bad people getting shot with their own weapons. She'd sort out exactly how she did it when they were safe in Irundail. Right now, she didn't want to think about it.

Crell and Carabella pulled Ghortin closer to the center of everyone when his injured leg buckled.

Within a few moments, the arrows stopped completely.

They brought the two injured scouts back to the group. Luckily, neither was seriously hurt. Crell waited until they were being treated, then nodded to Sorcha and Filian to join her and the three ran toward the direction the arrows had come from.

Calle calmly positioned herself over Ghortin.

"See here, I'm fine. Just a flesh wound." He struggled to get back to his feet, but Calle pushed him back with a finger.

"Stay."

Jenna grinned—Ghortin had again met his match. "I hope they have them on the run." The shield she'd been holding vanished. "That hurt." She shook out her arms to relieve the pin prickles flowing up them from the spell residue.

Ghortin yelped and she feared he'd been hit again. Then she saw him patting down his vest pockets. He pulled out the taran wand and held it close to his ear and mouth. "You have horrific timing. I assume you've made it to Irundail?" He barked a laugh and then motioned to Jenna. "They're fine, not in Irundail yet, but someone needs to hear your voice."

Jenna took the wand. The rangers were still covering Ghortin and Carabella, although it seemed the attackers were dead or gone.

"Storm?"

"Yes, what's happened?" His voice was magnificent to hear, but far fainter than it usually was through the wands. He might not be on the water anymore, but something was still disrupting their magic.

"We found some of Crell's rangers, then we were attacked." She gave him a few more details, but it would be best if they got moving. Once Crell and the other two returned, anyway.

Storm filled her in on his end. Even though they'd been delayed, he still might get to Irundail before them.

"Tell them we're on our way when you get there." Jenna wasn't going to say anything mushy, not with a bunch of tough rangers around them.

"Deal. Take care. We'll touch base when we can, but we plan on riding hard." He paused. "I can't wait to see you again." His voice was warm but low, and Jenna figured he had people around him as well.

"Same." The wand cut out.

After everything they'd all been through over the past few weeks, she wasn't upset anymore about his trick to keep her in Lithunane.

Lithunane. She felt the blood leave her face as she handed the wand back to Ghortin.

He paused before he put it away. "What's wrong, child? He said they were okay."

"They are. But I realized what could have happened if they had forced us to stay in Lithunane." Granted, Ghortin was a mastermage, one of the most powerful mages in the land. And Jenna herself wasn't a slouch. Her magic was far more unpredictable but usually strong.

Yet they might not have survived what had happened in the south.

Another more painful thought struck her. Or could they have stopped the attack?

Ghortin shook his head. "Your mind is too busy playing what-if again. I can see it on your face. We have no idea what the outcome would have been if we were there."

Carabella wrapped her arm around Jenna's shoulders. "You know I disagree with my son regularly, but I agree with him on this. Looking into what could have been helps nothing." If they had stayed behind, Carabella's inability to use magic might have caused her to be lost in the attack.

Jenna let out a long breath and hugged Carabella. "I know we found out a week ago, but I think I was ignoring it."

Ghortin patted the taran wand and slipped it back into his vest. "When Crell returns, we can see if she can reach Garlan or Rachael with her wand. This one will need to recharge." Taran wands were powerful old magic, but they weren't long-lasting and needed time to recover.

Crell and her two rangers returned, dragging a body behind them.

That wasn't the standard ranger procedure that Jenna recalled. She stepped back as the

body was brought before Ghortin—still on the ground with Calle nearby. No one was going to hurt him, but Calle figured that included hurting himself. He wasn't getting up until she said so.

"A present?" Ghortin leaned forward to see the man's face. There wasn't much left.

He was human, or so it looked. But his face was beaten bloody.

"Who beat him up?" Jenna peered down at the body. There were also injuries on his hands and arms, but there was nothing serious. Of course, magic didn't leave marks unless it wanted to. "And who is he?"

Crell frowned and nodded to Filian.

"It's hard to be sure with his face as it is, but this looks like the mage who sent us up here."

"Where were you when the mage sent you? And how long ago?" Carabella might not be able to use magic at the moment, but she still had excellent magical senses. Came from being immortal. She'd moved closer to the dead man, but now slowly backed away.

"It was five days ago, two after the attack. We had split into smaller groups and were trying to rescue the last refugees from the two closest villages to the capital. This mage ran out of a building, screaming for us to run. Next thing we knew, we were in the middle of nowhere."

Sorcha studied the mage's body. "This was him. But it's not now. We need to get away."

They'd said that none of their mages had made the trip up here, but Sorcha must have some magic ability, as she looked terrified.

Carabella shook her head. "I'm too limited in what I can do. But yes, someone help the injured and move away. There is something wrong with that body."

Crell paused by the mage. "Wouldn't it be easier to remove him?"

"No!" Sorcha's response was fast and sharp. "I have little magic, not a mage, but she's right, there is something wrong. Don't touch it." She helped one of the injured rangers, and two of the taller ones helped Ghortin and the other injured rangers move away.

Jenna made sure the horses and belongings were moved as well. The horses were remarkably calm during the entire thing, but she knew Ghortin couldn't keep them that way if another attack came.

Everyone was back in the woods, but nothing happened.

Just as Jenna was going to suggest they move on, the body exploded.

Jenna crouched down along with everyone else—the spell Ghortin had on the horses still held, luckily. What was even better, the trees mostly blocked the green goo that exploded with the body.

"A demonspawn? But why would he have tried to save the rangers?" Jenna fought to keep the terror out of her voice. Demonspawn could appear as anyone they'd killed.

"That's a good question," Crell responded but made no move to go out there. "That body was the only sign we saw of anyone or anything when we searched for the archers who attacked us. No tracks, no other bodies, only him."

Ghortin glared at the green mess outside of the woods. "Can someone find any of the arrows that were shot at us? My arrow got lost, unfortunately." He raised a hand to the ranger who'd wrapped his leg. "Not your fault, I didn't think we needed to keep it either. I believe we need to see one of them now, though."

Crell nodded to two of her rangers and they jogged off.

Jenna studied the injured rangers. They would need horses to ride and so would Ghortin. "Can we get the injured on the horses? I don't know about Carabella, but as long as we take it slow and my pack stays on my horse, I can jog." They still had a few days to get to Irundail, and this would significantly slow their time. But the need to get moving was strong.

"I shall have no trouble keeping up, I assure you." Carabella adjusted her scarf. "But yes, I agree we should get them on horseback immediately."

Crell nodded. "Once my rangers are back, I want us further off this main trail. A lesser-used one would be better given the recent issues. I hope they can bring back some arrows. There's something more than a little odd about an attack that solid breaking after only a few minutes."

Ghortin opened his mouth, most likely to say he was fine again, but shut it when Calle, Crell, and Jenna all glared at him. "What? I was going to ask for some help getting on my horse." Judging by the rapid change of expression, that was not what he planned to say at all.

CHAPTER FOUR

STORM HELD OUT THE TARAN wand to Edgar. "Let's get Keanin and get on the road. They're okay now, but they fell under attack."

Edgar had to pry the wand from his hand. "You might say they're okay, but I don't think you believe it."

"I don't. Arrows don't come from nowhere. They're still a few days out of Irundail. Plus, they won't be able to move fast unless they get more horses." Storm busied himself with adjusting his pack on one of the horses. He was more worried about Jenna and the rest than he'd been before being able to speak to them.

"They'll be fine." Edgar turned Storm toward him. "We have enough to worry about getting ourselves there."

Diath had kept his back to them but turned to face them now. "I see Keanin … and Talia. He's moving fast. She's trying to catch up without looking like it. He's furious."

Edgar and Storm shared a look. Keanin often went through a lot of emotions, but until fairly recently, anger was rarely one of them.

"Can we leave now?" Keanin had his pack and picked a horse to put it on. He was in the saddle before anyone could respond.

Storm had known him his entire life and had never seen him like this. If his jaw got any tighter, it was going to snap.

Talia stopped trying to catch him when she realized

he found the others but still jogged up. "Keanin, I'm sorry—"

"No. Say nothing more to me. *Ever.* Say what you want to them. I'll be on the other side of the alley. Waiting to leave." Keanin whirled his horse and trotted off.

Talia was pale, but she gave a small smile as he rode away. "Good." Her voice was low, but Edgar and Storm heard it. Diath did as well, judging by the way he took her arm.

"What did you do?"

Storm wanted to ask the same thing, but it was better coming from her brother.

She looked up with unshed tears in her eyes and shrugged. "I told him that I never felt that way about him. That I had a lover who was coming back and we would be wed soon." She nodded to Storm and Edgar. "He was going to ride with you, then once you got to Irundail, sneak back here. It's too dangerous and he's needed in Irundail. I saw how strong of a mage he is; he has a destiny. Now he won't mind leaving me behind for good."

"I wouldn't count on him not returning," Storm said. "He can be stubborn."

"I know." She gave a small smile. "Please don't tell him the truth." At their nods, she came closer and shook their hands. "Thank you. Goddess speed and fair travels. I believe your older sister is a cleric of Irissanta, yes?"

Storm smiled as he mounted his horse. He had one of the spares tied behind him, and Edgar had the remaining two. "Kaytine, yes she is."

"I shall send prayers for you all via her." Talia made a unique gesture with her left hand.

"She would be honored to serve." It was thought that the clerics of the collection of deities known as Irissanta, or the goddess of good, could facilitate prayers. Talia was obviously a follower.

With an actual smile and a few wipes as the tears came, Talia nodded. Storm and Edgar rode after Keanin.

"I know why she did it, but that's going to be horrible." Storm had dallied at being in love when he was younger, but had never been certain if the women were in love with him or the knowledge that he was a prince.

Then he'd rescued Jenna. He fell hard but didn't admit it for a long time. It changed how he thought about love and being in love with someone. He knew Keanin's feelings toward Talia were real.

And he knew she shared them.

"It is. But for him to think about coming back alone? With everything that's going on?" Edgar shook his head. "Let's see how he's doing. I agree, we need to get on the road."

Keanin looked like a statue as he watched the sea. He'd gone further than simply to the other side of the alley and was off to the side on the road out.

"Ready to go?" Edgar kept his voice light as they approached.

"I can't get out of here fast enough." Keanin kept his face toward the water but quickly wiped at his eyes before turning around.

Storm had planned to not say anything, but Keanin looked too devastated. He rode to him and clasped his shoulder. "I am sorry."

Keanin blinked. "Thanks. It's better if I stay angry." He gave them a tight nod and turned to the road.

Edgar shrugged and took the lead. Storm motioned for Keanin to follow Edgar, and Storm followed behind. He didn't completely believe that Keanin might take off. He was too upset to not have believed Talia's words, but it was still better to keep him in the middle of the group

Storm would also notice if Keanin was looking too pensive. They might not have known Talia for long, but with what they'd gone through, Keanin would know what kind of woman she was. And that she'd lied to him. But that would only happen if he got past the punch to his emotions.

Hopefully, that wouldn't happen until they were secure in Irundail and Ghortin could monitor Keanin.

The ride out wasn't fast. Heavily loaded wagons as well as single riders heading out of town as well. Despite that, some folks were heading back in. There were a few smaller villages further north and their people might have felt safer being in Erlinda.

All three men stayed quiet as they moved away from the town. Keanin took a brief pause at the top of the rise that would give the last view of the docks. He said nothing, but nodded to himself and quickly resumed following Edgar.

"Do you want me to take one of the extra horses? I should have thought of it before." Keanin nearly sounded normal.

Edgar waved him off. "We can switch up tomorrow. We'll only be stopping for a few hours at night. I have a feeling we should have been in Irundail a few days ago."

"Agreed." Storm looked back over the town, but mostly to make sure no one was following them. "Do you have any more taran wands in Irundail? I would like to leave one with Justlantin and my mother."

"Good thinking. I have a few in my room in the castle in Irundail. I'll try to reach Rachael or Garlan once this one recharges."

Keanin looked back at Storm. "You spoke to Jenna? How is she? How are they? Are they out of Strann now?"

His chatter almost sounded normal, but Storm knew Keanin had gotten good at suppressing his feelings. But with the amount of things that had happened to him, Keanin might need a bit of distraction. Storm filled him in on his talk with Jenna.

"I'm sure they'll be fine." Keanin waved his hand in the

air. "With all those rangers? No one can touch them." There was a line of worry between his brows that he was trying to play off. Jenna was like a sister to Keanin and he was clearly worried as well.

"That's what I told him. Now, let's pick up the pace to something an old grand da wouldn't be able to beat." Edgar didn't wait for responses but gave his horse a few words and they took off.

Ghortin swore when a ranger brought him an arrow as they headed down the road. Then three more. And they were all the same. Ghortin motioned for them to take the extras to Crell.

"These are our arrows. Well, not ours, but they belong to the Lithunane standing guard. How and why are they here?" Crell held the three she had and looked at them as if they were deadly snakes.

"That, my friend, is why I was swearing. And magically, I'm not sensing duplicity. These were fired from guards in Lithunane." Ghortin continued to twist the arrow around and scowl at it.

Jenna took the arrow from Ghortin as he waved it around. "But how? And why? And again, how? You're saying we were being shot at by our own people? Where are they?" She knew she wasn't the best scout in this world or any other, but even she would have noticed a bunch of Lithunane guards shooting at them.

Carabella didn't take an arrow, but she narrowed her eyes as she glanced around. "A slip spell. Smaller than a portal. That gentleman who exploded had flung the rangers this far out of

harm's way. He wouldn't have done that if he was on the side of those demonspawn. But someone could have used a slip spell to avoid the arrows from the Lithunane guards and send them after the rangers—and us."

Jenna handed the arrow back to Ghortin.

"None of this makes any sense. Not to mention, the rangers were sent through how many days ago? And the arrows only came through today?" Jenna knew that while she was growing magically and could do much more than she could a year ago, there were still major gaps in her knowledge. She had never heard of slip spells. The only way that she knew for people to be flung to another place was with a lot of strong magic. The royal family had a spell in the Lithunane throne room that could do that in times of extreme danger. During the ballroom attack of a year ago, the spell grabbed Storm and flung him and Jenna to Irundail.

Unfortunately, since Resstlin was the only royal in the palace at the time of the recent attack, no one else could have used the spell to bring anyone north. He clearly hadn't had a chance to use it.

"Slips are tricky magic," Ghortin said. "I would guess that after the mage sent these rangers up here, he was caught. They didn't kill him, but contaminated him with something from a demonspawn, then opened the slip with his essence, and sent him and a barrage of arrows through."

"That's convoluted, but I believe you're right." Carabella gave a grin and rubbed her hands together. "Which means there's still a slip floating around that we can use."

"We're not going back to what's left of Lithunane. Until we know more of what happened, it's not safe. We have to get to the royal family in Irundail." Ghortin shot her a glare.

"How are you even my son? Are we certain you weren't a changeling switched at birth?" She rolled her eyes toward the heavens. "The slip is still active and will be for about another twenty minutes if my guess is right. You and Jenna are powerful mages—we find the wee thing, you reconfigure it, and we all go to Irundail. No harm, no fuss."

She looked far too pleased and Ghortin looked far too horrified.

"Is that possible? And it will take all of us?" Jenna looked at the surrounding rangers. They were incredibly hardy, but now three were injured. She had no background on these slips, but if there was something that could get them to Irundail faster, and with less risk, she was for it.

She wasn't sure she believed that no one was after them.

"*If* we can find it. And *if* we can change the spell." Ghortin shook his head as he turned to Jenna. "There's a good reason that I never taught you about slip spells. They are unpredictable and unstable. If the body was still here, we could determine when he came through. Did the rangers and he appear at the same time? Or did he appear now when the arrows did? Time should be immediate with slips, but this one might not have been. And that is disturbing."

"If it fails, it could still take us days to get to Irundail, instead of minutes." Jenna waved her hand around. "But look at us. It was going to take days, even with all of us on horseback. And getting more horses could expose us to people we'd rather not meet." She didn't point out that while she wasn't the same woman she'd been back home in Los Angeles, she also hadn't trained for long, cross-country walking.

"We are in Traanafaeren though," Sorcha said. "That should give us some safety."

Carabella responded first. "Yes, but we're in the open lands. Few live this far north and east. And the Empress of Strann would have recently found out that the heir to Traanafaeren is dead, and the capital has fallen. There is no doubt that she will start sending troops to secure more of these lands."

"What she said." Crell made sure her people on horse-back stayed there. There were some complaints that they were fine, but she glared them into place.

"How do we find this slip, then?" Jenna asked.

Ghortin waved for her to come alongside his horse. "We should start walking the horses, but slowly. I have a feeling of where it is, but if we have unfavorable watchers, we don't want them to realize what we're doing. Particularly if they might have come through the slip themselves."

They soon formed a line down the trail, walking slowly.

They'd only gone a short distance when Ghortin stiffened and stopped his horse.

"It's to our right. Lingering between those two thin white trees. I believe it is watching us."

"The spell is sentient?" Jenna knew there were some of those, and the idea freaked her out. Trusting a sentient spell that could send them miles away—or in the completely wrong direction—was concerning.

"Not really." Carabella shot Ghortin a glare. "But they can be capricious. The slip spell will realize that it will vanish soon, so appeal to that. If it helps us, it can exist longer. Ask it to help and tell it where we need to go. Horses too."

Jenna scowled as she realized Carabella was telling *her* not Ghortin. Made sense, Carabella couldn't do magic and Ghortin currently couldn't get off his horse.

She stalked over to the thin white trees, her hand out toward the faint whirling between them. Ghortin had similar trees around his cottage. His white trees had to do with magic protections and maybe the spell felt more at home staying near them.

Great. Now she was giving the spell emotions.

"Hello there. I'm Jenna and I'd like to ask you for help." Feeling a bit silly, she explained what they needed the slip spell to do and why it should help them.

"Tell it to open before the walls of Irundail. We don't want it triggering a panic by crossing them and it probably would be bounced back anyway. The Keepers should block it." Ghortin nodded encouragingly.

Good point. Having visited Irundail only once, Jenna knew that the Keepers, towers that sat atop the eighty-foot-high walls at the entrance to Irundail, were infused with ancient magic. When secured, they could keep even the most powerful mages out.

There hadn't been a response from the spell, but she added the new instructions.

And still nothing.

She repeated the request two more times and got the same nothing back. Turning to tell the others this wasn't going to work; she was knocked back by a flash of blinding light and the world vanished.

Chapter Five

STORM KEPT WATCHING KEANIN, BUT aside from a tick on his cheek if Talia's name was mentioned, he seemed to be his normal self. Edgar was pushing them hard and after a day and a half, they were cresting the last hill before Irundail.

The massive walls and the Keepers could be seen in the distance and Storm felt a pang of loss. Although Irundail was the original capital of Traanafaeren, he'd grown up in Lithunane, only coming up here for family events.

Or major threats to the crown.

He shook his head. His older brother Justlantin would become king now. A better choice than Resstlin, but even Storm wouldn't have wanted it to happen this way.

He knew Justlantin wouldn't have wanted it either. Storm had threatened to remove himself from the royal lineage on more than a few occasions, and Justlantin wasn't too much different.

It was ironic that out of the four eldest children in the royal family, three didn't relish being king or queen. Perhaps his sister, Lilltkin, only a few years younger than him, would be more agreeable. The babies of the family, Princess Saysa and Prince Whealt, were too young to even think about.

"What's that?" Keanin wasn't looking toward Irundail, but at the hill next to them. Which appeared to be shaking itself apart.

"Do you feel anything magically? That's not natural." Edgar had some magic, but not on Keanin's level.

"I can't tell." Keanin frowned and held his hand out. "It's a spell of some kind and seems to be muddled in on itself." His golden eyes went wide and he backed his horse down the trail. "And it's coming this way."

The trail was too narrow and full of shrubs to easily get away from the swirling ball of magic that was coming for them. Edgar and Keanin held up their hands to raise shields when Storm shouted for them to stop.

"Don't! I somehow sense Jenna!" He barely got the words out when the spell slammed into them and a mass of rangers, horses, Jenna, Ghortin, Carabella, and Crell tumbled into them.

Either Keanin or Edgar had put a spell on their own six horses to keep them calm. While they weren't hit by the others, they were far too close for the animals to remain calm otherwise.

"Jenna!" Storm dropped off his horse and waded to her in the mass that had landed in front of him, helping rangers to their feet as he went. "What … how…Ghortin? What did you do?"

He picked Jenna up before Ghortin could respond, and, ignoring the people all around, kissed her soundly.

"There's no court to impress this time," she said softly as she traced the dark markings on his face, "although this would have caused some concern." But she wasn't going to complain. A few weeks apart made her realize how wonderful it felt to be with him again. With or without elaborate facial markings.

"I don't care. And this was part of my disguise." One more quick kiss and he pulled her with him as he went to Ghortin. Who was still sitting on his horse but now looking like a startled owl. "Again, what happened?"

"There was a slight misjudgment on my part concerning a borrowed slip spell. How long has it been since Jenna spoke to you?"

Jenna gave her mentor a questioning look but didn't say anything.

"A day and a half," Edgar responded first. He and Keanin got off their horses and made sure the rangers and Carabella were fine.

"What?" Jenna turned to Ghortin. "You said it would be immediate." She hadn't felt anything beyond the flash of light and slamming into the ground here.

"He simply refuses to admit when he makes mistakes." Carabella sniffed as she dusted the imaginary dirt off her clothing.

"I said, it *should* be immediate." Ghortin folded his arms. "But, against my concerns, it did get us here."

Jenna shot Ghortin another glare, then turned to Storm. "We left, using a borrowed slip spell, an hour or so after I spoke to you. We've been drifting in some weird limbo for a day and a half." She shoved the worries of what had happened to them into a dark corner of her mind.

"You look all in one piece." Keanin's smile was less exuberant than normal as he pulled her from Storm's arms and gave her an enormous hug. "I've missed you."

She hugged him back tightly. "I've missed you too, all of you." She smiled at Edgar. "But if we're all with the same pieces we started with, what say we get past the Keepers and into Irundail?" It might be residual from being in that slip spell for over a day, but she felt far too exposed out here.

Keanin offered Carabella his horse. She declined at first, which resulted in a wide-eyed look from Ghortin. Then Keanin whispered something to her, and she blushed, then nodded, and got on his horse.

Storm brought his horse around for Jenna. "You should ride as well."

"I can walk this far. I wasn't certain about jogging for a few days."

Crell pointed out that Sorcha had landed badly and was limping—much to Sorcha's embarrassment.

Another ranger, also injured and hiding it, took Edgar's offered horse. The three extra animals didn't have saddles, but no one else seemed to need to ride.

Jenna and Storm walked down the slope with their arms around each other toward the entrance of the massive obsidian walls.

Once her injured people were taken care of, Crell jogged up to join them.

"Did you tell him about where the arrows came from?"

Jenna felt her cheeks warm. "No, I think that slip spell scrambled my brains." She briefly told Storm that the arrows fired at them came from Lithunane through the slip spell. She knew there would be a much larger discussion of everything once they got inside Irundail, but Storm should know now.

"How is that possible?"

"No idea, lad, no idea." Crell kept pace with them as they approached the massive gates of the Irundail. They weren't gates so much as vast slabs of obsidian that appeared to have extended from the walls and rose so far up it was impossible to see the magical Keepers sitting above them.

Fifteen guards stood in front of the entrance, and Jenna was certain there were as many, if not more, watching them from the woods around them.

"Halt! Who approaches!" The leader of the guards stepped forward. He was kelar, but a foot or so taller than Storm.

"Are you blind up there?" Crell was not in a mood to be trifled with. "It's Prince Corin, I'm Ki' Crell, and you might also notice, Lord Keanin, Sir Edgar, Mastermage

Ghortin, Carabella, and Lady Jenna. We're tired, injured, and need food and rest."

Storm hid his grin but pushed his hair back out of his face and removed his eyepatch. "This is nothing but makeup."

"You look like a sell-sword to me. And we already have one Prince Corin inside. Not all the rest of you, but he was escorted here by Lithunane guards. Begone or we will use force."

Storm's smile fell and he released Jenna to put his hand on the hilt of his sword. "When did this impostor arrive?"

Edgar walked closer and Ghortin rode his horse forward but said nothing. Jenna noticed Ghortin pulling in magic as Edgar had already armed himself.

"A day ago. They ran fast and lost most of their horses."

"I would never ride horses to their death. Let me speak to my mother." Storm took another step closer to the guard.

The guard laughed. "That, my friend, will never happen. You could look similar to the prince without those tattoos. But you're not him. Last warning, be gone."

Ghortin gave a nod to Storm and rode even closer to the guards. "Who do I look like?"

"You're trying to appear as Mastermage Ghortin. Nice attempt, but he's shorter than you."

"No, he's—I'm not. I'm on a damn horse. Now, who do you think helped create Irundail? All those years ago. As in, my magic is part of this entire place."

"Now see here, old man…"

Keanin pushed his way to the front, dodging when Storm tried to grab his arm. "You know me. What you don't know is that I've had a horrific past few weeks." He stepped within striking distance of the guard and the rest of the guards moved around them. "I'm also a magic user. And if someone pretended to be Prince Corin, they were most likely using some sort of demonspawn magic. I don't like demonspawn." Before the guard could respond, Keanin muttered a few spell words, and the guard, and those closest to him, all flew a few feet in the air. "You have possible demonspawn, or at the least, followers of Qhazborh, inside Irundail. Let us in, or I will force my way in." His voice was low but deadly serious.

Jenna knew Keanin was a strong magic user, she'd helped train him on more basic things. But this was way above anything he should be able to do. Or her, for that matter—although to be fair, she'd never tried. That Storm and Edgar didn't look surprised meant this wasn't the first time it had happened.

Ghortin had warned her that grief and heartbreak could be powerful motivators for magic—Keanin was showing that.

Ghortin wasn't surprised. He nodded to Keanin to lower the lead guard to the ground and pushed the guardsman in the chest with his foot. "Now, lad. We can stand out here all day, waiting until Lord Keanin gets angry enough to throw you all over the gate, or you can let us in. With escorts, if you'd like."

The guard looked to the rest of his people still being held in the air. He opened his mouth to say something when the gate on the left opened.

Edgar and five of the rangers ran forward but stopped when Tor Ranshal, roughed up, but not injured, came out.

"Thank the stars you're here." Then the seneschal turned to the guard. "Are you blind? Obviously, you are because you let that demonspawn in. Come on everyone, we need you."

Keanin released the guards with more care than he had their leader, and then, horses and all, they ran in through the gates.

Tor Ranshal had about thirty guards with him, and he ordered half of them to go outside of the walls and relieve the current guards. The rest would escort those guards back for questioning.

"How did you get here so soon?" Ghortin patted his friend on the back as he rode alongside him.

"Garlan found a mage who could work with Rachael to get a slip spell for us. We were a bit off and ended up a few hours' ride south of here, but we saved a week or more of travel. The fake Prince Corin had just arrived, and Rachael and I were concerned that we weren't allowed to see him."

"What happened? You look like you were in a fight."

"A scuffle with a guard. The fake Lithunane guards escaped before they were found out—I don't think they were demonspawn, and neither does Rachael. But they all fled Irundail after escorting the fake Corin in."

"Where is the one pretending to be me?"

Jenna was walking next to Storm, but she had to look twice to make sure it was him. He still sounded like he was going to kill someone, but he was far calmer about it than normal. Keanin wasn't the only one who'd changed on their trip.

"He's locked in your chambers. He wouldn't speak to your mother or anyone. Kept insisting that his love was dead, so he had no reason to carry on."

"What?" Storm shook his head and turned to Edgar. "Can you take these marks off my face? There's going to be enough confusion as it is."

They were approaching the massive mountain that sat in the Irundail valley which was home to the castle of Irundail on its top level. The mountain had three levels, the first being smaller family homes, the next being the more well-off merchants, shops, military, etc. Then the top level had the castle, the House of Healing, and the Helaermage House. Jenna had forgotten about the odd mystics as they remained in Irundail. But they had been critical in saving Storm the first time she'd been here.

Large farms spread out in the valley beyond the mountain along with a few small villages. The population of Irundail declined as more people moved south.

Sadly, that would now be changing.

Tor Ranshal stopped and spoke to the guards at the bottom level. A few commands later, the guards from the front of the gates were being escorted to be scanned for possible influence.

Or the guard captain was just a jerk.

They were halfway up the wide road to the upper level when something hit Jenna in the head. Not externally, but inside. She felt herself tilting to the side as the sudden pressure in her head grew worse.

"What's wrong?" Storm held her up and Crell looked ready to help push her if she fell over the other way.

"I don't know … something isn't right…" Between one blink and another—Jenna wasn't in Irundail anymore.

CHAPTER SIX

———◆———

WELL, SHE WASN'T *ONLY* IN Irundail. She could still see it, and the concerned faces of Storm, Crell, and a lot of others, but she also saw a faint jungle. A familiar one that was some sort of access point for people on the chaotic realm.

"Oh no," she whispered, but kelar and derawri had excellent hearing.

"What's wrong?" They echoed each other.

"I think I'm where I went when I vanished before." There was no way to know if talking about it could impact Carabella, but as she had no idea where she was right now, she was going to be careful.

Crell got it. Storm looked more concerned.

Meith appeared in her narrow range of vision. He was a cuari, one of the ones lost when they tried to take over everything, and had helped her when she'd been trapped on the chaotic plane. But, unlike the last time she'd seen him, he didn't look like he'd just lived through the end of the world.

That was an improvement.

"There you are." He looked past her. "And them as well. They can't see or hear me, but this is quick. Run. The castle is going to explode. You have to flee."

"What? No." Jenna shook her head until his image vanished and the jungle of the chaotic plane disappeared. She looked at Ghortin. "I got a message. The castle is under attack, and it's going to explode." She ran, quickly joined by others who could run. She felt a brief wave of dizziness. That had to be Meith trying to get back to her but she kept running. Meith had his own agenda for her. And it was often something she didn't agree with.

She saw a flash of what he'd seen as the royal family, what was left of them, was about to be blown up.

Not if she could help it.

Tor Ranshal grabbed a guard and told him to start moving people off the mountain.

Ghortin scrambled off his horse in front of the castle and hobbled inside. Crell got him into a chair inside the door and forced him into it. "Stay here and be magic support. My injured rangers, stay on your horses and help direct people to keep going down the levels once they get outside."

"How do you know?" Storm had only heard a brief version about when Jenna had been snatched off to the chaotic plane a few weeks ago—but this wasn't the time to explain.

Jenna saw Carabella running forward. "Can't explain now." She gave a pointed look at Carabella. "But I believe it. Where is your room?"

"You think the fake prince is going to blow up the castle?" Crell nodded for the rest of her rangers to come forward. "All of you, get everyone out of the castle and keep moving down. Some of you warn the House of Healing and the Helaermage House."

"The images I got were vague about the source, but I think that your copy, whatever he is, is the cause." Jenna wished she could speak to Meith longer and without worrying about Carabella getting sucked into a soul-stealing magic ball.

"This way." Storm watched as the rangers went to save his family. Jenna could tell he wanted to go with them. But they might not be safe no matter where they went if they couldn't stop the explosion.

"Jenna and Keanin," Ghortin called from his chair, "use

your magics on this. There's a good chance that the person in that room is a magical construct." He waved his hand. "Which I realized I haven't explained to you. Treat it like an evil ball of magic."

Carabella glared at him. "Those would have been a good thing to teach them. I might not be able to use magic, but I can coach them."

She caught up to Keanin and Jenna, and they, plus Crell, Edgar, and Storm raced up the stairs.

"Any idea when this explosion will happen?" Storm stayed alongside her as they ran up the stairs.

"Not a single clue. I was ordered to flee, so I'd guess fairly soon."

Storm laughed. "And that was the forceful 'no' I heard. Good to know you haven't changed in the last month."

"I don't like being told what to do. And don't think I've forgotten your stunt. Let's save Irundail, then have a serious talk." She flashed him a grin. Yes, providing they didn't blow up, she was going to have a talk about what he did, but it was hard when she kept smiling about being around him again.

Two guards stood outside of the pair of ornate doors that Storm led them to.

"Halt. No one can enter."

Storm looked at his friends. "Have I changed that much? I still look like me, right? The marks are gone?" Not waiting for an answer, he spun on the nearest guard. "I'm Prince Corin, you can accept that or not. But we need you out of the way."

The guards didn't have a chance to respond before they were flying up to the ceiling.

Jenna turned to Keanin. "After this, you and I are so talking about your magic."

He grinned and spun the guards once, then set them down at the end of the hall.

Crell faced them. "Get people out of the castle and off the mountain. It's going to explode."

"Magic, lots of terrible magic," Edgar added when they hesitated—both guards paled, nodded, and ran down a back stairway.

Carabella paused in front of Storm's former bedroom and tilted her head against the wood. "It's a construct in there and an unstable one at that." She stepped back. "Keanin and Jenna go in first and do what I say. Keanin that floating trick is good, do that. Jenna, wrap what he lifts in every confinement spell you can think of. It has to be tight."

That seemed fairly simple for saving an entire castle from exploding, but Jenna wasn't going to argue.

"The rest of you, be ready to fight. No magic, as long as Keanin and Jenna hold things—but there will be violence."

That sounded more like the status quo that Jeanna knew.

Once everyone nodded, Carabella stepped away from the door. "Blast it, gently."

"Gently?" Jenna and Keanin said simultaneously. When Carabella smiled and motioned toward the door, they shrugged.

"Together on two? A gentle blast?"

"My lady, you have always been the center of charm and wisdom." Keanin bowed.

"One, two…" they hit the door at the same time with what Jenna hoped was a gentle enough blast. The doors didn't fly apart, or fall off their hinges, but they did pop open.

Carabella followed Jenna and Keanin through the open doorway without using magic, which was hopefully a sign that she remembered her situation.

Keanin magically grabbed the odd figure in front of them. It might have looked like Storm at some point, and it was still about his height, but otherwise, it looked like a mutating, un-defined blob. A walking blob who was now being held up against the ceiling by Keanin's magic.

"Wrap him now!" Carabella's fingers twitched, and she looked ready to cast the spells herself.

Jenna flung every containment or restrictive spell she could think of at the thing and kept spinning spells around it.

The creature yelled, then all of her spells were pushed as far as they could go as it exploded.

Keanin couldn't keep the small pieces up in the air, and they dropped to the ground, forming foot-high warriors. They were green and had long twitching arms that reached the floor and ended in nasty-looking claws.

"Damn it, you didn't say there would be nuits." Crell swung her short sword and lopped the heads off two of them.

"We stopped the explosion, but now these things are attacking?" Jenna backed up as one charged her. "What are they?"

"Not sure about stopping it." Edgar used his daggers to hit two more. "But we have to keep these from getting out of the castle. Hopefully, they were the only source of the potential explosion."

"They were the thing pretending to be me?" Storm was fighting them off but it wasn't that much of a fight.

"It's complicated, but in a way, yes. Magic Constructs must have a base form and are tricky to create." Carabella killed one with her sword. "The thing was probably only created hours before it arrived." She wrinkled her nose at the green ooze on her blade.

Jenna jumped as one of the little things bit her leg. Luckily, it hit her boot, but she swore she felt a tooth graze her—and she was wearing leather boots and thick socks.

"Watch out!" Storm grabbed her with one arm and

lifted her above the creature, and then Edgar sliced it. "Did it get you?"

"It hit my boot…but I don't think it…" The rest of her words vanished as the world went black.

———◆———

"I told you to get out. Are all people from your world this stubborn?" Meith hovered in front of her.

Every part of her body screamed in pain as she tried to adjust herself and figure out where she was.

She was on a cot and the chaotic plane jungle was looking far more solid than it had earlier.

So was Meith.

"What happened? That thing barely scraped my leg. If it even did that." Once she stopped trying to move, the pain settled down to a dull ache.

"Oh, it got you. Yes, it did. Kalinuits are short-lived, barely alive, evil constructs. Ones that were eradicated until the portal was forced open again. What my people did was wrong—except when we expunged things like them."

"My body hurts so much that I can barely move. Can you help me?" Jenna tried to turn to look at him better, but even that was impossible.

"It's unlikely that I will be able to do much. I pulled you out of there once I realized what had happened— your friends destroyed the rest of the creatures, by the way. But I have little energy left."

"Then how do I get better and get back?" To test things, she tried lifting her pinkie on her left hand. Nope. Soul-shattering pain shot out all over her body.

"You don't. Not right now. The poison those things carry would have killed you by now if you'd stayed where you were. I delayed that by bringing you here. But until my strength returns, I can't do much more." He peered closely into her eyes. "There is a sadness when you look at me that wasn't there before. You saw a future me." He nodded. "And not a good one."

"If I tell you what I saw, can you stop it?" What she'd seen was her former world, Earth, attacked by horrific monsters from the portal. Enough damage to not only lead to its destruction, but that of her current world, and the chaotic plane itself.

"No!" He waved his hands. "I am sorry. But the future isn't solidified, even if one has seen it. Telling me or any-one with Power of it will only lead to attempts to stop it. Which could lead to the event that was trying to be avoided and the destruction of all that we know."

CHAPTER SEVEN

M EITH TOOK A DEEP BREATH and settled down from his agitated state. "Time issues are touchy." There was weight behind those words.

Jenna forced her rising panic to settle down. *Her* instinct was to race out of there and change the future. That she currently couldn't move at all and had no idea how to stop things from heading into that awful future didn't help. And one of Meith's warnings from the future had been to not let her current world go to war. Something that was already in progress with the brutal attack on Lithunane.

Knowing that acting on what she knew could cause it to happen would have shattered her head. If it wasn't already so painful that blinking caused waves of pain.

"I need to get back. This poison or whatever that thing left in me needs to be removed. There must be a way." She almost mentioned that with the number of cuari trapped up here, anything should be possible. But only Meith ever helped her before.

"I don't know how. It's beyond me. Eventually, you will be able to move, but you'll need to stay here. Forever." His long face, which seemed to change a bit each time she saw him, looked drawn and sad.

Jenna hadn't felt anything from her mental roommate, the lost god Typhonel, for a while. But she felt a stirring in her head now. And she didn't think that mentioning him to Meith, or any cuari, was a good idea. Typhonel was lost in the void beyond the portal when the rebelling cuari threw him in during their attempt to throw over the gods and goddesses.

The rest of the deities stepped in at that point and removed all but one hundred of the cuari who were trying to defend the deities. The actively aggressive cuari had been removed from existence. Ones like Meith, who didn't take part, but also didn't try to stop the others, were sent to the chaotic plane. The one hundred cuari who fought back against their kind on the side of the deities, like Carabella, had their memories erased and were returned to the world to guide and protect the three newer races.

Even after stopping the cuari, the collected deities hadn't been able to retrieve Typhonel or destroy the portal.

"*Are you here?*" Communication with Typhonel was always dicey. He'd inhabited the bodies of the Protectors for hundreds of years—the single, specialized Guardian who was to be the one to shut the portal when the time came.

As far as they'd been able to figure out, he'd not been able to communicate with any of the prior Protector incarnations.

Jenna was pretty sure that his becoming aware and conscious of her was another sign things were going bad fast. But she welcomed his guidance and abilities. When she could reach him.

"*I am,*" Typhonel's voice was so faint that she barely heard it.

"*Can you help me?*" She focused on what had happened in Irundail and the poison. Sometimes images communicated better.

"*Not good. I can help, slow the body, and reverse the damage. You must leave this place,*" his voice was a little stronger, but still muffled and distant.

"*He says I need to stay.*" She looked at Meith so Typhonel was aware of him. She wasn't sure if calling names for either of them to the other wouldn't explode the chaotic plane or something.

"*Conflict. Need…back home.*" The words were choppier now.

The surrounding jungle shook and Meith looked around in shock. "What have you done?" His eyes went wide and he backed away. "You aren't here. There. No." He might claim to not have much Power, but he waved his hand and Jenna's world went black again.

"Jenna!" Storm yelled as he ran to her.

She'd ended up on the stairs outside of Storm's room and felt like she'd been run over by a massive truck.

"Stay back!" Ghortin leaned on a chair in the hall, but his voice was strong enough to stop Storm and the others from running toward Jenna. "You were bitten by a nuit, yes? Your friend took you to save you?"

Carabella was nearby but looked like she wanted to run forward. A sharp glare from Ghortin kept her in place.

"Yes. And another stepped in." She tapped her head. When no burst of pain shot through her, she smiled. "I think they—" A delayed reaction, pain spasmed through her body.

"*Hold still. The mastermage and I can fix this. But you must stay still. Need a third to anchor. The prince loves you?*" Typhonel's voice was still faint but less choppy.

"*Yes.*"

"*Then him. Others…go.*"

Jenna quickly told everyone that they needed to leave aside from Ghortin and Storm, but couldn't say why.

"There is a guest room next to mine. We can move her there." Storm hadn't run forward yet. Ghortin seemed to still be waiting for something, but Storm wasn't going to wait much longer.

Ghortin held out his hands as the rest of the people in

the hall, including Keanin, who's golden eyes were full of tears, left.

Jenna felt herself being lifted into the air and, feeling like she was on a cloud, drifted toward the open door. From Ghortin's grin, it was his doing.

Edgar and Crell were the last to leave and nodded solemnly before turning down the stairs.

"*Why do they all have to leave?*" Jenna asked Typhonel as she drifted into the room.

"*You could explode—there were things left in you. Your friends will have a compulsion to keep moving down the mountain and gather anyone remaining from the other levels as they go. The explosives inside you would destroy this entire structure. I don't intend that to happen.*"

That was a terrifying thing to learn, but she felt a bit more confident at Typhonel's tone.

The cloud holding her drifted down to the bed, then vanished. Ghortin, using Storm to support him, limped in.

"Haven't you gotten that taken care of?" She'd been gone for probably close to a half hour; a good healer could have fixed his leg in minutes.

"There wasn't time. You were attacked, vanished, and then popped up on the stairs moments later. I was only up here as I'd begun hobbling up not long after you lot came up here." Ghortin took a seat and Storm came to her and took her hand.

"It was longer than that...never mind. Time in that place is odd. Let me check what needs to be done." She started to reach out to Typhonel, and then a thought hit her. "You should know that the reason he wanted everyone else out was that something was left in me and this entire mountain might explode." That she was calm while saying it showed how truly crazy her world had become.

Storm squeezed her hand. "That's always the chance. Well, maybe not exploding the entire mountain, but dying. Over the past month, I've realized that I can't protect you, so I might as well stay with you." He glanced over to Ghortin. "Someone has to keep an eye on you mages."

Ghortin nodded. "I'm certainly not leaving, but thank you for the warning." He rubbed his hands together. "Now what feats of magic does your mental friend have for me to do? Something grand and dangerous?"

Jenna smiled. "Let me find out." With people watching her, she felt better closing her eyes when trying to reach Typhonel. It felt odd staring at someone while talking to another person in her head. "*We're ready, I guess. What do we need to do?*"

She had a moment of panic when Typhonel didn't respond, but then he came back.

"*Something is trying to block me. I will need to go away after this. However, for now, I need the mastermage to simply funnel magic through you. The prince should hold your hand and focus on how much you mean to him.*"

"*You'll do everything else? Shouldn't I be doing something?*" That seemed like a handful of effort for something as large as possibly blowing up a mountain. Ghortin was going to be sorely disappointed.

"*Yes. I need more strength and emotion to make this succeed. We might still not be able to do it. As for you, try to not explode.*"

Typhonel rarely, if ever, expressed emotions, but that might be a small attempt at a joke. She wondered if emotions and humor, like his physical form, were lost in the void. She opened her eyes and told them. Ghortin sputtered, offering feats of magic, but Storm finally cut him off.

"I'll send love, you send Power. That's it." He smiled to soften the tone, but Jenna saw the tension in Storm's jaw. It was also in his hand where he held hers, but she could tell he was trying not to crush her fingers.

"Begin."

"He says, begin." Jenna wanted to help, even though he said not to. She instead took a deep breath as waves of love and admiration flowed from Storm and massive amounts of pure Power came from Ghortin.

Typhonel's presence became stronger than it usually was as of late, but unlike their first encounters, he didn't take her over. The world felt as if it had frozen in time and begun moving at lightning speed simultaneously.

Pain hit her hard, the same pain from before but even more so.

"Don't let go." Typhonel's voice was back to being distant. Or it might have come from herself. She took a deep breath and hung on to the feelings from Storm. Immediately, she felt calmer.

A few more minutes, or what felt like that, and the pressure and pain vanished. She opened her eyes to see a tired-looking Storm, still holding her hand, and an exhausted Ghortin, collapsed in his chair.

"Is it gone? Are we all safe?"

"Yes. I must leave now." There was a slight change inside her head, which indicated he was gone.

She released Storm's hand and gently pushed herself up. "It's over."

Storm blinked and shook out his hand as if it had fallen asleep. "And we're all still here." He gave her a quick kiss.

Ghortin pulled himself up into a more normal seated position. "Speak for yourself. I feel like I've been drained of half my life. That was long."

"No, it wasn't." Then Jenna looked out the open window. Twilight had fallen. "How long have we been in here?"

"At least six hours?" Ghortin stood and stretched. "I lost track of time after the first few."

"You're standing." Jenna grinned.

"I…I am. I'm completely healed. Not sure if all that

Power I donated was worth fixing an arrow wound, but at least I got something."

"And I'm healed and not going to blow up the mountain." Jenna swung her legs off the side of the bed. "I think we need to let everyone else know, though."

"I agree and I am grateful that you are uninjured and did not explode." Ghortin went for the door, then muttered to himself, and pulled up some mage lights along the stairs. "No one was here to turn on the lights. It's going to be a long walk to get everyone back when they'll probably be gathered past the gates."

"True, or you could use your taran wand and have Crell and Edgar bring everyone back." Storm patted Ghortin's back.

"Aye! I think all that Power going out has hindered my brain." He patted his vest and pulled out the taran wand. A few minutes later, Crell, Edgar, and Garlan responded that they were herding the population of Irundail back inside the gates.

"Now what? I won't be able to sleep with the thought that more of those…nuits… whatever they were, being around." Jenna shuddered. The almost-dying bit was bad, but those little critters were worse.

"I can do a sweep." Ghortin took a deep breath and shook his head. "Rather, I can guide Keanin and other younger, non-drained mages to do a complete sweep. It will take all night to get to the outer areas, but I'll have them work in stages." He saw Jenna's face. "Don't worry, we will clear this entire mountain before dinner."

She relaxed, and Storm dropped his arm around her shoulder.

"Not the way I'd envisioned our reunion. But I'm glad we're together." He kissed the top of her head.

She reached up and rubbed his hand draped over her shoulder. "And I've mostly forgiven you for that stunt you pulled." Her smile dropped. Those housemaids who had followed her around for gossip from the prince's fiancé quite possibly were all killed in the attack.

"What's wrong?" He pulled back.

"I made some connections about the people who were lost in Lithunane. We have to win this fight for all of them." The housemaids were young and full of life. None of them, or anyone else who died down there, deserved to die.

His face grew somber. "Agreed."

The three walked down as the sounds of carriages and riders came up from the second level. Lights were being lit on the first level and were traveling upward.

Jenna, Storm, and Ghortin waited in the front hall area for the rest to come in. The castle staff raced in first and then Crell, her people, Keanin, Edgar, and Carabella.

"You are a sight for sore eyes!" Keanin scooped Jenna up and swung her in the air. "There was this nasty compulsion spell pushing us to keep going down and out. Ghortin I assume?" He set her on her feet and narrowed his eyes at Ghortin.

"It wasn't him," Jenna responded before Ghortin could. "Long story that we can't discuss here, but yes, I nearly exploded and the compulsion spell was a just-in-case situation."

"Dinner will be ready in an hour; I think everyone needs food and cheer right now." Tor Ranshal and Rachael came in with the final stragglers.

Jenna had already hugged him, but she embraced Rachael tightly. "How are you?" Rachael was old, far older than most kelar at nearly two thousand years old. But within the past month, she'd aged significantly.

"I'm ready for this to be over, to be honest." The smile she gave Jenna was a sad one. She meant more than only the fighting. When Rachael had first met Jenna, she'd hoped that Jenna's appearance was to replace her as the primary Guardian. Alas, Jenna's destiny was something else, as the Protector incarnation, the one who would close the portal. So, Rachael was still here. "I am still worried about those who are making their way up here from Lithunane." Her smile lifted. "But it is good to see you. And the rest."

Tor Ranshal marched off with a pack of chefs. Many of them already magically preparing for an incredibly fast dinner. Tor Ranshal might have lost his magic a year ago, but he was still the castle seneschal—regardless of which castle or palace he was in.

"Where is the royal family?" She hadn't seen the queen or Storm's siblings in a long time, but she knew they would be noticeable.

"They went in a secret entrance," Rachael said. "The queen and heir particularly want to see you, Storm. Things were a bit jumbled while waiting, but they were concerned that you didn't come to find them."

"I was up here. Jenna got exposed to a nuit, and she was saved, but I was needed." He was trying to avoid things like missing god, exploding mountains, and magic. They were still in the open entrance hall.

Rachael was aware of Typhonel, but it took Jenna grimacing and tapping her head to catch on. "Oh my, it has been a long week." She patted Jenna's hand and nodded to the two of them. "I think you should rest, and you, young man, should go find your family."

Jenna was going to say she'd been resting for the past six hours or so, but the truth was, she felt exhausted. "I'm afraid I don't have a room yet."

Keanin was talking to Ghortin but perked up at Jenna's comment. "That I can take care of. Before I am recruited to cleanse this place." He held up a small group of spell bubbles. "I already started. But I can work on the stairs up to the floor that has your room. Which is near mine, by the way. Storm will need to be moved to that floor as well. I think his old room will require cleansing at an entirely different level." He held out his arm with a nod to Storm. "Go visit your family and tell them I'll see them at dinner." He smiled but there was a sadness lingering there.

Jenna knew that Keanin, having been raised by the royal family, thought of them as his own. And from what Jenna understood, they felt the same. Judging by the look on Storm's face, she wasn't the only one who caught the oddness of his statement.

Storm nodded and then took the stairs up two at a time. Keanin released his spell bubbles and they darted around the entire area and then called up more as they ascended the stairs at a more normal pace.

Jenna squeezed his arm. "How are you?" She hadn't known everything that had happened to him during their separation, but she knew that horrible things had happened to him. And even if she didn't know all that had occurred, there was a difference in him. He appeared the same and was trying to act the same, but there was a brittle edginess to him now that was never there before. Like Rachael's aging, Keanin had changed.

CHAPTER EIGHT

KEANIN CLAIMED TO BE FINE and chatted about local gossip he'd picked up while he and the rest of Irundail waited at the gates to come back. That was typical of Keanin—but it was obvious to Jenna that his heart wasn't in it. He kept chatting as he set her up in a spacious bedroom, one clearly designed for high-ranking visitors.

She wasn't going to complain, especially when the bed was probably larger than the living room in her former apartment in Los Angeles. It was all she could do to not dive into it the moment she saw it. Instead, she turned to face Keanin as he readied another group of spell bubbles to send out into the hall. "How are you *actually* doing?" She took his hands after he sent the minor spells off to cleanse the floor they were on.

He tried to flash his normal smile, but it fell short. "I can't lie to you, can I? It was easier with Storm and Edgar—they knew what happened and were fine with me not talking about it. Much." He gave a small, genuine grin. "But being here? Around so many people? And the royal family? I don't know how to act. What to say. Anything. They'll be expecting the old me." He looked up with tears in his golden eyes. "That man is gone."

Jenna hugged him tightly and pulled him into her room when she heard voices coming down the hall. She shut the door and rubbed his upper arms. "The people who love you will understand. It might take a while to get used to, but they won't stop loving you. You're the brother I never had, and I'm certainly not letting you go, no matter how you change."

His returning hug cut off her air but was worth it. "Thank you. I love you like a sister, but only because you and Storm belong together. That boy was in a state every time we heard of something going wrong with you folks. There were a few times I think Edgar was debating using a sedating potion on him."

Against her will, Jenna felt a yawn force its way out. "Sorry."

"Hey, being attacked by nuits and almost exploding takes a lot out of a person." He kissed the top of her head. "I have important mage duties to perform—how odd sounding is that? Anyway, I shall see you at dinner. Go rest."

He was out the door and gone before she could respond.

She dropped her pack on a chair and climbed on top of the bed. Carabella had shown her how to set an alarm when Jenna had complained about there not being such things as alarm clocks in this world. It was a simple timing spell that she barely completed before falling asleep.

She felt as if she'd just closed her eyes when the spell tried to shatter her head. Once she woke up more, she realized it wasn't that bad—but still nasty. She shut it off and then looked at her wrinkled clothing. Even before sleeping in them, her current clothing wasn't suitable for dinner. Especially dinner with the royal family. This was a basic meal and not fancy, but despite that, she didn't want to make a poor impression. She and Storm weren't actually engaged, but she thought that maybe someday that would change.

Once they saved the world, anyway.

Unfortunately, she didn't have a lot of clothing options in her pack. A soft knock at the door broke her away from looking at her clothes spread out on the bed.

A castle maid smiled and held up a floor-length dress. "I was told this should fit and make you feel better."

Jenna took it. Not fancy, but far better than her current collection. "Thank you. From who?" She was grateful, but with all the magic flying around, if this was a magically created dress, she might have to stick to what she had. Becoming nude in front of the royal family if a spell dropped wasn't the way she aspired to be noticed.

"Lady Rachael. She said it's not magic."

Jenna laughed. "Tell her thank you as well."

The castle maid gave a small curtsy and went down the hall.

It was a lovely, simple gown. Light blue and green with long flowing sleeves. When she was younger and reading every fantasy book she could get a hold of, she would have said this was a princess-in-waiting dress.

She took a quick bath and changed. Rachael might not have made it out of magic, but something made it fit perfectly. Jenna felt a slight magical tingle as she put it on.

There wasn't much she could do with her hair, so she brushed it out. After a month on the road, the temptation to change into pajamas and crawl under the covers was strong, even with the lovely gown.

Then her stomach rumbled. She hadn't used much magic directly, after that misguided slip spell, but she had no idea what all she'd been through had done to her reserves. Right now, she was starving.

She opened the door and realized she didn't have a clue where the royal dining room was. She'd been in Irundail for a few weeks over a year ago, while Storm recovered from almost dying. But she didn't roam around the castle much. Certainly not in the royal areas.

"There you are," Crell's voice coming up the stairs was welcome. Her hair was damp and she had fresh clothes on, but they were serviceable hunter-type clothing. "I had a feeling no one would recall that you had no idea where to go." She stood back. "Lovely dress. Shall we? I could hear your stomach on the floor below this one."

"Ha. But thank you about the dress. Rachael sent it. How are your injured rangers?" They walked back toward the stairs.

"They'll recover. Although it has been expressly requested that we never travel via slip spells again. Even if the option is death." She grinned. "I think they were joking."

"I'm with them. That wasn't fun." She stopped and turned to Crell. "Is there anything I should know about the royal family before we go in? I met them briefly, but haven't spoken to any of them much." Aside from blessings from Kaytine and the queen when Jenna and Ghortin saved Storm's life.

"You dealt with the most difficult one—Resstlin. I speak no ill of the dead, but he'd always differed from the rest. Prince Justlantin is an unassuming man. He'll make a fair king, I believe. The rest are mostly harmless." Her smile was full of affection for them.

"That's not as reassuring as you might think. Still, it is nice to be in a building. One that hopefully no one will try to burn us out of." She was going to continue ignoring the almost blowing-up aspect.

"Now, life on the road isn't always that bad." Crell tried to keep a straight face, then dropped it. "Even for me, that was a long trip. I think once we save the kingdom, and possibly a world or two, I might get a farm in the back of this valley and retire."

Jenna peered down at her with an eyebrow raised but said nothing.

"You don't think so? Eh, you might be right. And we have a lot of work between then and now, so who knows what will happen by the end of it." They approached a pair of wide, carved doors with two pairs of heavily armed guards in front of them.

"Ki' Crell, it is good to have you back. I am glad we did not lose you in Lithunane." An older human, one who looked enough like Tor Ranshal that Jenna did a double take, came out of a side chamber as they approached the guards.

But where Tor Ranshal's thin face was kind, this man looked like he'd been sucking on lemons. All of his life. And his words were flat. He'd probably given that same cheerful greeting to everyone who'd made it here so far.

"I am glad as well. Lord Siralan, might I present Lady Jenna, also formerly of Lithunane, Lady Jenna, this is Lord Siralan. Tor Ranshal's cousin."

The human noble gave a slight bow, then narrowed his eyes. "The fiancé of our Prince Corin? Interesting." He looked her up and down. "I would have expected you to at least have a little kelar blood, as the royals are kelar. If you will excuse me, I find I have another engagement."

Without waiting for a response, he swept away down the corridor. Difficult to do without a ballgown or long cape. But he did it.

Jenna almost said something when he got out of sight, but then noticed the stoic guards not looking as stoic as they had when they'd first walked up. Instead, she gave a nod to Crell.

Crell stepped closer to the guards. "Are you planning on not letting us in? You did hear that man acknowledge who we are."

The tallest guard tightened his grip on the pike he held. "All guests must say their names aloud for the spell." He lifted his pike to point out a small swirling ball practically hidden in the decorated ceiling.

Jenna felt the magic coming from it, but not what it was designed to do exactly. She'd ask Ghortin when she found him.

Crell shook her head, but raised her voice, "Ki' Crell."

The ball glowed a light green and the guards stepped aside.

Jenna moved forward. "Jenna Reilly." The spell bubble turned red and the guards stepped back into place.

"Do not move."

Jenna froze. She knew she'd been through a lot, but she was pretty sure she was still herself.

Crell, however, moved back toward Jenna. "Don't come any closer. I trust this woman with my life and will defend her."

"The spell will bring forth the helaermages. You can go inside if you would like Ki' Crell, but your companion will have to wait."

Jenna wished she still could call to Ghortin in her head. For a while, after he'd gotten his body back, they could still communicate mentally. That had eventually vanished. It would have helped clear this up.

"I'm not leaving her. You need to get Mastermage Ghortin out here."

"The door must remain under guard by all of us. You must wait."

The sound of people coming up the stairs made Jenna turn around. Three helaermages. Their brown cloaks and hoods were familiar. Helaermages were a different type of mage, ones with a heavy dose of mystic, but they had helped save Storm's life.

"Jenna? Is that you?" The first one who approached, a derawri judging by the height, threw back his hood. Dantil had been kind when she'd been here before. Most of the helaermages didn't interact with others, but Dantil was different. He smiled and took Jenna's arms. "It is good to see you, my child." He turned to the guard. "Why were we called?"

The guard again used his pike to point to the spell bubble. "She is not who she claims to be. Prince Justlantin has said we must lock up all people who do not pass this test in the Helaermage House."

"As far as I know, I am still me. Not even Ghortin is in my head this time." Jenna's concern had grown until Dantil arrived. Crell was an excellent fighter, but fighting their way out of Irundail would be madness.

Dantil looked at the two other helaermages, said something softly to them and they left. "I can determine if there is anything dangerous here. Do you accept my verdict?" He watched the guards carefully.

"We should get Prince Justlantin."

"You said you couldn't get Ghortin for me. How come you can now go inside and get the Heir?" Jenna folded her arms; she was quickly going from mildly freaked out to annoyed. It had been a long and exhausting day and her nerves were fraying.

"With helaermage Dantil here, I can send one person in. To request Prince Justlantin." He nodded and the guard next to him opened the door and slipped inside.

Crell shook her head. "I understand, trust me. But she *is* Jenna."

Dantil motioned for Jenna to move away from the guards and the door. Crell looked ready to follow, but he shook his head. Crell was angry, but she stayed in place and focused her anger on glaring at the remaining three guards.

"Child, I know you. I knew you when you carried that stubborn Ghortin in your head. You are you." His deep brown eyes were worried. "But there is someone else inside you. Which is what triggered that spell. You are not *simply* Jenna."

Jenna knew then who'd triggered it—Typhonel. But he'd vanished and she didn't sense him at all. Not that he had a lot of places to go to. This wasn't where or why she wanted to have this conversation, and she wished

Ghortin or Rachael were here. The guards gripped their weapons with more force now.

"Can you cast a spell of silence around us?" She watched the guards as she dropped her voice to a whisper.

Dantil glared at the guards but nodded. "Hold still for a moment. There, we're silenced. No one can hear us. What's wrong?"

"Do you know Rachael of Lithunane?"

"I know of her. She, like Tor Ranshal, is a Guardian."

Jenna gave a relieved sigh. It was too hard to figure out who could know what. But if he knew of the Guardians, this should be okay. She hoped.

"Okay, I'm sort of like them. Only I'm a Protector incarnation. And I have someone in my head." She took a deep breath. "Typhonel. He might be what's triggering the spell bubble, but I can't tell people about him."

CHAPTER NINE

DANTIL ROCKED BACK ON HIS heels. "The lost god? Interesting. My people have dedicated much study to finding what was his end. Many of us believed he lived on incorporeally even as his body was lost to the portal. I would like to speak to him at another time. But right now, this causes an issue. Any official event in the castle will have those spell bubbles and probably more. As Prince Corin's fiancée, you can't not attend."

"That's another thing, the fiancée situation—Storm made Prince Resstlin think that was the case to keep me in Lithunane. But until it's been cleared up, you're right."

Dantil raised his eyebrows but only nodded. "I think we can tap into the Ghortin issue to keep them from questioning further. When we get back out of this spell of silence, go to the door, and state your name and Ghortin's name. I'm planting an essence of him to block that of the lost god. It should hold for a few weeks."

He took a deep breath and Jenna felt a spell flow over her like a warm coat. Then the silence spell dropped. And the door opened to the guard and Prince Justlantin. He reminded Jenna more of Storm than of Resstlin, even though he was shorter than his younger brother. And he had their mother's kind, deep brown eyes.

Dantil bowed. "Good evening Prince Justlantin, I believe I have found the problem. A year ago, the consciousness of Mastermage Ghortin resided in his apprentice's head. While he is no longer living there, I sensed the residual presence. I believe that is causing a conflict for the spell bubble."

The prince nodded. "I recall when that happened. Can this be resolved?" He gave Jenna a small smile but stayed within the range of the guards.

Jenna didn't blame him after everything that had gone on.

"I believe it can, Jenna?" Dantil smiled and motioned for her to step closer to the door. "Repeat your name and Ghortin's."

She nodded, stepped forward, and quickly stated her name and Ghortin's. The spell bubble flashed green. She kept the relief off her face, but she was grateful this worked without exposing Typhonel.

"I am honored to meet you in person, Lady Jenna. Please come and join us." Prince Justlantin nodded and went back into the room.

"Thank you, Dantil," Jenna said as she and Crell went past the guards.

"You are welcome. Give my regards to Ghortin." Dantil pulled up his hood and went back down the stairs.

This was not the formal royal dining hall, but more like a fancier family dining room. The table easily fit the people already there, and there were two empty seats next to Storm.

Prince Justlantin took his seat at the end of the table and nodded to Ghortin. "There was a bit of an issue with someone's past residence in his apprentice's head." His smile showed that he wasn't upset about the situation.

Ghortin looked up from his conversation with Tor Ranshal. "What? That spell bubble out front?" He shot a concerned look at Jenna and she gave a slight head shake. He smiled. "Sorry about that, Jenna, I do leave a presence even after I've left a place. Don't worry, we can look into it later."

Tor Ranshal and Rachael shared a worried look but shoved it aside for smiles and nods.

The rest of the table was introduced, with Kaytine and the queen again expressing their thanks for what she'd done for Storm a year ago. Storm's younger sister, Princess Lilltkin, was as lovely and charming as she'd appeared at the ill-fated ball over a year ago. The two youngest royals, the twins Princess Saysa and Prince Whealt, were well-behaved children. It was difficult to determine their ages. At the ball over a year ago, they'd appeared to be about five or six, and now they looked closer to ten.

Prince Justlantin introduced his wife and apologized that their children were too young to attend this evening.

The conversations dropped to a murmur as platters of food came out. Jenna tried to keep from lunging at them, but it was a difficult thing. Like the bed in her room and sleeping, it felt as if she hadn't eaten in a month.

Once she'd cut the edge off her hunger, she studied the rest of the guests. Keanin was sitting between the Saysa and Lilltkin, regaling them with his exploits. He nearly seemed like himself, but there was a tightness lingering around his eyes.

Judging by the way Edgar kept watching Keanin, Jenna wasn't the only one to notice.

Carabella sat on the other side of the queen and whatever the two spoke of caused both of them to shoot knowing glances at Jenna and Storm.

Considering that Carabella knew full well that the engagement was a ruse, Jenna wondered what they were talking about. The grin that Carabella flashed her way didn't settle her nerves at all.

The queen smiled at her as well, but she'd aged in the last year. When Jenna had seen her a year ago, they still held hope that the king could be rescued—not realizing he would be dead within days of being captured. To lose her eldest son in Lithunane compounded the blow.

Kaytine was a cleric of the goddess Irissanta and kept one hand on her mother's shoulder while the two spoke. Most likely she'd been in Irundail since the king was lost. She was no longer in line for the throne, having removed herself when she followed the goddess and normally lived in their temple island halfway down to Lithunane.

"What are they up to?" Storm noticed them as well.

Crell laughed and lowered her voice. "I'd say matchmaking, but you two are fairly well matched. They could be planning a wedding."

Storm patted Jenna on the back as she took an inopportune drink of wine at that moment and choked.

"Don't worry, I'll clear that up with my family tomorrow. Although, this isn't a good time to plan a wedding, regardless. We're facing war."

"Aye. That's why we need to make happy plans, too." Crell nodded. "It's important to look at what will come about when the dying is over."

"Good point," Jenna said. "But being your fiancée hasn't been that bad." She felt another twinge at the thought of what might have happened to the staff of the Lithunane palace.

"Really?" His blue eyes were mischievous. "That's good to know." He rose to his feet and coughed to gain the attention of those at the table. "As many of you know, it was believed that Lady Jenna and I were engaged. I need to make a correction, however." He looked down at Jenna and then held out his hand for her to rise.

Jenna wasn't certain how she felt about this. Being thought of as his fiancée hadn't truly been bad.

"I was unable to ask her properly before, nor could I present a ring." He tilted his head toward his mother as he pulled out a lovely ring encased in delicate diamonds. "Jenna Reilly, will you marry me?"

His question hit her hard. She hadn't been expecting it

and while part of her had hoped for it at some point, she didn't think now was the time.

Crell kicked the back of her leg.

"Yes! I mean, yes, of course, after all the… well, yes." She put her hand up to wipe away an errant tear.

Storm grinned and slipped the gorgeous ring on her finger as everyone in the room clapped. She wasn't sure how many of the family members knew that they hadn't truly been engaged before, but the grins from her friends were wonderful.

"I believe we need a toast." Tor Ranshal turned to the head server. "Five bottles of sparkling wine from the Enari province if you please."

The man nodded and vanished.

"Five? You're planning for more than a toast. Unless you're planning on inviting my rangers in." Crell pushed aside her glass of ale at Tor Ranshal's words.

"I want to make sure we have enough for a proper celebration." Tor Ranshal smiled, but it felt more like Keanin's joviality, hanging on the edge. He wanted to celebrate because of what was coming.

Jenna leaned into Storm's shoulder and looked up at him. "The ring is stunning. I could have said no, you know." The ring had so many stones of varying sizes that it looked different with every turn.

"That's why I was so glad you said you didn't mind being my fake fiancée—I figured the odds were in my favor. And that was my grandmother's ring. Justlantin had his own made for his wife, and Resstlin never married. My mother thought you might like it."

Both of them looked at the queen and smiled. She smiled back, but there were tears of happiness in her dark eyes.

"I can't wear it to war, though." She watched him carefully. He'd pulled the royal fiancée trick on her to keep her out of harm's way before. While he had apologized, and said he realized he couldn't stop her from being endangered, she wasn't certain she completely trusted him about that.

"That is why I have this one as well. Nothing fancy, but you could wear it when we leave Irundail. If you want." He looked embarrassed as he held out a simple gold band. One that looked uneven.

"Is that the one you made?" Crell blurted as they served the sparkling wine in tall glasses.

Storm looked past Jenna to Crell and smiled. "It is. I'm glad you never let me throw it away."

Jenna looked at the ring in her hand. "You made this?"

"When I was younger. I felt that when I found the woman I would marry, I wanted her to have something I'd created. Well, after seeing Justlantin do so. Of course, he does have magic, so the ring he made turned out better."

Jenna closed her hand over the smaller ring. If it wouldn't upset the queen, and possibly the rest of the family, she would have swapped rings immediately "This is the best ring. Ever. I will be proud to go into battle with it on my finger."

Crell pounded her back. "Spoken like a true warrior."

Storm smiled. "I'm glad."

"Now, might I officially raise a toast to Prince Corin and his fiancée, Lady Jenna?" Tor Ranshal stood and raised his glass. Everyone else stood as well, although the younger royals appeared to have glasses of non-bubbling fruit juice.

Jenna slipped the second ring on and raised her glass as well.

The rest of the evening was a blur. After the massive feast, everyone had to come by and admire the ring, extend their best wishes for the happy couple, and in many cases, hug Jenna and Storm.

The evening was winding down, and Jenna felt a sadness flow over her as she looked at Storm. In the time that she'd been in this world, she'd accepted this was her home. Even when she was offered a chance to return—she realized Earth wasn't home anymore.

But becoming engaged made her wish she could tell her family. And introduce Storm to her family and friends. Without them freaking out that she was back from the dead, in their view, and marrying an elf.

Storm was talking to Edgar on his other side, so Crell spotted Jenna's melancholy first.

"What's wrong? I thought you'd be happy?" Crell had been Storm's nanny as a child and the one who gave him the nickname Storm. She knew how difficult he could be at times.

"I am. Very. Until he asked me, I didn't know how much it meant to me." She sighed. "I'm just missing my family on Earth. I love all of my new family," she hugged Crell, "but this would be something to share with the people I loved back there." Her throat closed up. She hadn't felt the loss of her old life this hard since not long after she arrived here.

"It's completely understandable. You should feel what you feel."

"Thank you." Jenna looked over at Storm as he and Edgar debated something that happened on their trip. "I guess he's a decent consolation prize."

Crell laughed and offered to refill her wineglass.

"No, thank you. Between the food, excitement, and possibly the longest day in any world, I'm wiped out." The yawn she couldn't repress made her eyes water. "I think I'm done."

Storm heard that and looked over. "I should have thought of that sooner. May I escort my fiancée to her sleeping chamber?" He gave a bow that Keanin must have been coaching him on.

"I think so, but I wanted to hear about your adventures." She put her hand up to cover another yawn as she got to her feet.

"We promise not to talk about them until the morning. You look exhausted." Crell also got to her feet, but she took her wineglass with her. People were moving around and she was aiming for Tor Ranshal.

"I wasn't going to say that." Storm's smile pointed out that he thought it as well.

"Thanks, you two. Do I have to officially take my leave?" She figured they might excuse any slight breaches of etiquette, but no reason to start on the wrong foot.

"No, this really is a family dinner. My mother and Kaytine have already left."

"Good. I need about a week of sleep." Jenna nodded to those people who noticed them leaving and let Storm escort her out.

"I am happy to officially be your fiancée, by the way," Jenna said as they stopped in front of her chamber door. And then gave a massive yawn. "Sorry."

He looked down at her with a smile. "You've had a fairly eventful day. And I am extremely glad you said yes." His kiss was gentle and he was still smiling when they broke apart. "Get some rest. Tomorrow will probably be hectic, to say the least."

Jenna gave him another quick kiss and went into her room.

Jenna didn't even remember showering, changing, and crawling into the massive bed. But she swore she'd only been asleep a short while when she heard people running past her door.

She rolled over and put one of the million pillows over her head. Someone in this world needed to invent earplugs.

Then reality woke her up. People running in a castle

was a bad thing. She threw back her covers and quickly changed into a tunic and leggings. She wanted to wear her new slippers—they felt like walking on clouds—but that wouldn't be a good idea if she needed to go outside. Her boots had seen better days, but they worked.

The hallway outside her room had windows that showed her morning was in place…early morning. While there wasn't an alarm as would be happening for a full invasion, there was more noise, and the obvious trying to not be making noise, going on downstairs. She knew Keanin and Storm had rooms on this floor, but hadn't found out where they were. Going around knocking to find out didn't seem nice.

She also had no clue where Ghortin, Carabella, or Crell were rooming. With a shrug, she jogged down the stairs.

To see Edgar, Keanin, and Storm fully armed and heading out the front door of the castle.

CHAPTER TEN

JENNA RAN AFTER THEM. SHE didn't think Storm would take off after proposing, but he was a flight risk if he felt he had a cause.

Edgar and Storm were holding on to Keanin, but not stopping him, only slowing him down. He was fighting hard, but he was heading for the stables.

"I have to get her; it'll take too long for them to bring her up."

"What's going on?" Jenna ran up behind them.

Keanin spun around to her and Storm and Edgar released him. "Jenna, do you remember sending Tor Ranshal and Edgar into the castle from the gates when they arrived badly injured last year? Can you do it again?" He sounded calm, but his jaw was clenched. And his golden eyes were wide with fear.

Storm turned to her. "People we left in Erlinda were attacked, some of them escaped and came here. They are getting close to the gates, but they're in terrible shape." He kept watching his friend but didn't stop him as Keanin ran for a horse.

"That wasn't me, it was Ghortin." A year later, she still wasn't certain how he'd done what he did. It was magic far beyond her current level. And he wasn't in her head now.

"What was me, child? What's happened?" Ghortin, Carabella, and Crell came into the stable. All three looked a bit disheveled from sleep, but Crell and Carabella had swords. Edgar also got on a horse, neither he nor Keanin bothered with saddles or tack.

"Unknown assailants have attacked people we know. They're being chased outside of the gates; we have to get down there and rescue them. Can you and Jenna bring them in magically?" Keanin responded.

Jenna turned to Ghortin. "Like you and I did for Tor Ranshal and Edgar."

Ghortin shook his head. "That was an unusual combination of Jenna and myself, I'm not sure how we did it." He stepped back as Keanin and Edgar raced out of the stable at his words.

"Follow us!" Keanin yelled as they rode off.

Storm jumped onto an unsaddled horse as well. "Can you try? One of the injured is close to Keanin."

"Definitely." Ghortin magicked four saddles on four horses. "Go, we'll catch up to you."

Storm turned to a sleepy-looking stable boy. "Under my orders, call out the guards—there's a problem outside of the gates. We need a full complement out there immediately." The boy nodded and ran back toward the castle.

Storm nodded to Jenna and raced off after his friends.

Carabella and Crell were already on two of the horses, so Ghortin and Jenna followed.

Jenna was grateful for Ghortin giving them saddles— she wasn't an amazing horsewoman and this wasn't the time to try bareback.

Crell took the lead, with Carabella close behind.

"Are we going to be able to do it? I have no idea how you did it before."

"I don't know, but with what we now are aware of, that we weren't at the time, I think it was more than only you and me," he dropped his voice, but Carabella was far enough ahead not to hear them. "Work on contacting your friend. I know he vanished, but I think we need *him*."

Jenna mentally reached out to Typhonel, but as they drew closer to the gates, there was still no response.

The race down the three levels of Irundail and across the stretch of land separating it from the wall and gate was a surreal ride. She'd never seen or felt Keanin's terror like this. He was trying to control it, but it wasn't working.

She and he had always had a connection of sorts, and right now he was trying to mask a serious panic attack. Someone in that group was dear to him—but there was also a layer of guilt to his feelings.

"How did Keanin know something happened to them?" Ghortin rode after their friends at a good pace.

Jenna shrugged as she hung on to her horse. "No idea. We'll have to ask when we catch up to him."

Keanin, Edgar, and Storm were racing across the flatland toward the wall. The gates weren't open, but she didn't think that would last long once they got there. Keanin's magic had grown and changed in the time they'd been apart—he might see if he could blast the gates if they didn't open fast enough.

Jenna and her friends were on the stretch leading to the walls when the left gate opened and Keanin's horse sprinted out of it. As they grew closer, Jenna saw Storm and Edgar arguing with the guard. But unlike yesterday, the guard nodded and sent more people, along with Storm and Edgar, out the gate.

Crell and Carabella drew their swords as they raced through the open gate.

"I didn't bring a weapon." Jenna's brain caught up to that fact.

"You and I *are* weapons," Ghortin said. "Have you reached him?"

"Not yet."

"Keep trying."

A group of guards stayed near the gates, and judging

by the looks on the faces they passed—the argument had been about them staying there. The fighting was close and they wanted to be part of it. More guards were coming down from the castle, but until reinforcements were there, these couldn't leave the gates unguarded.

The sun had risen enough to see the fight up ahead. Foul creatures pinned a group of twenty people down.

Creatures that she recognized. "Demonspawn?" Jenna immediately pulled in the nastiest spells she could find. She would welcome Typhonel's assist, but her fury at those things would cause them a lot of damage.

Keanin was off his horse and in the thick of the fight, using sword and magic as he cut his way through the demonspawn. With yells, Storm and Edgar jumped off their horses and joined the battle. The guards that rode out with them went to another group.

Jenna felt the horse under her panic at the demonspawn. "Leave your horses!" She got hers to stop so she could get off, and so did Ghortin. Crell and Carabella did amazingly graceful dismounts and then dove into the fighting.

All the horses ran back toward Irundail as the guards called from the castle arrived at the gates.

Jenna still didn't feel Typhonel, so she focused on what she could do. Her most violent spells would have worked well if the demonspawn weren't so close to the people they were trying to save. One kelar man was listing heavily as he fought off three of them to keep them away from a blonde woman who had collapsed at his feet.

Keanin was decimating demonspawn on his way to get to the two—so those were most likely his friends. But the demonspawn were drawn to him and made his progress impossible.

Jenna raced through to the man and woman just as one of the remaining two demonspawn stabbed the man in the stomach with a barbed tail.

Jenna yelled and sent the two demonspawn a few hundred feet backward. Then smashed them into the ground.

Keanin was still fighting the growing number of demonspawn as Jenna got to the injured pair. Storm and Edgar were near him but were also trying to help the injured.

Jenna ran to the two injured kelar. "I'm a friend of Keanin's." They were bleeding badly and the woman was unconscious. She tried once more to reach Typhonel, but nothing. And Ghortin was too far away to help her. She grabbed ahold of both of them, fighting her memory to recall that spell. She felt a force of what she wasn't sure of, but with whatever it was, she got herself and the two dying people to the castle.

Jenna gasped and dropped to her knees as they landed on the front stairs of the House of Healing. Every part of her body felt ripped apart, but they made it. A guard ran forward.

"Get help. They're dying." She heard the guard yell for assistance, then the world swirled around her for a moment. She closed her eyes and tried to clear her head, but opened them when she heard the sounds of people running toward her.

"Jenna! Are you injured as well?"

Jenna smiled. Maggie. The most efficient healer and mother hen she'd ever seen. Four more healers were checking on the injured pair.

"It's good to see you, Maggie. I'm fine, just some magical kickback from getting them up here. They're seriously hurt." She wished she could go back and transfer all the injured up here, but while she had successfully done it this once, there was no way she could magically even light a candle right now.

Maggie helped her to her feet as the other healers got the pair on rolling cots. "Come with us."

Jenna wasn't going to disobey her, not to mention that

the world still seemed off and she felt like her head was going to split open. She followed them as they went inside the House of Healing and into a smaller healing room on the main floor.

There were more healers there and soon the injured were surrounded by magic and healing medicines.

They drew a curtain to separate them, and Jenna panicked. Had one already died?

"Easy child," Maggie said. "We will need to operate on both, but I feel we can save them. Who are they?"

Jenna shrugged. "Not sure. These two were part of a group of people that Keanin, Storm, and Edgar knew in Erlinda. They were chased here by demonspawn. That's what hurt them. And there will be more injured coming." Something she would have said earlier if her brain hadn't been so scrambled.

"Demonspawn." Maggie looked ready to snap something large in two with her bare hands. "Thank you, child. Now go wait for your friends. I will keep all of you apprised." She turned to one of the other healers. "Please prepare the larger rooms."

Jenna nodded and went to the castle. Again, the feeling of needing to help rose, but she had nothing left. And if Typhonel had helped get them here, he never said anything. Counting on him wouldn't be an option.

She found Tor Ranshal and explained what had happened. "They're going to need help to get the rest of the injured up here."

"I'll send wagons. You need to sit. You look pale."

"I feel pale." She forced a smile. "Is it possible to have food sent to my room?" She was having increasing difficulty focusing on Tor Ranshal and being around more people would be worse. And she needed food badly.

"Yes, child. Ahh, Rachael. Could you escort Jenna to her room and see she gets fed?"

Jenna hadn't seen Rachael, but she came around the

corner. "Of course. Come with me." She smiled and took Jenna's arm.

Jenna began to tell her what happened, but Rachael cut her off. "After you've recovered a bit." She nodded to Tor Ranshal.

He flagged down a passing page and ordered wagons and more guards to be sent to the gates immediately, then went out the front door.

Jenna waited until she was sitting in a comfortable chair by the window in her room, with a full pot of tea and a mass of food, before she told Rachael what happened.

Rachael's face grew grimmer and her hands clenched. "Those things need to die. On the other front, the spell of translocation you did is a dangerous and tricky one. You say Typhonel didn't assist? Nor Ghortin?"

"As far as I know, no. If Typhonel helped, he never made his presence known. Ghortin wasn't near me. When I saw that Keanin was trying to get to that man and woman, I cut through to them." She ate some more toast. "It was odd. The demonspawn were fighting Keanin, and keeping him away from the victims, but they hadn't hurt him when I left. I know his magic has changed in the past month, and he is an impressive swordsman, but it was like they weren't *trying* to hurt him. Only to hold him in place."

"That could be bad." She whistled and a tiny mouse-like, but with wings, construct appeared in the window. "Take this message to Ghortin and the others. They need to protect Keanin." The construct gave a chirp, then flew away.

"A scree. I forgot about those." Jenna smiled and got to her feet. "I feel better and should get back there. Especially if you think Keanin is in danger."

"You're in danger too. And you're exhausted." She frowned, then spoke quickly. "Close your eyes, stand on your left foot, and touch your nose with your right index finger. Now."

The last word was a low-level compulsion spell, and Jenna did what she asked. Or tried to. She felt herself losing balance the moment she closed her eyes and hit the middle of her forehead with her index finger. Before falling over completely. "What happened?"

"It is as I feared. Something has severely depleted you on many levels. That spell you cast is my thinking. You overextended yourself and now your very balance is lost. You wouldn't be able to help any of them out there right now."

"I need to do something."

"You have. You sent help to them and I've warned them about protecting Keanin. I'm not sure why the demon-spawn are acting as they are, but it can't be a good thing."

Jenna looked out the window as the first wagons came back, all escorted by guards. But she didn't see her friends either on horseback or in the wagons as they rolled over to the House of Healing.

"I could help over there."

"You are stubborn. You take after Ghortin that way," Rachael sighed. "Fine, but you get a healing draught first and you can't use magic. Do you agree?"

Jenna hesitated as a gray and yellow swirling drink appeared on the table. Ghortin wasn't the only one who made nasty concoctions. "This will heal me?"

"It will keep your brains in place. And start healing your balance." She picked up the glass but pulled it back when Jenna reached for it. "No magic. At least for a day. Do you agree?"

Jenna sighed. "Yes, I promise."

Rachael peered at her for a few moments. "There is a bit of the chaotic realm in your eyes. Something happened when you did your spell. Not only no magic but no going to the chaotic plane to get more Power for at least a few days. That is most disturbing and something I didn't notice until now." She handed to drink to Jenna. "Drink up, then we'll go to the House of Healing."

Jenna drank the mixture and as bad as it looked, it tasted like water. She put down the glass. "Not that I'm complaining, but that wasn't bad."

"Ghortin has to stop making his potions taste so vile. Gives the rest of us a terrible reputation." She headed for the door but turned back quickly. "If you start feeling dizzy, or odd, or—"

"If anything odd comes up, you'll be the second one to know. I promise." Jenna cut her off with a smile.

"Okay. I trust you. But with your fiancée and friends all out there, I doubt I could get you to stay here."

"Probably correct."

Rachael was a good four inches shorter than Jenna but she was a fast walker. Jenna was jogging by the time they got out of the castle.

The wagons appeared to have all come back, and single riders were now crossing the plane below. The gates were shut and a mass of guards stood nearby. Keanin rode up from the second level. He jumped off his horse and ran into the House of Healing.

Jenna felt relief as they followed him. He was safe, and even though he obviously cared about the pair she had rescued, Jenna knew there was no way he would have left Storm or the others if any of them were injured.

"We might want to catch him; I can feel his panic from here and Maggie might still be working on the two you brought up. Stopping Keanin and saving lives might not be mutually possible even for her." Rachael walked faster.

Jenna *was* jogging as they entered the House of Healing. Keanin was already arguing with two stoic-faced guards outside of the ground-floor healing room as Jenna and Rachael caught up to him.

"You don't understand, I need to see her." Keanin had his head lowered, but Jenna felt a spell growing in his right hand. "I *will* see her."

CHAPTER ELEVEN

JENNA RAN FORWARD AND GRABBED his other hand. "Keanin, let the healers do their work. They can't if you're in there."

He spun but relaxed when he saw it was Jenna. "I have to help her. It was my fault; they should have come with us when we left Erlinda."

Rachael came alongside him and clasped his right hand with hers. The spell he'd been pulling up vanished. "Your terror would be projected on all the injured in that room—including the one you are taking irrational blame over. You would hurt them." Rachael was usually gentler about her admonishments, but Keanin needed something stronger right now.

"I…I wouldn't want that." He freed his hands and rubbed them across his face. "I made one hell of a mess."

Jenna pulled him away from the door, and the two guards who were studiously looking over his head but hadn't moved. "Come over here. I'd like to hear how you were responsible for a bunch of demonspawn attacking." She kept her voice low.

"I wasn't." Keanin didn't protest when she pushed him into a chair down the corridor, and she and Rachael stood in front of him. "But I should have made them come with us." He looked up. "You saved the love of my life and her brother. Talia and Diath."

Jenna smiled. At least he said saved. It meant he still had hope. "You were trying so hard to get to them. When I saw my chance, I took it." She took one of his hands and squeezed. "I'm glad you found someone."

It was odd that he hadn't spoken of Talia before. Speaking of his latest loves was something the old Keanin did on an hourly basis. This was another change—but she also felt it was more than that.

"I did. Then she told me it was all a ruse to save her brother, and we left Erlinda without them." He dropped his head. "My bruised ego almost killed them."

Storm, Edgar, and Crell came running up.

"Because she didn't want you endangering yourself by coming back to Erlinda alone." Storm had a slice on his upper right bicep, and all three of them looked roughed up, but he had no problem hugging Jenna.

"I...probably would have." Keanin looked down with a frown.

"And then the demonspawn would have you as well. By the way, Hon and Flini were injured, but feisty enough that I had to order them to ride in the wagons up here," Edgar said.

Keanin gave a small smile. More friends from their adventure.

Jenna wanted to ask why the demonspawn were trying to take Keanin and not kill him, but the look on all three of their faces said this wasn't the time.

Keanin's face also indicated that he wanted to say something else to Storm, but turned to her instead. "Thank you for getting them up here."

"I'm glad whatever I did worked."

"And she's not to use magic for at least a day. If any of you notice her appearing dizzy or disoriented, come get me or Ghortin immediately." Rachael was watching her closely again.

All three kelars and Crell nodded and Storm's concern transferred from Keanin to her.

She started to say she was fine when a healer apprentice

came out of the healing room. "Maggie says you may come in now. The rest of the injured are in the larger room." She nodded to Jenna but stepped back as all five moved toward the door. "I'm not sure about all of you?"

Storm, Edgar, Crell, and Rachael nodded and stopped walking.

"We can wait here. Keanin needs to go in with Jenna, though." Storm squeezed Jenna's shoulder.

The apprentice studied Keanin and then nodded.

"Take a few deep breaths." Jenna held onto Keanin's arm and slowed his rush. "Your energy could hurt them. They will be fine, you saved them. Don't forget that."

He looked down with tears in his eyes. "*You* saved them. I won't forget that."

Jenna felt his terror ebbing. It was a good thing that she didn't have this type of connection with anyone other than him. Feeling his powerful emotions was difficult enough. "We *all* saved them. Now let's see how they're doing."

Maggie waited for them inside the door. "They are stable and conscious. They would like to see you. Both of you. But keep it quiet and brief. They need further time to heal."

Jenna raised an eyebrow at that. Neither should have been aware enough to know what she'd done.

Keanin nodded and went to the closest bed—the blonde woman. They had taken the curtain between them down, and it was clear by their faces that they were siblings.

Jenna held back, but the dark-haired man waved her over. "Thank you. I saw you save us. Not sure exactly how, but I was losing a lot of blood. My name's Diath."

"Glad I could help. I'm Jenna."

Keanin looked up from his conversation with Talia. "And she's engaged to Storm." He flashed Jenna a genuine smile. "Diath is a bit of a lady-killer."

"Good to know." Jenna grinned at Diath but he shrugged. "I won't bother you much. You need rest, and Maggie is a fierce guardian. But when did the demonspawn start after you?"

He gave a half-cough. "From the start, but we didn't realize it. Bands of what we thought were simple soldiers from the north struck Erlinda. We needed to get as many people out as we could. We were a few hours away from here when some of those traveling with us turned into demonspawn and attacked."

Jenna frowned. "That doesn't make sense. If they wanted to kill you; they could have done it earlier in your trip. Or waited until you were closer to here if that was their goal."

"Agreed. We lost a lot of good people, but because of Keanin, you, and the others, we're here now." He yawned.

"And you need to rest." Jenna nodded and left the room. She needed to speak to Ghortin.

Who luckily was in the same waiting corridor they'd left the others in, along with an oddly silent Carabella.

"How do we know the injured who were brought up aren't demonspawn?"

"Well, they were bleeding red…"

Storm and Edgar shook their heads.

"They can do that for a while before they go green." Storm put his hand on the hilt of his sword.

Ghortin got to his feet. "I ran a low-level spell over the injured, but it might not have been enough. We need to see all of them. Including Keanin's friends." He marched toward Maggie's healing room. Spoke softly to her and motioned for the rest to stay outside.

He came back a minute later. "They are clear. Let's go find the rest."

"Were there any who weren't seriously injured?" Jenna asked Storm as they ran upstairs to the larger healing rooms.

"A few. We made them come up in the wagons with the others. And they are waiting in a room in the castle under guard to be checked out. We'll need a mage to go over them. But not you. No magic, remember?" Storm still looked worried about her.

Rachael patted Storm's arm. "Good lad, keep an eye on her. I'll go check the ones in the castle, maybe with Crell to assist if any cause trouble?"

"I'll get a few of my rangers as back up on the way over to the castle." Crell followed Rachael out of the House of Healing.

"I checked though." Ghortin paused and narrowed his eyes. "Or did I? Now I'm questioning myself."

"Demonspawn aren't mages, right? But could they be working with one to make it seem like things were okay?" Jenna hadn't felt any blanketing spell, but she'd only been down there a short time. Carabella was with them so she didn't want to mention who would most likely have been working with a group of demonspawn—Sacaranz.

"Aye, they could." Ghortin nodded to the guards outside the larger healing room. "I need to see the injured."

The guards paused long enough to make Jenna wish she'd stopped to get her weapons. But then they opened the door.

The room was organized chaos, with healers and assistants racing around trying to save lives. Jenna felt a twinge of guilt at disturbing them—but if there were demonspawn, they needed to find them. The demon-spawn in hiding could have attacked the group escaping from Erlinda at any time. Yet they'd waited until now. Something else was planned.

Ghortin went to the main healer in this room, an exceedingly tall kelar man with long gray hair pulled back into a braid.

Jenna had only seen few gray-haired kelars. He was probably close to Rachael's age.

"Mastermage Ghortin, it is good to see you. What can I help you with?" He was a force of calm in the surrounding hustle. But he still redirected two healers in the time that he greeted Ghortin.

"Loxsin, good to see you, it's been too long." Ghortin shook the kelar's hand. "I need to check on the injured." He dropped his voice. "Demonspawn."

A flash of pure anger crossed Loxsin's thin face, but he recovered. "I can search as well. After the ball in Lithunane, I went back into my hermitage and learned everything I could about them."

Ghortin nodded and he and Loxsin took opposite ends of the room.

Carabella looked around. "Since I can't use magic, and we have enough physical muscle here, I'm going to assist Rachael and Crell." She patted her sword and a wicked-looking dagger. "I can back up Crell and her rangers if anyone gets feisty in the castle." Her tone was such that she was looking forward to it.

Storm nodded and Carabella left.

He turned to Jenna and they made a blockade in front of the door along with Edgar. "She's far more subdued than usual. And accepting of her situation."

"That's relatively new. She eventually realized what would happen if she used magic on our trip, but this silence is recent and worrying." Jenna didn't know how much Carabella would confide in her. But they'd become close in the last month, so hopefully she'd open up. Something clearly concerned the cuari woman.

"More to keep an eye on." Edgar watched Ghortin, Loxsin, and the injured. "I thought we'd be safe here for a while, but it appears not."

"I'd hoped to have at least a few days before the next tragedy." Jenna sighed. She also continued to observe the people in the room, but aside from any of the patients suddenly becoming demonspawn, she wasn't certain what she should be looking for.

Ghortin and Loxsin took their time casting spells and examining the injured carefully.

Then they met in the middle of the room.

There were no demonspawn among the injured.

Ghortin and Loxsin spoke for a bit, and then Ghortin came back to them at the door. His frown was at odds with not finding any demonspawn.

"Nothing?" Edgar got out before anyone else.

"No. Which is good and bad. The demonspawn wouldn't have behaved as they did without a plan, and if the people whom Rachael is examining are also not demonspawn, then we have no idea what that plan is." Ghortin nodded to the door. "We need to go back to the castle."

Jenna was the closest to him on the way out of the House of Healing.

"I know I can't use magic right now, but wouldn't it be a good idea to train all magic users for whatever detection spells you and Healer Loxsin used?" She wasn't sure what they'd been using and the slow way in which they checked each patient pointed out that it might not be workable in a fast-paced fight. But it was better than nothing.

"I came to the same conclusion. And we need ways to speed the process." Ghortin's look was grim as they entered the castle.

They were heading toward the rear of the first floor where the uninjured remained locked up when screams echoed through the hallway.

CHAPTER TWELVE

THEY ALL RAN, WITH STORM and Edgar quickly taking the lead. Edgar might be short for a kelar, he was half-human, but that didn't slow him down. Jenna and Ghortin kept up as best they could. She might need to take up jogging once everything settled down.

The door they were running to was ajar and there were no guards in front of it. Neither of which was a good sign.

Storm and Edgar hit the partially open door and had their swords out before Jenna and Ghortin got into the room.

Rachael, Crell, Carabella, and three rangers stood in the center of the room surrounded by twenty people. All of whom were standing and screaming. If they were demonspawn, they hadn't changed yet.

"Rachael?" Ghortin took a few deep breaths. Running wasn't his strong suit.

"It's okay. There is a spell on them, probably why they show few injuries. Yet, they aren't demonspawn." She sounded far calmer than Jenna was feeling.

"Can you make them stop screaming?" Ghortin looked like he was going to forcefully find a way if she couldn't.

Jenna agreed. The screaming was discordant and made her eyes twitch.

"They're working whatever was done to them out of their system." Like Crell, Carabella had her sword raised. "Rachael cast a spell on them. They stopped doing what they were doing and did this. It is annoying though." Her left hand twitched as if itching to cast a spell.

"They'll come out of it soon. It took myself and our three ranger friends here to figure out the spell." Rachael continued to smile and nod at all the screaming people.

"Aside from trying to split our heads, what's the point?" Edgar also looked ready to cast a spell but held back.

"That is unknown. The scream spell was embedded deep within all of them and was to trigger a far nastier spell. But it was not set-up to start for a few days. Whatever it was, it was growing in power. The situation would have been far worse had we waited. It vanished once I broke it and I have no idea what might have already been triggered." Rachael nodded as the people stopped screaming. One by one, they blinked a few times and then collapsed.

Four guards came running up with swords drawn at the same moment. "What's happened?"

Rachael flashed them her sweetest smile. "There were issues and they sent you on a mission. Which you completed gallantly. Thank you. Resume your posts, please."

Jenna felt the tail end of a compulsion spell flow over the guards. They nodded as one and stood outside of the door.

"Oh, please shut the door if you would. And don't let anyone in without asking us first."

The nearest guard shut the door, and Rachael slumped forward with a sigh.

Storm caught her before she fell, but she patted his arm.

"I'm fine. Just a lot of tricky magic in a short time. These were not demonspawn, but that spell on them was one I'd never heard of. We had the options to try to find out what it was, or clear them of it before it grew worse." She shook her head as she looked over the collapsed people around them. "I didn't think we had a choice. The spell residue might tell us something about what it was."

"They're okay then? Only sleeping?" Jenna looked down at the woman closest to her. She appeared to be simply sleeping, but magic could be tricky.

"Yes. And they might be for a while. I felt their exhaustion as the screaming ended. I'd like to keep them together as they recover. But not in the House of Healing just yet." Rachael looked exhausted as well. "We need to find better ways to screen people."

Edgar looked between Rachael and Ghortin. "When we were in Khelaran, I was able to use a spell to uncover hidden demonspawn, I tried to use it during our fight in front of the gates, but I couldn't reach it. I'd like to see if you two could help me figure it out."

One of the rangers, a tall kelar woman, nodded. "Agreed. I've not heard of a spell like that but it would be helpful."

"I think all the mages in Irundail need to learn it. And once whatever this was has been determined, screen for it as well." Ghortin tilted his head as he studied Edgar. "There could be some blocks restricting your access to the spell. We can sort it out." Then he turned to Jenna. "But not you just yet. I agree with Rachael. You need a magical time out."

Carabella smiled and dropped an arm around Jenna's shoulders. "We can sit out together. I want to do some research while we're here on sorting out freeing my people." She held up her hand as Ghortin, Rachael, and Jenna all opened their mouths to protest. "I know. I can't see or hear some things. That's why if I have help, I'll be less likely to trigger something bad."

Jenna shrugged. "I'm fine with helping her. If you try to train me on the demonspawn reveal spell, when I can't practice it, I'll forget it. Doing something is the way I learn tricky things."

"See? We'll accomplish so much!" Carabella sounded

close to her normal self, but there was a tightness around her eyes that hadn't been there before they came south to Irundail.

"I can get interviews going with the less injured people over in the House of Healing and find out what they noticed on their trip here." Crell looked at the people sprawled out on the floor. "And get these folks into beds. I doubt that the screaming was a new plan of attack for demonspawn."

"Agreed." Rachael went to the door and spoke to the guards, then returned. "I've asked them to set up a secure room with cots for these people. And guards. I don't sense anything from them—not like I did before—but it's better to be cautious."

Once the unconscious people were sorted out, Storm came to Jenna and Carabella. "I could help research if needed, but I think I'd be of more help investigating the ambush location outside of the walls."

Carabella smiled. "Thank you for your generous offer, but I believe that Jenna and I have it covered." Her eyes darkened. "But do be careful out there. There was an odd feeling when that attack was happening, one I couldn't specifically nail down without my magic. Take some mages with you. Not everyone needs to learn this spell at the same time."

"Agreed, smaller groups are easier for training on this level of magic. But since Edgar utilized something like it before, I think he should sit in on the first group." Ghortin finished up with the last unconscious person to be wheeled out of the room.

Crell nodded to the three rangers. "Me and these three can go with Storm. Keep him out of trouble."

Ghortin nodded as they left the room. "We'll do the lesson in the House of Healing; I'd like to get Keanin involved."

Edgar laughed. "Good luck prying him away from Talia. He fell hard the moment he met her and fell even worse when she chased him off. With the attack, he's probably never going to leave her side."

"Is she a magic user? That could get bad." Jenna had images of an overprotective Keanin being magically hung by his heels somewhere dark and dismal.

Storm turned back as they walked out. "No, but she's a guard captain in the Erlinda forces—she might use weapons on him if it doesn't ease up, eventually."

Jenna was looking forward to hearing more about the two of them, and more details about the rest of their adventures. The taran wand limitations meant only the most basic information got out to her and the others in the past month. She agreed with the potential for Keanin to become obsessive, though.

"Cheer up, Jenna. You get to spend time with me, trying to find the rest of the cuari." Carabella's smile still wasn't reaching her eyes.

Jenna returned the smile. She figured that once they were alone, she'd see if Carabella would open up. She'd seemed fine yesterday, so it was hard to say what had changed.

Ghortin and Edgar, with four unknown-to-Jenna-mages whom Ghortin grabbed along the way, left for the House of Healing. Storm gave Jenna a quick kiss, and then he, Crell, and her rangers headed for the stables.

Carabella turned down a long, narrow hallway in the castle.

Jenna hadn't spent a lot of time in Irundail, but she knew she'd never gone this far back into the castle. The area they were heading toward was dark, musty, and seemed to be ancient.

"Ah, now I feel better." Carabella pushed open a heavy wooden door. "This area was the first place we built when we came here. Well, after the walls and the Keepers. This land was pretty wild back then, and we were still recovering. Or trying to."

Jenna watched her as she tried to smile, but failed. "You miss them, don't you? The friends you lost fighting that thing in the Markare?" Ghortin, Carabella, and a small group of adventures including Storm's grandfather, had created Irundail long ago when a battle to stop a monster in the Markare went bad and they had nowhere to go. They'd stopped the creature, but they'd lost people. Coming here was probably bringing back painful memories for the ancient cuari woman.

"I do. And who we were back then. I haven't been back here much in the past thousand years. Only a few visits more recently." She gently ran her hand along a heavy wood bookshelf. "This library was always my favorite."

An old derawri came scuttling up, adjusting a pair of glasses perched on his nose. "Welcome to the…Carabella?" His jaw dropped and he stopped.

"Wilty?! You old dog. I would have figured you would have retired decades ago and set up that farm you always spoke of." Carabella's smile reached her eyes this time as she ran forward and engulfed the tiny derawri.

He might be about half her height, but that didn't slow down his enthusiasm as he returned her hug.

He stepped back. "I tried a few years ago. Still have the farm at the far end of the valley. It's lovely, but I was bored to tears. No one to talk to about the old stories. About the old days. Here they have to let me ramble on."

"I might join you out there once we get these minor problems taken care of. Maybe we can form our own group of old warriors." Carabella motioned to Jenna. "This is my dear friend Jenna. She's technically Ghortin's apprentice."

Wilty scurried forward. "Prince Corin's fiancée? I am honored to meet you." He took her hand and smiled.

"Did that hooligan Crell travel north with you all as well?"

Carabella laughed. "Yes, she did. She and some of her rangers are with Corin checking out the attack from this morning."

Wilty's eyes went wide and he soundlessly pulled out two chairs around a massive table, then took the third for himself. "What happened?"

Carabella filled in most of it, and he looked ill when she said demonspawn.

"I'd say I should have stuck to retirement, but this is larger than simply Irundail, isn't it?"

"We're looking at a war. One that will pull in all the known lands." Carabella was immortal, and she never looked older than someone in her thirties—until now. But then she shook it off and appeared fine after a few moments.

Wilty nodded. "We will be prepared. War is more than swords and magic. Knowledge will be needed. Speaking of which, something more than my friendship sent you here today."

"Truly spoken. Even more so, as I had no idea you were here. I would have come here sooner had I known." Carabella gave him an abbreviated—mostly because of things she couldn't speak of, and things she couldn't know—version of what had happened in the last month.

"You have come to the right place. Whoever took your people will have left traces." Wilty got a gleam in his eye as he got to his feet.

Jenna got to her feet as well. "But how can ancient books lead us to freeing the cuari now? Have they been kidnapped before?" She enjoyed research. Finding hidden answers to mysteries had been the best part of graduate school in her prior life. But she was having a disconnect with something happening now that had no precedent.

"Ah! There is always a trail in the past. One has to

know where to look." He led them into the stacks of books.

"There's some information that Carabella can't hear." Jenna hated bringing it up, but if Wilty was going to help them, he needed all the details.

"I keep forgetting that." Carabella shrugged. "It's annoying but true. Do you still have the silence rooms?"

Wilty smiled. "Indeed. Where do you think I take my afternoon naps?" He detoured down a narrow walkway between the tall bookshelves and stopped in front of a large, dark cube. "Make yourself comfortable." He waited until Carabella entered the room and the door clicked. Then his smile dropped. "Even though that room will block all light and sound, it would be better to move away a bit. I'm glad you said something. I can't solve a problem with missing pieces."

He nodded when he felt they were far enough away.

Jenna told him about Sacaranz and the chaotic plane. She couldn't explain who Sacaranz was. The idea that the original cuari had tried to take over the world eons ago wasn't something she was free to tell. That would be up to Tor Ranshal and Rachael. She might be the Protector, but they were the Guardians and had been securing this knowledge for hundreds of years. She would mention to them that Wilty might need to be included.

"They trapped them on the chaotic plane? That's not good. They can't stay there long."

"They can't. We need to remove them within a year from when the first ones were taken, and time is running out. We believe that getting them back is crucial to winning the coming war, destroying the portal, and ending the demonspawn for good."

He nodded and silently sorted his thoughts. Not that Jenna blamed him, even telling him only part of it was still staggering.

"This changes what we need to be looking for, of that

I'm certain." He paused and tilted his head. "Might I ask you an unusual question?" At her nod, he continued.

"You're not from here, from this world, are you?"

CHAPTER THIRTEEN

———

JENNA FROZE. THAT WASN'T SUPPOSED to be common knowledge, but Wilty was asking to confirm something he felt he knew. She finally nodded. "I am. Sort of. It's complicated."

Wilty's smile was gentle. "I am a mage and head librarian. I can sense things that are hidden. You have an odd duality that I've not seen before."

Jenna took a deep breath and summarized her arrival.

He took her hand. "I am so sorry. Both for the loss of the woman who was mindsacrificed and as well as for you being torn from your former life." His eyes held tears as he peered closer into her face. "Do you miss it?"

"I would say no, that this world and the people in it are more than enough. And this place *is* home to me now. But there were family and friends back there that I will always miss. At the least, I wish I could comfort them that I'm still alive and doing okay." She thought about the current situation and the upcoming war—maybe not that part.

"It must be a hard thing, but know that I feel you are exactly where you're supposed to be." His tiny, wrinkled face broke into a huge smile. "And perhaps, once things have settled and slowed, I can help you contact those from your prior life. At least long enough to reassure them." He released her hand. "If there is nothing else that she can't hear, we probably should let Carabella out. No one likes a cranky cuari."

She'd been in there less than ten minutes, but Carabella

appeared bored and feisty when they got her out. But the sorrow that Jenna had seen earlier was gone. Maybe it was simply being in Irundail and the old memories haunting her. Wilty might not have been in that initial campaign, but seeing him had helped Carabella.

Wilty led them down into a small locked room—and the research began.

They were digging through some scrolls when a young kelar page came hurrying into the room.

"I'm sorry to disturb you, Master Wilty, but they requested Lady Jenna back in the House of Healing."

Jenna was about to ask who requested, but the boy was so on edge that she feared any question would cause him to panic. "Guess you two are on your own. I'll come back if I can." She followed the page out.

He relaxed when they got out of the library.

"Who sent for me?" She waited until they were walking down the steps of the castle.

"Lord Keanin. There's something wrong with magic."

Jenna wanted to ask him why the library disturbed him so much, but his words shook her. "Thank you, I know the way." She didn't wait for his response but started running. The page might have misspoken, but he said *magic*, not *Keanin's magic*. As she ran, she ignored Rachael's decree to not use magic and tried to pull up a simple spell, a light. It was faint as she ran away from the castle, briefly grew stronger, and then vanished when she got to the House of Healing.

Swearing under her breath, she ran to the room that Keanin, Talia, and Diath had been in.

Keanin stood near Talia, but she was asleep. A glance showed that her brother was as well. He left them and met Jenna at the door. "There you are. There's something wrong with the magic here. I can't call up even a simple spell, and the healers are losing their ability as well."

"When did it start?" She tried to pull up even the mage

light spell, but there was nothing. She might have her own magic issues, but that wouldn't have been the case for others.

"I don't know for certain; I hadn't tried to use any recently until one of the healers came in and asked me and other mages about it. Maybe a half hour ago." He was worried, but not hysterical, so Talia and Diath must be asleep naturally.

"We need Ghortin."

"I sent a page for him as well, but they haven't come back yet."

Jenna nodded. She had no idea where Ghortin was doing his class on revealing demonspawn, aside from somewhere in this building. But others could find him. "Have you seen Maggie?"

"She was in the larger healing room. I didn't want to leave them." The way he moved his hand to the hilt of his sword indicated that lack of magic or not, no one was getting to these two.

"I'll send guards back here for outside the door. Stay inside here." She started out, but he caught her arm.

"You think we're under an attack?" His golden eyes were wide.

"Yes, not sure how it was done, but I think someone is trying to take out Irundail's magic. That can only be a precursor to an attack." She shut the doors as she left, grabbed two guards, and ordered them to guard the door—it was handy being a royal fiancée, a lot fewer questions—and ran toward the larger healing room.

There were guards already on this set of doors, but they recognized her, so stood back as she ran inside. Maggie was barking orders and looked frantic. She spotted Jenna and ran over. "All of our magic users lost their ability to cast spells. I've sent for helaermages, but this is horrific."

"It just happened? Keanin said it began a while ago. I didn't notice it in the castle, but I did on the way over here. I think it's spreading. Ghortin is somewhere in this building with a bunch of magic users. Can you send a scree to lead me to him?"

"The scree should still work—they're a different type of magic." Maggie nodded and held out her hand. A scree appeared from somewhere. "Take her to Mastermage Ghortin." She looked at Jenna. "Please sort this out quickly."

Jenna nodded, then raced off as the scree flew to the door and then out as soon as she opened it.

The tiny construct flew upstairs, coming back a few times as it could fly far faster than Jenna could run.

It finally stopped in front of a room.

Jenna thanked the scree, knocked in warning, and then went in.

Ghortin was stomping around in front of a group of mages, swearing. "Jenna! Something's happened to our magic!"

"Just now?" At his annoyed nod, she told him about Keanin and Maggie. "I think it's spreading slowly instead of everyone getting hit at once. Whatever it is."

"This is bad, extremely bad. I need to speak to Tor Ranshal and Rachael."

Edgar jumped to his feet. "I'll warn any mages with Storm. If it's only inside Irundail, they might still have magic." He was gone in a moment.

"Are there diseases that destroy magic? If this was a single spell, everyone should have been hit at once, right?" She might have only been in this world for a short while, but she'd done a fair amount of reading on magic.

"I've never heard of such a spell, but if it did exist—yes, everyone should have been struck at the same time. Not spreading out slowly like a contagion. We need to report this to Prince Justlantin. Everyone who can fight needs to be armed."

It wasn't as satisfying as hoped that Ghortin came to

the same conclusion she had—this was an attack. Taking out all the magic users in Irundail could have horrific results.

After telling the rest of the mages in the room to spread the word and get arms, Ghortin led the way back to the castle and the throne room.

Another spell bubble similar to the one outside of the dining room the prior night flared, but after the second try, it cleared Jenna.

Prince Justlantin sat on a throne and appeared to be holding a regular meeting with nobles, but he looked at them with a start as Ghortin bulldozed his way through the waiting courtiers.

"Can any mages in here access magic?" Ghortin called out loudly as he approached the throne with Jenna trailing behind.

A few worried faces indicated that none of them had noticed anything off—the worry expanded as they tried minor spells and found nothing. Whatever it was, it had hit here as well.

"What's happened?" Prince Justlantin flicked his fingers for a spell, then frowned at the lack of result, and motioned for Ghortin and Jenna to come forward.

"The valley is under attack. It's a spell to block magic, but it's spreading slowly, instead of all at once. You might want to order everyone who can fight to arm themselves and get those who can't into safe quarters." Ghortin moved close enough to the throne that dropping his voice meant only Jenna and Justlantin heard him.

Justlantin's eyes went wide, but he immediately called forward the guard captain and told him to do what Ghortin said, then stood in front of the assembly. "There has been an attack against magic. I need all able-bodied people who can fight to arm themselves and prepare to defend Irundail. Get anyone who can't fight into the back shelter immediately."

Jenna had never heard of the shelter, but it made sense—there was no such thing as a completely secure place in this world. Probably not in her world either, she just never noticed it when she was there.

"I'll need to warn my family." Justlantin was calm, but he moved quickly. He didn't run but ducked into a side passage protected by two guards. "These two are with me, but don't let anyone else through." Both guards nodded and patted small squares on their hips.

Jenna would have to find out later what those were and why only two guards were needed to protect the royal back rooms.

Ghortin looked worried as he glanced back at the guards as they followed Justlantin. "We don't know if static spells are impacted yet."

"Good point. I can have more guards sent." But Justlantin didn't stop moving.

Those squares were static magic of some sort and not something she'd seen or heard of before. Static magic was set and stored spells that could be triggered at a later time. From what she'd read, they could even be used by a non-magic user. But they were tricky to create and took a lot out of the mage who made them.

Ghortin said that maybe in a few dozen years he'd work on teaching her how to make them.

The back area was homey and relaxed and appeared to have chambers, big ones by the size of the doors, for all the family members. All except Storm.

"Isn't this area secured? Could the family stay here?" Jenna kept her voice down, but it made sense. The more people they had to move, the greater the chance of something going wrong.

"Yes. It is. But there is another more secure space even further down. I need everyone to get into it. Lilltkin will probably argue, but I need her to stay there too." Justlantin knocked on the doors facing the hall. His wife and children, along with the queen, Kaytine, Lilltkin, and a male derawri who Jenna had seen with the two youngest royals, were all in the hall immediately. Along with a group of household staff.

Justlantin motioned to Ghortin to tell them what happened. As he predicted, Lilltkin immediately demanded to stay out of the shelter and fight with the others. She was almost as tall as Storm, with long, rich red hair like their mother. She was also so thin and willowy she looked like a strong breeze could snap her. But the look on her face was pure Storm on the level of stubbornness.

Interestingly, the queen agreed with her daughter. "Justlantin, she is a warrior like Corin. You can't protect her forever."

He looked ready to argue, then shook his head. "Fine, but please be careful."

"I need to stay out as well, little brother." Kaytine smiled. "I might not have access to my magic, but the goddess will help protect against this attack. I need to be involved."

"It seems I can't argue with anyone. But I assume my mother, youngest siblings, and the house staff will go into the shelter with my wife and children?" Justlantin didn't seem like a pushover, but he appeared to have a far better acceptance of the forceful personalities in his family than Resstlin had held.

The queen smiled. "Yes. We will bring along all the castle staff since our area is large enough. It will leave more room in the regular shelter for people coming in from the lower levels."

"I've had runners sent out for everyone in the valley. We will get everyone safe." He looked like a combination of Storm and Resstlin but was far calmer than either.

"Where is Carabella? Perhaps she's heard of something like this," Kaytine asked as the derawri escorted

Justlantin's wife, his children, the two youngest royals, the queen, and twenty staff down a long hallway.

"She's in the library. I need to get my weapons, but then I'll get her. She's with Wilty." Jenna noticed that Justlantin and Lilltkin were arming themselves. Then Kaytine went to a hall cabinet and added throwing knives to her cleric ensemble.

She smiled at Jenna. "The goddess wants us to protect who we can, however we can. I will fight if needed." She turned to Justlantin. "But I'd like to speak to the helaer-mages."

He nodded, then looked at Ghortin and Jenna. "I'll be gathering forces to protect what we can. Once you are armed and have gathered Carabella, please join me in front of the castle. I believe she has something that will help us. Providing that static spells aren't impacted by whatever this is." He frowned. "The item she created should have been able to be triggered here. I tried it but it's not responding."

Ghortin looked like he wanted answers. But instead, he led them out of the royal area. "You're going to have to lead the way to Carabella. If she and Wilty were working together, we could lose them in the stacks for ages."

"As long as they haven't gone too far from where we were." Jenna picked up the pace. She wanted to get her sword first, then find Carabella, but this new information changed things. She'd get her weapons after she dug Carabella out. "Do you know what Justlantin was talking about?"

"No. But since my mother hid from me for almost a thousand years, she could have set something up at any time. I hope it's not something that she has to cast herself, though."

Jenna agreed as she pushed open the library doors and eventually got going in the right direction. She had been focused on the page who'd come to get her on the way out, so she hadn't paid as much attention to where she'd started as she should have.

She heard their soft voices before she saw them.

"Jenna! Crisis averted?" Carabella was barely visible from the collection of books and scrolls piled around her.

Wilty looked the same, but he'd been focusing on a scroll, so the look he gave them was owlish.

"No, the crisis is bad," Jenna explained what was happening.

"And Justlantin seems to believe you might have something that will help, but he can't trigger whatever it is from here. And we're not sure if the static spells are impacted as well." Ghortin seemed to be trying to read the top books upside down. He loved research and Jenna knew he hadn't had as much time for it as he would have liked as of late.

"I have something I set up a year ago. That's not good that the remote trigger isn't working, but I always have a failsafe." Carabella nodded and got to her feet. "First I have to get my sword, and then we have to climb. Thank you, Wilty, I suggest you go to the shelter."

He got up as well. "I've done some adjusting to the library. Once you three are out, I'll secure the library. Nothing will get inside here." His face was grim, but his voice was confident.

Carabella nodded and pushed them out of the library.

"What do you mean climb? Prince Justlantin said you'd set something up. Isn't it here in the castle?" Jenna kept up with her, but when she wanted to move, Carabella was fast.

Ghortin kept up a steady pace behind them, but he didn't sound happy about it.

"It was about a week after you all left the last time. The ballroom attack in Lithunane was shocking, so I created a static spell cover for this valley. It's magic-based, but it's protected, so hopefully whatever this spell is won't have affected it."

"A cover?" Jenna glanced back to Ghortin as they ran up the stairs, but he shrugged.

"Yes, quite ingenious and something I forgot about until you mentioned it. Don't say anything Ghortin, I am old enough to forget things from time to time. Anyway, the cover should act to block magic attacks—or physical ones using magic to break in here." She waved at them as she turned off a floor before Jenna's room. "I'll meet you at the bottom. Wear something you can hike in."

Ghortin's sigh was audible as she vanished. "That's like her. I'm afraid that while I am mostly recovered from the arrow to my leg, I'd better not push things, so you'll need to go with her alone."

Jenna shrugged as they got to her floor. She used to hike back on Earth but hadn't done much here.

She ran into her room and changed clothing—wishing she had jeans and hiking boots—then grabbed her sword belt and sword.

Carabella was at the bottom of the stairs, pacing. "Excellent. Let's get going. Ghortin's gone back to the House of Healing since he can't do this journey. We can't even check if other static magic is working as I used the chaotic plane to anchor this one. Hopefully, we can activate it."

"Great. Where are we hiking to?"

"The top of the wall. Not the Keepers, but near there." Her grin was far too perky.

It was going to be an ugly hike.

CHAPTER FOURTEEN

—

"YOU CREATED SOMETHING TO PROTECT all of Irundail, but you have to hike to the top of those monsters to activate it? Isn't that kind of pointless?" Everyone who needed protection could be dead or captured by the time they triggered the cover. The walls were massively high.

"No, sadly, it should be able to be triggered by the royal family in the castle. However, the lack of magic down here probably severely impacted the trigger device, something I will have to adjust once this is over. I felt it when we got out of the library. It should still work, but it will need to be set manually."

Jenna looked at the walls. "I didn't even know there was a way up to the top. Unless we have to hike that ridge to get to it?" The mountain range that surrounded the Irundail valley was massive and even taller than the gates and walls at the front. It connected to them, but there wasn't a nearby way up that she could see from this distance.

Again, Irundail could have fallen to whoever was attacking them by the time they got there.

"Ha! I am far trickier than that. Let's get our horses, then prepare to be amazed." Her grin was full Carabella, which was both nice and scary to see.

Jenna sighed and followed her to the stables.

The way down the mountain was organized chaos as families made their way to the top and the defense shelter. Jenna figured the reason that most people weren't panicking was that they didn't understand what was happening. She could pick out every magic user by the lines of concern on their faces, however.

They might not be fully aware of what was going on, but they knew that not being able to access their magic was bad.

Jenna watched the open area between the mountain and the gate walls. Storm, Crell, and the rest were still out past the walls, but she didn't see anyone coming back. She'd figured they would return once Edgar told them what was going on, but it looked like they chose to stay out.

"I know we have no idea what this spell is, but could it have gone past the walls? Shouldn't the Keepers have blocked any spell from coming in?"

"It might be," Carabella said. "I've heard of magic blanketing spells, but a few centuries ago, and never this large. Something is tickling my memory, but staying out of reach. I wasn't certain until we got up here, but I think something has weakened the Keepers from the inside."

The Keepers were a pair of towers on top of the walls that guarded the gates against magic attacks. They were supposed to be insanely powerful, but as Jenna found out a year ago, they'd faltered before. That something had gotten past them again was bad.

Jenna had a flash. Giant, bat-like monsters attacking Tor Ranshal and Rachael back in Lithunane. And Carabella passing out when the creature's name was spoken—dakair. They were invisible when at their strongest, but Jenna saw them before with help from Typhonel. Who she still couldn't reach. The dakair had drawn out all the magic in the room, then worked on trying to kill Tor Ranshal and Rachael.

"Oh no." She kept her words low, but Carabella had exceptionally good hearing.

"What? You've heard of something?" She gave a bitter smile as she watched Jenna's face. "Something that judging by your appearance, I can't hear." She raised one hand as they rode across the open plain. "Don't fret, I've mostly accepted that there are things I can't hear unless I wish to pass out. It is most annoying, however. Do you know how to stop whatever you think it is?"

The dakair were from the lost time in the past when the cuari were more than the current one hundred. Since none of those one hundred knew anything about that time, any terms from then caused them serious problems.

For thousands of years, it wasn't a problem. In the past year, more creatures and things from that long-lost time were coming back.

Jenna nodded and kept her mouth closed. If it weren't that Carabella was the one who created whatever this thing atop the walls was, she'd try to lock her up with the others. Two of the dakair had taken out Tor Ranshal and Rachael with ease—she shuddered to think how many would be needed to overwhelm the Keepers and remove magic from the entire valley.

Not to mention what would happen if it was the dakair and they finally attacked instead of only stealing all magic in the valley.

"Since I can't know what has spooked you so badly, let's pick up our pace, shall we?" Carabella didn't wait for her to respond, just nudged her horse gently and took off.

She turned to the right, away from the gates themselves, far enough back that while Jenna saw there were guards still on this side, she couldn't see who they were.

A thick line of trees twisted its way up the hillside directly beyond the solid rock of the walls themselves. Carabella was already off her horse and speaking to it softly when Jenna caught them.

"The horses can't go up this. But they'll wait here as long as it is safe." She nodded to Jenna's horse, who nodded back.

Since Carabella couldn't use magic, this horse trick was something else. Jenna got off her horse, adjusted her sword, and followed Carabella into the trees.

The trail was invisible from outside the forest, but while narrow, it was well-defined.

Carabella smiled as the climb grew steeper. "This is a good sign. I tied the spell I left to the one keeping the path hidden. No one has been here since I created it, but it's still clean and open."

When this war was over, and the cuari were free again, Jenna needed to sit down with Carabella and have her teach her how to tie spells directly to the chaotic plane. Jenna used to pull her magic by going to the plane—until things got weird there—and Ghortin thought it was odd and explained that no one did it that way.

Maybe she simply did things more cuari-like than other mages.

The trail would have been relaxing if it weren't for the fact that the fate of Irundail and everyone in it was at risk. And that she'd had to shove aside the worry for Storm and their friends with him about ten times in the past five minutes.

"I can hear the worry in those sighs. Don't worry, they're safe. They'll all be—" Carabella cut herself off and froze, her hands slowly raising.

Jenna walked a few feet behind her and hadn't seen the human man blocking Carabella's way until another step. He pointed a sword at Carabella's throat.

A shadow moved alongside Jenna, and a woman fighter came out. She was kelar and had her hair pulled back so there was no doubt that the top tip of one of her ears was gone. Khelaran so disfigured their worst criminals before they were executed. Unfortunately, they didn't seem to be good at keeping those prisoners in their own land or executing them. There were more than a few of them during that fight in the Markare a year ago.

The king of Khelaran denied knowing how they'd gotten free.

Jenna had more warning than Carabella had, so she got her sword up and blocked the attack from the woman.

Carabella took a step backward, and even holding the kelar woman at bay, Jenna saw a familiar smirk.

Only Carabella could be that cocky with no magic, and her sword still in its sheath.

The woman fighting Jenna lunged again, and again Jenna blocked her move.

"I figured we were wasting our time up here—no one would be stupid enough to escape by climbing out. But orders are orders." The woman's moves at first seemed relaxed. As Jenna demonstrated more of her sword skills, the kelar woman fought back harder.

"Come on, stop playing around. We have orders to bring in anyone we catch." The man wasn't paying attention to Carabella as he chastised his companion.

Bad move with a cuari. Granted, she still wasn't appearing very cuari-like at the moment. Her eyes still had the spell on them to make them appear human, and her ears were covered by a bandana.

She moved so fast that even though Jenna expected it, she barely saw when Carabella dodged around the man's sword, shoved his arm up with a snap, took his sword, and held it at his throat. His broken arm hung uselessly. But he said nothing.

His partner jumped forward, which allowed Jenna to disarm her. Although not with the same amount of flair as Carabella used.

"Now, we only need one of you to tell us what's going on and who's behind it. Who's going to chat first?" Carabella pushed forward with her borrowed blade, nicking the side of the man's neck. "Seriously. One. We only need one."

"Don't say anything! She's a damn cuari." The kelar woman yelled and then dropped to her knees when Jenna kicked her legs out.

"Smile when you say that." Jenna kept both swords crossed at the back of the woman's neck. They didn't have time for questions, and these two were low-level grunts. She would, and had, killed to defend herself or others, but killing in this case would be hard for her. But knocking them out and tying them up in the bushes would work.

Carabella kept watching the human man. "I'm losing my patience. And my young friend there has *no* patience. Ten seconds."

"I'm not—"

"Nine."

Jenna had to bite her lip to keep from laughing. Carabella had spent a long night when they were on the road and neither could sleep, telling Jenna of her life as a pirate a few hundred years ago. Had she let out an 'argh', the tone of her voice would have matched a movie pirate from Jenna's home world easily. However, Jenna doubted Carabella would ever run like Jack Sparrow.

"Fine. We're here with the—" His words were cut off in a gurgle as the kelar woman got a slim dagger out and threw it at his throat before Jenna could move.

Then she bit down on something in her mouth and fell over dead.

"What the?!" Jenna jumped backward as a corrosive liquid carved its way into the rock the woman collapsed on.

"Come on, that's not good." Carabella kept her stolen blade and ran up the hill. "Followers of Qhazborh use that poison—it can explode."

Jenna picked up speed and they kept running. They

slowed when an explosion shook the ground and almost knocked them over.

The path behind them was gone, but amazingly, there wasn't a fire. The amount of damage indicated they would have been killed had they stopped to search the bodies. And there was a terrific chance that they wouldn't be going back down the way they came up.

"So, she killed him and herself so we wouldn't find out that they were working for Qhazborh?" She kept glancing back for signs of smoke or fire. Growing up in Los Angeles had given her a healthy terror of fires.

"He might not have even known what she was. I heard it in his voice. He was going to tell us the plans. A follower of Qhazborh wouldn't have even thought about doing that. We need to hurry and get this protection up. Things are worse than we thought."

Jenna had a lot of questions, but she agreed on getting whatever this thing Carabella created up and working immediately. Dakair? Followers of Qhazborh? Hopefully, like the two they'd just seen, not everyone was working together nicely.

She shuddered at the thought of all their enemies joining forces.

The rest of the climb was uneventful, although Jenna and Carabella kept their spare swords out. Mostly because there was nothing else to do with them and neither wanted to leave weapons behind.

Jenna didn't think they were being followed, but she noticed that the closer they got to the top of the walls, the more Carabella kept looking behind them.

Jenna didn't think it was because she feared a forest fire.

The trail kept going to the left so that the top of the walls was finally in sight. Carabella moved to the edge of the woods but didn't go out in the open.

"I want to make sure that there is no one else following us." She continued to watch the path they had come up.

As far as Jenna saw, this was the only way up, but hopefully, that wasn't the case. Yes, they could probably make their way back down without a trail, but it would be slow going. And there was no guarantee that this creation of Carabella's would work.

And even if it did, it might be a while before it fully restored magic depending on what the source was. Time spent wandering lost in the woods wasn't a great option.

"Okay. Stay low, there are most likely enemy archers out there and we'll be visible until we get to the block." Carabella stretched her shoulders and crouched down.

"I don't see a block." Jenna leaned forward in case she wasn't looking far enough. Nope, nothing but an empty, dark, and extremely smooth surface. One that looked to her that would be easy to slide off of. It was about ten feet wide, far too narrow in her opinion to be running across at this height.

"Oh, I forgot. This isn't magic but it'll help." Carabella touched the side of Jenna's face. "Close your eyes for a count of ten."

Jenna shrugged and did so. When she opened them again, there was a low obsidian block sitting in the middle of the wall walkway about twenty feet from where they crouched. It looked to be made of the same material as the walls, but Jenna knew that alone hadn't been enough to hide it from her.

"I know. And, no, I did not use magic." Carabella shrugged. "Well, I used cuari magic over a year ago. The echoes of our magic linger. Or in this case, something told me to make it function without new applications of my magic. When we get there, I'll need your help to make it work."

"I don't have magic, remember? How can I help?" Jenna was working on quelling a fear of heights that she never knew she had.

"Nothing beyond brute force is needed, my dear. You and I together will have to push that lever over."

Jenna squinted at the black box. Eventually, she saw a black pole that could be a lever. That would involve them both standing up. Hopefully, it was close enough to the center that any archers from the ground below wouldn't see them.

A horrific thought hit Jenna. "There's no way to let *our* people know it's us up here. What do you think Storm, Edgar, or Crell will think if they see two shapes up here?"

Carabella swore. "I never thought I'd say I missed those taran wands, but I do, and you're right." She watched the box as if it would help them out. "We'll need to stay low, move fast, and think good thoughts toward Kaytine's goddess. Are you ready?"

Jenna wanted to say no, but nodded instead.

Carabella crept out from the trees onto the slick black surface. Jenna followed, also keeping low. Luckily, the surface appeared slicker than it was and had a roughness that helped with not slipping and sliding to her doom.

"Watch it." Carabella turned back to her. "You nearly stood."

Jenna lowered her position and they scurried to the box. She wanted to look over the non-Irundail side to see if she could find Storm. But the chance that he, or someone with him, might shoot at her stopped that.

There was a brief pause as yelling was heard on the Irundail side. Jenna and Carabella froze and crouched low alongside the box. Then the sounds faded.

Carabella scowled and motioned for Jenna to move closer. "I believe those were our forces. It sounded like they were taking positions for an invasion."

Jenna took her word for it. As she'd found out during the last month, Carabella had exceptionally good hearing.

"What do I need to do?" The lever, such as it was, appeared to be part of the odd box itself.

"We both get on your side and push it down." She tilted her head and sized it up. "I didn't make the most helpful design with this. I believed that the trigger that the royals had would work."

They moved adjacent to the lever, with Jenna closer to the bottom, and Carabella taking the riskier position of being on the end. To get it to move, they were going to have to stand up.

"On my count of three. Rise, push, and pray no one sees us." She waited for Jenna to nod, then counted down. At three, they stood and put all their weight on the lever.

It didn't move.

"Is there any other way to move this thing?" Jenna felt like everyone on both sides of the walls had spotted them. The lever wasn't moving at all.

"No." Carabella took a deep breath and put all of her weight on the end of the lever. "It shouldn't be this hard."

As she got the last word out, the lever dropped a bit and Jenna pushed down harder. Just in time. Two arrows from past the gates flew over their heads as the lever went to the ground, taking them with it.

CHAPTER FIFTEEN

THREE MORE ARROWS FLEW OVERHEAD but bounced off the air on the Irundail side.

Carabella leaned against the block and grinned. "At least the physical aspect of the shield kicked in. Going to be difficult to assess the magic part if no one on our side can use magic yet. But, as even the physical defenses have magic making them work, I'm going to assume the protection against outside magic is functioning as well."

No more arrows flew over their heads, but Jenna was ready to crawl back to the trees. No more arrows didn't mean there weren't archers down there. "How do we get our magic back? The shields are good, but if we don't have magic and whoever is launching this invasion does, we're still at a disadvantage."

"Indeed. But I think we've done what we can here. Let's get to the trees and discuss it on the way down." Carabella looked around. "People on our side could still hit us by accident."

Jenna dropped to her knees and crawled as quickly as possible. She wasn't certain how they were going to go down, as they'd destroyed the trail.

They got to the shelter of the trees as they heard more yells come from below. One voice bellowed louder than the rest, and Carabella smiled. "That's my son. I'm glad he's stepping in to let them know what's happening. Even if he is doing it exceedingly loudly."

"I'm glad you know what he's saying, I only hear yelling." Jenna wanted to get through these woods, but her legs were shaking. "I don't know what's wrong…I can't stand." She was already starting to sit when her legs buckled completely and she landed hard.

"Jenna!" Carabella kept her voice down but still had urgency as she grabbed her arm. "What's happened?"

"I don't know. I feel odd. Something is—" The world went black, then back on like a light switch. "Wrong. Oh, no." She was back in the jungle that was the chaotic plane. "Hello?" She struggled to her feet. The odd exhaustion was gone now, but this was possibly the last place she wanted to be right now. "Meith? Are you here?"

The only sound was the wind sharply passing through the trees.

Damn it. He'd been here before, but as she had no idea how large this illusion was, or the chaotic plane itself, she didn't want to go searching for him. Not to mention that time seemed to be fluid here and she didn't want to run into the Meith from that dystopian future again. Ever.

"Jenna?" The voice was so faint that at first, she wasn't sure she heard it. Then it came again, a little stronger. But it wasn't Meith—it was Carabella.

No, no, no. Carabella couldn't come here. Keeping her away from whatever had taken the rest of her people and trapped them up here was a major goal.

"Who is that?" Meith spoke behind her, in the opposite direction of Carabella's voice.

"Meith?" Jenna spun. He looked like the version of him that she'd seen originally, so that was good. The confusion on his face was not.

"Jenna? I sent you back moments ago."

"Which time?" She didn't hear Carabella anymore, so hopefully however her voice had come through, it had only been her voice and not her.

"Oh, dear. You're not from the same time as the one I sent back. We just met. How did you come here?"

"No idea. I won't tell you what's going on, but things aren't good. I was talking to someone and then, mid-sentence, here I was. How did I end up here the first time?"

"I'm uncertain." He frowned and walked around her slowly. "I see the differences. You've been on some adventures, but you're not much older. Good. Were you perhaps speaking to another cuari when you were brought here?"

"Yes."

"Good. I blocked one as I found you here. You need to tell her to watch where she goes." He clearly knew she'd been speaking to Carabella. The first time Jenna had come up here, the other cuari had already been taken— so it wasn't hard to figure out who she was speaking to.

"Is there a reason for me being here? The timing wasn't great." It was interesting that when she used to travel to the chaotic plane to replenish her magic, it didn't look at all like this jungle.

"There's something different about you this time. The prior time, alas, I can't speak to anything that might have happened in my future, the chaotic plane pulled you in for unknown reasons." He leaned forward, like he was sniffing her, then rocked back. "You brought yourself here this time. Interesting."

"So, I am physically here? I used to access the chaotic plane for my magic when I was starting—but it was in my mind, I didn't physically go here."

"Yes. You brought yourself here. Maybe for magic?" He nodded with a smile. "That must be it. Very impressive."

"But I don't feel like I can pull in magic. I can sense it, but this isn't right." She motioned to the surrounding jungle.

"Probably not. But if you focus, it will be. I feel a sense of urgency from your cuari friend. We haven't been able to help the rest of the one hundred, but I think I can help her." He took a thin band of hammered copper from off his wrist. "Give it to her. It will help protect her and give her access to her magic of long ago. I know our times are different, but right now, I feel you need help."

Meith was a cuari as well, but unlike Carabella, he hadn't tried to stop the other cuari when they attacked the deities thousands of years ago. He also hadn't tried to destroy them. He and the rest of his kind lived trapped on the chaotic plane.

Jenna took the band. "Thank you. Now, how am I going to access the chaotic magic?" The words were barely out of her mouth when the world spun. Meith was nowhere in sight and the surrounding area appeared as the chaotic realm she used to see in her mind. Bright colors, exotic and entrancing shapes. She closed her eyes to pull in what she could.

Then she was back in the woods. She was still on the ground, still clutching the band Meith had given her, and Carabella was looking panicked.

"Oh, child! What happened? Cuari can vanish as they need to and when they have their full magic, but as far as I know, you aren't cuari."

Jenna got to her feet and dusted herself off. The debilitating weakness was gone. "I took a trip. Again. Only this time I might have gone there because part of me wanted to." She held out the slim band. "I can't say the name, but someone said to give this to you. They said it would help protect you in order to use magic. It will be limited, though." Part of her was afraid to give Carabella the band. She had no idea what 'long ago magic' meant, nor what might trigger the cuari-stealing spell bubble. But even once this crisis was resolved—and it was a pretty large one—they were going to need more help to free the rest of her people and win this war.

Carabella looked at the bracelet but didn't reach for it. "That looks old, extremely old."

Jenna had a moment of panic. Extremely old could

be before the cuari were removed and the one hundred who remained had their memories wiped.

"I think I had one like that a long time ago." She smiled but still didn't take it. "It was when the new races: kelar, derawri, and humans, were coming into their own. We still had to observe them carefully, we always do, but that was a good time." Her face softened as she thought back to those early days.

Jenna let out a sigh. Those were old days, but ones in which the remaining one hundred cuari were already in place.

Carabella tentatively reached out for it, as if she expected it to vanish. She touched it, then put it on her wrist. "I would be interested to know who had this. Can you say if they are one of my people?"

"I still haven't seen the trapped cuari on the chaotic plane. But the one behind this meant no harm." That was the closest she could get.

Carabella nodded and patted the bracelet. "It is odd. I don't recall it having anything to do with magic before." Then her eyes went wide and she was flung backward into a tree.

Jenna ran to her. She shouldn't have given it to her. She didn't think Meith meant any harm, but his version of reality wasn't the same as what was here.

Carabella held out her hand as she got to her feet. "Don't worry, I'm not hurt. Nothing but a bit of a shock. It is pulling forth my basic magic." She looked around the forest. "The magic I had long ago. Watch." She waved her hand and every rock around them lifted into the air, then dropped.

Jenna held her breath. If that spell bubble showed up, she wasn't sure she could break Carabella free.

Carabella paused as well; her head tilted as if daring something to grab her. Then she flicked her hand and the rocks rose again, switched places, and then dropped.

And still no spell bubble.

"This is amazing. My magic isn't as strong as it should be, but when we were first put in place, our skills were limited as we guided and watched over the new races."

"And you did magic. Did your protecting block out there stop the magic drain?" Before Carabella could answer, Jenna tried picking up a few rocks near her. She laughed when they rose easily. "Maybe it did."

"Or maybe this bracelet is working outside of the spell. It feels out of time. And if you took magic directly from the chaotic plane, it could work differently as well. We need to find the others." Carabella looked down the hillside, then took off at a jog.

Jenna dropped the rocks and scrambled after Carabella. "The trail is still gone, remember? Moving a few rocks around is something, but you and I might be the only functioning magic users in Irundail at this point—I don't think we want to waste what we have on debris." She didn't mention body parts, but that was on her mind. The two they'd fought had been in the center of the explosion—literally.

"Ye of little faith. I *do* have some trail skills that have nothing to do with magic." She darted in between a clump of trees and what could be a trail. If someone focused on it enough.

It was more a deer path, but Carabella was scrambling down it like a goat.

Jenna stayed as close as she could—that spell bubble hadn't popped up yet, and hopefully using magic from long ago meant that it wouldn't. But she didn't want to be wrong and let Carabella be captured and trapped with the other cuari simply because she couldn't climb down a wooded hill fast enough.

There was a rustle in the bushes up ahead, but Carabella didn't even slow down. However, she raised her fist. Two thugs, clothed similarly to the two they'd run into on the way up, except both were male, kelar, and had fully intact ears, rose into the air.

Before Jenna could say anything, Carabella flung them up through a gap in the treetops and back toward the walls.

"No time to deal with these people." She continued her jog down, somehow finding the thinnest gaps that constituted a trail. "They appeared surprised at my magic though, didn't they?"

"Probably because you threw them in the air. But yes, they looked surprised."

"Good. They deserve to be startled. We made Irundail to be impossible to break into when we created it. I'm not going to have a bunch of losers messing with that." Carabella jumped back with a yell as an arrow came right for her.

"I said no!" The arrow hit the ground, but Carabella had it back up and flying toward whoever sent it. The shadowy shape down near the bottom of the hill yelped and ran away. Two more followed it.

"Hopefully, that wasn't one of our people." There was no way to tell from what little Jenna saw.

"Why do you think I only injured them? But we need to get out of these trees and find my son."

The rest of the way down was empty of attackers, but Jenna ended up with plenty of tree and shrubbery bits in her hair and clothing. She tried to imagine how Carabella made it through unscathed, but it was beyond her ability.

"Where is everyone? We heard Ghortin before." The guards were still at the gates, but no sign of Ghortin or any of the rest of their friends.

"We did. I have a feeling that he joined the fight outside the gates." Carabella shook her head as she ran to her horse and got on. "It's better to fight there. He doubted that you and I could block the attacks. That child."

Jenna didn't get on her horse as gracefully as Carabella, but she made it and patted the horse's neck to thank her for sticking around.

Then Carabella was off.

"Okay, girl, follow the crazy woman." The mare nickered and then shot off after Carabella's horse.

Jenna wasn't completely certain which was better, moody and sad Carabella, or feisty and fierce Carabella.

The guards at the gates all came to attention and shouted for them to halt and raise their hands.

Jenna had a moment of panic when Carabella lifted only one hand. She was afraid the cuari was going to throw the guards in the air. But she brought her horse to a halt and raised both hands.

Jenna rode up alongside her, also raising her hands. Which was a stupid way to see if magic users were unarmed. "I'm Jenna, Prince Corin's fiancé. This is Carabella, Mastermage Ghortin's mother. I'm sure you don't mean to stop us." She rode ahead of Carabella. Hopefully, Carabella wouldn't get jumpy and shoot off a spell before Jenna could talk them through the gates. With luck, someone had at least heard of her. If not, they'd certainly know Ghortin.

"Aye. I recognize you." A tall kelar guard captain nodded slowly. "I'm not sure you want to go out there, as magic isn't working outside the gates either." He not only knew who they were, but he also knew they were magic users. It wasn't good that the magic issue was also outside the walls though.

"We're fine. We can fight with swords, and we have important information for the ones outside." Carabella lowered her hands and nudged her horse forward.

The guard captain watched them—Jenna was sure she was a sight to see after their mad run down the hill through the trees. She'd be picking out twigs from her hair for days. He finally nodded and the guards pushed open one gate.

Carabella took the lead, bowing to the guards as her horse ran past. Jenna smiled as she rode behind her.

The gate slammed shut behind them as they rode out toward the hills. There was no fighting here, but from the sounds of it, it wasn't far.

They'd crested the third low hill when they saw the fight. It was slowing down with what could only be magic—and their side was losing badly.

CHAPTER SIXTEEN

THE ATTACKERS WEREN'T SLOWING DOWN at all. "No magic? I'd say someone has some and it's not our people." Carabella paused in her race forward, assessing the fighting.

At first, Jenna couldn't find her friends, but then she saw the familiar long dark brown hair of Storm as he raced his horse through the enemy. Well, he appeared to be racing, but the movements of him and his horse were slowing down. Once she spotted him, the rest were easier to find. Ghortin was using his sword, something unusual for him, although Jenna knew he was a gifted swordsman. He vastly preferred to fight with magic. He was also slowing down in his movements. The same with Crell and Edgar and the Irundail guards.

"We need to break that spell." Jenna wasn't certain of the range of her current magic, nor how long it would last.

"Aye. And to do that we need to find the one…HA!" Carabella yelled as she pointed to a tall kelar with a mass of deep red hair back in a tail. Not surprisingly, he had the clipped ear tip of the Khelaran prisoners.

"Seriously, are they executing any of them up there?" Storm, Edgar, and Keanin had filled her in at dinner about what had taken place while they'd been in the kelar homeland. But what were the odds that they'd run into two escaped death row prisoners in the span of an hour?

"Doubtful. There were rumors they were being used

as agents for the crown for the past few years. Unfortunately, the cuari who were investigating it are indisposed at the moment." Carabella's voice sounded like she'd almost come to terms with her captured people. The way she clenched her fist indicated she hadn't. "Can I blow something up? Please? It won't be what I could do normally, but sending that one into the air doesn't seem like enough."

Jenna agreed with the thought. "Good idea, but he's too close to our people. Maybe send him into the air, move him away, and then blow him up?" She knew a magic user able to slow down a hundred fighters probably would fight back. But whatever Carabella did might distract him enough to drop his spell.

"I can do that. You're going to ride in with magic and sword, I presume?"

Jenna grinned. "Indeed. A few spells should push back the attackers and give our people a chance to fight." The decreasing speed of their people scared her. If they didn't pull this off, they would be slaughtered.

Carabella ran forward with a yell, not for any reason that Jenna could tell aside from that she wanted to and was cocky enough to let that red-haired kelar mage know she was coming.

He barely looked over. Clearly, he was confident in his slowing spell. That was another issue—Jenna felt that dakair might be involved in the magic drain, but didn't see any.

Of course, they'd been invisible when they'd first discovered them in Lithunane. Warning Carabella wouldn't work, she was already lifting the mage in the air. Not to mention she would pass out if she heard the name. With only two functioning magic users on their side, they couldn't lose one.

Jenna needed to get to Ghortin.

The kelar mage screamed as he was torn off his horse, flung high in the air, pushed past the battle zone, and exploded.

Carabella grinned but only had a moment before a human fighter lunged for her. She had drawn her sword, so fought back that way.

Jenna worked her way around to Ghortin. The slowing had stopped, but judging by his scowl as she saw him try to use a spell, the blanket on magic remained.

Aside from the one Carabella blew up, it didn't appear that any of the enemy fighters were using magic either.

"Ghortin!" she yelled as she got closer, but couldn't yell her suspicions where Carabella might hear them.

"Jenna! Watch out! Some spell slowed us down!"

"Carabella took care of the mage who cast that spell." Her horse dodged through a gap in the fighting and they came to his side. "I think there are dakair here. We got Carabella's shield up over the valley. She's currently accessing some of her original magic." She waved him off when he started to speak. "Long story, she's safe for now. I got some magic from the chaotic plane and my *friend* helped her. But I don't know how to make the dakair visible if I'm right."

He smiled, then repeated the spell. Jenna said it three times softly until he nodded that it was right.

She put the weight of the chaotic plane behind her words as she shouted them. She was operating on the fact that if it were the dakair, they appeared to need to be close to their targets. But in her mind, as she shouted the words, she was sending the spell to every dakair within a hundred miles of Irundail.

At first, she thought it hadn't worked—or she'd been mistaken in her belief that the dakair were behind this magic dampening. Ghortin fought off another sword-swoman and Jenna took a deep breath to yell the spell again.

Suddenly, massive bat-like beings began appearing on the fighting field. "Kill those things! Carabella, turn away!" It looked like Carabella had created a shield around herself and her horse and it darkened at Jenna's yell, but she wasn't close enough to be certain. Nor to tell if Carabella had passed out or not.

Storm, Edgar, and Crell led the charge toward the dakair. It was interesting that the creatures had wings, but they were all landing as they were exposed. Some fell hard and didn't appear to be getting up again.

There were fifteen of them, twelve that hadn't died on impact. They were dead within minutes. The rest of the attackers ran or rode off without looking back.

Storm rode to her and took her hand. "Not sure what you did, but thank you. Things were getting a bit dire. It felt like our attackers were speeding up."

"Not completely sure what I did myself. And actually, that kelar mage was using a spell to slow all of you down. But we need to go back inside the gates. At least a few of the attackers were in the valley."

He nodded and turned to the guards. "Clean up the grounds. Burn the enemy dead, bring in our own. I don't want to risk bringing healers out, so get wagons to bring in our injured."

Edgar and Crell rode over.

"What of us?" Edgar flashed a smile at Jenna. "And I assume that's Carabella in that shadowy box?"

Jenna looked back. Yup, Carabella's shield still held. "Long story, probably let Ghortin figure out Carabella's situation." She quickly filled them in on everything, including the attackers inside the gates.

"Those gates never opened once we came out. How did anyone get in?" Crell looked ready to hunt down all the attackers herself.

"A question for later," Storm called over a human guard. "Dothia, can you monitor things out here? We have more problems to deal with inside." She nodded and rode back to the rest, barking orders as she went.

"I like her. She's like a human Crell." Jenna smiled.

"I'll take that as a compliment." Crell turned and went back for the gates.

Storm gathered twenty more fighters and a group of Crell's rangers, as they made their way to the gate.

Ghortin tapped Carabella's shield and it vanished. Then he caught her when she fell off her horse. "We'll be right behind you. Just need to wake her up, she's fine." Which answered the question of if she'd seen the dakair or not. At least she'd triggered the shield before the spell knocked her out.

Jenna nodded and rode with Storm, Edgar, Crell, and their small group. She didn't know how to find any remaining attackers—or if any had gotten onto the mountain.

"Where did you see them before?" Storm asked as the gates opened and the group rode through.

"In the forest at the sides of the walls. They thought we were trying to escape. Which makes me wonder if there's a way to get in over there." She hadn't put the comments together with a possible trail into Irundail until now. But it had been a hectic morning and she still felt a bit off after her trip to the chaotic plane.

"Damn, there hadn't been a way in, but there could be one now." Storm turned to Crell. "Can you and your rangers search the hillside next to the gates? Getting here should be impossible from the other side, but stranger things have happened."

Crell nodded, whistled for her rangers to follow, and they ran toward the forest.

"What's on the other side?" Jenna knew she saw a map long ago, but didn't recall it.

"A sheer cliff over the ocean." Edgar glared at the woods. "Something that no one should have been able to hike up. Ever." He looked like he wanted to follow Crell's rangers. Then shook it off and leaned low over his horse.

"If those things are dead, shouldn't the magic issues be gone?" Storm rode close to her.

"I don't know. I'd think so. But I still feel the same." She shook her head. She tried to spell all the dakair within a hundred miles, but the odds of that happening were slim. Not to mention Carabella's shield over the valley. "Damn it. I didn't think of Carabella's shield. It would have blocked my spell against any dakair that already got inside here."

Shouting an unfamiliar spell while riding at close to full speed wasn't the best idea—but there weren't many options. They'd already seen that the attackers could still use some magic. It took a few tries but, like before, dakair appeared in the air and either crashed or descended on their own. There were ten nearby, but there could be more of them farther down the valley.

They needed to get to the mountain in case there were already attackers there. They didn't have time to kill all the dakair by sword. She focused on a spell, one that should destroy the dakair where they were. Her magic felt odd, like it was borrowed, not how it normally felt even when she went directly to the chaotic plane for power. It also felt limited. But they had to destroy the dakair.

She cast the spell, attaching it to the images of the dakair only. Even she was surprised to see small bursts of flame dot the valley. Hopefully, it wasn't wishful thinking that she saw a few lights at the far end as well.

"That was you? Well done!" Edgar yelled as he rode on her left. "My magic is still gone, but it could take a while for the influence of those things to vanish."

"Are you okay? You look pale." Storm's blue eyes were dark with concern.

"I'm fine. This is a weird magic I'm using." She took a deep breath and forced a smile. She didn't feel fine, she felt excessively drained. But they needed to save the people on the mountain. Yes, they'd hopefully managed to get the entire population to safety, but there was always the chance a few hadn't made it.

Or someone found a way to break in.

They raced up to the first level. Guards were standing at the bottom but relaxed when they saw Storm. "We haven't seen anyone, your highness."

"They might have been here before the crisis began. Keep half of your men here, then do a systematic sweep of this level." At the man's nod, Storm rode up the ramp to the second level and repeated his commands to the guards there.

"Where are the rest of the guards?" Edgar frowned as they reached the top level. "Between the ones out front of the gates, those guarding the gates, and the two groups we just saw, that's less than a quarter of the guards in Irundail."

"That's a good question," Storm yelled and his horse increased speed. There were no guards visible at all on this level.

"This is bad," a guard captain with them said. "I'd like to check the barracks." He raced off to the left as soon as Storm agreed.

Storm kept up a steady stream of muttered swear words as they rode in.

"Were they all out when you left? I don't recall even noticing when Carabella and I came out." Jenna thought she'd seen more up here, but was focusing on other things at the time. "Maybe they're protecting the shelters?" That sounded lame even as she said it. The guards wouldn't have left this level unprotected.

"Something is wrong." Storm raced toward the castle, then down a narrow path between it and the House of

Healing. "Keep watch!" He yelled as they went behind the castle.

To find a pair of massive heavy metal doors blown open.

CHAPTER SEVENTEEN

———

STORM HELD HIS HAND UP as he brought his horse to a halt. Right inside the shattered doors were the bodies of at least a dozen Irundail guards. "I need five guards to stay here. Use your horns if anyone approaches who isn't Ghortin, Crell, or Carabella."

Jenna had seen the horns at the sides of the guards here, but they hadn't been common in Lithunane. This made sense, considering that the Irundail valley was about five times the size of Lithunane.

The guards who stayed in place remained on their horses and spread out in sight of each other. The rest got off their horses and followed Storm.

Jenna was next to Edgar as they marched forward. "Can you feel your magic yet?" She dropped her voice low.

"I don't know." He held out his sword and muttered a word. At first, nothing happened, but then it glowed lightly. He dropped the spell a moment later. "That's something, but not much. I'd say hopefully those dakair are all dead, but their spell is lingering behind. I'll keep my blades out."

Jenna nodded. Edgar wasn't a big magic user, but the fact he could call a little up did bode well that magic was returning to Irundail.

Whether it would be in time to help them was another issue. She might be the only functioning magic user in the valley right now, and she still felt like something about it was wrong.

The shelter appeared to be a massive cave hewn out of

the same black rock that the walls and the cliffs backing Irundail were. It had some features, mostly torches, and raised banks that had once held weapons, but if she'd stumbled upon it, she would have thought it was simply a cave.

"Where is everyone?" she whispered to Storm.

"The actual shelter itself is farther inside, but no one has ever broken those external doors before." If he clutched his sword hilt any tighter, his fingers were going to snap.

"How many times has someone broken into Irundail and gotten up here?" She understood his terror, but it wouldn't help right now.

He gave her a tight smile. "Excellent point." He picked up his pace and they jogged down the tunnel. A small group of guards stayed ahead of Storm and Jenna, cautiously looking behind each large rock they ran across.

They soon heard the distinctive sound of sword fighting.

"Spread out. I need one person to stay back in case we fall. They'll need to warn everyone else outside." Storm looked down at her, but Jenna shook her head.

"Not me. I might be the only one with magic right now. You need me."

"I know, but there could be things here we aren't aware of yet. Something destroyed those thousand-year-old doors." The look on his face said he agreed with her but still wasn't happy about it.

"And was probably magic." She held his arm. "I understand, I do. I don't want you down there either. But this is who we are right now. This entire world is at stake." Actually, according to Meith, far more than only this world. It was better not to think about the implications right now.

He tilted his head back and closed his eyes, then opened them, and nodded to a guard. "Fosst, stay here. If we fall, get the word out."

The guard bowed and walked back a distance. Not far, but enough that hopefully he could flee if they fell.

"That's not a good thought. I have missed much."

Jenna stumbled when Typhonel's faint voice popped up in her head. Storm had moved forward, so she mentally updated Typhonel about what was happening. *"Can you help? My magic is odd and limited."*

"I'm not sure. There is something still blocking me. I can try. I'd rather you weren't killed."

If she had been speaking to him face to face, she would have probably given him an odd look. He was definitely showing a bit of a sense of humor.

Hopefully a good sign, but unusual. Sadly, there was no guidebook for what was normal with displaced deities taking up residence in your head.

She ran to keep up with the others as the sounds of fighting increased.

The shelter doors appeared to be shut, which was good news. If possible, these doors were even larger than the ones they'd come through. The bad news was that the fighting in front of the doors was fierce and even with Storm, Edgar, and the guards they brought, they were still overwhelmed.

Edgar raced ahead of the rest and attacked two enemies who'd pinned down an Irundail guard. The fallen guard was alive but had collapsed with his left leg twisted oddly.

Most of the energy-sucking weirdness connected to her chaotic plane magic was gone, but Jenna still didn't feel like her normal self—nor like her regular magic had returned.

Taking a deep breath, she lifted five enemy fighters into the air. She understood now why Carabella had used that trick. It disabled the attackers and didn't put as much magical strain on the mage as a more destructive spell would.

She wasn't certain what to do with them once she got them to the ceiling of the cave, however.

"Let me try."

Jenna felt a surge of energy come from deep inside her mind then all five of the attackers exploded. Raining bits over everyone else.

"I am sorry. That wasn't my intention."

Jenna shrugged when the others turned to her. "Sorry." There wasn't more to say, but she felt bad. And grossed out.

While unwelcome and unexpected, the rather grisly demise of some of their fighters made the enemy pause. Not long enough to make a huge difference, however. Even with those five gone, they still had far more on their side.

Then she looked past the fighters. Not all of their enemies were fighting—a group was blocking a smaller group behind them. "They're trying to break open the gates!"

Storm looked where she pointed, and Edgar darted toward them. Only to be slammed back as a spell shield shoved him into the air.

Jenna dodged an attacker and then hugged the wall. Yelling hadn't been a great idea, but she'd probably drawn more attention by throwing those five fighters into the air. *"Typhonel, we have to get that shield down."*

"Agreed. I will need you to help, but your magic has an odd tinge to it."

"They used dakair to drain magic in the valley, I borrowed this magic from the chaotic plane."

"There is something more…but not now. Follow my lead."

Images flowed through her mind, showing the construction of the shield being used against them. She doubted she'd remember most of it, but Ghortin would have been impressed. If it wasn't being used by the other side. The ones working on trying to break open the doors were the same ones who created the shield and the magical lines between them and it showed where it was keeping its power. They were using low-level magic combined with explosives. So far, the explosives kept sputtering out the moment they touched the metal of the doors. There was a functioning static spell on the gates, but she had a feeling the enemy would get around it soon.

A rush of power, the magical kind, hit her and it took her a moment to realize it was Typhonel and her magic from the chaotic plane slamming into the shield. Would have been nice to have had a warning.

She yelled a spell word she'd never heard before, then added, "Duck!" and the shield exploded.

At least this time there weren't body parts.

Edgar gave her a nod. Then he and four of the Irundail guards ran forward to stop the people trying to break open the doors.

The fighting around her continued, but Jenna nearly collapsed when the energy from Typhonel vanished. She tried to reach for magic as an attacker charged her, but there was nothing there. Luckily, Crell and Carabella had worked on Jenna's sword skills while they'd been on the road to Strann and she'd become fairly proficient.

She blocked the attack but found movement was becoming increasingly difficult. Trying to call for Typhonel did nothing, and most of her friends were locked in their own battles.

Then an arrow struck the man she was fighting. A short and stocky crossbow bolt that was strong enough to pierce his leather armor.

"Jenna! Duck!" That was Crell's voice.

Jenna didn't duck so much as collapse, but it still got her out of the way as the archer behind her fired three more bolts into the fighter and he fell.

Crell ran forward and grabbed Jenna's arm as her rangers charged into the fight. "Are you injured?"

"Not physically, but something is pulling the magic and energy from me."

"*Dakair.*" It was Typhonel's voice in her head, but so soft that it sounded like the wind.

"Damn it. There might be more of those things here, but I don't know if I can expose them."

"The dakair?" Crell kept her voice low. "Carabella is out front with Ghortin and the guards."

"Could you get Ghortin in here?" Jenna got to her feet and stumbled back from the fighting. The attackers trying to get into the shelter had stopped once their shield fell, but that meant their number was now added to the active fighters.

With Crell's rangers joining in, they were almost equal, but not quite.

Crell nodded and helped Jenna to a rock along the wall and waited until Jenna sat on it. "Stay here." Then she raced off.

The feeling of exhaustion grew stronger. Her trick of destroying the dakair in the valley hadn't reached here. The shelter itself might impact magic. Hopefully, Ghortin had regained enough magic to help, but they'd have to hurry. The dakair in here—if that was what was doing this—would quickly undo any magical gains Ghortin or any other mages had retained.

Her magic still felt odd, but mostly intact. But her energy levels were slipping away at an increasing pace.

She tried again to reach Typhonel, but there was still no response.

Ghortin and Crell came running down the passageway.

"You think there's dakair in here?" Ghortin was already pulling up a spell.

"*He* said so, but I can't reach him now. My energy is draining." It was odd. The more her energy vanished, the stronger her magic felt. Great, she might be able to cast some wicked spells if she didn't land flat on her face when she stood.

Ghortin muttered a spell word and helped her to her feet. Together they cast the spell she'd used to expose the dakair.

Magic flowed from her, still odd, but strong. And three dakair—larger than the others they'd seen—appeared. They weren't in the air but realized when they were no longer invisible.

And they were pissed. They looked at her and Ghortin as they flexed their wings for an attack. The magic-draining powers of the dakair were horrible—but so was their ability to simply rip people apart.

Two Irundail guards and three of the enemy were killed as the dakair attacked them to get to Jenna and Ghortin. They might have been on the same side as the invaders initially, but they didn't care who they killed now.

Crell and two more archers fired bolts and arrows into the lead dakair, but while they hit it, they didn't kill it.

Jenna pulled up a spell and swayed to the side. Whatever was draining her was still strengthening her magic. Not the best tradeoff in a fighting situation, but things could be worse.

"Lean against the wall," Ghortin yelled as he aimed spells at the three dakair with only moderate results.

Jenna felt an overwhelming disgust at these three. "Stop!" She reached back to her first days of magic and grabbed the command word she'd used to stop Ghortin so long ago. It slowed them down, but they kept coming.

Not sure if it came from her or Typhonel, but a surge hit her and she flung fire at them. It was a magical fire so it only hit the three dakair. At first, she thought they were going to survive that as well. They were out of options. Then the dakair yelled as a single voice, burst into flame, and vanished.

Better than dropping flaming dakair body parts all over, but still upsetting.

"Did you?" Ghortin blocked the sword of one of the enemies.

"I didn't make them vanish. And I can't reach my *friend*." She felt her energy coming back, but fear as well. Those three dakair were stronger than the others. That someone might have saved them when they vanished was disturbing.

The fighting surged as the invaders tried to escape and, failing that, continued to fight. "Get one alive if you can," Ghortin yelled to the Irundail fighters. So far, that looked doubtful. If they couldn't escape, the enemy was fighting to the death.

CHAPTER EIGHTEEN

"DON'T WORRY, I GOT ONE," Carabella called out from behind them as she came down the passageway. Luckily, she'd not come in until the dakair were gone. She'd used her elevation spell and was pulling along a kicking and yelling enemy behind her like a balloon.

"You never stay where you're told." Ghortin didn't sound surprised.

"Nope." She came to where Jenna still leaned against the wall.

Carabella searched Jenna's face. "Feeling better?"

"How'd you know? But yeah. We had some complications."

"I feel it." Carabella shrugged. "Hard to say why or how, but I sense you now."

The fighting ended as all the enemies, aside from Carabella's prisoner, were killed. None of them begged for mercy and, in fact, seemed to be set on being killed if they couldn't escape.

Ghortin and Storm ran to the interior gates of the shelter and pounded on them in an oddly specific pattern. Made sense when Jenna realized it. There was no other way to let the people inside know they were safe.

The gates didn't budge at first, but then one door opened a crack. Storm stepped forward and helped pull the door open.

Tor Ranshal and Rachael were right behind the guards coming out, opening the door fully and the second one as well. The way Rachael held up her hands in the air as she magically pushed open the gates indicated she'd recovered some magic. Hopefully, all the mages were recovering now that the dakair were gone and the shield over Irundail would stop further attacks.

Rachael dropped her spells and ran forward to hug Jenna. "By the stars, you have some strength in you. I felt it even through these monster gates and walls." She pulled back and tilted her head. "Yes, something has changed. We'll look into it once we clean everything up." She looked around at the trampled bodies and body parts. "I don't believe we need to stay here."

They turned away but stopped when Storm came out of the shelter with his brother and mother. He was close enough that Jenna noticed he didn't look happy.

"I thought you were going to the royal shelter?" Storm asked Justlantin.

"There was too much panic, we needed to be seen to support our people. The twins, my wife, children, and Lilltkin are with the entire castle staff in the royal shelter." Justlantin looked around the chamber. "You and your people did an admirable job here. Thank you."

Storm shook his head. "But how did you get Lilltkin to go into a shelter?"

"I convinced her that we needed fighters inside the shelter as well as outside." Justlantin nodded. "It was the truth."

Jenna didn't want to bring up what just happened… but it needed to be said. "Do we know they weren't attacked also?"

Crell nodded. "Once we cleared the woods—there were only three fighters—we went to the castle. The library and the royal shelter remain intact and sealed." She shrugged. "It didn't even appear that any fighters had entered the castle."

"Nor the House of Healing." Keanin came down the passageway with his sword in one hand and a spell bubble in another. A heavily armed blonde kelar woman strode next to him.

"Talia?" Edgar came up as well. "Thought you were still injured?" He took her arm in greeting.

Talia grinned as she looked at Keanin. "Keanin is more than simply a pretty face. When he was able to access his magic again, he protected the entire wing, then sped up my healing and that of Diath's. My brother is remaining on guard back in the House of Healing."

"I'm grateful to hear that. Let's go back to the castle where we can discuss this more comfortably." Prince Justlantin was carefully not looking at the bodies around them.

Rachael and Tor Ranshal nodded.

"I agree, Your Highness. We have much to discuss if the valley is secure," Tor Ranshal said.

Carabella brought down her prisoner and the guards secured him and marched him off. The rest of the guards began the cleanup.

Ghortin paused as they reached the shattered outer gates of the shelter. "I never thought those would give way." He touched one ragged edge gently. "The spell they used was an old one. But we can make certain it never happens again."

Carabella didn't touch the gates, but a brief sorrow crossed her eyes as they passed. Most likely, long-lost friends had helped create those gates.

Storm came up to Jenna. "How are you feeling?"

She gave him an odd look. She had no physical injuries and since he was magic numb, he wouldn't be able to sense things being wrong that way. "Why does everyone keep asking me that? I'm fine." One dark brown eyebrow arched into his hair in disbelief. "Okay, I'm mostly fine. There were some odd issues, but I'll recover." She leaned into him. "You're fine, right?" He looked like someone who'd been fighting for a while, but his movements indicated that most of the blood on him wasn't his.

He dropped his arm around her shoulders. "Stiff. But I'll be fine."

They reached the horses and the guards they left to watch the way out. Storm nodded to one. "Please return the horses to their stables."

"What happened to the rest of the Irundail guards?" There seemed to be more of them than before patrolling the grounds, but she couldn't be certain.

"They were hit with a spell in their barracks. It's wearing off slowly, but they should be fine," Edgar responded.

"Very good." Prince Justlantin held his arm out for his mother as they entered the castle. "I suggest everyone take a brief rest, change, whatever is needed. Then we will convene the council in two hours."

Everyone nodded and dispersed. Jenna would have liked to see what the royal shelter looked like, having seen the impressive regular one. But she also desperately wanted a bath and a change of clothes.

Storm escorted her to her door and then kissed her. "I'm grateful your magic came back."

Jenna gladly returned the kiss. She was going to mention the chaotic plane aspect, but that could wait. "I'm glad that you're such an excellent swordsman."

He grinned and left for his room.

Jenna got inside her room and nearly dropped to the floor as a new wave of exhaustion smashed into her. Her magic surged through her, making half a dozen items in her room float in the air.

"Typhonel?" she asked out loud but didn't hear or feel a response. More things went into the air and mage lights flickered on and off. She slid to the floor as her legs gave out.

At the same time, she felt as if she could magically single-handedly take on and win a battle against the entire Strann empire.

It was as if she'd had way too much caffeine, but simultaneously had no food for a week. Not a fun feeling, and she didn't even have the energy to open her door and call for help.

She tried concentrating on the trinkets floating around to make them hold still. They continued bobbing about as if part of some deranged dream. If they sang or talked to her, she was going to find a way through the door.

Stopping them didn't work, so she focused on the odd surge of magic going through her and forced them down.

They fought as if they had minds of their own, but finally dropped.

"Typhonel?" She still didn't feel him, but something was causing this weirdness.

"Jenna?" That wasn't the lost god, but Meith. A moment after she heard her name, he appeared in front of her.

"That can't be good—how are you doing this?" He was faint, but he looked happy to see her. How he got here was another issue. He'd never appeared to her outside of the chaotic plane before.

"Thank all, I thought we'd lost you. The magic you received from the chaotic plane is fighting now that your magic is returning. You have to release it."

"But I used to pull in magic from the chaotic plane all the time—it's the same magic, right?" At his frown, she forced herself to stagger to her feet. "Right?"

"Yes and no. What you normally would use is the same as all magic on this level of existence. But that wouldn't have helped you in this case. That magic would have vanished once you returned here. Suppressed just as before. You received a boost of cuari magic. Something you held longer than I expected, to be honest. But you need to release it now."

"You could have warned me." She felt like she needed to sit again, but forced herself to remain on her feet.

"I was afraid if you were aware of the circumstance, you might cause it to fail. Human minds are delicate. Now take a breath, and release it." His eyes flashed oddly as he spoke.

"Why can't you take it back?" Something was wrong with him, but she couldn't tell what. Something beyond him popping into her room—even only semi-transparently.

"It's how this works. You need to release it to *me*." Meith's voice changed and became deeper.

"What attacked me when we first met?" She moved away from the door and into the corner of her room. The feeling of wrongness increased. Cracks began showing on Meith's face. Dark ones that had a fire within them.

"That is not important. The cuari magic will destroy you if you don't release it." The being pretending to be Meith solidified.

"No. It is important, and the real Meith would know." She pulled in the overwhelming magic Power and aimed it at the fake Meith. He staggered at the hit and returned to being transparent. "Who are you?" She sent another bolt his way, but there wasn't a lot left in her.

"I am Meith. Now release the power to me." The cracks in his face grew wider and she recognized the actual face behind them. "Sacaranz? You have no power in this valley, or with me." She pulled in the last of her magic and focused it on the image.

Sacaranz snarled, then he vanished.

This time when Jenna slid to the floor, she didn't think she was getting back up.

"Jenna?" A confused Meith reappeared. "You called me here, what's wrong?" He ran to her, as transparent as Sacaranz from before, and then dropped next to her.

She flinched away from him. "What attacked me when we first met?" Sacaranz could have doubled back.

"Two sciretts." He scowled. "Two changed ones that I still need to deal with. Why? What's happened?"

There was no way she could explain it, but more than the answer, she knew in her gut that this was Meith. "I don't know. My magic has felt odd the last hour." She told him the rest, including what she believed was Sacaranz trying to get her borrowed magic.

"That isn't good. Not your reaction, nor that the abomination could sense it. It was correct, however, I had to give you cuari-focused magic or you wouldn't have any Power when you returned here. I feel the magic of here returning and I will release the cuari magic. It should have let go on its own, but something kept it with you even as your magic returned." He touched her forehead gently.

Jenna would have fallen to the ground if she wasn't already sitting. As it was, it took a lot of energy to keep leaning against the wall. But the weird, too powerful, and at the same time, too weak feeling left. "Is there anything I need to worry about? How did he take your appearance and get in here? Can he do it again?" Slowly, her normal magic felt like it was returning. She still wasn't ready to stand up again, however.

"He must have followed the cuari magic you were using, and even with the shield covering this valley, he was able to partially get through. Now that odd magic is gone from you, he won't be able to do so again."

Another thought hit her. "What about Carabella? She has that bracelet you gave her. Is she in danger?"

"Never fear, that is an artifact and as such, he can't access it. However, please remind her that it is limited in what it can do." He began to fade.

"Thank you, Meith," she said before he vanished.

She sat for several minutes. It was hard to believe she'd only gotten up a few hours ago, with everything that had happened. But there was nothing to be gained by staying on the floor. She rolled to her knees and got back to her feet. Still a little wobbly, but it felt like her magic and energy were recovering as she grabbed some fresh clothes and went for a bath. Whether the hot water that filled it when she turned the knob had come from a water heater or magic, she didn't care. It was the best feeling in the world right now.

The warm bath was far too comfortable, and she'd dozed off when a knocking at the door to her room rousted her.

"Hold on." She quickly dried herself off and dressed. They had provided a fluffy robe in her room, but it wouldn't be good form to swing open the door to a guard or household staff wearing that. She didn't concern herself about propriety before the engagement became real, but now she figured she didn't want to embarrass the family.

Crell smiled when she opened the door. "You look better. Ready to get something to eat and attend the council meeting?"

Jenna wasn't sure how long she'd been in the bath, but it couldn't have been that long. "I thought we were meeting in two hours?" She stepped back to invite Crell in. She'd gotten dressed but was still barefoot.

"Yes, and we still have a little over an hour. But there is a lovely pub not far from the castle, The Drunken Squirrel. I figured some fortification might help you recover. Not to mention, these full council meetings can go on for longer than necessary." She tilted her head and smiled. "Although, as I said, you look much better already."

Jenna sat and put on socks and her boots. She thought about something a little fancier, but trekking to the pub might not be the best for fancy and uncomfortable shoes.

"I feel better, but whatever that was, it wasn't fun. Have the other mages regained their magic?"

"They have and they are saying they felt stiff and sore when it came back. I hope whatever you and Carabella triggered over Irundail holds. We have a serious fight on our hands and we can't win if we can't even protect our base."

Jenna nodded and got up. "I think I could get behind a nice meal and an ale. It's been a crazy morning."

"Aye, it has." Crell led them out.

The guards were recovered from whatever attacked them, at least judging by the dozens marching around. Jenna had a feeling that all the uninjured were out in force on the mountain and in the rest of the valley.

"Oh, and be prepared. Even though Storm officially proposed to you last night, Prince Justlantin will probably make a formal announcement of the betrothal soon. The gossip chain from the first unofficial one didn't reach out of Lithunane. So, the news will be fresh."

Jenna looked up to see a large, rambling wooden building up ahead. By the wooden sign of a squirrel collapsing against an empty ale bottle, it was pretty clear what it was. "I get that the court needs to know, like it or not, Storm is still in the line of succession. But is a council of war the place for it?" She briefly rethought her clothing choice. But even the boots fit what she was, a mage trained to fight. She'd try to keep from embarrassing the new in-laws, but she wasn't changing who she was.

"It is. War has been looming over Irundail since even before Lithunane was destroyed. Sorry to say, but the romance between you and Storm will soften things after our recent attack. Even if only briefly. If Prince Justlantin only spoke of the attacks and war, things would fall apart quickly. You two becoming engaged, particularly now, will give people hope."

"Great. I guess." Jenna wasn't sure how she felt. It made

sense, but she still had some terrible memories of the prior fake engagement and the nobles in Lithunane. Luckily, they went into the pub and the low-level cheerful noise distracted her.

It was easily two stories high with a row of tall windows up top, but little else. It felt like most of the pubs she'd run across so far in this world, cozy, even for its size, and with a vaguely English feel if she'd been back home. But this one seemed more comfortable. Possibly because, unlike the ones they'd stopped by on the road to Strann, no one was going to try to kill them. Hopefully.

A few derawri yelled and waved to Crell, and she waved back but shook her head at their invitations to join them. "I think we need some downtime."

The table she took them to was small and might fit one more person, but it would be close. Jenna had a feeling that the selection was on purpose.

"Is there something wrong?" Jenna asked as they took their seats. And some heavenly smells wafted by as a server darted over to a nearby table to drop off platters of food. Whatever they were having might be what she wanted by the smell alone.

"Only wanted to see how you were doing. The last month has been a little hectic. Before we found out about the destruction of Lithunane, I'd hoped there would be time to recoup before the next onslaught. Between that and what just happened, I don't believe we have that luxury. Plus, I wanted to make sure of your intentions with my favorite ward." She tried to look fierce but couldn't hold it. The server came by to see what they wanted. "Trust me to order for you?"

"Ale or food?"

"Both."

Jenna laughed. "Sure. But I liked the smell of that." She pointed to the other table. It looked like a bowl of stew and a platter of bread and meat.

"Our special." The server smiled broadly.

"Two stouts and two of those. And she's engaged." Crell laughed to take the sting out of her observation.

The server nodded, but his smile dimmed a bit. "Right up."

"Did you think he was flirting because he smiled?"

"That way? Yup." Crell flashed a smile as another server brought over two heady mugs. "This is what we need after every battle. Wonder if I can get Prince Justlantin to agree to make it a decree in the land?"

Jenna took a tentative sip, then a larger one. The knots she didn't even know she had in her back released. "I could get to like this place."

CHAPTER NINETEEN

B Y THE TIME THEY'D FINISHED the mountain of food and discussed everything under the sun, Jenna was ready for a serious nap. But unlike before, it wasn't a magically caused energy drain. She'd asked Crell if they had wedding party attendants in this land, and then immediately asked her to be her lady of honor once she confirmed they did—what would have been her maid-of-honor back on Earth.

"Of course! I would be privileged to do so. You can have as many as you want, but most brides stick with two."

"Good to know. I was thinking of asking Carabella as well." There was no way a wedding would happen until they won this war. But she now agreed with Crell's earlier assessment of Justlantin announcing their engagement—it was nice to have something fluffy to distract from the horrors that would come soon.

Crell finished her second ale and nodded to Jenna to finish hers as well. "We should get back for the meeting." From the tone of her voice, Crell might have been a close confidant of the royals, but she wasn't a fan of the council meetings.

There was more traffic entering the castle than Jenna had seen since they got there. Most of them were exceptionally well dressed and looking a little snooty about it.

"Okay, is my clothing going to be a problem? I could change." Jenna frowned. "Although I don't have any formal clothes up here." That might need to be taken care of at some point. The ones that were made for her were left in the Lithunane palace. And were now destroyed.

"No. This is a meeting of war, even with Justlantin using your engagement to bring in less doom and gloom. You and I look like fighters. Which is what we are." She marched up the stairs and led the way to the back of the castle.

This chamber was close to the throne room, and Jenna would bet the two were connected in the back, but it was less ostentatious and more functional. The only banner was that of the royal family. A group of probably close to a hundred chairs were spread in semi-circle rows around a dais in the front which didn't hold a throne, but seven well-appointed chairs.

"We don't have to go to the stage, but we should sit in the front row." Crell walked forward, having to dodge around non-moving groups of gossiping nobles. The room wasn't full and most people were standing around chatting.

And giving Crell and Jenna judging looks.

"Crell! Jenna! Over here!" Keanin, Talia, and her brother waved from the front row off to the right.

Crell waved back and shrugged at a pompous-looking kelar who'd been approaching them with purpose. He looked at Keanin and stopped heading for them.

"Shouldn't these people know who you are? That guy looked like he was coming to kick out the riffraff."

"Sadly, Lord Keanin is far better known, especially up here, than me. Oh, they'll sort it out, eventually. And with the introduction of Prince Corin's fiancée, we'll become people to talk to. But we'll escape out the side door when this is over."

Keanin rose as they approached and made introductions to Talia and her brother. "I'm not sure that I formally introduced you all, but here we are."

Talia smiled as she shook Jenna's hand. "I'm glad to meet you. Every time something bad happened on your end, Storm was ready to find a way to Strann, even if he had to walk or swim. It's a good thing that he's not a magic user, he would have tried to transport himself to your side."

Jenna grinned back. Talia was tall and athletic, with short blonde hair and a fighter's grace. She was beautiful, and her face had an open honesty that Jenna liked immediately. She was perfect for Keanin—and completely unlike anyone Jenna had ever seen him with. Jenna knew that at some point, she'd find out what had happened to him, but she was glad he'd found Talia.

"Thank you for keeping an eye on those three for us. Well, Edgar can take care of himself." Crell grinned at Keanin's fake look of surprise.

"I'll have you know that Storm and I were fine." Then he shrugged. "Not really, but we're here. Now ladies and gentlemen, please sit and try to stay awake." Keanin still looked like royalty, but there was a difference to him. One that went further than the sword he now wore.

Diath had said his hellos at being introduced but remained quiet after that.

Edgar came up and sat next to Diath on the edge of the row. "Did you know that Hon and Flini have joined the castle guards?"

Talia shrugged. "Not too surprising, they were furious at the attack on Erlinda. I had a hard time convincing them to come here."

Jenna looked around and saw Ghortin and Carabella making their way down the main corridor to the center front-row seats. They were dressed elegantly, and Carabella gave no one a doubt that she was a cuari as she regally nodded to people as they passed.

Ghortin spotted Jenna and the rest as they took their seats and gave a nod. Jenna smiled. His dressing up was all Carabella's work—if he could, he'd never wear fancy clothing.

A guard with a trumpet went onto the stage and blew three clear notes. The people who still hadn't taken their seats immediately did so, and the chatting stopped.

Jenna wasn't certain who would be in those seats beyond Prince Justlantin, and based on his absence, Storm. But she wasn't surprised when it was also the Queen, Kaytine, and Lilltkin. The final two seats were for Tor Ranshal and Rachael.

As castle seneschal and official advisor to the royals, Tor Ranshal was used to events like this. But the normally unflappable Rachael didn't appear happy at being up there. Most people only knew her as a common hearth witch and friend of the royal family—if they knew her at all.

And she liked it that way.

Clearly, Justlantin felt it was important for her to be front and center now.

Her worried frown eased a bit when she saw Jenna and the others. And she even flashed Ghortin and Carabella a small smile when she spotted them as well.

Prince Justlantin rose to his feet. "Thank you all for this quick assembly. As you know, we are facing attacks on Irundail. Sadly, sooner than expected. The people attacking us are powerful, but so are we." He gave a nod to Ghortin and Carabella, as well as Jenna's group. "More of our fighters are heading north every day. However, our pushing back the invaders, and stopping their attempt, might aid us in keeping the enemies from Irundail for a while."

There was a mild round of polite clapping and Jenna wasn't sure if most of the people in the audience even knew what they were clapping about. When Justlantin had said a council meeting, she'd believed it would be full of generals and other fighters. This group appeared to be nobles.

She turned to Crell but didn't say anything.

Crell nodded. "Don't worry." Her words were so soft that even the woman sitting on the other side of Crell didn't turn.

Justlantin gave a brief, extremely so in Jenna's opinion, summary of the attack and how it was stopped. That she and Carabella were 'forces for the kingdom' indicated he didn't trust his nobles and courtiers completely.

"Before we adjourn, I'd like to share some happier news." He turned to Storm, who rose, then nodded to Jenna to do the same. "I am pleased to announce that Prince Corin has formally selected his bride. I would like to introduce Lady Jenna Reilly to the council of nobles. She shall receive the same accommodations and treatment as any member of the royal family. I would also like to point out that she is Mastermage Ghortin's apprentice and is also skilled with a sword." He smiled. "Welcome to our family, Lady Jenna." The entire royal family, along with Tor Ranshal and Rachael, rose to their feet clapping.

Jenna gave a bow and felt her face grow warm. Hopefully reminding them that she was a mage and dangerous would keep most of the nobles clear of her. A glance at the calculating looks on the faces of those around her showed that was probably not going to be the case.

Tor Ranshal led the royals off the dais, with Prince Justlantin nodding to the collected nobles before he left.

The audience rose and began chatting.

And shooting more questioning looks in her direction.

Keanin grabbed her arm, and with Crell on the other side, they all went to a small door to the far right.

They weren't fast enough, as some nobles followed them. Edgar had left his seat earlier and reappeared to cut them off.

"So sorry, there are private functions to be dealt with." His smile was pure royal knight as opposed to royal spy. "You understand."

As he held them off, Keanin opened the slim door and they escaped. Edgar shut and locked it behind him. "Don't worry, once they get used to you, you won't be as interesting. We're in a fight that could destroy this land as well as others, and they're more interested in royal gossip."

Jenna looked back at the door as they went down a narrow corridor. "That wasn't what I'd expected as a war council. Although why wasn't Armsmaster Garlan here?"

Keanin laughed as he kept walking. "That was simply to appease the nobles. They're probably planning what to wear at the royal wedding, more than how to survive. There are some good ones in that group, but for the most part, they aren't going to help fight this. The real council of war will be in a few minutes and will have the actual discussions."

Jenna smiled at how far her friend had come. When she first met Keanin, he would have been one of the ones worrying about the proper clothing for a royal wedding. She doubted he hadn't thought of it at all, but he could now multitask.

Edgar joined them. "Garlan is keeping low. He's working on other tasks that it was thought better most people didn't know of. Even when he was helping fight against our attackers, he was incognito."

"They are afraid of traitors in the nobility?"

"There could be," Edgar replied. "The strikes were too well done, and the attacks in the valley itself indicated an awareness of certain aspects that wouldn't be common knowledge. That was another reason for the council—mages will surreptitiously scan all the nobles before they leave."

"And here we are, the true war council." Crell turned with a smile as Keanin stopped in front of another narrow door, but one with a pair of heavily armored guards blocking it.

Keanin stood still as a mage ball up near the ceiling scanned him, then everyone with him. No questions this time, and the mage ball seemed far more elaborate than the others Jenna had seen around the castle.

A soft chime was heard and the guards nodded and stepped back from the door.

This room was far smaller than the last and there was no dais or fancy chairs. There were seats, but the people inside were standing and talking in small groups. Along with Ghortin and Carabella, there were a handful of better dressed nobles. But most of the people were high-ranking military and guards judging by their dress.

Including a solid kelar-human man whose rough face lit up when he spotted Jenna.

Garlan was the Armsmaster of Lithunane and a member of the royal family's inner council for decades, according to Keanin. However, he hadn't gotten along with Prince Resstlin when he'd assumed the throne.

Garlan had worked hard during Jenna's time in Lithunane to train her to be a competent fighter. He grabbed her in a hug, and then finally set her on her feet. Such behavior was unusual for the gruff man, but Jenna knew where it came from.

He'd been worried about her roaming the wilds on their way through Strann.

"It is good to see you. And I heard that you're going to make an honest man of young Storm." His face was dark from traveling in the sun and had more lines in it than it had only a month before.

"I figured someone needed to. It's good to see you." She wanted to say more, but Prince Justlantin called for attention from the front of the room.

"Please take your seats. We have much to discuss." As he spoke, castle staff came out bringing trays of light foods and carafes of tea.

From the smell of the tea in the teapots, Jenna figured it was very strong tea. An old Irish classmate used to say that tea should be strong enough for a mouse to walk across. Just by the smell alone, she had a feeling a fleet of mice could safely cross the liquid.

Keanin frowned as they set up the tables for the food and drink. "That's not a good sign. Glengelen tea and food? We're not getting out of here soon."

Storm joined them and put his hand on Keanin's shoulder with a smile. "Don't think of trying to escape."

"But…fine. I'm getting some tea first though. Staying awake will be difficult." Keanin stalked over to the table, grabbed two cups, filled them, and returned to hand one to Talia. "You'll need this. Trust me." With a forlorn expression that completely reminded Jenna of the Keanin she'd first met, he sighed and took his seat.

"Did you want some tea? Keanin is being overdramatic," Storm asked Jenna as she sat. This crowd was far more casual and there were still some conversations taking place. Even Justlantin was speaking to Tor Ranshal.

"I am not." Keanin sniffed and sipped his tea.

"Maybe later." Jenna grinned at Keanin.

Storm just shook his head and sat.

"I'm going to sit with some of my crew. We can catch up later." Garlan's smile was as odd as his hugging her, but it was good to see.

"He thinks of you as his ward," Crell said. "He shared with me how worried he was when I took off after you three from Lithunane a month ago. I've never seen him like that."

Jenna only had time to smile in response before Justlantin and Tor Ranshal stopped their private conversation, and everyone took their seats.

Ghortin, Carabella, and Rachael took seats behind Jenna and the rest of her friends.

Jenna was lost within ten minutes as Justlantin launched into an update of the forces still coming up from the remains of Lithunane and an update of the conditions in the former capital.

They'd left enough troops to protect the outer areas of the city which hadn't fallen and the surviving nearby villages. Mostly, the attackers fled once the palace was destroyed but damaged nearby villages as they retreated. They'd been dressed plainly, with no flags or banners, but it was determined that it had been a contingent from Strann. How they'd gotten there with no one seeing them, was another issue and one without an answer.

The Traanafaeren troops coming up from Lithunane were making sure that there were at least minimal forces to protect the remaining areas.

Justlantin nodded to Garlan and he continued.

"There aren't enough surviving troops to protect all the smaller towns and villages in Traanafaeren. Even before losing so many in Lithunane, our forces weren't enough. If this war is going to take place here, we have to merge the civilians into groups that we can protect better. And recruit more fighters."

"Won't bringing them into fewer groups make those places larger targets?" One noble asked as the surrounding ones nodded.

"We're in a unique situation. Our entire country could quickly become a battlefield—and as much as I hate to say it, probably will. There are some strategic areas that we can move the populace to that will help us protect them. Even with the recent attack here, I think the coastal towns and smaller area villages should evacuate into Irundail." As Garlan spoke, one of his people rolled out a large board with a paper map tacked on it.

There were already a dozen small circles in red that matched the large red circle in the center of Lithunane.

CHAPTER TWENTY

HERE WAS ALSO A RED 'X' over Strann and a question mark over Khelaran.

"Yes, although neither country has officially declared war, Khelaran and Strann have to be treated as questionable or hostile. Especially if the things we've heard about the bulk of the attackers being from Strann are true. Dewari is staying clear of things for the moment, but we hope they will join us."

Jenna glanced at Crell, but her face was as immobile as stone.

"Even with the attack on his capital, King Philia of Khelaran still believes this is a Traanafaeren issue and is not related to an attempt on his kingdom." Justlantin nodded to Storm. "Could you, Edgar, and Keanin fill us in on the events of your trip out of Lithunane and then to Khelaran?" He nodded to include Talia and Diath—Jenna knew the two siblings had helped the other three greatly.

The three stood, but Keanin didn't look happy.

"I think Edgar would be the best to tell the tale. Keanin and I can add in as needed." Storm remained standing but nodded to the spymaster.

Jenna had heard part of the events. She watched Keanin's jaw tighten as he looked ahead during Edgar's emotionless discussion of the problems they'd had in the south. When he finally ended with a vaguely worded attack on Keanin—she knew there was a lot more behind it.

She would wait and ask Storm about it in private.

Keanin was like a beloved brother to her and during that brief explanation, he looked ready to run out of the room or be seriously ill.

Edgar briefly mentioned demonspawn when he spoke of the attack in Shettler's Point, but he was talking so fast during that portion that even if someone wanted to question him, they wouldn't have been able to. He then moved into a longer description of their approach to Erlinda after dumping their stolen ship. And their trip to Craelyn, the Khelaran capital.

A few insistent people wanted to focus on the demonspawn menace, but Edgar kept looking at Keanin and ignoring them.

Storm cut in on one of the questioners and looked around the room. "There were demonspawn trying to stop us every step of the way. I'm sorry if some of you believed that the threat from them was over after the fight in the Markare last year. They are still around, still deadly, and part of the force trying to destroy us all. If you'll let Sir Edgar get the rest of our tale out, you will hear they are changing—and not in a good way." Storm glared around the room.

A few muttered comments and chagrined nods later, the questions stopped.

"Thank you." Storm nodded to Edgar.

Edgar continued, mentioning Mikasa and her ladies— he added they were fairly certain that all of them were demonspawn by that point. There were more mutters from the crowd, but they didn't ask questions. Mikasa had been Storm's fiancée-turned-traitor.

The rest of their journey brought voiced questions, but they were intelligent ones, interested in the kraken that Storm and the rest had freed. Even Ghortin looked intrigued but remained silent. Most likely, he would wait until they were in private to launch his barrage of questions.

Kraken were mostly myths, but every once in a while, a reputable sailor reported seeing one. That one had been held captive on a known pirate island—then freed by Keanin and the others— intrigued everyone in the room.

The discussion veered into saving the Khelaran king and most of his court from the demonspawn.

And Keanin's major role in it. He continued staring ahead, ignoring the muttering around him. Lord Keanin was well known in both courts as a flighty noble. People were already looking at him differently as more information came out.

Jenna watched the people around them. Those quickest to question demonspawn involvement were now the ones turning the palest. She had a general idea of what her friends had faced, but things had been far closer to them not surviving than she'd heard after the fact.

Edgar turned to Talia. "I would ask Captain Talia Cilone of the Erlindan guard to explain what happened after we left."

Talia got up and locked her arms behind her back in a military-at-ease stance. "The day after these three left, we were invaded by sea and land. As is now clear, there were already demonspawn hiding within the town. As the only large port in northern Traanafaeren, we were of significant interest. I originally thought that the attack came from Khelaran and perhaps our freeing of the king and his people had been reversed and the demonspawn claimed power. But it became clear these were not from Khelaran—or at least not officially so."

Talia continued speaking of the attack and that many of the citizens of Erlinda had taken to the sea to escape. The boats that had brought in the invaders didn't go after them.

"We brought about thirty fighters with us here. There were too many who couldn't or wouldn't make the long trek to Irundail. We hid at least four hundred in the Zalin Pass shelter. There is an old safe-hold there from when Traanafaeren was new. They should be safe; however, they will need more supplies as there was little warning when Erlinda was attacked. And we could only leave a dozen fighters with them."

Carabella nodded. "I know that hold. It will help your people stay safe. But I agree on more fighters and a few mages to help protect it." She looked at Justlantin. "It could be a safe place for some of the smaller villages in the area as well, and could easily hold another four or five hundred people. Ghortin, myself, and our prior companions created it when we first set up Irundail as a safe location for those traveling in from the coast." Carabella turned back to Talia. "As for supplies, do you know of the land in the back of the cavern? There are self-contained, and self-controlling farms back there."

Jenna watched the exchange.

"Diath and I used to explore it when we were kids and I'd always wondered who created the shelter." Talia shook her head. "But I'd never seen or even heard rumors of anything beyond the main caverns. If something there can help supply food and water, they will welcome it. There were only two mages we could spare to leave with them. Plus, any who might have been with the civilians." Then she turned to Justlantin. "After we left them, we were attacked close to the gates of Irundail. Had your people not come out when they did, we wouldn't have made it."

"Thank you, Captain Talia. If you have both recovered, it would honor us to have you and your brother fight with our troops. Plus, any of your group who feel able to do so."

Even with magic, injuries could take time. Diath still looked pale. But he nodded when Talia did.

"We would be honored, thank you. But I fear we need to get more protection back to the civilians we left in the shelter."

Carabella rose to her feet this time. "I believe that I could take charge of that duty. I will bring some of the fighter mages and what warriors Prince Justlantin can spare. There are many secrets built into the Zalin shelter that only myself and Ghortin know." She looked down at her son with pride. "And I fear that he needs to remain here."

Justlantin paused, then nodded to her. "Very well. We will work on getting you a group and supplies."

Jenna knew Justlantin had little to say about Carabella going or not. Even without being able to access most of her magic, she was a force to be reckoned with.

"Perhaps before you leave, you could share with Ghortin any other hidden protections you might have set up in Irundail?" His smile was soft. He'd known that she'd created something to protect the valley—she'd shared it with the royals. He also knew her well enough to know there was a good chance she had other things that she hadn't shared.

Carabella gave a small bow. "Agreed. Ghortin, Garlan, you, and I should have a chat before I leave."

Justlantin and Garlan nodded to each other and the heir called an official end to the council.

It still wasn't as in-depth as Jenna expected, but there seemed to be many moving parts to this war. And she'd never been involved with a war before. Small groups were breaking up, and Justlantin and Garlan circled to each, discussing specific assignments.

Storm, Edgar, and the rest of her friends all stayed together.

"Do we get assignments?" Jenna didn't enjoy battles. But with her unique skills, and that lost god connection in her head, she couldn't sit on the sidelines. Nor would she let the love of her life or her friends face danger alone.

"You'll all be working with me." Rachael beamed at them as she walked up. The tiny white-haired kelar woman looked frailer than before. But there was a fire in her eyes. She was long-lived, even for one of the kelar. But she'd been the primary Guardian of the cuari books and of their true history. She couldn't die until a replacement came—or the things she was protecting were no longer an issue.

She grinned when Talia and Diath took a step back. "Oh, even you two. I am Rachael, and I'm relieving you from standard duty at the moment. We are charged with dealing with the true issue behind this war. Magic will be helpful, but so will a willingness to fight for our lives." She looked around at the smaller councils of war going on around them. "Even if we win the physical battles and defeat our opponents, we will not have won the war until we have destroyed the portal in the Markare permanently."

Jenna and Storm knew of the portal, and that several things had to happen before they could destroy it— such as it needed to physically reappear and they needed to free the rest of the one hundred cuari. She was fairly certain Crell and Edgar knew some of the details, even if not the full specifics.

Talia and Diath appeared confused, and Keanin looked terrified.

He shook his head and took a step back. "I can't go there. Not into the Markare, and definitely not to the portal. We can't destroy it. No one can. Ghortin, Carabella, and their extremely powerful friends couldn't do it. Why do you think we can?" His voice got louder and he had a death grip on the hilt of his sword.

Talia put a comforting hand on his arm and Jenna first thought he was going to shake it off. But he took a deep breath and relaxed instead.

"We have much to discuss, and it shouldn't be out here." If Rachael was concerned about Keanin's behavior, she didn't show it. "I have secured our own place to discuss this further. It will be coded only to us, Ghortin, who will join us once he sends Carabella off, as well as Prince Justlantin, and Wilty the librarian. Even if the door is forced open, no one but us will be able to enter the room."

Storm took Keanin's other arm. "You know I will protect you with my life. We all will. You need to be part of this if we have any chance of making it work."

Keanin closed his eyes and finally nodded. "Lead on."

Storm released his arm, but Talia grabbed Keanin's hand tightly.

"I won't let anyone hurt you, I promise." Talia leaned into him. She was an inch or so shorter than Keanin but held him up easily.

Rachael nodded as if there were no objections and waved for them to follow her.

They were heading back to the castle library. Not that surprising since she'd mentioned Wilty, and Jenna wasn't sure if he ever left the place.

Wilty came scurrying out as they entered and grinned as he greeted Rachael. "I have the planning room all set, even put out refreshments. A more substantial late dinner than what was out in the war room." He grinned at Jenna. "Very good to see you again. I am saddened that Carabella won't be joining us, but her duty is also important." As he spoke, he led them deep into the library, even further than Jenna had gone before. "I have some other tasks to address before I can join you, but I have provided scrolls and books that might be of assistance."

He paused in front of a pair of ancient oak doors, ones

that looked older than Ghortin's three thousand years. Which was far older than Irundail itself.

The room he led them into looked like what it was, a study hall within a large library. Aside from the fact that there were no windows and a dozen spell bubbles hung all over the ceiling.

He waved his arms to encompass the entire room before them but kept them all outside the doorway. "Welcome to the most secure room in Traanafaeren. Possibly the entire world. Before you can go in, we must magically examine you. It won't hurt at all, but these spell bubbles will make sure you're who you claim to be and that you stay that way every time you come inside."

Rachael stepped forward and a light flowed over her. Then changed from white to green and she stepped inside the room. "I have already entered, so what I went through is what will happen each time you come in. The first time will be a little longer. Jenna?"

Jenna shrugged and took a step forward. There was a slight cooling of the surrounding air, but then the white light appeared. A few moments later, it turned green.

After that issue in the royal dining room, she was still wary of the scanning spells.

Keanin was the last, but Jenna didn't think it was because he feared being scanned. It was more as if he feared this would lock him into a path that would eventually lead him back into the Markare. Jenna, like Talia, Storm, Edgar, and Crell kept an encouraging smile on her face as he finally moved forward.

It went slower this time. The scan seemed to process something that it hadn't with anyone else. But then the white light appeared and turned to green.

"There, now that we're all set, let us begin." Rachael nodded to Wilty as he closed the door. "This is going to be shocking news to some of you, and it cannot go outside of this room. Literally. Anything spoken in here can only be said to another person from in here. If you try to speak of it around anyone not of this group, you won't be able to say anything."

Diath narrowed his eyes. "I still don't understand why Talia and I are included in this highly secret group. We're not even from here."

"I know. And until I saw you both unconscious in the sick ward, I had no idea who our missing two who were mentioned in the books were. This will get complicated for you, but you two must be included."

"Missing two?" Talia was still holding Keanin's arm but frowned. "So Diath and I are simply ordained to be here? We weren't planning to come to Irundail until Erlinda was attacked and we had no choice but to flee."

Rachael shrugged. "Many things in life are planned by a higher purpose. Some are not. I believe that you two were supposed to be here and are essential, as are all of you, to completing our task. I wasn't speaking lightly when I said that if we fail, all the physical battles that our people give their lives for will be for naught."

CHAPTER TWENTY-ONE

S ILENCE FILLED THE GROUP FOR a few moments, then Wilty pointed to a table with food and surrounded by chairs. Another table of equal size, loaded with scrolls and books, sat in the corner. "As I said, I do have other tasks at the moment. But I will be back later. I believe this evening's meeting will mostly bring everyone up to speed. It's been a long day for most of you already."

Rachael waited until he secured the door behind them and everyone had a plate of food before starting. "As I said before, this information may come as a shock to many of you. I'll be short and blunt—the three current races were not the first in this world. The cuari were. There were far more than the current one hundred, and they were all extremely powerful."

Jenna saw varying looks on the faces around her. She and Storm might be the only other ones in the room who knew this. The rest appeared to be at varying levels of surprise and confusion.

"The deities, as we now know them, were also more numerous and not grouped as they are now. Trust me, there are far more than three." Rachael waved her hands as Talia's confusion deepened. "That will come, never fear. Thousands of years ago, when it was only their world, the cuari created a portal that crossed all dimensions in the center of the land. The Markare was a lush and lovely place back then. This portal used the power of the land, and a lot of magic from the cuari, to send beings they didn't like to other dimensions and distant worlds. The deities finally told them to stop—they didn't."

Rachael sipped her tea. "A war broke out between the deities and the cuari. When it was over, one god had been lost to the portal, and the cuari who'd led the attacks were unmade by the might of the gods and goddesses they'd fought. Ones who didn't attack, but also failed to help the deities, were banished. Pulling in the Power to unmake the bad cuari, and to securely banish the ones who didn't help the deities, is what turned the Markare into the desert it is today. The one hundred who had tried to help the gods and goddesses against the rest of the cuari were mind-wiped and set to guard the new races. Carabella fought on the side of good, but she can never know." She turned to Jenna. "Tell them everything."

Jenna took a deep breath; she knew that Rachael wanted her to tell them about where she came from, as well as about Typhonel. It was hard to hold secrets that tight and then share them with others. She trusted both Rachael's judgment and Keanin's—but Talia and Diath were total strangers.

"I'm not from this world. A mage, one who it appears is one of the supposedly unmade evil cuari, was testing the Power between worlds a year ago and pulled my consciousness from my world to the body of a newly made mindslave." The look of horror on Talia and Diath's faces said they weren't strangers to mindslaves.

The followers of Qhazborh ritually sacrificed the minds of these victims, leaving a mindless husk. It destroyed their enemies but left their body functioning enough to join the forces of Qhazborh. Jenna still had nightmares of what had happened to the woman she replaced.

"This mindslave was the Protector and knew how to close the portal. But when her mind was sacrificed, that was lost. There was an echo of her when I first came here, but never anything about the portal. That echo has been silent for quite a while." She sort of missed it but hoped that the woman's soul was now at rest.

Rachael took over. "I am a member of a small order tasked with protecting the true knowledge of the cuari. I am a Guardian. The woman whom Jenna was pulled into was the Protector—the one who would live their life ready to destroy the portal when the right time came. We never knew, throughout the thousands of years of watching this world, what made the Protector different. We now know. The god whom the original cuari threw through the portal, lives in the Protector. His name is Typhonel and like everything spoken in here, you cannot repeat his name to others."

Everyone except Storm looked shocked and turned to Jenna.

"I'm still me, you guys. I've simply had help."

Crell gave a small smile. "Those first fights when we fought together when you destroyed the enemy but had never killed before. Him, I presume?"

"Yes. He wasn't much more than a strange force in my head then. One that partially took me over and controlled my actions when I fought. It's only been relatively recently that he's been able to communicate. And he's not here most of the time."

"So, how do we destroy this portal?" Talia recovered first, but unlike Jenna's friends, she wasn't putting together what they had known of her with what they now knew.

Crell nodded. "I'm glad you cut through to the issue. The portal has been studied by many, and two thousand years ago Ghortin, Carabella, Storm's grandfather, my great-great-great grandmother, and a few other adventurers crossed out of Khelaran to fight a monster that had come through the portal and was attacking the desert tribes. They destroyed the creature at a substantial loss, but even with their collective abilities couldn't destroy the portal, but only closed it and let it sink into the sand.

They crossed to this land and created Traanafaeren while they recovered from their injuries."

Diath looked around. "Keanin mentioned this before, but now that I understand more, I'll ask it again. If they couldn't destroy it, how can we? And I don't understand why it matters. The world has continued on this long with it open. How is that a problem now?"

"Excellent points. Like your sister, you get to the essential parts. Which might be why you two have been pulled into this." Rachael looked far older than she had for a few moments, then shook it off. "The deadly creatures we have been seeing in the past few years: sciretts, ertin, and many more who have been attacking the lands are from the portal. It is appearing and opening more frequently now and the followers of the god Qhazborh, which was actually a group of gods and goddesses on the side of evil, are trying to open it permanently. They and a few surviving cuari who were supposedly unmade, including one named Sacaranz, the mage who led the ballroom attack in Lithunane a year ago, want to bring it to its full power. Effectively destroying this world as it pulls life-power from all the other worlds and creates a world of their liking. It would be the end of life as we all know it."

The room went silent.

"My parents died investigating the portal. I almost died twice within the Markare. But with all of you supporting me, I will do whatever needs to be done to end this." Keanin's grip on Talia's hand was tight enough to turn his knuckles white.

Talia didn't flinch. Jenna was so glad those two found each other. Keanin had gone through something horrible in the Markare, but when Talia looked at him, it was clear that she'd protect him from anything. And he already demonstrated that he'd do the same for her.

"Thank you, Keanin. I know coming into this room

was hard for you. Even with all I've told you that this group needs to accomplish, there is one more thing we must resolve before we can work on the Markare and destroy that portal for all time." Rachael looked at Jenna and nodded for her to speak again.

Jenna looked around the group. This wouldn't be a surprise to Crell, as she'd been with Ghortin and Jenna when they found out. But it probably would be a shock to the others, even the ones who knew about the missing cuari. "We first have to rescue the missing ninety-nine cuari. They are essential if we're to have any chance of destroying the portal."

"Do we know where they are? How are we going to rescue them without a lot more people?" Keanin got out before anyone else could.

"We do." Jenna looked at Rachael, but she nodded again. "They are being held on the chaotic plane. Yeah, sounds impossible, but they have them captured up there. Oh, and the cuari who didn't help the gods and goddesses all those thousands of years ago? They're up there in sort of limbo and I'm friends with one of them." She hadn't discussed the specifics of much of this, even with Ghortin and Crell. When they'd been on the road, there had been too much of a chance that Carabella would overhear.

"His name is Meith. I was pulled up into the chaotic plane a month ago, but we don't know by whom. Meith rescued me and put me back here. But there were time issues involved. The chaotic plane isn't as stable as I believe it once was. I was sent back to my home world, then here in the future. In both cases, the worlds were being destroyed."

"And this Meith person can't explain why?" Edgar asked.

"No, he's fluctuating as well." She looked at Rachael. "Even you don't know this, I would have told you earlier, but things have been hectic. While I was in my room a few hours ago, Sacaranz appeared looking like my cuari friend, Meith. Meith had given me some cuari magic to counteract the magic draining dakair. Sacaranz wanted me to give it to him."

Rachael paled. "There are several dangerous points in that. When we're finished, I'd like to work with you alone." At Jenna's nod, she turned to the others. "I'm not trying to exclude any of you. For this to work, we can't afford to keep secrets, but I need to figure out what's happened first. It won't be much fun for you to sit around watching Jenna and me staring at each other."

Diath yawned and Jenna and a few others echoed it. It wasn't that late, but considering the day they'd had, it was amazing any of them were still awake.

Rachael nodded to Talia and Diath. "And you two are recently healed. I do apologize. Time to complete our tasks is crucial, but wearing you out won't help anyone."

"You've given all of us a lot to think about," Edgar said. "Was there going to be more this evening?" Unlike Talia and Diath, he looked ready to head out on patrol.

Of course, he hadn't recently recovered from horrific wounds as they had. Even Jenna was

surprised at their quick recovery. Keanin's magic might be new to him, but he was quickly finding new ways to use it. The healing arts were complicated.

"There was, but as I spoke, I realized that processing major changes before going about to fix them would be prudent. I was expecting Wilty to be back before we broke up, but I can fill him in on anything that he didn't already know. Which, honestly, would be little. He seems to know everything. Ghortin already knows all of this, and right now it's more important that he works with Carabella before her trip."

Keanin got to his feet. "Then, if it is all the same, I feel I should escort my wards back to the House of Healing."

Talia laughed; then saw he was serious. "I'm fine."

Diath nodded in agreement.

"I have learned that while magically enhanced healing is helpful, people still need rest and to be monitored." Keanin slowly nodded as if he were the head schoolmaster.

"Maggie threatened you, didn't she?" Jeanna grinned.

Keanin gave a sideways smile. "She might have put it that way. I could bring these two out, but they need to spend a few nights in the House of Healing. Or else."

"Or else what?" Diath asked as Talia got to her feet, but he remained seated

"She left it open, and I don't want to find out. Trust me, neither do you." Keanin motioned for Diath to get up. "If all of you will excuse us, we will call it an early evening."

Rachael laughed. "Never get on the wrong side of a healer, especially one as powerful as Maggie. The rest of you can go as well, aside from Jenna."

Jenna knew that Rachael would need to know of the cuari books they'd found along the way to and in Strann. Well, the intact ones. There was a pile of pages of at least one, reportedly two, in a chest that Ghortin had magically tucked away in his cottage far to the south. That no one, even Rachael and Tor Ranshal, had known about these two books until they'd been found was shocking. Then there was the actual third book they'd found and still hadn't been able to open, let alone read. Jenna had a difficult time sorting out why, if she was the Protector, these books were being so difficult.

Crell and Edgar nodded to the rest and left, discussing defenses. They might have been recruited for this separate task, but neither would let that take away from what they did every day—protect the people of Traanafaeren.

Keanin escorted Talia and Diath out with a bow to Jenna and Rachael.

Storm came to say good night. Wilty showed up at the doorway and Rachael went to talk to him.

Storm grinned as Rachael led Wilty away from the room. "She's not subtle but good at what she does. This isn't a very romantic engagement, I am afraid." He peered down at her with a soft smile.

Jenna stepped into his embrace and held him tightly. "It's better than the first time. And once we save the world, we can work on romance. But no taking off without me this time." She pulled back and poked him in the chest. "I will hunt you down."

He stooped to kiss her with enough conviction that she decided he was trying to apologize for before.

"I promise. We can die together running into the maw of the portal with our swords waving."

"That's much better." She gave him a quick kiss. "I think I hear Rachael and Wilty coming back. She's speaking far louder than normal."

Storm returned the kiss and then nodded. "Agreed. I'll see you in the morning. Sleep well." He passed Rachael, Wilty, and now Ghortin as he left the room.

Ghortin stopped Storm for a few words, but they were too low for Jenna to hear.

Then he followed the other two in.

"Carabella is gathering a troop to head to the Zalin shelter. They will leave tomorrow after the breakfast council. I believe we need to discuss a few more things before calling it a night?" Ghortin went to the table of food, gathered enough for a small army, and then sat.

"Are all meetings in Irundail given with food? Not complaining, but it is odd." Jenna hadn't noticed it elsewhere. But she'd eaten enough in the past few hours that she didn't think she needed to eat for a day or two.

"It helps increase the number of people who show up." Ghortin gleefully put away a few rolls.

Rachael watched him with a fond smile. "It also is a

time saver, which is the real reason for it. Guaranteed food at a meeting means no wandering off or eating elsewhere. King Daylin started it after a few too many people ended up at the pub for extended meals instead of at the meetings."

"Will Carabella be safe at this task? I'd heard she'd been gifted with some unusual magic?" Wilty poured himself tea but didn't get food.

Jenna turned to Rachael. Most likely Wilty was someone who could know everything, but it was best to be certain.

At Rachael's nod, Jenna explained briefly about Meith, what he was, and where Carabella's current magic came from.

"Another cuari, but not of this world. Fascinating." Wilty's eyes went wide. "That bracelet has her old magic? Powers unaffected by the spell against the cuari in the here and now. Oh, had we known that would work before they were all taken, we could have saved many." His sips of tea seemed aggressive, but they appeared to be aimed at himself. "I should have known."

Rachael laughed and patted his arm. "Old friend, no one aside from the Guardians knew the true story of the cuari until recently. And even we had no idea what had happened to the ones who weren't part of the one hundred, yet weren't unmade. Jenna found that out for us."

Jenna shrugged. "I'd like to claim that logic led me to it, but if I hadn't been pulled up into the chaotic plane, I would have never known. None of us would have."

"Which might be why you were so drawn to going directly to the plane when you first arrived here, come to think of it." Ghortin pushed aside his plate. "I've had dozens of apprentices over the decades and never had a single one do what you did to access Power. I don't even know that I could get to the chaotic plane directly like you have. And with what's going on now, I'd be too concerned to try. Perhaps some part of you, Typhonel, or the echo from the mindslave, knew you would need to be connected to it."

Chapter Twenty-Two

"AND THAT IS WHERE THEY'RE holding the rest of the current cuari." Wilty scowled into his teacup. "I have a feeling there are many things that we have missed along the way."

Jenna jumped in on that comment. "One is why the books of the cuari are being so difficult to get and read when they were designed to help the Guardians and the Protector handle the cuari and destroy the portal for good. I get that they could only be used at the right time, as nothing else worked. But come on, I have a god in my head—I think the time is right."

"I'm not a Guardian nor Protector, but I have to agree," Ghortin said. "And why was I able to read the one cuari book prior to my abduction, but not now?" He turned to Jenna. "Are you carrying any of the books?"

"No, I didn't think bringing them along was a good idea. They're hidden in the box you made in your library back in your cottage." It had taken the full week of their trip down from Strann for Ghortin to get her to a point where he felt she was ready to use the magic storage.

He'd first tried explaining it, but action always worked better than theory for her, so after a day, she got him teaching her the real deal. It felt like when she used to go to the chaotic plane for magical Power, but Ghortin scowled when she pointed that out.

She continued to see the connection; she simply didn't mention it to him anymore.

"Excellent, now you've stored things there, can you get them back?" Ghortin folded his arms as he dropped into his teaching mode.

"He never gets past that, does he?" Wilty laughed. "I recall when he lived up here—he could terrify students by nothing more than lifting an eyebrow."

Jenna joined him in laughter and raised her left eyebrow steeply. "This? He tried that when I first came here—but it's harder to intimidate an old college student." She turned to Ghortin who was trying to look fierce, yet also trying not to laugh. "I believe I can successfully get them back."

"That might be a good idea." Rachael stood. "But let me secure this room." She waved her hand at Wilty. "Nothing against your library, this is an amazingly secure location. But one can never have too much magical protection with all that's been going on." She nodded to Jenna; her current concern was prompted by Sacaranz breaking in before.

Jenna felt the spell as Rachael cast it. Regardless of her secret standing as a Guardian, Rachael had mostly presented herself as a common hearth witch. The spell that flew around the room was anything but simple.

Ghortin gave an approving nod as Rachael tied the spell to the four magic users and sat back down.

"Now, I believe you should be able to access the mage hide." She nodded to Ghortin. "Or whatever he is calling it."

Jenna called up the hidden storage spell. It wasn't hard, beyond the fact that it bounced around. She'd accused Ghortin of making it do that on purpose, but he insisted it was part of the spell itself.

At the time, Carabella had muttered that *her* spells like that didn't bounce.

Ghortin ignored her.

Eventually, Jenna reached into thin air to get the books.

It was always disturbing to see the open storage area when just moving a bit to the side showed nothing. The hidden storage portal was part of Ghortin's library back in his cottage to the far south. The dimly lit library itself was beyond the magical storage box. She grabbed all the books that she had in there, including the non-cuari ones that Carabella had lent her, and stacked them on the table. She was closing the portal to the library when a dart shot out of it.

She ducked and barely missed getting hit. Ghortin, Rachael, and even Wilty, all had spells up and ready to go. Access to the portal vanished, but Jenna wasn't sure if she did it or not.

"What was that?" Ghortin growled as he stalked to the wall that the dart stuck out of. "I don't have any defenses like that in my library. Well, nothing that should attack my approved apprentice. And I *never* use darts." He didn't remove it from the wall but held his left hand over it. "No magic, no poison."

"It still could have done some damage if it had hit one of us." Rachael bristled with defensive spells. No mage near her right now would think she was a common hearth witch.

Ghortin muttered the spell words to open the magic storage portal and scowled when nothing happened. On the third attempt, with several shields between him and the space he was trying to call up, it flashed open.

Jenna stayed on the edge of being able to look inside, but hopefully far enough away that if another dart came through, it would miss her.

No darts, but the box rattled.

"That's new." She started to lean in closer but held back. The only protections in there should be from her or Ghortin. And she knew neither of them had done that.

"And unwelcome. Someone has invaded my cottage!" Ghortin looked ready to climb through the box to find the culprit. Never mind that the box was about four feet in the air, and not very wide.

"You won't fit." Jenna sized up the box, then looked down at her hips. Rachael would fit better, but she should still be able to make it. "I might."

"Neither of you have the slightest idea what's on the other side. We have the books; your cottage will be fine." Rachael held to the right of Ghortin as if ready to grab him. Aside from her body hanging onto him, making sure that he couldn't fit—she wouldn't have been able to stop him if he forced the issue.

"There are important things in there. They can't be left to thieves! And they are inside the vortex, or they couldn't be in the library. I need to go through, chase them out, and secure the vortex and the cottage. I can do it if I'm there." He was sizing up the space again and stepping back for a running jump.

Jenna nodded to Rachael, then jumped into it before he started running. It was a tight fit, and the invisible sides, top, and bottom all felt like cold metal. There would have been no way for Ghortin to fit. Short of a shrinking spell—which, he assured her long ago, did not exist.

Jenna looked back into the other room once she jumped into the library. "You'd better get me back out of here when I secure the cottage." After spending her first few months in this world in Ghortin's cottage, she knew where Ghortin's traps and supplies were. That someone had not only made it in but had found their way into the vortex was disturbing.

Ghortin's vortex was unique in the world. He'd created it when he was coming into his own as a mastermage. When he was too new to realize it should have been impossible. It was an unending sector of space that was attached to his cottage and contained his libraries, labs, and mythological artifacts. When Jenna first arrived, he'd set her up in a bedroom inside of it. He wasn't completely sure how much of a danger she might be, so he wanted a way to keep her from rampaging the country-side if she was dangerous.

By the time he'd realized that she was safe, she'd gotten used to staying in the vortex and kept her room in it.

"Are you going to close it?" She was in the main library's workroom and there was no one else around that she could tell. The mage lights were coded to increase at movement and only went fully on when she jumped out of the box.

"No. I can move this around and follow you." Ghortin grunted at something either Rachael or Wilty said that he disagreed with. "Eventually follow you. It might take me a while to get it going. But it needs to stay open so I can stop these thieves." At least he was no longer trying to figure out how to crawl through the box.

"Keep an eye on him, Rachael."

Rachael looked at Ghortin and shook her head. Her expression said it all: his cuari mother couldn't keep him in line, the odds weren't good for anyone else. "Where are you going first?"

"I'm going to find backup." She grinned at the con-fused look on Ghortin's face. "The elementals, they can go anywhere." Before he could respond, she ran into the center of the library.

She wasn't surprised when, while there was a lot of faint swearing coming through the box, it stayed in the workroom she'd left. She didn't know much about those storage passages, but she knew they were old magic and difficult.

And she'd crawled through one to the other end of a country gripped in war. Not the brightest move, but she didn't see an option. The risk of enemies having access to Ghortin's vortex and all that was inside of it was ter-rifying.

A massive, lumbering desk stood in the middle of

the library, then it scuffled back a few feet as Jenna approached. "Hello! It is good to see you." The huge desk was sentient, after a fashion, and also mobile. And it had its own personality, much to a young Storm's chagrin. As a child who visited Ghortin's forest often, he'd been chased by the desk a few times and still flinched when it moved. Jenna made friends with it when she lived there. "Was there anyone recently in here?"

She put her hand on the desktop, but all she felt was a contented purr. If there had been someone, they were gone now. "If any strangers do come in, can you trap them for me?" An even louder purr-rumble. "Thank you." She patted it once more and walked to the wall. Like the rest of the vague-looking beige walls, this wall was completely solid, giving the impression of no way out.

"Hello? I'd like the door to appear, please. And also, I'd like to talk to you." There were an untold number of elementals inside the vortex. Specks of light and energy that looked more like random dust motes caught in a sunbeam than sentient beings. Ghortin treated them as servants, ordering them about.

Jenna made friends with them.

She'd even used them once to chase Ghortin out of wherever he'd been hiding in the vortex early in her stay here. Which was why she thought of them now. If someone was hiding in here, the elementals should be able to chase them toward the entrance of the cottage.

The elementals should also appear and create the door in the library wall at her call. But nothing happened. "I'd like the door, please." She put a little more force into her words.

A thin glowing line appeared in the general shape of a door, flickered once, then held. Jenna touched the center and the door inside the outline vanished. "Thank you. I would like to speak to you."

A mass of glowing lights surrounded her as she stepped into the hall, but they felt more curious than hostile.

To be fair, she had no idea how they kept track of time, and it had been over a year since she'd been there. She held out her arms with palms up. "I'm a friend, remember?"

They continued buzzing around her, but not coming closer until five of them broke off and went to her hands. After a moment or two, they settled on her fingers and glowed brightly. The rest didn't land on her but flew closer. They'd either remembered her or decided she was safe.

Her prior communications with them were simplistic, but enough for them to find Ghortin and chase him toward her a year ago. She needed a little more than that this time.

"Has anyone been in here besides me recently?" She tried imagining the passage of time for them. Her prior experience had shown they reacted to emotions and thoughts as well as words and intentions.

The elementals buzzed about as if discussing things, then came back and gave her a mental nod.

"Are they still here?" It was difficult to feel them in her head, far more subtle than they'd been when she lived here—but also more advanced.

Again, the mental nod.

"How many?" She wanted to ask more, like where were they, did they have weapons, and how long ago they got in. But this communication was tenuous at best. Since she'd lived here, they'd become more attuned, but she wasn't sure they had the time for that rapport to build.

The original five flew up as one and came close to her face. A number came into her mind.

"Four?" At the affirmative from the elementals, she looked down the misty beige hallway. "Which direction?" Hopefully, whoever these invaders were, they hadn't gone deeper into the vortex. If so, she'd have to send the elementals to chase them to her.

The elementals went down the corridor which led to the solid part of the cottage. It was still upsetting and concerning that someone had broken in, but if she could at least get them out of the vortex, that would be a start.

The elementals flew faster and Jenna jogged to keep up with them. Yup, they went to the doorway to the main part of the cottage. Even though elementals were part of this world, Ghortin had told her they couldn't go out of the vortex.

She paused before going out the doorway. "Thank you, my friends. I wish you could come out into the world; you would be a great boon to our cause."

The five elementals closest to her flared in brightness and a single word, "*done*" echoed in her mind. A word coming from thousands of voices. Then the flashing lights all raced out of the doorway and into the cottage.

She had a feeling it might be a good idea that Ghortin hadn't been able to follow her. He probably wasn't going to be happy about this. Even worse was that she had no idea how she'd done it. "Wait! Some of you need to stay in the vortex and guard it. Unless it's Ghortin, Storm, or myself—don't let anyone inside there."

"*Turn.*" The same all-one voice echoed in her head. She looked back and saw more elementals down the vortex hall. There were new ones or ones she hadn't seen before. The number with her didn't appear diminished.

"Not sure how that happened, but let's find who broke in here." She felt a tingle as she crossed the doorway and ducked as a dart shot out at her.

CHAPTER TWENTY-THREE

THE DART HADN'T BEEN AIMED well but was still too close for her liking.

The elementals on this side of the vortex swarmed toward the kitchen and low-voiced yells and the clanging of pans were heard.

Jenna ran around the corner, her hand raised for a spell to blast apart whoever was in there. Then came skidding to a halt. There were three injured derawri fighting off the elementals and a fourth one unconscious on the floor.

Tigan, Crell's second in command of her deathsworn, scowled at her through the haze of buzzing elementals. "What took you so long?"

"Don't attack them—these are friends." Jenna wasn't sure if she needed to speak out loud for the elementals, but she figured it wouldn't hurt.

The elementals circled the derawri once more, then came behind her.

Tigan held a heavy skillet but set it down when the elementals backed off. "Thank you. We've been trapped here for a week, not able to get out or see what's happened to the rest of my people. My mage finally broke into that whirling place and we found the library. Then that box in the air opened and I heard you. I tried shouting, but you didn't hear me. I was hoping someone would notice the dart." He looked down at his unconscious companion. "He barely survived getting us through the vortex and I had to drag him out. Where are the rest of you?"

Tigan was short and stocky, like many of his people,

and had a perpetual scowl. But right now, the relief on his face was so clear that he appeared ready to hug her.

"In Irundail. I'm confused though. Crell said you were all sent back to Derawri when we left Lithunane over a month ago."

"Aye. And we went. But my people are fighting their own battles and we were magicked back down here. Julin is my only mage; they did not send the rest with us." His scowl was back and his hand clenched.

Deathsworn rarely admitted to having mages in their ranks. His obvious concern at the few he had being missing was unusual.

The description sounded a bit too much like what had happened to Crell's rangers a few days ago.

"How did you get into the cottage?" There were a lot of why questions, but those would be for later.

Tigan let out a deep breath. "We were sent down here against our will at the end of the fall of Lithunane. We saved some people and they escaped in a caravan to the north, but we had too many injured to travel far. I hid most of them in Ghortin's secret cave in the forest, then broke in here for food. Whoever sent us here gave us no supplies."

"Ghortin isn't going to be happy that you could break in. Nor that your mage was able to get into the vortex."

Tigan grinned. "I will deal with him when we get back there. I was truly hoping you weren't that far away and could help us."

"Sadly, no. We're all in the castle in Irundail, including Crell. Your dart got our attention, but we can't bring forces down through that mage box. You don't know how you were sent down? Or why?"

"No. We were setting out to defend Derawri, as ordered by Ki' Crell. In the middle of our strategy meeting, the room filled with smoke, and myself and many of the deathsworn were suddenly outside of Lithunane. No warning, no time to grab more weapons. The only reason we didn't fare worse was because of who and what we are."

"I heard Lithunane fell quickly." Jenna still had trouble thinking of the lives lost there. Shoving it aside to save others wasn't easy.

"It did. Even if we had a hundred more of my people, we couldn't have stopped the collapse. Whoever was behind it had planned the attack for a long time, and had far more people than Lithunane could muster. I was no fan of Prince Resstlin, but I believe that his ignoring the warnings given to him about the danger contributed to the fall. He sent two thousand guards to the Mark— are two days before the attack under mysterious advice." He looked at his unconscious mage and two warriors. "I have three healers back in that cave. These injuries aren't bad, but they will get that way if not treated."

"I should be able to get us out of here." Jenna wasn't sure why the cottage had let Tigan break in but then blocked them from leaving.

She, and half the flock of elementals, including the five who seemed to want to stay nearest to her, went to the front door. She had a brief twinge of sadness as she crossed the front room. Things had been far less deadly when she'd lived here. They were still dangerous and more things were happening than they knew—but before that ball, the world seemed like a calmer place.

She felt a jolt as she touched the handle. And it wouldn't turn. "I live here, you stubborn door. Let me out." The elementals with her flew to the door and a nearly out-of-hearing range conversation took place. Bits of sounds floated in the air.

Jenna grabbed the door handle again, still felt a slight tingle, but the door opened this time. "Thank you. I will tell Ghortin you did your duty." She turned back to the kitchen and she held the door open. "Get your people and any supplies you can take out while I keep this open." She'd thought of visiting her old room. She'd been whisked up to Irundail during the ball a year ago with only the clothes on her back. But the door still didn't feel happy about letting the intruders out. Standing with it propped open against her back was prudent.

It was early morning here, whereas it was night back in Irundail.

Tigan carried the unconscious mage out, and the other two helped each other. A group of elementals circled the pair and seemed to be assisting.

"Thank you." She spoke to the ones closest to her but nodded to the rest. "But are you certain it's safe for you to be out here?" She kept the door open and Tigan went back and dragged out piles of food and supplies.

She had no idea Ghortin had that many stores, but he had been trapped in places of his own making before, so a hidden storeroom of long-lasting supplies wasn't completely surprising.

The elementals buzzed around the area, and a faint confirmation came through her head. It was handy to have some communication, but it would be nicer for it to be clearer.

She shook her head—communication. "Didn't you have a taran wand?"

Tigan dragged out the last bit of supplies and stopped right outside the door. "I did, and still do, but it wouldn't reach anyone. I left it with my people in Ghortin's cave to keep testing it. The fact that they didn't reach anyone in Irundail doesn't bode well."

"No, it doesn't. I know they've had trouble with them." There was the sound of horses nickering from around the back of the cottage, and the door pushed on her. "Hold it a minute. Tigan, do you need anything else? This door wants to close." She had planned to crawl back into the mage box after this was resolved, but she didn't feel she should leave the deathsworn in such a critical situation. Not to mention she wasn't sure about what she should do about the elementals. The ones that had come outside were exploring the area, but not going beyond the thin white trees that circled the cottage grounds.

Bringing them through to Irundail might be a troubling situation. For the same reason, she couldn't let them loose here.

"We have what we need," Tigan said as he brought a final bag of supplies out.

The sounds of horses again came from behind the cottage as Jenna let the door close. "Did you have horses?"

"Not originally." Tigan grinned and whistled. "The deathsworn don't normally use them. But we saved these from the guard stables of Lithunane." At his whistle, a herd of close to a hundred horses came around the corner.

"Wow, that's impressive. They look well fed." Ghortin had always kept a few horses in his stables, but she never thought about them unless they were going for a ride.

"Ghortin has a collection of magical stables way in the back, on the edge of the forest. They seemed to have been ready and willing to feed them." He looked up as another twenty came around the corner. "And we're gathering more. Now, let's load up some wagons. We need to get to the cave. I'd thought maybe some of my people would have come here when we didn't come back after a few days, but I don't see any signs."

The elementals were flitting between the horses, but while the animals noticed them, they didn't appear concerned.

They quickly found two wagons, small but workable, and loaded the supplies, the unconscious mage, and against their will, the two injured derawri. They were battered, and the woman's leg looked chewed up, but neither wanted to ride.

"How were these two injured?" She knew derawri were stubborn, but if Tigan had left most of his people—including the injured—in the caves, these two shouldn't be here.

"We were attacked not far from the cottage. The beasts are dead now, but they did their damage. A troop of ertin, sickly looking, but still fierce."

Jenna reached for her sword before recalling she didn't have it and that all of her weapons were back in her room in the castle of Irundail. Maybe she could try to get back into the cottage and find something to use.

Ertins were the first monsters she'd run into here, and she'd hoped to never see them again. "You need to check them for poison once we're inside the cave. Trust me." Storm nearly died after being bitten by one of the nasty things. She pulled up the most powerful spells she could think of, holding them in her mind in case they were attacked, and then called out to the elementals. "I need you to guard these wagons and us. There are evil creatures about."

The elementals agreed and seemed far too excited about it as they zipped around the wagons and spread out.

"We did kill them all, their bodies were left past those white trees." Tigan didn't look offended, simply curious.

"I believe you. But I have a bad relationship with those things." She couldn't even mention the name and found herself again reaching for a sword that wasn't there.

Tigan saw the movement. "We have extra weapons in the cave. But I agree we should move quickly." He looked at the elementals as he led the first horse and wagon. "Are those coming with us to the cave?"

"No idea. As far as I know, they've never been outside of the vortex." She led the second horse and wagon but waved to the five elementals who were staying closest. "Actually, can you leave some of your companions behind to guard the door? In this case, it was good that Tigan could break in, but we don't want others to do the same."

A group of bright lights broke off from the mob, circled them, and then went to the door and darted around the flowers near it.

The rest of the elementals hung close to the wagons. When they were a short distance from the cave, the elementals vanished. Jenna would have thought that perhaps they were at the edge of their range, but they'd all shot to the right before they disappeared. They might be after something.

"What's that smell?" Jenna kept her hand steady on the horse's halter, but her stomach sank as the odor hit her. Ertin were like a nasty combination of a large greyhound and a velociraptor—and they had a unique smell. To her, it smelled like rusting metal, but that would be hard to explain to Tigan.

"It is ertin, but far away. We need to get the supplies inside and then send the horses back to their stables. The stables are protected."

That was a good thing to know as Jenna was mentally trying to sort out how they were going to fit the horses into Ghortin's cave.

The cave front was as she expected—completely closed off by large stones from the inside.

Tigan went near the rocks and shouted a few words in what she assumed was derawri. There was a rumbling and the stones began rolling back.

Unfortunately, the ertin smell was either getting stronger, or she was freaking out over it and was making it seem stronger. Jenna had hoped to never see, or smell, an ertin again in her entire life.

They got the stones removed and were halfway through bringing in the supplies when the distinctive howling and yipping came from deep in the forest.

Tigan ducked into the cave and came out with a short sword and sword belt and handed them to her. "I know you're a magic user, but a solid sword is always good to have."

"Thank you." Jenna buckled on the belt and then continued tossing supplies to the next derawri. The ones who'd come out looked in decent shape. With luck, the supplies weren't too late for the injured.

Jenna removed the horses from the wagons and led them back to the cottage.

"I can do that; you should go in the cave." Tigan stuck out his chin as he frowned.

"No offense, but I'm the one with magic. And I've faced these things before as well," she said as he took a breath to argue. "You need to protect your people, and I'm not letting these horses get caught up in whatever's going on." The howling grew louder. "Close that cave!" She didn't look back as she ran between the two horses. There was no way to know if these ertin would attack them or not. Ghortin said that ertin were normally controlled by a magic user. Which might or might not be a good thing in this case.

Tigan said nothing more, but she heard the stones moving back into place behind her.

"Come on, let's get back to your safe area." It would have been nice to have known that the stables were magically protected when she and Storm had first been stalked by the ertin the last time.

Knowing Ghortin, that might have been a more recent addition that came following that attack. He was constantly updating the cottage and the forest around it. When he'd been living here anyway.

The howling increased and while the horses didn't panic, they did pick up speed.

The stables were in sight and the horses that had come

to the front yard area before were back behind the barrier—at least it appeared so.

She followed them into the stable yard as the howling behind them increased.

The ertin came into view, chased by a swarm of lights. The elementals appeared to be making a game of it but the fallen ertin behind them, four that Jenna saw, indicated what they were doing was deadly.

Jenna stayed right inside the stable yard. Hopefully, the magic barrier that Ghortin had left would keep her and the horses safe. If the elementals didn't kill the final three ertin before then.

Another ertin growled and then collapsed. Two left. Then one.

The final ertin fell two feet from the entrance to the stable yard. The elementals flew over the horses and danced in the air.

The horses didn't seem concerned and most went to the back of the stables for food.

Jenna kept her sword out as she left the shelter of the stable yard. None of the fallen ertin moved, but she made sure she had a spell ready to blast them with as well as run them through if needed.

She used the tip of her borrowed sword to nudge the first one, but it seemed to be withering in front of her eyes. The same with the trail of its companions behind it.

Holding up her hand, she mentally called to the elementals. "What did you do to them?" Within the vortex, the elementals were workers, they created things or removed things within the field of magic that functioned in the vortex.

This was new.

Images hit her, but they were too disjointed to sort out. "Only one of you." When they all paused and sent confusion to her, she modified it. "How about you five?"

Since the ones who stayed closest to her had already separated themselves, hopefully, they could function as their
own entity.

"*Life. Energy. Gone.*" Those words weren't as clear as if
someone had spoken them, but the result was the same.

The elementals had simply removed the life force of
the ertins.

Chapter Twenty-Four

JENNA FELT A CHILL FLOW through her. It was a good thing that these elementals were on their side. But what if they hadn't been? Did Ghortin have any idea that they could do this? She would have thought he would have mentioned it if he did.

Which meant that like escaping the vortex, they were developing new skills.

"Okay. That's good." She stepped back as the nearest ertin body crumbled to dust. "Creepy, but good. Do you know of any more of these creatures in the forest?"

The five spokes-elementals glowed brighter for a moment, then dimmed back to normal. "*clear.*"

Either their communication was getting better, or she was developing a skill in understanding them.

With a nod, she walked back to check on the horses, they were eating and relaxing as if nothing was wrong.

Maybe it was part of Ghortin's spell on these stables. Or they intuitively knew more about the elementals than she did.

If there were no more ertin about, she needed to get back to the cave. Hopefully, Tigan's taran wand worked now.

The stones still blocked the cave entrance, and sadly her derawri was limited to a few swear words picked up from Crell. She doubted those would be appropriate.

"Tigan? It's me, Jenna. The ertin are gone now."

"That's good. They took out three of my men." The voice behind her was male and human. The point of a sword tapped her back. "Not sure who you are, why you're out here, or what you're yelling at rocks for. But my people and I haven't had fresh food or water since we got lost in this place. Keep your hands up and turn around slowly."

Jenna took a calming breath and did as she was told. The speaker didn't have enough of an accent to tell which side he was on.

The ragged band of men and women, human, kelar, and derawri alike gave her the first clue. The battered Lithunane livery confirmed it.

"I'm on your side." As she spoke she wished that she hadn't. Even though they appeared to be Lithunane guards didn't necessarily mean that they were. Or even if they had been, that they hadn't been working for the other side. The city fell too quickly for there not to have been traitors to the crown involved.

She did note the poor condition of the group, and the red blood, not demonspawn green, marking most of them. Storm and Edgar had spread the word that demonspawn could now bleed red before bleeding out their natural green—but some of the wounds looked deep given the bloody bandages.

"I'm not working for Strann or Khelaran." She kept her hands up, but that wouldn't help them being up against a mage as they were. The spell she held in her mind and right fist would strike them off their feet on the first pass, and knock them out on the second.

Hopefully. It was one she'd created on the way back from Strann. It had a limited range and duration, so she wasn't certain she could get everyone. There looked to be about fifty soldiers surrounding her.

"Lady Jenna?" The female voice came from the back of the group. Then the speaker came out of the group.

At first, Jenna didn't recognize her. She was wearing

a tattered and ill-fitting uniform of the castle guard and had her left arm in a crude sling.

"It's me, Baliana, I was one of your ladies' maids in Lithunane."

Her smile brought it back to Jenna. Baliana was one of the floofy dress brigade. But she'd been kind. "Baliana! It's so good to see you!" Jenna stepped forward, but the guard blocking her wouldn't budge. "I simply wanted to greet her. And if you are all actually from Lithunane, you should recognize me as Prince Corin's fiancée. Not to mention, that you would know that I am a mage. And a damn good one." She let sparks fly from her fingers. They were showy but useless, yet they got the point across.

Baliana put her good hand on the foremost guard's arm. "It's her, I can tell. I told you that I trained as a cleric."

"And as a horse trainer, hired guard, and lady's maid." He gave Jenna a studied look. "I saw you briefly in the castle. But there have been demonspawn working with our enemies. Ravenhearst said he'd be back as well."

"If you see him, kill it. I saw the real Ravenhearst die." Jenna lowered her arms.

Baliana ran past the guard captain and hugged Jenna. "Sorry to be so informal, but we feared you had died on the road with Mastermage Ghortin, Carabella, and Crell."

"It's good to see you." Jenna looked at the group of guards. "All of you. But Ghortin, Carabella, and Crell are all alive and secure in Irundail."

"We'd heard rumors you were all killed." The guard sheathed his sword. "How and why are you here?"

"She was helping us." Tigan remained so quiet before he spoke, that Jenna didn't even know he was there.

The stones were still in place, but he and three of his people now surrounded the guards with bows drawn.

Jenna smiled at Tigan then turned back to the guard. "It's complicated. Now, are we all friends?"

"Yes, but what is that?" The guard captain nodded toward the direction of the cottage—more importantly, the stable. A mass of bright dust motes and horses were coming their way.

"I'd wondered where they went. Don't worry, they're on our side. But don't do anything aggressive." She'd been so caught up in the entire mess that she hadn't noticed the elementals had gone back to the horses before she got to the cave.

The horses slowed down and a few nickered greetings.

"Our horses? What magic is this? We lost them in the fall." A tall kelar guardsman reached out to one of the animals with a look of wonder.

Tigan shrugged. "We ended up at the stables in the palace at the right time and released them. They followed us here." He handed the taran wand to Jenna. "Hopefully it will work better for you. Maybe the magic box you came through is still open."

Jenna had thought about that, but she had a feeling she'd need the elementals' help to get into the cottage. If he didn't watch it, even Ghortin might need them to get into his own home when this was over.

"If you will excuse me for a moment." She nodded to the guards. The taran wands weren't well known, and if possible, it would be better to keep it that way.

The guard nodded as his people went to the horses.

"I will keep watch." Tigan folded his arms and kept an eye on the soldiers. His two companions lowered their bows but didn't put them away.

Jenna smiled in thanks and went behind the cave. A clump of elementals, including the five that had latched onto her, followed. "I'm not sure if you can help, but this magic needs a boost. When I speak, help me reach Ghortin." There were others with the taran wands, but he would be the best for them to focus on.

She held up the wand close to her ear and mouth. "Ghortin?"

There was a pause, then an anxious voice. "Jenna? Where are you? I had to close the way into my library." His voice was tinny and hard to hear, but it was him.

Jenna nodded. "Long story. In brief, the elementals are out of your cottage and I believe they are helping me reach you. Tigan and a bunch of Crell's deathsworn are in your forest, along with a group of Lithunane guards."

"That's a lot for being gone such a short time. Crell is in here now and is clearly impatient to speak to Tigan. Storm has joined us and wants you back up here. Rachael and I believe we can get you back up here, but we can't bring the others."

Jenna carefully looked over the guards. There were only a few injured guards and soldiers, but she knew the derawri had some as well. "Can you find a way to bring me and the injured up there? I think we need to get them to a safer place."

"I'm not sure. OW! What was that? I think there are elementals in here!" Ghortin sounded like he was running.

"They might be trying to help?"

"By shocking me to death? Oh, hold on a bit." Ghortin's voice vanished for a moment but the connection seemed to still be there. "Okay, no idea what you did to my elementals down there, but they have indicated that they can bring a few of you this far. Won't tell me how, and it's my magic they're working on…but they can do it. Go to the clearing past the caves—bring the injured. Keep the wand open so it doesn't have to recharge."

Jenna walked back to the guards and Tigan. "We might be able to get your injured up to Irundail. But not the rest of you."

Neither the guard captain nor Tigan showed anything but relief.

"We will continue our fight and work up our way to Irundail as we secure the land. Thank you for trying to help our injured." Tigan gave a small bow then opened the cave and brought his injured out.

The guard captain had six injured, including a slightly argumentative Baliana, to bring to the clearing.

"I can fight. And I am good with horses." Baliana wasn't happy.

"And you have a broken arm. You can fight for Irundail once you're healed," the guard captain said gently, but with a bit of exasperation.

Jenna stepped in. "We do need more people in Irundail, and their healers are the best."

"Fine." Baliana lifted her good shoulder. "Truth be told, it hurts a lot."

Once Jenna, Baliana, and the collected injured were together, Jenna reached out to Ghortin. Yes, keeping the taran wands a secret was important, but she didn't have a choice.

The elementals near them began circling the group of injured as she spoke to Ghortin. "Hold on a minute, I need to give the wand back to Tigan. Then beam us up." She laughed in her head at her joke that no one else in this world would get, then tossed the taran wand to Tigan.

The world exploded in a flare of sparks that she hoped were the elementals.

CHAPTER TWENTY-FIVE

———◆———

THEN THEY WERE BACK IN Irundail. Not in the castle, but at the mouth of the alley between the castle and the House of Healing.

Not all the elementals remained with them. But the five who appeared to be her liaisons, plus a few hundred more, zipped around and lit up the night. Jenna was grateful they were staying nearby. With all that had happened to the people of Irundail today, the last thing they needed were nosy fluffs of light and energy shooting through their houses.

Storm, Crell, and Ghortin came running out of the castle with more trailing behind.

Storm grabbed Jenna and held her tight. Then put her down as a dozen elementals buzzed in his hair.

"It's okay, these are good people." Jenna shrugged to Storm then turned to Ghortin. "I didn't know they would come with us."

"Can you ask them to confine themselves to your room until we get this sorted? I appreciate their assistance, but I am at a loss as to what to do with them. I have a feeling they won't take my command to go home." Ghortin's hair was ruffled and Jenna briefly wondered if the elementals had recalled harassing him a year ago and wanted to play again.

Jenna focused on thinking of her room. "Okay, here's my room, can you all go there and wait? All of you that are already here, at any rate." The last thing she needed was to have *all* of them up here.

The main five flew close to her, circled her head, and then they all vanished.

Maggie came running up with a fleet of healers and cots. None of the injured, even the recently conscious deathsworn mage, wanted to get on the cots.

Maggie changed all of their minds in a moment—even a Dewari deathsworn who made Tigan seem light and cheerful.

Of course, it hadn't hurt that Crell was standing next to Maggie with a full scowl of her own. Even the injured Lithunane guards paid attention to Crell.

Baliana climbed on a cot, although she pointed out that it was her arm that was broken, not her legs. "Thank you, and it is good to see you again, Lady Jenna."

"Just Jenna if you please. It's good to see you as well." She smiled as a healer quickly rolled the cot away.

"She was one of the lady's maids from the palace of Lithunane, wasn't she?" Storm kept his arm around her, but so far hadn't chastised her about her adventure.

That was a good sign, but one she doubted would last.

"She was. And it sounds like she has many other skills." Jenna leaned into Storm. She'd only been gone a short while, but she knew how she'd feel if their positions were reversed.

Rachael studied the dark sky. "Night's coming into itself, I think we need to rest before long." She held out her hand before Ghortin could comment. "But I agree that we need a *summary* of what happened in the south. In the library."

Wilty nodded vigorously and led them back into the castle.

Storm kept his arm around her shoulders as they followed. Judging by the newer additions to the group, the news of her adventure had traveled.

The war room was far more crowded than when she left. Everyone from earlier was present, plus Prince Justlantin and many of his advisors. Wilty made certain there were seats for all, but no food this time. Jenna wasn't certain of the time difference between the two ends of the country, but it seemed to be long enough that it was early morning in the south and night was settling in here.

Rachael had a bit of news as well. While Jenna was gone, Dantil and his helaermages verified that the odd screaming some of the Erlindan survivors did was a spell. It shut down the Keepers long enough for the dakair and others to get past. Had it activated later, when it had built up more strength, it would have kept them open permanently. A different attack than the one on Lithunane, but one as potentially deadly.

Rachael nodded to Jenna. She kept things brief but detailed what had happened since she crawled through the spell box.

Storm went pale at her mention of the elementals. "Those were them outside?" He didn't fear them as much as the animated desk back in Ghortin's cottage, but they still weren't good friends.

"Yes. I think Ghortin will have his hands full with them when this is over." She looked to Ghortin, but he was muttering to himself and looking annoyed.

"These troops who were sent to the Markare before the collapse, were they who found you?" A military captain sitting between Tor Ranshal and Crell asked.

Jenna shuddered. "I hope not. They said two thousand were sent to the desert and there were less than fifty that I saw. But hopefully, Tigan and the Lithunane guards can find the others."

The soldier nodded. "We'll speak to the injured soldiers in the morning, thank you for bringing them back."

"Can these elemental creatures be used to spy on our enemies?" Another gruff-looking soldier, a woman this time, asked.

Ghortin answered first. "I'm not even sure how they

got out of my vortex, let alone anything else they've done. They've gone far beyond what I created them for and until I get a chance to examine them—in the morning—we'll have no idea if they can be more helpful than they already have been."

Prince Justlantin watched the room, then gave a small nod. "I say that everyone needs to get some sleep. We have received hopeful news, but the immediate need will be to continue protecting Irundail and the surrounding areas. We defended ourselves this time, but war will be here and I feel we will need to ride to meet it."

The room went silent at his words, and then people broke up and left.

At a nod from Ghortin, Jenna stayed and waited until it was only her, Storm, Ghortin, Rachael, Tor Ranshal, Crell, Wilty, and Prince Justlantin.

"I won't keep anyone long, but I did want to reiterate that while I created the elementals, I have no idea what they have become," Ghortin said. "We need to proceed cautiously with them, and I don't think any plans should be made to use them."

"I gathered as much." Justlantin turned to Jenna. "For now, can you continue to keep them in your room?"

"I can try. They seem to listen to me more or less, but I can't promise anything."

"That's the best any of us can do." Justlantin gave a nod and left.

Ghortin, Rachael, and Tor Ranshal stayed behind with Wilty, most likely planning on ignoring Justlantin's order to sleep.

Jenna walked out with Crell and Storm.

Crell lowered her voice as they went down an empty hall. "I'm glad that Tigan and the ones who were sent down with him are fine, but I find it suspicious that some of my rangers were sent up here, and then he and a group of my deathsworn were sent to Lithunane. As far as we know, no other groups have been moved that way."

"Agreed. It sounded as if your rangers were sent north to save them during the battle in Lithunane," Storm said. "I doubt the same would be said of your deathsworn."

"Tigan had nothing else to go on, but he said he'd be reaching out now that he got his taran wand to work again. Although he might not be as happy that the elementals could be needed for that." Jenna fought a yawn, but it came out anyway. "Sorry, folks, I'm done."

"Go sleep. I'm going to sort out some ideas as to who in Derawri might have sent them. Although the why is a more difficult answer. After I do another check on the injured." Crell nodded to them and continued down the hallway.

"Not going to say you shouldn't have done what you did." Storm gave a soft laugh as they walked to her room.

"But you thought it." Jenna paused outside of her bedroom. She'd love to invite him in, but there were a few hundred elementals inside. Not to mention, fatigue was hitting her hard. The day felt longer than most weeks.

"I did. But you are who you are, and risks come with the territory. And, you might have given folks up here hope for some resistance in the south. Especially if they can find that regiment that Resstlin sent off." He shook his head. "I don't like to speak ill of the dead, but what could he have been thinking?"

"That Lithunane was invincible." Jenna slipped into his arms and pressed her head against his chest. "Although not as protected as here, there were still enough fortifications and soldiers left to make him believe that. The question would be why did he send them—was it someone trying to pull away forces before the attack, or did he actually have information about something going on in the Markare?" She almost hid her yawn this time.

"Excellent points. But if you yawn once more, I might

take it personally." He leaned down for a kiss. "Go to sleep, if those elementals will let you."

"Thanks. You should as well. Or I could send some of them to help?" She knew Storm often went with little or no sleep, but there wasn't a reason to now. Even if he might not believe that.

He stepped back and raised his hands. "I'll be good. Sleep well and please keep them in your room."

"Deal." Jenna went into her bedroom, but there were no elementals. Maybe they went back to Ghortin's cottage. "Hello? Elementals?" She turned on the rest of the lights, but there was no response. "I hope you didn't go to the wrong room." If they had returned south, that was one thing. She wasn't sure how they could help up here, but they could use everything they had. But it could be horrific if they invaded the wrong room.

She'd bathed and changed into sleepwear and was crawling into bed when the elementals buzzed into the room.

They came through the outer wall and window, and there'd been no yells of terror, so hopefully they hadn't gone into any occupied rooms in the castle.

"What am I going to do with you? It's great you're out and about, but for now can you stay in this room?"

The five flew closer to her, buzzing around her head for a moment, then gave an affirmative. Soon the rest of the elementals faded into the desk. The five stayed near her.

Jenna had wondered where the elementals went when they weren't opening doors or being called to do something by Ghortin. She hadn't thought about them literally fading into the woodwork.

The five near her circled the room once, flashed brightly, and then settled around the door frame.

Feeling oddly protected, Jenna fell asleep.

The next morning was blissfully free of yelling, the sounds of running, or any strange creatures in her room. Aside from the soft glow of the elementals coming from the doorframe and the desk. The daylight coming from the windows was bright enough that if she didn't know the elementals were there, and was looking for them, she might not have noticed.

Wishing she'd closed the curtains better before she went to sleep, Jenna rolled out of bed and went to the window. It was too late to pull them tighter and go back to sleep now, the amount of sun peeking through made that clear. But it would be nice to get a feel for the day.

And hope no disasters were waiting in the courtyard below.

The five elementals joined her at the window and went to the glass as she fully pulled back the curtains. Considering that they could go through the fabric, she figured they were being polite.

She let out a sigh. The yard in front of the castle looked calm and lovely. There was a soft mist rising from the bottom two levels and already people were going about their day. They were heading into war, she knew that. But it was nice to have some calm. Even if only for a while.

A strident knocking on her door burst the illusion. Her sleep clothes covered everything, but she slipped on her robe as she, and the five elementals, went to the door.

She didn't feel it was paranoid that she pulled up a blast spell as she unlocked the door. Not after the past few months.

"There you are." Keanin smiled at her, but there was a lot of worry on his handsome face. "Can I come in?"

Jenna shrugged, released her spell, and stepped back.

The elementals remained closer to the doorway but it was still only the five.

Keanin saw them but came in anyway. His smile dropped as she shut the door.

"What's wrong?" Jenna motioned to the small table and chairs near the window and followed him when he sat.

"I'm concerned about Talia." He held up a hand as Jenna got to her feet. "Not like that. Between Maggie and myself, she's completely healed. Did Storm tell you how she and I left things in Erlinda?"

"Vaguely. You were planning on sneaking back there, alone, after Storm and Edgar reached here." She folded her arms and narrowed her eyes a bit to show him what she thought of the idea.

"A blunt way to put it, but yes. I'm in love with Talia. But I also feel that Erlinda is going to be a crucial point in this fight and we need to get it back." He closed his eyes. "I didn't think it would fall that quickly though."

Jenna reached forward and took his hand. "I know your magic has changed a lot, and so have you. But if they had that many invaders, I doubt even you could have saved the town."

He opened his eyes. "But…yeah, you're right. I think what's getting me is that I was so willing to believe Talia's lie about not loving me. She didn't even have to convince me." He dropped his gaze and studied the grain of the table.

"And you've never had that happen before. Have you ever been seriously in love? Not your love of the moment, but a deep love?" Keanin had always been a flirt and a lover, but she'd never seen it go further than that.

He looked up sheepishly. "No. There were a few times in my youth that I thought I was…but after meeting Talia, I realized they weren't real. She's so unlike who I normally was attracted to."

"Extreme understatement." Jenna laughed. "Can I

make an observation? She feels the same way you do. The reason you believed her back in Erlinda was because you feared what was between you two wasn't real."

"That…makes sense I guess. But how do I get past this? When this battle is over, I intend to ask her to marry me. How can I do that when I'm not sure I believe what we have?"

"There are no guarantees. Not in times of war or peace. You have to trust in what you have. Have you talked to her about this?"

"No. Well, a lot was going on." He gave a defensive grimace when Jenna shook her head at him. "There was."

"Go find her and talk this out. If for no other reason than the fact that both of you are going to be needed in the coming battles, and neither of you will be at your best until this is resolved." She honestly felt that from the little she'd seen of Talia, nothing, not even her own heart, would stop her from doing what needed to be done.

However, emotionality could seriously mess up a mage. Keanin's training was questionable at best. His magic had been suppressed until a year ago and he was extremely Powerful, but not very trained.

And something traumatic had changed his magic wildly.

"You are as wise as always. Storm is a lucky man." His smile wasn't up to normal, but more realistic than when he came in.

"You used to call him Corin."

"I know, but after all of these years I've realized that Storm is who he is." He got to his feet with a sigh. "I should leave my best friend's fiancée to her morning preparations. Breakfast will be in the royal dining hall in an hour. And I now need to go speak to Talia." He gave a bow as elaborate as the ones he used to do in court.

Jenna gave him a hug when they got to the door. "Just remember, she loves you. It will work out."

His hug back was tight and he sighed. "Part of me knows that. I'll let that part talk."

CHAPTER TWENTY-SIX

ONCE SHE SENT KEANIN OFF to talk to his true love, Jenna took her bath and dressed. Somehow, more appropriate clothing had appeared in her closet at some point. She thought of Ghortin as he'd done the same when she first arrived in this world. Nothing fancy, just slightly nicer versions of her tunic, leggings, and boots that she normally wore.

The five elementals vanished after seeing Keanin to the door and none of them reappeared when she got ready to leave. "You're all okay staying here for now, right?"

Silence.

"Can the five at least show themselves so I know that you're staying?" There was no way she was letting Ghortin escape after breakfast until he and she had a meeting with the elementals.

The five appeared near the frame of the window.

"You didn't go outside again, did you?"

They stayed flittering around the window.

"Seriously, these people here have had a bunch of bad stuff happen, they shouldn't be harassed. Or investigated." She found it difficult to glare at a bunch of floating dust motes. Especially when they kept going behind her.

"*Yes.*" The voice in her head sounded disappointed, or it could be that she felt it did.

"Thank you. Stay inside. We'll work something out, I promise." She left and managed to find her way to the breakfast room with only three wrong turns. The smells of eggs, bread, and meat drifting down the hallway helped.

There were groups of tables instead of a single large one as for dinner. Crell, Keanin, Talia, Edgar, and Diath were at one and Crell waved her over to a saved seat.

Jenna kept her grin to herself as she noticed the way Keanin and Talia were looking at each other. There was no doubt that Talia was a fierce fighter, but she had seriously fallen for Keanin.

Diath noticed Jenna looking and laughed. "They've been that way all breakfast."

Jenna sat in one of the two empty chairs next to Crell. "Any word on Storm?"

"He's been locked in a family meeting since dawn. The only ones not included are the twins." She pointed to a separate table where the youngest royals and their nannies ate quietly.

Ghortin, Tor Ranshal, Rachael, and more of their cronies were at another table and appeared to be doing as much debating as eating.

Jenna had planned on asking him if anyone had heard from Carabella and her group but figured she'd wait. She'd been drawn into some of Ghortin's debates before and found it was better to wait and ask him about things afterward.

She shrugged as she watched him debate an older woman human who she didn't know. He might be busy for a while. "Has there been any information about Carabella?" She wasn't certain how far of a ride it was to the Zalin shelter, nor how many people rode with her. But Edgar said he'd given her one of his extra taran wands.

"Not yet." Edgar looked over at Ghortin and his group. "Or if there was, we haven't been told about it. The wands seem to be working better now, but not sure how long that will last as I'm not sure what was causing them to have problems before."

"Could they be working better because of the elementals?" Crell passed around a bowl of rolls. Most of the food was in a buffet at the far end of the room.

"It might be," Jenna said. "They definitely helped with boosting Tigan's taran wand. Have you spoken to him yet?"

"Yes, I had no trouble getting through. He did say there was a group of elementals following him around like baby goats. The rest appeared to have returned to the cottage, but he didn't think they were going inside. Or at least not staying there."

"At least they're good for something." Jenna took a roll. "The ones up here were out last night when we had our brief meeting in the library. Hopefully, no one noticed them." She wasn't sure how likely that was, but they were able to hide well.

Storm came stomping into the breakfast room and sat next to Jenna. "Morning everyone." He ripped apart a roll.

"Did Justlantin do something? He's the easygoing one of your bunch," Keanin said.

"No. But Garlan had more information arrive this morning from his people coming up from Lithunane. They found another troop of Lithunane soldiers. They told him that Resstlin actually sent two groups of fighters into the Markare, not one. The two thousand fighter company went to the south, and then a few hours later, a smaller troop of under a thousand was sent north. The ones who just made it here were from the northern group. They were attacked two days ago and got separated from the rest of their unit. Monsters came out of the portal—and they didn't sound like ertin or sciretts, but they vanished immediately. The thirty who arrived this morning are being scanned by the helaermages."

Jenna looked over to Ghortin's table. That sort of information should be shared with him as well. He and Carabella were the only people still alive who'd fought a creature from the portal—one that wasn't an ertin or a scirett. Unlike the ertin and sciretts, the thing they fought more than a thousand years ago hadn't been something from this world tossed out by the original cuari—it was something from another plane completely.

"Does Ghortin know?" Ghortin was still animatedly discussing something with one of his tablemates.

"No. He will, everyone will." Storm looked around. "Why is no one eating?"

"We were waiting for you, but shouldn't we be off seeing what these monsters were? And killing them?" Edgar looked ready to jump up and ride to the desert immediately.

"Storm and Lilltkin can't go into the Markare." Keanin's hand shook as he tried to pour some tea. But he refused to add to his comment.

"I have to go. And from what my little sister vehemently said, the only way to stop her is to tie her up." Storm got up and pulled back Jenna's chair. "We need food, it's going to be a long debate and research-filled day. They won't go anywhere until they know what they're up against."

"Research is harder than fighting in my book." Talia got to her feet and pulled Keanin up as well.

Keanin still looked pale but he followed Talia like a lovesick dog. They'd had their talk. Jenna watched the two as they debated various food offerings. It was a good thing that he found someone so strong. Jenna had a feeling he was going to be crucial in resolving whatever was happening in the Markare.

And destroying the portal.

As the Protector, Jenna's primary purpose in this would be to destroy the portal at all costs. All the other battles were pointless if they couldn't remove that thing from existence. Original discussions had suggested that they find a safe place for Jenna to hide in until that time came.

Rachael and Tor Ranshal had shut that down immediately—the Protector's final job was to destroy the Portal, but she had many smaller jobs before that could happen. She had to be allowed to fight.

Jenna was the only one happy about that decree. She didn't like fighting, but there was no way she'd let Storm and the rest of the people she cared about in this world go into danger without her.

Edgar changed topics and brought up the elementals when everyone returned with their food. That was a safe thing to talk about, as no one knew much about them. "I think we can do a lot more with them than Ghortin ever imagined. How well do they communicate?"

His spymaster side showed now. Jenna imagined him thinking of thousands of spies to gather information without being seen.

"Not well." Jenna laughed as he deflated a bit. "But, they've done some changing in the last year, so who knows?"

"I'd like to be included in whatever talk you and Ghortin have about them. There might be other ways we can use them," Edgar said.

Jenna flashed him a grin. If anyone could sort out how to use them as spies, it would be Edgar.

"My concern is again, why did Resstlin send away half of the Lithunane troops?" Storm shook his head. "I think whatever was at the bottom of that choice will help us understand what we're up against. So far it's the followers of Qhazborh and Sacaranz and whoever he has with him. Is he the only one of *them* roaming around? How do we know if the ones who were destroyed were really destroyed?" The fact that Sacaranz was not only a cuari, but one of the ones who had openly attacked the deities and supposedly been unmade when they lost, wasn't common knowledge and it needed to be kept that way.

The people in this room were all close to the royal family, but even they couldn't be told this.

"Have you asked Kaytine? Could she ask Irissanta?" Jenna noticed that Talia's eyes perked up at the goddess's name.

"No, I should have thought of that." Storm nodded. "I'll wait until I can get her away from our mother."

"How is the queen holding up?" Keanin kept his eyes on his plate.

From his frown, like Jenna, Storm had caught on to the oddness in his voice. "She's doing well, she's a fighter. But she's had a lot of grief lately. And she wonders why you haven't visited her."

Jenna saw the look of concern that flashed across Storm's face and she agreed. Keanin was all but part of the royal family.

"I've been busy. We were under attack…ow." He shot a look at Talia, who looked innocent but had clearly done something to his arm.

"They are your family. You need to visit them as soon as possible." Talia's smile grew brighter and was almost scary.

"Don't try arguing with her about family. Trust me." Diath laughed at Keanin's expression. "You won't win. I tell you as her brother, surrender now."

Keanin flushed but then nodded. "I will request an audience with her Maj… Areania as soon as possible. Are you happy?"

Jenna knew she wasn't the only one to catch him begin to use the queen's title. But Storm looked satisfied.

"And I'll make certain he follows through." Talia flashed another blinding grin, then went to get more food.

"These elementals. Can they go through anything?" Edgar asked.

"I thought you were going to wait for our meeting? But as far as I know, yeah, nothing stops them. But they'd never been able to leave the vortex in Ghortin's cottage before." Jenna paused. "I think I let them do so. When I said goodbye at the threshold of the vortex, I mentioned how I wished they could come out. I heard the word, 'done' in my head and they came out."

Crell shrugged. "There could be a connection between you and them. Ghortin created them but you changed them. I think I need to be in this elemental meeting as well. After I find a mage to send a message to the rest of my deathsworn in Derawri."

Talia smiled. "I'd heard of the deathsworn, never met any though. Your people are fearless. A few thousand of you and this war would be over before it starts."

Crell laughed. "The deathsworn are fierce, but also hidebound—they aren't flexible. Although after speaking to Tigan that might be changing. A great fighting force has to be able to be fluid with the situation. The deathsworn have a lot of rules. Although I can command them, I am not one."

The discussion broke down into a tactical analysis of different fighting styles and the hope that more of the forces in Erlinda had escaped before the town fell.

"I still believe that the ocean will be important for this fight." Keanin held up his hand before Jenna could respond. "Yes, the Markare is as well. But I have an odd feeling there is something that we're missing in the water."

Edgar laughed. "You're missing your kraken friend?"

"It wasn't a bad beast. It didn't want to eat everyone. The odd communication between us was fascinating— after the fact." He looked over to Ghortin's table. "Do we know if those creatures were originally from this world?"

"How could massive sea monsters travel from the middle of the Markare to the ocean?" Edgar asked then frowned. "Not to say there couldn't be a second portal under the sea. That would mess things up."

Everyone turned to Jenna.

"Hey, I'm still sorting things out, but I can ask Rachael and Tor Ranshal. But from the little I saw; the focus of those books was on the portal in the Markare. The kraken might be naturally of this world." She shoved aside the shudder at the idea of a second portal, one at the bottom of the sea. Her world would change once this was over—hopefully, the important parts would stay intact. But once her purpose as the Protector was completed, and with luck, Typhonel was released, she might not be who she was now.

Like the idea of an underwater portal, she crammed that into a dark corner of her mind.

"Talia and Diath, what tales do your people have of the kraken? Like everyone else here, I have little knowledge of them." Crell pushed her plate aside.

"Not much, sadly," Talia said. "They were more myth than anything else until we ran into that one. The pirates kept it trapped on their island to hide their location from others. That might be the only one."

Keanin shook his head. "I don't think so. When it left for the deeper ocean, it felt like it was going to find others. Think about it, we know there are other lands somewhere beyond the ocean, but as far as I know, no ships sent from Traanafaeren or Khelaran have ever made it back. Something is taking them."

"We don't know that it's not whoever is on the other side of the ocean or the mysterious lands to the far south. There are a lot of 'ifs' right now," Storm added.

While it was nice to be discussing threats most likely not being conducted by beings trying to destroy the world, Jenna wasn't as relieved as she'd expected as the discussion broke down the theories of kraken.

Part of her feared they were just another danger, and the thought of a portal under the ocean was terrifying. Granted there hadn't been a mention of such a thing, but there was a chest back in Ghortin's vortex that contained a pile of pages that were thought to be two cuari books—ones that neither Rachael nor Tor Ranshal had ever heard of. Unfortunately, it hadn't been stored in the same place as the cuari books.

She'd need to check on what the plans were for getting the chest back. Because of its size, a different type of spell was used when they hid it.

"I'd bet that Wilty would have some good books on kraken," Crell finally added. "Not to distract from our current crisis, but if Keanin's hunch is right, we might need to know more about the ocean beasts. We can't let any angle be ignored."

"Now what is everyone here being so animated about?" Ghortin came to their table and Jenna noticed that many of the guests had left and the majority of tables were now empty.

"Kraken, at the moment," Jenna answered. "But we need to talk to and about those elementals. Crell and Edgar want to join us."

Storm got to his feet. "I'll go with you too. I need to tell you about the family meeting this morning. I know they'll pull you in, but you might as well know now."

Keanin blanched when Talia asked if he wanted to sit in on the meeting about the elementals, so instead, she asked him to take her and Diath on a tour of the city.

Keanin rose and bowed with an elaborate wave of his hands. "Of course! There is much to recommend, fair is Irundail."

Jenna smiled as they left. It was good to see the old Keanin reappear, if even for a short while.

Ghortin, Storm, and Edgar walked ahead as Storm filled Ghortin in on the monster attack from within the Markare. And the additional missing troops.

"That look isn't good." Crell nodded toward Ghortin as he turned in profile at Storm's information. "My family kept the stories alive of what happened in that desert a thousand years ago. But it was so far in the past that they are little more than myths. To have survived that horror and have to face such things again…that's not good."

"No, it's not." Jenna stopped walking as an odd feeling hit her. One that had been lurking in her mind since they'd fled Strann, but she'd tried to ignore. "I need to ask you for a weird promise. It's not based on anything but a gut feeling. And it might go against what you would normally do."

Crell took her arm. "That sounds ominous. But I can't agree to anything until I hear it."

Jenna waited until Storm, Edgar, and Ghortin had rounded the corner to the stairwell. "I might need to do something drastic to shut that portal when the time comes. Don't ask what, I'm going off some weird stuff in my head. But whatever it is, Storm will try to stop me. Others might as well. *No one can stop me.* No one. You have to hold him and anyone else back. It could mean the difference between saving this world and destroying it." She wished she had more to go on, but the chill that hit her at the idea of a second portal under the ocean had remained and emphasized her emotions.

"That's a serious request and I know you wouldn't ask if the situation wasn't dire." Crell looked up into Jenna's face for a few moments before nodding. "I will keep Storm and the others from stopping you in the Markare. Even if it means your life." She held out her hand to clasp Jenna's elbow.

Jenna duplicated the motion, grasping Crell's elbow, and nodded. "Thank you. I wish I could tell you more, and this could be my imagination running wild, but I feel better knowing you'll be there."

"I am honored to be of service. But I truly hope it doesn't come to that. I've already made extensive plans to be the nanny of your children. Find us all a nice farm near the woods some place with a stream for fishing. I'd rather that goal wasn't destroyed."

"I'd like that. It sounds like a normal, even boring, life," Jenna hugged her. "Now let's go catch up with them, or they'll come looking for us." Her relief at Crell's agreement took the edge off the fear, but it still lingered. The trick would be to keep it hidden from Storm.

Storm, Edgar, and Ghortin were standing in front of her door, debating something. Well, mostly it was Ghortin pacing in front of her door while he muttered disparaging words about people keeping secrets and Storm adding a few words from time to time. Edgar stayed back and silently watched them.

Storm smiled as they came up but then frowned as he saw something lingering on Jenna's face. "Is everything okay?"

Jenna forced a smile. "Just girl talk. Best sword for horse battles, that sort of thing." She kept her voice light, but not too much so—Storm would figure something was wrong if she tried too hard to hide it.

She opened her room and invited them in. "I'm afraid we'll need more chairs." Her room was large but there were only the two chairs at the table by the window.

Ghortin waved his hand and three more chairs appeared. "Now, where are those miscreants?"

Jenna looked around but even the faint glow from before was gone. "I told you not to leave this room." She spoke the words as she also thought them. The elementals seemed to work on both levels.

The window and the wall alongside it filled with light as a few hundred elementals flew through. They were zipping around far more than she'd seen before.

"Easy, there!" Ghortin held out his hands. "Where were you and what's wrong?"

The elementals settled down and Jenna's five came to her. "*Bad. Valley.*"

She looked to Ghortin to see if he'd heard the elementals, but he was busy dealing with a bunch of them crowding around him.

"They said, 'Bad valley.' Ring any bells?" They had to sort out better communication with the elementals if they were going to be able to use them for anything.

"Maybe? There's a smallish canyon in the far back of Irundail valley. Its name is Flotin Crere. It means bad valley in the old tongue because it's unstable and treacherous." Ghortin swore and held up his hands to the elementals. "Is something wrong there?"

"*Bad things there.*"

This time everyone heard them, at least from the reactions on the faces of her friends.

"I have to say I'm not fond of them speaking in my mind." Crell tilted her head as she spoke. "They can't see inside our minds, can they?"

Ghortin watched the elementals as they began to slow down. "Not that we know of, but they are evolving. Their references are still limited, but I think we need to go see what's happened there. Out of all the places in this valley, that should be the last one anyone from the outside could have gotten to."

CHAPTER TWENTY-SEVEN

—◆—

"WHAT ARE WE TALKING ABOUT? Can we do it with us and my rangers? Or do we pull in some of the Irundail troops?" Crell got to her feet. Discussions were fine with her, but she preferred to fight.

"How bad is it there?" Jenna spoke and thought the words.

"Not good. Small space." Again, it looked like everyone heard that in their heads.

"I'd say us, your rangers, plus Keanin, Talia, and Diath. Get them used to working with everyone." Edgar nodded to Jenna and Ghortin. "And you two can get used to working with Keanin's new abilities."

Storm nodded. "Agreed. We'll need horses, so let's meet at the stables in a half hour. I'll track down Keanin and the other two."

"What about the elementals?" Jenna asked as everyone headed toward the door. "They aren't great at staying in one spot."

Ghortin gave a narrow-eyed glare at a clump of them, but whatever he told them mentally didn't get the result he wanted. His frown deepened.

"The biggest issue of them roaming around is stirring fear in the general population." Edgar shrugged. "I'll get the word out that they are part of a new defensive spell by Mastermage Ghortin and not to be feared."

"Thank you. They won't listen to me." With a huff, Ghortin marched out of the room with the rest following.

Jenna turned to the five elementals once the others were gone. "Thank you for telling us. Can you and a few dozen of your companions join us in the bad valley? The rest should keep watching the rest of Irundail." As she spoke she envisioned the entire length of Irundail as seen from a map.

"Yes."

Jenna left them to sort out who was coming with her and who would do a patrol as she added weapons to her outfit. At first, she stuck to her sword belt and throwing knives, but then added her bow and quiver. She hadn't had as much practice as she'd like with it, but she probably wouldn't shoot any of their people.

"Okay, let's go. The ones coming with me need to stay close. Can you be any clearer as to what is wrong there?"

"Bad. Bad beings. In bad valley."

Jenna waited to see if there would be more coming but that seemed to be it. Yup, they needed to work on communication.

Crell and a group of a dozen rangers joined her on the way to the stables. Crell's rangers always looked like they were getting ready for an undercover operation in the deep forest.

Which they often were.

"Any idea where the rest of your rangers are?" Less than half of her group had been flung up from the south.

"I'm hoping they're beating up a bunch of enemies in the south. My mages should be with them, so I have one of the castle's far-speaking mages trying to reach them. But they need a specific person to reach out to and so far they haven't been successful." A twitch in her jaw was the only indication of her concern that they couldn't be reached. "They are also still trying to reach the rest of my deathsworn in Derawri. There is some interference to the north that they can't get past."

The mages who controlled the far magics; far-speaking, far-seeing, and more, were a different type of magic user than Ghortin or Jenna. He'd tried explaining how their abilities worked to Jenna during one of her early lessons, but all it did at the time was confuse her.

Everyone except Ghortin was already in the stable and getting their horses ready. Talia was extensively armed with a sword, short bow, and crossbow. Also, a bandoleer across her chest which held a row of throwing stars. Diath stuck to a long bow and sword.

"I've updated Justlantin on what's going on, and that the elementals will be roaming the town." Storm came up with a saddled horse for Jenna. "He did say that the far-seer mages were able to see Carabella and her group. They were going into the Zalin shelter a few hours ago."

"That's good. I miss her, but she's probably best working with people less likely to trigger a reaction." Jenna climbed on the horse. If they were going to use Irundail as a base, she'd need to find one to use regularly. While larger than the mare she'd been using on the road, this one seemed calm and confident. She laughed.

"What's funny?" Storm brought his horse alongside hers.

"Nothing really, just recalling my first ride on horseback in this land. I seriously wanted Ghortin to have us walk from his cottage to Lithunane instead of ride." She rubbed her horse's neck. "I will never think of these wonderful animals that way again."

Ghortin came bustling up patting his vest. He only carried a sword and walking staff that she could see, but most likely had many weapons hidden around him.

Rachael was right behind him and came to Jenna. "I think you need to take this one with you." She handed over the third of the cuari books—the one they'd found in Strann. "No, I don't have a logical reason for it, only a strong hunch."

"Thank you." Jenna took the book and tucked it in

her tunic pocket. "A hunch from you is worth more than most people's absolutes." She turned to the elementals darting in and around the horses and riders. "You need to stay within eyesight of us. *Our eyesight.*" She wasn't even sure what kind of eyes magical dust motes had.

Once everyone was set and ready, Edgar took the lead with a pair of Crell's rangers on either side.

Keanin rode between Talia and Jenna and appeared far more comfortable going into an unknown danger than he ever had before.

Jenna still recalled having to break him out of his room in the palace of Lithunane and pull him out from under his covers. He'd changed significantly in the month they'd been apart.

Diath rode with Ghortin, Crell, and the rest of her rangers at the back and seemed to fit in with them. Jenna wasn't sure what to think of Talia's brother, but the fact that Storm and Edgar trusted him was enough for her.

"You're thinking again," Storm said as he rode on Jenna's other side. "Or are you trying to get more information from those elementals?"

"Pondering changes, and the realization that when I was here before, I never got past the mountain. This valley is lovely."

"It is. We used to come up here for vacations and to make sure all of us kids understood where we came from. I wanted to build a cabin in those woods. Keanin would rarely leave the castle."

"Now, that's not fair." Keanin broke from his tour for Talia and waved around the rest of the valley. "I went out. Once. It wasn't my fault that I wasn't an outdoorsy person like you. There were far more interesting things to explore in the castle and the mountain." He rode easily in his saddle but had his left hand on the hilt of his sword. He was trying to appear relaxed, but he wasn't completely successful.

Jenna drifted closer to him. "Are you noticing any-thing?" She and he had an odd magic connection and could work together sometimes. Or had. She didn't know if the new Keanin's magic worked the same.

Keanin noticed her glance at his hand and smiled, but didn't move it. "Just my normal level of paranoia. But your little friends seem to be impatient about things." He nodded to the clump of elementals flying in front of them.

Even her main five were zipping around more than before. But they hadn't tried to communicate with her or the others so, hopefully, there wasn't anything new to worry about.

"They seem to have their own agenda. I'm hoping they'll notify us if things go bad." She looked around as they rode. It was possibly the most serene place she'd seen in this world. The massive obsidian-colored cliffs that surrounded Irundail set off the trees and farmhouses as if they were works of art. "This is a beautiful place."

"Maybe we'll live here once this is resolved." Storm looked far more at peace out here than he did in the castle.

Jenna hoped Justlantin and his children would lead long fruitful lives as kings and queens. Storm wouldn't make the best king and had recently convinced his mother and Justlantin to move the kids in line before him—if they were old enough. She shivered at the thought of her being queen. While she didn't have the same mindset Storm did, the idea of her having to rule people wasn't a great one.

"Good idea. Crell has already claimed status as nanny." Jenna flashed a smile back toward her friend.

"All settled then!" Keanin waved toward the darker clump of trees they rode toward. "Just take care of a few things, get back the cuari, destroy the portal, once it opens of course, and we can all put down roots here. I do want to be on Irundail mountain though."

Jenna happened to be watching Storm's face at Keanin's words, and she saw a brief look of concern. Whatever it was, she'd get him to share it when they were alone.

"Something is moving up ahead, let's run." Edgar and the two rangers with him took off even as he called out.

A group of elementals stayed alongside them.

"There should be nothing back there. It is a closed box canyon and the valley walls are the highest there." Ghortin remained lost in his thoughts as they rode but he was focused now.

Jenna agreed with the walls being the highest. The path to get to the top of the walls at the gates had been disturbingly high. As she got a clearer look at the canyon and walls ahead of them, she couldn't imagine anyone climbing these.

Her family would hike in the summers when she was young. The highest they'd done was Mount Whitney. These mountains appeared to be about three times that.

The narrow entrance to the canyon was choked with massive trees and there was no sign of a trail.

That didn't slow down Edgar, the rangers, or the elementals as they raced into the small forest.

"So much for caution." Ghortin rode closer to Jenna now as Crell and the rest of her rangers began to drop back and spread out.

Good idea if rescuing became an issue.

Jenna slowed her horse down as they entered the forest. She was a better horsewoman than she'd been a year ago, but still couldn't compete with her friends who had grown up riding.

The forest looked different than the one she and Carabella had hiked through near the Keepers. The trees were thicker and wider.

And they made noise.

"Are they talking? Please tell me that they aren't speaking?" She'd loved reading about the Ents in The Lord of the Rings while growing up and watching them in the movies. But that didn't mean she needed to meet any.

"It's only the wind. But it's not a wind that is anywhere but here." Ghortin scowled as he looked around. "And it's one coming from further in this canyon. Can you ask your elemental friends where the danger is?"

Jenna was going to point out that *he* created the elementals but dropped it. He was focusing on the trees and looked like he was trying to taste the wind.

She had to call them a few times before the group of five came back. The rest were flittering around the trees ahead of them.

Even Edgar and the two lead rangers were slowing, the trees and bushes were too dense, and they had to pick their way through as there was no path.

The five buzzed in front of her in what she was beginning to realize was their way of acknowledging her.

"Where are the things who were out here? The bad things?" Mostly, she didn't want to have all of them go deeper into this place if there was some danger coming up behind them.

The rangers in the back spread out far enough to reach from one end of the canyon to the other and Keanin and Ghortin had their hands cupped to hold spells of some kind.

"*Path.*"

Jenna was getting better at figuring out if the elementals were being heard by anyone other than her. Right now, all of her friends were watching the trees but didn't change expressions or twitch at the elementals' words.

"There's no path," as Jenna spoke, a thin line appeared through the trees and led off to the right.

"Tell your friends thanks." Edgar turned toward the right. The canyon wasn't that wide but searching all of it with the number of trees involved would have been a problem.

"Can you show me what we're looking for?" Jenna focused on asking the elementals for help but also made sure her horse continued in the correct direction.

"*Bad things. Not many.*"

She sighed and looked at the others. "Still no idea what we're facing, aside from that they're bad and there aren't many of them." Which hopefully was good.

Edgar mentioned using the elementals for spying, but she didn't see how that was going to be possible. At least not without more work than they had time for.

A familiar and unwelcome smell came through the trees. "Ertin." She looked around to see everyone else had picked up on it as well. Talia and Diath had their bows out as did many of the rangers. Crell had her crossbow loaded as she looked through the trees.

Keanin had brought his bow and quiver with him, but it stayed on his back as he was still holding the spell he'd called up. It was starting to crackle as bursts of lightning showed through his fingers.

Everyone either had a spell, a sword, or a bow and arrow out and at the ready—except Jenna. Something was wrong. Even though she smelled the ertin, it seemed off.

She stopped her horse and mentally gathered all the elementals to her. The path they'd lit remained visible in an echo of their light, but they all surrounded her horse. "Are these ertin in truth?" As she spoke, she mentally focused on the way the elementals had killed the ertin around Ghortin's cottage in the south.

"*No.*"

Not as helpful as she hoped but it did explain why she felt things were off and why the elementals hadn't taken care of these ertin as they easily did the ones in the south.

"*Ma-gic.*" The word came through clearly, but oddly

broken. Considering the elementals were made up of magic, they should know what it was.

"They say there's no ertin, but something of magic." She called to her friends as the elementals turned around and continued into the canyon. Black walls surrounded them on three sides now and the open entrance coming into the canyon felt far away. If there was something deadly in here, this would be a great place for an ambush.

Jenna followed and motioned for Edgar to hold back as she took the lead. The feeling of something being wrong grew stronger. She felt it in the air, but she couldn't tell if it was something they could fight.

Chapter Twenty-Eight

———◆———

THE FOREST GREW DENSER, AND her horse slowed. It didn't feel like he was doing it intentionally, but he was slowing regardless. Jenna's movements still seemed normal, but she had a feeling that if she were walking instead of riding, she'd face the same invisible resistance as her horse.

Something was pushing them away from the back of the canyon.

The smell of ertin vanished, but it was replaced by the smell of death. Old death. She pulled up a spell and kept her other hand on the hilt of her sword. Although he continued slowing down, her horse didn't seem at all disturbed by whatever was going on around them.

Which meant that it might not be real. If there were a physical threat here—such as a random pack of ertin— the horses would all be racing to get away.

Good thing that he was fine as she was trusting him without hands on his reins.

The elementals hung closer to Jenna and her horse as if they were afraid.

"Jenna? Where are you?" It was Storm, but he'd been right behind her moments ago. He wasn't now.

Twisting around on her horse, she couldn't see any of her friends or Crell's rangers. The forest was clear, no fog or mist, but they'd vanished. Or she had.

Soon more of them were calling for her. Not loudly, but clear enough that she should be able to see them.

"I'm here!" She yelled, but her voice seemed to bounce back at her. "Elementals, you still see me, right?"

A sharp affirmative came from the cluster, but they still appeared eerily disturbed.

What could scare magical balls of fluff? And how had she and her friends been separated?

She took a deep breath, sheathed her sword, and pulled out the cuari book that Rachael had given her. The third of the cuari books had many odd spells worked in with ancient history.

But something had pointed Rachael toward giving it to her for this adventure. So there most likely were spells or information that she could use here. Hopefully.

"Child. You aren't what your predecessors were." The voices were wispy and flowed around her. They weren't scary on their own, but the elementals were hiding in her clothing. She had no idea why they hadn't simply vanished, but they were comforting in a way.

Her horse didn't appear upset, but he did come to a halt. His ears were forward and he seemed more interested in finding a snack than anything else.

"Who are you? What are you?" She flipped through the cuari book.

"We came from before. We're coming back. You and your friends will die."

Jenna looked up from her book, but there was still no one around except for the elementals. She did know one thing; it seemed the beings most likely to threaten death were unable to complete it. If the voice or voices could kill her right now, and wanted to, they'd have done it.

She nudged her horse forward. He flicked an ear but resumed walking. "Elementals? Do you sense anything? Is the voice the bad?"

"*Yes. No. Not here.*"

Sort of helpful. "How are you going to do it, if you don't mind me asking?" She continued flipping through the cuari book as her horse walked forward. There had been a particularly nasty spell inside that she recalled, she just needed to find it. And be able to cast it. Then hope that disrupting whatever these disembodied voices were doing would snap her back to her friends.

Storm and the others continued calling her name but their voices were so faint she barely heard them. This canyon wasn't big enough for that kind of distance.

"We will rip the flesh from your bones and destroy all of this world."

She looked up from her book. "But how? You should have a plan, you know." She realized that even if whatever was speaking to her was bluffing, she should be concerned.

But an odd calmness flowed over her once she opened the book. She wasn't alone. There was no way to rationalize it, but she felt as if all the Protectors from the first one to the woman whom Jenna replaced, were with her.

Weird, but she'd take it. And ask Rachael if she knew this would happen when they got back.

"We will destroy you."

"You already sort of said that. How about we talk face to face?" The canyon narrowed at the end into a long meadow, but the trees lined the rock walls and pointed to a cave. It looked like a massive lava tube and the wind from before seemed to be coming from it.

Jenna found the spell she wanted; it would freeze anything within her vision for at least five minutes. The risk would be not looking at her horse. Hopefully, the elementals would be immune, but if not, she'd apologize later. The comforting feelings from other Protectors told her she'd made the right choice.

The entrance of the lava tube was as tall as a single-story building and about twice the width. When the lava from eons ago burst out of here, it was massive. She peered closer at the walls. Or when it burst through the direction she was walking. She'd taken a geologic survey class a long time ago and this place felt like the lava had been escaping away from here, not going into the Irundail valley.

Made sense, the valley was probably the remains of an extinct volcano.

The elementals created light for her to see as they moved further into the tunnel, but now her horse was agitated and refused to go forward.

She patted his neck, then slid off the saddle with her book and sword. The moment she was clear, he whinnied, turned around, and trotted back out.

"Can some of you make sure he gets out okay?" A dozen elementals took off after her horse. Hopefully, even though something had separated her from her friends, her horse would be safe.

"I'm here, when are you going to destroy me?" She kept the spell balanced delicately in her mind. Once cast, she wouldn't be able to use it again for about six hours—or longer. Waiting until they showed themselves was crucial.

Walking further into the cave supported her theory that this was the direction the lava burst out. It was becoming larger rather than smaller and either some of the elementals had gotten way ahead of her, or there was a tiny bit of light at the end. Indicating an exit.

Even if whatever had caused the elementals' worry was no longer here, she needed to keep going. Because no one knew of another way into Irundail didn't mean it wasn't a danger.

"Is the magic bad still here?"

"*Yes. No.*" Possibly the worst answer. Or at the least the most useless.

The elementals were spreading out the length of the tunnel she'd already come down, but as far as she could tell none of her friends were in here yet.

"Can you be more helpful?"

The mental image of a shrug wasn't what she'd been hoping for.

"Fine." She continued walking toward the speck of light at the end.

"Hello? Scary voice who wants to kill us all, here I am." If the beings behind the voices didn't show up soon she was going to have to release the freeze spell she was holding. Some spells could be held for hours or longer, depending on the spell and the mage. From the way this one was draining her, this spell wasn't one of those.

No responding voice. It was as if once she'd come inside the lava tube, the voices vanished. Or maybe that was how they were going to kill her and they already brought her into their trap.

That thought stopped her and she took a moment to regroup. The feelings of the Protectors before her were still there, but growing fainter. Maybe they knew she was doomed too.

"Okay, let's see where this goes. Elementals, are there any living beings down this way?" She walked along the elemental-lined path.

"*Yes.*" That came from her five.

"Are they deadly?"

"*Unknown.*"

"Seriously, when we're back in the castle we are building some sort of real communication," Jenna muttered and walked faster. She had to release the freeze spell. With any luck, she could call it up fast enough if needed. But her head was aching from holding it so long.

No more voices and the light at the end grew larger. The wind she felt before was growing stronger but the feelings from the other Protectors all but vanished when she put her book away. Them being with her had never happened when she tried to read any of the cuari books before, so hopefully she'd be able to get them back once this was done.

For something as old as this tunnel was, it had surprisingly little debris. Especially considering the wind that was coming through it.

"*Typhonel? Are you here?*" She should have tried to contact him earlier, but he often didn't respond.

"*Yes.*" It was interesting that he and the elementals sounded so different in her head. The elementals were more a feeling than words, although her mind translated. Typhonel was words. But he sounded incredibly faint.

"*Can you help me or guide me, or give me a clue as to what this place is?*"

"*You shouldn't be there.*"

Great. Faint, vague, and not helpful.

"*Wonderful, but I am, and I'm going to keep going. But I could use some help. What's down here?*"

The wind picked up and leaves flew inside. The opening ahead of her was large enough to see green through it, but no real definition. Which was as much because of the wind as the distance. It was difficult to see well when she had to squint most of the time.

"*It is where it began. I can't stay.*" She usually could tell when Typhonel was gone, but this time it was as if he'd slammed a door in her mind.

"Fine. No one will help me; I'll go on my own." She was to the point of crawling to stay upright against the wind when it abruptly stopped and she stumbled forward.

Rather, the elementals formed a wall and blocked the wind.

"Thank you." She stood and called forth the freeze spell again, it felt easier this time, but still noticeably weighty to hold in her mind.

The entrance was massive, clearly where lava had forced

its way out however many thousands of years the explosion happened.

And she was a few hundred feet over a tree-filled ground; one with a vaguely diffused light in the sky. At first, she thought it was fog or clouds, but a closer look showed her that it was the ceiling of a massive cave.

CHAPTER TWENTY-NINE

JENNA STEPPED BACK AS A weird combination of vertigo and claustrophobia slammed into her as she looked out over the cliff at the cavern spread out before her.

It was a mini world. At least one with plants, and birds, if that was what she saw in the distance, and some sort of light source.

She dropped to the ground as it overwhelmed her.

Literally.

There was a horrific tearing at her soul. An old spell shoved at her—she wasn't supposed to be here. Not that she knew where here was.

An earthquake shook the massive cavern in front of her. Trees swayed and more birds flew into the air.

"Elementals? Is this what the 'bad magic' was?" They'd stayed in the tunnel behind her, but her five came cautiously forward.

"*Bad. Not time. Leave.*"

"Not helpful. If I go back to my friends, is the threat gone?" The earthquake was short, and the cavern went back to whatever it was doing. It was as if she were looking over a jungle in South America—a big one.

The elementals buzzed around each other as if in conversation. "*Bad gone. For now.*" That seemed difficult for them to put together.

Jenna stayed seated but looked out over the world in front of her. It was terrifying. Magic was strongly behind it as waves of Power flowed over her. And was probably contributing to her feeling of desperately wanting to leave. The spells around this place were ancient and didn't want visitors.

Yet, the trail that hugged the cliff down to the floor was oddly tempting. She got to her feet and took a step away from the ledge.

She felt the threatening voices from the canyon behind her weren't connected to what she was feeling now. This was more like she'd crossed a no-trespassing sign, but the armed guards hadn't shown up yet.

And going down there would be an extremely bad idea.

She got to her feet and walked backward into the tunnel then turned and started jogging. The elementals swarmed around her and lit the way out. "When we get back you're telling me what just happened."

"*Yes.*"

That was hopeful to hear, but she wasn't certain they could do it.

Voices echoed down the tunnel from the canyon. Familiar ones. She ran faster. Luckily for her, the elementals flew to stay ahead of her and kept the path lit.

"Storm!" she yelled as she ran, but the voices were still too faint to hear well.

The light from the canyon opening grew brighter, but none of her friends were visible yet.

Then the voices went silent. Jenna didn't have time to slow down and pull up the freeze spell, but it slammed into her mind the moment she thought of it.

Possibly not the best option, but she would use it if she needed to.

She stopped running once she got out of the tunnel and into the canyon. Her friends were coming her way, but in slow motion. They were still on horseback, and

Storm had the reins of her horse tied behind his. But like that spell thrown by the mage in front of the gates, they were coming to a halt as their movements became slower.

Jenna swore and released her freeze spell. It wouldn't be helpful right now, but something else might be. Someone had to have cast this on them, she just couldn't see anyone. She ran to Storm and shook his arm.

And fell back when he and his horse, hers as well, suddenly burst into normal speed at her touch.

"Jenna?" Storm whirled around, but the others were still moving at slow speed around them. "What's happened to them? Where did you go?"

It was weird that the two horses returned to normal when Storm did. She hadn't touched them.

"You've been spelled, or this place is a spell. Let me test something." She touched the arms of Edgar and the two rangers with him. She was ready for it this time, so jumped back before they and their horses returned to normal speed.

"Keep moving toward the tunnel. I'll fix the others." She got Crell and Ghortin, then worked her way through the rest of the group. Once freed, the others might have been able to help, but the hair-rising weirdness she felt right now said she couldn't take that chance.

Something was coming into the canyon—something they didn't want to meet.

Once everyone was free and gathered in front of the tunnel mouth, Ghortin turned toward the canyon forest with a glare.

"An old harvester trap. A spell to catch game. Or enemies. They're incredibly unstable. Designed to slow prey to make it easy for the kill."

Edgar snorted. "It was stable enough to catch us— including a mastermage. Does anyone else have a disturbing feeling? As if we're still being hunted?"

"Maybe it's a leftover from that trap spell?" Diath

sounded hopeful, but his face didn't show it. He had magic and looked agitated. All the magic users did.

"No, it's not." Ghortin pulled up a shielding spell, then a second one. "We need to get out of here. Now."

Jenna felt it too, an odd pressure all around them. As if something massive was coming from the front of the canyon and was going to suck out their souls when it reached them. Considering the voices she heard earlier—there might be something behind it.

Crell took a deep breath and looked around. "But where? This is a closed canyon."

A trickle of sweat rolled down Jenna's spine. One that had nothing to do with her brief run through the tunnel. Terror froze her. She shook it off and took the reins of her horse back from Storm, but didn't get into the saddle. "The tunnel. There's something in the back of it. A weird world or something. Maybe there's a way out."

The elementals vanished at that moment. No way to know if it was because of the thing coming toward them, or because she mentioned going into that place they didn't like. Nothing seemed to bring them back. Ghortin tried as well and scowled when there was no response.

"And we could be trapped there." Keanin was holding enough magic to blow up everything around them. "We should stand and fight."

Something echoing in her head told Jenna they shouldn't do that.

"We're trapped here as it is." Edgar turned his horse toward the tunnel mouth. "I can cast a low light spell as we go, but we might want to spread out the magic users." He swung off his horse after getting a better look inside the tunnel. "And someone should spell the horses. Leading them will help, but they won't like this place."

Ghortin's spell on the horses was light but seemed to calm them.

Everyone got off their horses quickly and quietly. Judging by the looks on the faces around her, even the non-magic users felt the threat now.

Jenna called up her small light spell and led her horse inside the lava tube.

"What did you find in here?" Storm walked his horse alongside hers and kept his voice low.

She agreed with the low volume. There hadn't been proof of danger in here, but it felt like a place that needed quiet. "A weird massive cavern world. The elementals didn't like it, and that might be why they're gone. It was like a lost world. Jungle, warm, couldn't tell much beyond that as the trees covered everything below. But there appeared to be a broad trail that hugged the cliff and went to the bottom. No idea where it will go, but at the least, it will give us more room to fight if whatever was in that canyon follows us."

"Keanin and I cast a spell on the entrance to this tunnel." Ghortin didn't feel the need to be quiet as he came forward. "It should stop, or at the least slow down, anything that tries to come in from the canyon."

"And not stop us from escaping if need be?" Storm kept his voice low regardless of what Ghortin did.

"Of course not, lad." He nodded and stayed behind her and Storm. But a flash of worry crossed his face.

Jenna turned to watch Ghortin. He was a Powerful magic user and knew it. It was rare that he wasn't completely certain of what his spells could do. He gave a slight shrug at her questioning look.

The tunnel seemed shorter this time, but she'd also been here before. She gave another thought to the elementals, but there was no response.

The ground and walls shook briefly, then stopped.

"I believe that's something testing the spell you two

left." Crell kept her voice lower than Ghortin's but it still reached the front of the line.

"I agree," Ghortin said. "I might suggest we move faster."

Jenna and Storm picked up the pace. That rumble hadn't felt too bad, but better not to find out who was behind it.

The light of the hidden world was ahead of them as they broke into a jog.

And the floor and walls shook again.

"Yes, yes, that looks promising. Shall we run now?" Ghortin's tone was so unlike him that Jenna spun back to look. His face was creased in discomfort and Keanin also looked upset a few rows behind him. Whoever was trying to break in from the canyon side was causing pain for the two spell casters.

"Let's run." Jenna and Storm ran along with their horses toward the opening. "I have no idea how big this place is, or where it leads, but it will get us out of this tunnel." She looked at the cliff trail to the bottom. It was narrower than she'd initially thought, but would still be wide enough for the horses to safely make their way down. "Can you set another spell here to keep anyone from following us down in case there is something inside the tunnel?"

Ghortin shook his head as he came closer and looked at the world below. "Keanin and I are tied to the spell on the entrance. I can still use magic, but not a second one like that."

Edgar whistled as he looked out over the land below them. "This is impressive."

"Could Edgar and I create that blocking spell?" Jenna felt a creeping feeling that they were about to be out of time.

"I can teach you both. It's relatively simple. But it might drain your power." Ghortin pulled the two aside while everyone else either looked out over the world below them or stayed back and looked a bit ill.

He was right, it wasn't hard, but Jenna felt a tug once she and Edgar got their test spell up and then released it. It needed to be cast at the last minute to not interfere with her and Edgar getting out of the tunnel.

The ground shook longer this time and rocks began to fall.

"We need to go now!" Storm motioned for Crell and half of her rangers to go first, then everyone else. Finally, it was only he, Jenna, and Edgar.

"You go before us. We need to set the spell!" Edgar yelled to Storm as the shaking behind them grew more violent.

Storm nodded and he and his horse ran down the ramp.

Jenna and Edgar set their spell after they started down. Things weren't shaking here, but she already felt tugs on the spell as they moved away from it.

The world below them was more exotic up close than from overhead as they made their way down to it. Bright birds and flowers were in abundance and the sound of running water echoed around them.

Then the cliff trail shook. Luckily, no one was near the edge as it crumbled away in places. The path hugged the side of a high cliff, but so far nothing had fallen from above.

Crell and her rangers looked back to the others, then picked up speed. The horses seemed to agree and fought for their leads.

"Run!" Storm yelled, as another shake disintegrated still more of the edge of the trail. At this rate, there wouldn't be a path left before all of them got to the bottom.

They were almost to the ground when massive shadows flew overhead. Jenna chanced a look up and swore. Gigantic birds of prey, with wingspans easily twenty feet, circled above them.

They ran off the ramp as another quake, stronger than all the others combined, shook the ramp to dust. This time, parts of the cliffs far above fell as well.

CHAPTER THIRTY

———

TALIA PULLED OUT HER BOW and quiver and aimed at the birds above them. "Friend or foe?"

"No idea." Ghortin shaded his eyes; whatever caused the impression of daylight down here, it was brighter on the valley floor unless you were under the immense trees.

"I'd hold off." Crell also covered her eyes as she looked up. "They're looking for something to eat, not us—yet. Let's not give them a reason to change their minds." She squinted up the cliff face to the entrance they'd left. "You four can probably release your spells. We're not getting back up this way, but unless they have wings, no one can follow us either."

Good point. Jenna nodded to Edgar and they released their spell. Ghortin and Keanin did as well.

"Where do we go?" Jenna was used to her friends being unflappable. Clearly, Crell's rangers were, as well as Talia and Diath. But everyone was too calm for her liking. They were trapped in a strange hidden world, with few supplies, and no way back to Irundail.

Maybe she could freak out enough for all of them.

Diath handed his horse's reins to his sister, then walked a bit into the trees. "I think there's an opening in that direction." He came back and pointed to the left. Away from most of the trees and the larger part of the cavern.

"How'd you know?" Edgar swung back on his horse as the rest followed.

"I sent a low-level searching spell. There's salt water that way." Diath shrugged. "Maybe it's a way to the ocean."

Ghortin scowled, then cast a spell, and glared at the deep forest blocking the bulk of the place. "I can't tell what's in that direction. This place is extremely old and was created by magic so far beyond mine that I feel like a schoolboy."

"Cuari?" Jenna meant the original ones, but she wasn't going to clarify out here.

"That's my guess." Ghortin looked into the trees closer to them. "It is fascinating down here, and I would love to study it, but not now. Not to mention that I'm not sure how well most of us would fare living off the land."

Keanin shivered. "Whoever built this might or might not still be around, but I don't think they want us here. I was trying to reach out magically and got slapped."

"Then we go that way." Storm turned to Diath. "You figured it out. You and the rangers lead."

Crell nodded and the six rangers who'd taken the lead coming down joined Diath as they left the rubble of the broken trail behind.

Jenna continued to twist around, trying to take everything in. The how of this place was almost more interesting than the why. But it was close. Part of her wished Carabella was with them. The other part was glad she wasn't—especially if her people *had* created this self-contained place prior to the battle with the gods and goddesses. She sighed.

Ghortin was on her left with Storm a bit ahead of her on the right.

"What was that sigh for?" Ghortin asked it, but from the way Storm turned, it was clear he'd heard it as well.

"Carabella would love this place. Or not."

"Agreed. I won't contact her yet, but we need to tell Rachael and Tor Ranshal what happened. And that we have no idea where we are, or when we'll be back. Also, that no one should try to follow." Ghortin took out his taran wand, but there was no response from anyone he tried to reach.

Edgar got the same result when he tried his. "It's probably whatever is in these cliffs that are surrounding us. It's like a bubble made of stone."

"We can try again once we're out of this place." Crell was on the far end of the group and watching everything around her.

Jenna was glad that Crell sounded confident about their getting out. She was having serious doubts. What if this place was as it looked? A completely enclosed and self-functioning world?

She'd been on the road enough in this world to know that it was tough even with the proper supplies and equipment—it was going to be miserable with nothing but water bags and dried fruit and nuts. Crell's rangers were probably better prepared, but it still wouldn't be nice for them for any length of time.

The rest of them had figured they were only going to the canyon, not even going outside of Irundail, and hadn't grabbed much.

She tried reaching the elementals again, but none of them appeared. They hadn't been happy when she first found this place, and they might not be able to get in here. Or might not want to.

The trail in this direction was more open, with the heavy forests fading behind. Which made it noticeable when those massive birds flew over them a few more times. She doubted they'd go after people or horses, but that wingspan was impressive and frightening.

The walls surrounding them appeared more ragged and layered. Until she looked up at the ceiling again. The mages who created this did such a great job with so much magic that what would be the sky looked like an overcast day with diffused sunlight. She shook her head and went back to focusing on the horses in front of her. If she didn't look around, she could try to convince herself they were simply on a normal trail somewhere.

There were three of the dinohawks—as she was calling them in her head—flying over them now. Their heads weren't shaped exactly like pterodactyls, but their beaks were far longer and narrower than any bird of prey she'd seen at home. As she watched, a fourth one joined them.

"Are we sure we shouldn't be worried about them?" She asked as she pointed up. The birds were keeping up with them. They would fly ahead of the riders, then circle and hang behind them for a bit.

Ghortin glanced at the birds and shrugged. "I'm not sure what we can do. I'm thinking that this is the correct way out, so we need to keep going." He waved at the cliff walls on either side. They were still wide, but the cliffs appeared closer to them than when they started. "It's getting narrower."

"I'm ready in case we've misjudged them." Crell had her crossbow out and Talia and Keanin had their longbows off their packs and ready.

"They *are* hunting something," Talia said calmly. "Could be us, might be something else."

Jenna nodded but kept looking for the something else that they might be after. There were still trees along the walls of the valley they were riding through, but not enough in her opinion for anything to be hiding that would be large enough for the dinohawks. She kept one hand on the hilt of her sword and kept a few spells, including the freeze one, fresh in her mind.

They rode long enough that Jenna feared there was no way out. But the smell of the ocean was clearer now. Unless she was hoping so much for it that she was now imagining it. And so was everyone else.

"Three more birds coming up," Talia called out after she turned around.

"There's no way they aren't up to something." Edgar

shook his head at the seven shapes that now were drifting higher above them.

Crell motioned to the six rangers in the back of the group. "Four of us go left, three go right. Everyone else keep moving but slowly increase the pace. If there's something they're trying to flush out beside us, we'll see it."

Crell and three rangers broke left, the other three took right, and the ones up front with Diath increased their pace. Not hugely, but enough that everyone had to nudge their horses.

The dinohawks added an eighth member. There were now enough of them to cause this group some serious problems. Even the horses were getting skittish. However, that could be in part because of their riders' agitation.

Smaller birds rose into the air as Crell and her rangers ran through the thin stands of trees on either side. But nothing larger.

"You're ready with a spell or two, I presume?" Ghortin asked as he and Storm stayed alongside her.

"Two. One is the freeze spell I found in the book Rachael gave me. Are they hunting us or herding us?" The dinohawks did their fly ahead and then loop back behind the horses and riders' trick again.

Edgar moved up closer to Diath and the other six rangers. "I'd say herd, possibly intending to hunt. Does anyone see any covered area we can get to with the horses?"

That wasn't good. Edgar wasn't a hiding kind of guy, but he looked worried as they rode.

Aside from Crell and her six rangers who were still skirting the trees along the sides, everyone rode closer together.

They were getting nearer to what looked suspiciously like a dead end. The cliffs were closing in and unless there was a hidden way out, they were trapped.

"A cave!" Diath yelled as he and the rangers leading the group veered slightly to the right.

Crell and her group of rangers came out of the trees and joined them.

Jenna still wanted to know where the smell of the ocean was coming from. There was no way out that was visible, but the salty smell was getting stronger.

They were almost to the cave when two of the dinohawks dropped. Talia and Keanin fired, but the arrows went past the birds.

She knew how good of a shot Keanin was with the bow—even riding on horseback—he should have hit the bird he fired at. The birds went back up higher, but neither appeared concerned about the arrows.

Jenna looked around the cliffs that surrounded them. Those dinohawks might not have ever seen an arrow in this enclosed environment. Or someone was shielding them and the birds knew it. A shielding spell like that would need line of sight, so if someone was casting it, they'd be above the trees.

She continued to watch around them as they entered the cave. Diath and the rangers were already riding back out.

"It's a trap!" One ranger yelled as they tried to turn everyone else around.

Three of the dinohawks landed behind the group and crowded the front of the cave.

Everyone with a bow fired, but like with Talia and Keanin's arrows, something deflected the shots.

They were pushed back even though none of the birds tried to come into the cave.

Jenna saw piles of bones lining the far wall, this wasn't the first time those dinohawks had done this. A glance indicated some of the bones were animal, the rest human—or rather human, kelar, and derawri.

CHAPTER THIRTY-ONE

"HOW FAR BACK DOES THIS place go?" Ghortin sent a few low-level spells at the dinohawks as they crowded the entrance. They didn't seem affected at all but also didn't try to come in further.

"Was that a shield of some kind?" Jenna happened to be watching as one of Ghortin's spells failed. It appeared that for a moment, an iridescent bubble blocked the spell from the bird. She doubted the birds had magic, but someone around them did. It explained the arrows failing to hit their marks as well.

"I don't feel one." Ghortin shot off another low spell and watched the lead bird carefully. "Damn. You're right. That's an odd shield though. Old and sneaky."

"Is there a way around it?" Keanin was calm but had his bow drawn.

"Maybe with enough time. It's not like any magic I've seen before." Ghortin took a step closer to the birds. The lead bird matched him but didn't go further.

"So, we're stuck here until they pick us off? That's not going to happen." Crell looked ready to keep firing crossbow bolts until she got through. Or ran out.

"Move all the horses into this side cave. It's not a great option, but I can spell them enough to keep them calm." Edgar moved the animals into the smaller cave while muttering a spell under his breath. Immediately the horses settled down and appeared to drift into a doze.

"There's a tunnel in the back here and it's long. But there's no way to tell if it's a way out, or there's something worse at the other end." Diath answered Ghortin's question before he said it. He held his bow ready and kept watching the birds.

"Something has been feeding well." Talia tilted her head back toward the bones but didn't turn away from the birds.

Jenna wasn't thrilled about looking at the bones, but there was a chance they could help them sort out if the dinohawks ate the beings or something else did. Not that she felt they had much choice—those birds were three deep now at the mouth of the cave and no one was getting past them until whatever shield that protected them was disabled. Trusting that the rest of their group had enough eyes on the birds, she turned and walked to the grim bone collection.

The three races were represented but so were larger animals—including horses, judging from two skulls. All the bones were pale and brittle with age and dust. The horses could have been wild, but she figured that if people were living in this place they would have noticed their trip down the exposed trail.

So where did these come from? Something shiny glinted under a body toward the back. It said a lot about how she'd changed in the past year that she didn't flinch as she shifted the bones to get it. It was a dagger in a jeweled metal sheath. Both dagger and sheath appeared to have been there for a long time—possibly before Ghortin was out of short pants. But she was able to rub a lot of the debris off. The designs on them were stunning and while she'd seen some amazing works in Irundail castle as well as Lithunane, this was far more elaborate. It appeared to have an entire scene carved out between the dagger and sheath. Her nose was only an inch away when a tiny bolt of lightning shot out, hit her, and knocked her to the floor.

Storm was next to her in a moment. "What happened?"

Jenna sheepishly accepted his arm to get up but held on to the dagger and sheath. "I got nosy." She hadn't felt it before, but there was a low-level charge coming from the dagger. Not strong, but definitely magic. She held it a bit further away. "I'm not sure what this dagger is up to, but there's magic attached to it."

Storm reached for it before she spoke, but stepped back when she said magic.

"A magic dagger?" Talia stayed facing forward. "Maybe it's part of the cursed daggers we heard about as kids, right Diath?" She had a laugh in her voice, but Diath was serious as he stepped back to Jenna and Storm.

"Can I see it? Don't hand it to me, just hold it up." The look on his face and the tone of his voice were more concerning than the fact this thing had zapped her off her feet.

Jenna raised the dagger to his eye level. And turned it so he saw both sides. "There's a sheath out of metal too. But the dagger is what hit me."

Diath glanced at the sheath but then returned to focusing on the dagger. "The tales were about the dagger; nothing about a sheath. But I think this is one of a group of bewitched daggers. They were supposedly created eons ago by three mages who were trapped on an island off the Erlinda coast. The people of the, at the time small, village of Erlinda feared the three and stranded them out there. It was said the daggers could focus magic. And they could also fly around on their own." He shrugged when the dagger showed no signs of doing that. "Mostly children's stories, but if they did exist, that one looks old enough to be one. Oh, and once they've selected a person, you're stuck with it for life. Or until it completes its task. No one can take it from you."

"Those were myths, nothing more." Ghortin gave a final glare at the birds blocking the entrance, walked over, and grabbed the dagger.

Then was flung back with a lot more force than Jenna was hit with.

"Is your hand smoking?" Jenna ran to him, but the dagger shook when she got too close. "Knock it off whatever you are, or I'll feed you to those birds." The movement from the dagger stopped and she put it into the sheath. She was grateful when it stayed there.

"A little." Ghortin winced, spoke a soft spell, and shook out his hand. "Better now."

Jenna fussed with her sword belt and added the dagger sheath to it then buckled it back on. "Is this thing going to help us?"

Talia shrugged without taking her eyes off the birds. "No way to tell. They weren't real as far as I knew."

"And this might not be one of them, but some other cursed dagger. It was a popular thing to do a thousand years ago or so." Ghortin leaned forward but didn't even touch the sheath this time.

"It didn't help him or her though." Jenna looked at the sad pile of bones.

"How did they get here?" One of the rangers relinquished their stare off with the birds and stalked to the bones. He dropped low and dug through them. "There are more pieces of metal, buttons, a few weapons, and coins, all of them are at least a thousand years old."

"Could they have been living in that world out there?" Jenna asked as she watched the ranger pull out more ornate pieces. No daggers though. Or swords. Most of the weapons consisted of various knives or a few of the throwing star-type things.

"I don't think so. These designs are Erlindan." Diath joined the ranger in slowly looking for items within the bones.

"Unless there is another entrance, and these Erlindan fighters came through here and lost the fight with the relatives of those birds." Storm lowered his bow but not completely and he remained closer to the dinohawks.

From what Jenna could tell, the birds were waiting for something. As long as no one made a move toward them or the entrance, they stayed in place.

"Or there's a bigger threat further inside and they work together." Talia shook her head as she saw Jenna watching the birds. "Those birds are big, but that type of beak is more for scavenging. They could kill us, but that wouldn't be how they normally feed."

The dinohawks squawked and stomped their feet, but they didn't leave their positions.

At first, it sounded like there was an echo coming from the long dark tunnel at the back of the cave. Then Jenna and Ghortin looked at each other as they recognized the sound.

"Sciretts? Tell me that's not what that is." Jenna pulled out her sword and called up the freeze spell.

"That's what it sounds like. I'd hoped that since we hadn't seen them recently, that the group who attacked us on the way to Lithunane was an aberration." Ghortin dropped his voice. "The ones you faced, *elsewhere*, don't count."

Jenna understood what he was saying but the two she'd faced down on the chaotic plane were massive and terrifying. Not that sciretts weren't bad normally. They were. Odd combinations of a hyena, a large cat, and a baboon, they were nasty animals. Ones who shouldn't have been in this world anymore, but like the ertin, had started to find their way back.

Or someone brought them back.

The best way to defeat them was to outrun them. Something that they couldn't do within this cave.

The weird birds tilted back their heads, no longer making their screeching sounds, but instead creating a gurgling that was worse.

Crell shouted orders as she and her rangers all moved to the back with swords drawn.

Ghortin turned to the blocked front of the cave. "We need to drop the spell that's shielding the birds. We'll have a better chance against the sciretts if we're not in here."

Jenna and Keanin moved closer to Ghortin. Edgar and Diath, and possibly a few of Crell's rangers, were magic users also, but the three of them were the strongest.

"Are we going to keep blasting them and hope their shield cracks?" Jenna had no idea how to break these shields. There were low-level spells that could, in theory anyway, break down another magic user's shield. But nothing like the one protecting these dinohawks.

"In a way, yes. We're going to combine our Power, and drill a hole in it." Ghortin's glare at the birds now had a smirk. "It took me longer than I'd like to admit to sort it. Crell, are you all going to be okay back there for a few minutes? We might need to borrow a few archers once we drop the shield."

"Wherever those sciretts are coming from, it's a distance. They're getting closer, but slowly. Especially considering their sprinting speed. Maybe they'll die before they get here." Crell sent three rangers carrying crossbows over to Ghortin.

Ghortin turned to Jenna and Keanin then pushed Keanin to the middle, Jenna to the far right, and Ghortin took the far left. "Jenna, you, and I should take a single step forward. Keanin will act as our focus." He rubbed his hands together.

"But what spell?" Jenna and Keanin asked at the same time.

"This one." As Ghortin spoke, Jenna felt a wave of magic come from him. She couldn't speak for Keanin, but a glance back showed that he appeared as stunned as her. A complicated spell filled her mind and she found herself needing to cast this spell. She couldn't talk, move, or think. Just the spell.

They all sent it at the same time, yet arcs of magic from her and Ghortin flowed into Keanin. His magic hit the middle of the dinohawks.

The sound of glass shattering filled the cave and a human-sounding scream came from somewhere outside. With luck, whoever was behind the shield on the birds was at least seriously injured. Ghortin had warned her that while a tight connection to a spell made it stronger, it could also leave the magic user at risk. Judging by that scream, they'd been extremely vulnerable.

Crell's archers wasted no time and killed the first six of the birds before the rest screeched and flew off.

Jenna felt invigorated by the spell. Why was Ghortin teaching her spells the slow way? This was great. Then her legs buckled and she dropped. A similar thud behind her pointed out that Keanin had fallen as well and looked as shocked as she felt. Ghortin was still standing but looked a lot paler than before.

Which explained why this wasn't the best way of teaching spells.

Within a few moments, the spell she'd cast was gone from her mind, and feeling slowly returned to her limbs.

"The sciretts are here!" Crell yelled from the back of the cave as the hoots of the sciretts grew suddenly louder. They'd been closer than anyone thought.

Jenna tried to get to her feet, but it was as if everything from her hips down had turned to jelly. From the way Keanin was struggling, and still seated, he was having the same problem.

"Can you cast spells?" Ghortin teetered but could walk.

Jenna had a moment of panic when she reached to find something, and there was nothing. Then her connection with magic came back. It was odd that that a Powerful spell zapped her physical energy, but still left her with magic. But she wasn't going to argue. "I can."

"Me too." Keanin tried again to get to regain his feet but fell back. "Fighting from the ground is a bit much though."

"Aim for their knees." Edgar glanced back at them with a smirk.

"Funny." Keanin shook his shoulders and held his hand up. There was so much Power in whatever spell he held that Jenna was fairly sure they could have felt it back in Irundail.

The hooting became overwhelming and all Jenna saw was a wall of her friends. Then the sciretts were upon them.

CHAPTER THIRTY-TWO

AS SOON AS JENNA COULD get a clear shot she was going to fry some sciretts. She agreed with Keanin though—fighting from a sitting and trapped position sucked. She had to drop her freeze spell as freezing everyone in the cave wouldn't be optimal. She couldn't defend her friends if they were frozen. Also, there was no way to know when the surviving dinohawks, or the mage who was working with them, might be back.

The fighting was fierce and cramped as the tunnel the sciretts were coming out of was narrow. The defenders stayed in rows, but so far, none of the animals had made it past the first of the defenders. At least that she could tell.

"Jenna! Behind you!" Keanin yelled as he turned away from the back of the cave.

A tall shape covered in rags and holding a long, jagged sword crept toward her. She flung the spell she had ready, one that would attack the joints of an attacker, and he screamed in pain as his joints began to freeze and turn against him. He dropped the sword and stumbled away.

A single scirett then managed to fling itself over the wall of rangers. The long gashes on its sides showed where the defenders had tried to stop it. It ran for Keanin.

And exploded in a ball of ash as Keanin's spell hit it.

Scirett ash drifted around the cave as Jenna stared at her friend. She knew his Power and ability to use magic was changing, but that was a terrifyingly impressive spell.

Keanin didn't even look winded as he pulled in another spell.

Even if she knew how to cast that spell, whatever it was, Jenna knew that she'd end up as weak magically as she currently was physically if she tried to throw something that strong.

The sciretts became silent as they continued to fight until they were all destroyed. They could have run back to wherever they came from at any time, but they fought to the end.

Finally, Crell and Storm raised their swords and turned around.

"They're dead. Where did this ash come from?" Storm asked as he dusted the ash off himself. Pretty much everyone, including the semi-dozing horses in the side cave, was covered in a light coating of scirett ash.

"I might have used a bit too much force in my spell." Keanin pushed himself to his feet slowly. "The ash is from that scirett that got past you all."

Jenna managed to also totter to her feet this time. She hoped they got out of here and could ride. Walking wasn't going to be easy for a while. Her legs were now partially cooked noodles. Better than jelly, but not by much.

"I didn't see one get past us." Edgar looked around as if more were lurking in the shadows of the cave.

"It went right over all of you and you'd hit it a few times." Jenna watched as confusion crossed all of their faces. "None of you saw it, but Keanin and I did? Is that a spell?"

Ghortin stalked further into the tunnel that the animals had come out of, at least fighting had brought him back to full strength. He came back out. "Yes. Damn it, someone had spells on the sciretts. We're lucky only one made it past. That's an old and tricky magic and not unlike that shield spell on the birds. We need to get out of here. Immediately."

"That's what we've been doing." Crell walked over to

the horses. "Or trying to, anyway. Did you find a new way out and forget to tell us?"

"No. But there had to have been a connection between this place and the outside world long ago. Most likely near the coast or there wouldn't be the dead Erlindan adventurers in here. We find it, reopen it, and run. After shutting it again, obviously." Ghortin's smile was like he'd explained how to make toast.

"How…?" Storm shook his head. "Never mind. There has been a lot of weird magic going on, you'll sort out something. And I agree, we need to leave."

Jenna told them about the cloaked man who'd tried to attack her while they brought their horses out. The animals remained in their spell daze and would be kept that way until they were out of the cave.

"That's not good. That person could have been behind the birds or someone else entirely." Edgar moved toward the cave mouth.

"And you're not going out there looking for them." Storm took his horse and walked to the tunnel. "The mystery of this place and who is behind the attacks will have to wait."

Edgar gave a final look out the cave entrance then sighed and took his horse to the side. "I'll take the rear."

"And Keanin and I will create another block across the entrance to the cave," Jenna got out before Ghortin could. "You're going to be busy getting us out at the other end, right?"

He paused, then finally nodded. "Yes, good thinking." Ghortin followed Storm into the tunnel.

She and Keanin moved closer to the entrance to the cave, then together cast the spell that would block the opening.

"It's nice to work with you again," Keanin said as they finished the spell. "My magic has changed in the last month, but it always seems to be drawn to yours."

Jenna grabbed his hand and smiled. "Agreed. I feel stronger working with you." The old Keanin was still there, the changes he'd faced had modified him, but not destroyed him.

Keanin drifted back a bit and Jenna walked her horse past Edgar. She knew that at the first sign of any trouble behind them, Edgar would be gone. Storm knew that as well.

They went single file into the tunnel, the semi-sedated horses bobbing their heads but not paying attention to anything beyond the horse in front of them. Ghortin was two rangers behind Storm and let a few simple lights fly ahead of them. They didn't show everything inside the tunnel, but it was enough to keep from walking into a wall.

Jenna studiously ignored the piles of bones that lined the sides. She was grateful there wasn't enough light to see them distinctly.

"How are we going to know when we're at the end? And how are you going to open it without everything falling on us?" Jenna wasn't too worried, but the tunnel looked the same no matter how long they walked. Ghortin indicated that he could tell where part of it had been open long ago but didn't indicate that they were near it.

"Ah, ye of little faith. I can tell. It takes decades to develop the skills—"

"Most likely there will be a pile of boulders, stone, something," Crell cut him off with a laugh. "Sorry, Ghortin, since Carabella isn't with us on this adventure, someone has to keep you in line."

"I get no respect. But yes, there most likely will be indications. At some point, long ago, there was a passage." Ghortin walked faster and managed to get himself and his horse around the two rangers as well as Storm to take the lead. "And I believe it will be right around this corner!"

They turned the corner and aside from even more bones, there had to be an entire platoon in this place, the walls were still smooth. And in a dead end.

"This can't be right. Did anyone see a side tunnel?" Ghortin approached the solid-appearing walls and tapped on them in case it was an illusion of some kind.

"We would have noticed it." Storm patted his horse and then joined Ghortin at the dead end. "There has to be something here."

Edgar was still in the back and remained in the main tunnel. "I think something is trying to get into the cave."

"Jenna and I would have felt something," Keanin grunted and hung onto his horse's saddle as something hit him.

Jenna felt a wave of pain hit her as he spoke. Unlike the rattling when the prior shield was attacked, this one was being struck hard with the intent to hurt the caster as well as bring the shield down.

"Whether this was the way out or not, it needs to be so now." Jenna grabbed her stomach as another surge of pain came through. "Whatever is out there is taking that shield down and intends to kill Keanin and me to do it."

Diath came closer to Ghortin. "I've had some education about rocks. There might be a different feel to the place where there was an opening." He didn't seem confident.

Jenna wanted the waves of pain to stop ripping her apart from the inside. If he could help with that, more power to him. Storm was holding her upright now. The shield she and Keanin created still held but it wouldn't for long.

At Ghortin's nod, Diath walked slowly along the walls with one hand hovering an inch above the stone and his eyes mostly closed. He was almost to the end when he stopped and opened his eyes.

"This is weird. But it's here." He knocked on the stone

wall, then sent a spell into it. A line appeared that looked like a large doorway, then vanished.

"Are those elementals?" They hadn't appeared to be the same, but similar enough for Jenna to try and mentally reach out. And get no response before they vanished.

"That is an excellent question." Ghortin stood next to Diath. "Show me what you did."

Diath duplicated it and Ghortin joined him. This time the line of light held its shape. "Not Jenna and Keanin, you two focus on keeping that shield out front up, but Edgar and any other mages, come here and help us push. I was figuring we'd find a physical barrier, but it appears a mage or two closed this off."

Two of Crell's rangers were mages and they stood alongside Ghortin and Diath. After a brief set of instructions, all four physically and magically pushed the wall. The glowing lights flickered a few times, then held.

Just as Jenna and Keanin yelled as their shield was destroyed.

Storm grabbed Jenna as she fell and Talia held Keanin up. He was taller than her but she seemed to know what she was doing.

"Go!" Jenna got out through gritted teeth. The pressure from the mage who destroyed the shield spell back in the tunnel continued to eat away at her insides. Distance might be the only way to survive.

Ghortin and the three mages with him slammed spells at the interior of the lighted doorway. The wall inside of the lines vanished and revealed a cliff overlooking the ocean.

Ghortin was the closest and led the way out onto the cliff, but motioned for Jenna and Storm to take the lead. Getting out was great, but not if they couldn't shut the way out behind them.

Hopefully without destroying the rocky but clear trail down to the bottom.

Talia and Keanin were next, although it seemed as if Keanin was protesting leaving.

Jenna's focus was to get away from the pain before it killed her. He wanted to fight.

The cliff was broader than it appeared from the inside, but the trail to the coast was narrower than she'd like. But as long as they got out of here and the pain stopped—she'd do it.

Storm linked his arm to hers and they led their horses down. The horses were still under their spell doze and Jenna envied them.

Looking out past the narrow path they were going on was nice though. The ocean wasn't that far below—if she looked out enough. To the south, there was a large town, possibly Erlinda. Which might be running into the fire if that town was still under siege or had fallen completely.

As the pain inside began to fade, she appreciated being out of that tunnel, and the weird world behind it, even more as a cooling wind from the ocean reached its way up.

The rocks they were winding their way down appeared to be similar to the black rock that encased Irundail.

She, Storm, and their horses had made it down three switchbacks when a rumble came from above them. Ghortin appeared over the edge and motioned from them to keep going but didn't appear panicked.

"Is that Erlinda? Where's Khelaran?" They still weren't certain which side the Khelarans were on. But Jenna was still curious to see the other country.

"Yes, it is. Khelaran is behind that wall of fog." Storm pointed to what she'd assumed was a natural fog bank. Now that she noticed it, it was clear that didn't seem to be moving.

"Is it always like that?" The pain faded with each step. If she wasn't going down a tricky path, she'd start running to help the pain vanish faster.

"No. Their land routes are closely protected and take a long time to cross. But that bank is covering the ocean access as well. Whether King Philia is on our side or not, he's not taking chances."

Keanin and Talia were behind them and moving closer.

"It seems they closed that hole, but Ghortin suggests we move as fast as safe," Keanin said. His voice was stronger than before. "He's not admitting it, but I don't think he trusts that closing that passage didn't do structural damage to this mountain."

A slight rubble under their feet pointed out that Ghortin might be right.

"Can't we go anywhere without destroying the trail behind us?" Jeanna agreed that the ramp leading into that hidden world was better destroyed. But this one still looked like a long way down.

"As long as we can get off in time, it might be a good thing. We don't want anything from that cave world getting out anywhere," Talia said.

"Won't stop the dinohawks if whatever Ghortin did to close it falls." Jenna laughed at the confused looks that came her way. "Sorry, that was my name for those birds." Another thought hit her. "What if they fly into Irundail? That entrance was open."

"Your and Edgar's was when your spell fell, so they can get into the tunnel in Irundail," Keanin said. "But I felt the one that Ghortin and I left on the entrance in the canyon. When it fell it took down most of the rocks around it. That's closed now."

"That would have been good to know if we were planning on going back that way." Crell was a few riders behind them but the twisting path down put her right above them. "I agree in this case. But it could have been bad had that been our only way out. What's that?"

She kept leading her horse but pointed out over the

ocean. From here, they could see a few miles out. The water was mostly smooth. "Wait, it'll come back up."

Storm, Edgar, Talia, and Diath started swearing.

Edgar shouted out first, "A kraken!"

CHAPTER THIRTY-THREE

———◆———

FOUR OF THEM APPEARED WORRIED, and Jenna noticed that even though the creature was far below them in the ocean, they reached for weapons.

However, Keanin had a huge grin. "The kraken! I'd hoped he'd survived."

The monster was little more than a massive blueish-gray rock with tentacles coming out of the ocean at this distance. But since five of them recognized it, Jenna would take their word for it.

"That thing isn't your friend, Keanin." Storm's tone indicated this wasn't an issue when they were here before.

"You don't know if it's even the same one. Oh." Edgar's swearing was kept under his breath as two more blueish-gray stones rose out of the water. "Are they attacking that ship?"

They were far enough in the ocean that Jenna doubted anyone not at this vantage point would see as the three beasts closed in on a large sailing ship. The ship tried to change direction, but while the kraken appeared rock-like from this distance, they moved quickly.

Edgar brought out a long scope and shook his head. "There's no way that ship can escape."

They all watched in shock as the three kraken overwhelmed the ship and dragged it under the water. Within moments there was no evidence a ship had been there—or the kraken.

"Our people were using the larger ships to flee Erlinda and go down the coast. Are those things working for the attackers?" Talia clenched her sword tightly and appeared ready to race down and take on all three krakens on her own.

Jenna was rethinking Talia and Keanin as a good match. If they were that ready to charge foolishly into battle, neither was going to live long.

"The one I freed was a prisoner of a group of pirates. I don't think the kraken are on anyone's side." Keanin's happiness at seeing the kraken faded.

"That might not have been one of your ships," Edgar spoke a few spell words over his scope and shook his head as he peered through. "I augmented the viewing on this, there's enough rubble on the water to see a flag. Strann. And it was heading into Erlinda, not out."

"Isn't Strann a landlocked country? Why would they have ships?" Jenna didn't know much about ships in this world, but that had looked like a large one. That they probably were behind the attack on Erlinda wasn't a surprise—just how they did it.

"They don't. Or rather, they didn't." Storm shook his head as he resumed moving down the trail. "They would have had to transport them across land and enter the ocean either in Traanafaeren or Khelaran. Even with a lot of magic, that would be a serious undertaking."

"None of this is good, especially Strann having warships. And make no mistake, that's what it was. I felt the battle spells when it was being dragged under. And I believe we should move faster." Ghortin nudged them down the trail as another slightly stronger rumble hit under their feet. "Also, not good. The people we left behind are trying to breach the hole we made and that I closed. That won't be good for any of us if we remain on this mountain."

One look at Ghortin's face made Jenna want to sprint down, with or without her horse. It took a lot to worry

Ghortin, and his face was lined with concern that got worse every time he looked back to the top.

They were all jogging by the time they reached the bottom. Because of the sedative spell on the horses, that was more difficult than it should have been.

As soon as she and Storm reached the bottom, their horses shook their heads and looked around as if they had no idea how they got there. Edgar had released his spell. They mounted their horses as the rest of their friends came off the mountain.

The shaking grew worse.

Jenna readied a lightning strike type of spell. It wasn't that helpful against attackers on the ground as the angle to cast it was wrong, but if it worked as planned, it should take down one of those dinohawks if they escaped and came for them.

As with the trail into the hidden world, the path they'd come down crumbled. It didn't vanish completely, as the other one had, but massive boulders came loose from the sides and destroyed the path they'd been on.

With everyone on their horses, they raced out of the area. The cliffs weren't that far from the beach and Storm was heading that way.

Jenna continued to look back even once the rumbling and shaking stopped. If the way that Ghortin had sealed was open, she knew that the lack of a way down wouldn't stop those birds.

"Where are we going? Not that I would question Storm normally, but do we want to be close to the ocean?" Crell came up alongside Jenna's horse.

"The krakens won't come on land," Keanin yelled from his position in the crowd.

Looking back, Talia didn't look like she agreed with him.

Storm slowed as they hit the sand. Horses could run on

packed wet sand, but this was drifting dunes. Not something to be racing through.

"We need to stop. If that tunnel opened, we can't leave whatever comes out free." He reached behind him and pulled out his bow and quiver. Most everyone else did as well.

Keanin had his bow out, but as before, Jenna felt that he had also pulled up a spell.

"I don't think they broke through—my spell feels attacked but still intact. And if they do break through, that entire tunnel will collapse. Won't kill all of them, some might make it out. But it should stop the bulk of them." Although Ghortin was a decent archer, he was sticking with arming himself magically.

Jenna noticed that while he hadn't said it, Ghortin felt there were more than the three dinohawks who had escaped before.

That was a cheery thought.

The soothing sound of low waves meeting the beach behind them seemed completely at odds with the terror that would happen if those birds got loose. Although maybe they could get them and the kraken to fight. Keanin might trust the sea monsters, or at least the one he'd freed, but any creatures who could destroy an armed massive ship in moments were something she didn't need to meet. Ever.

A puff of dark smoke came from the top of the cliff they'd come down. Ghortin's left arm went up as if to cast a spell as he yelled at the cliffs. "Come on. Try once more."

Jenna looked at him closely. "You want them to come through?"

"I want them to try so my trigger spells can destroy that entrance for good. We do need to investigate that cave world, but not when we're trying to save this one. I couldn't use a larger active spell when we left without risking us not being able to get down. But if whoever is up there would expend a little more Power…" He glared at the top of the cliff as if he could force it to happen.

Either it was mind over matter or good timing, but another billow of smoke, this one larger and darker appeared and three flying shapes came shooting out. If there was anyone or anything with them, they were crushed as the tunnel and cliff collapsed.

"Birds!" Crell yelled. She'd switched out her short crossbow for a longbow almost longer than her. Her hands were steady as she waited for the birds to get closer.

The lead dinohawk swooped down and got one of Crell's arrows for its trouble. But it was also hit by a second arrow that didn't come from anyone in their group.

They were surrounded by high dunes covered in beach grass, but Jenna couldn't see anything in the direction the second arrow had come from.

"Whoever you are, stand down!" Storm yelled as Keanin shot down a second bird.

The third one figured things out and flew too high for even the longbow arrows to hit. "These are our kill. My people need food." The human man who spoke came out from behind a dune with two more people, a kelar and another human, close behind. They still had their bows ready, but weren't aiming arrows at anyone—yet.

None of the three looked good. Their clothing was tattered, and the leader appeared to have been a guard—or he had taken the jacket off of one.

Jenna was sure that while three had come out, they would have left some behind and out of sight.

"Tireli?" Talia didn't lower her bow; the third bird was still circling.

"Captain Talia? We feared you and those who left with you had been killed."

Talia nodded to Storm. "This is Tireli, he is, or was, one of the guards under my command. You stayed in the city."

"We should have gone with you. The attacks from the sea increased the day after you left as we sectioned off a part of Erlinda to defend. We got most of the non-fighters into safety, but I fear they will be found. We fled after two days with only what we had with us." He looked angry enough to snap the bow in his hands. "Erlinda has completely fallen, aside from a few small groups who remain hidden. At least we believe they haven't been caught yet."

"How many are with you?" Talia nodded to the other two.

"We have forty. I believe we're the last defenders still free. Aside from any you have." Tireli looked around for hidden fighters.

Talia waved to Ghortin and the rest. "Aside from my brother, these are all fighters from Irundail. It's a long story, but hopefully we can help." She appeared to be watching Tireli more than the bird still flying overhead but turned and fired as it dropped lower.

Keanin shot at the same time and everyone else looked ready to. The bird crashed into the beach.

"We can hopefully get these arrows back." Crell dropped off her horse. "But since we have limited supplies at the moment, we might want to start calling our targets."

Keanin shrugged. "We wanted to make sure that thing was dead."

Tireli whistled and a group of fifteen people came out. They looked as bedraggled as the first ones and three were already going to gather the nearest downed bird.

"It's only been a week since we fled, but that's a lot when you have nothing. The outlying farms have all been destroyed. Crops burned, livestock chased off or killed." Tireli watched his people gather the dead dinohawks, then turned. "You're welcome to come with us, but our supplies are short." He walked around a dune.

Ghortin swore and reached into his vest pocket. "Tireli,

we need to check something before we go anywhere. Some people are looking for us." Although they had mostly kept the use of the taran wands secret, he, Crell, and Edgar each took out their wands and tried to reach people who might be looking for them. Especially if they saw the canyon's end of the collapsed tunnel.

Tireli stopped but he and his people stayed in place.

Ghortin reached his mother before Crell or Edgar connected to whoever they were reaching out to.

"Ghortin?! Where are you? I came back to Irundail for supplies and they're telling me you were all destroyed in a cave-in at the far end of the valley." Carabella's voice carried extremely well out of the taran wand. Something that wasn't easy to do.

"Easy. We're all fine, we weren't squished by a tunnel. Just found a hidden world, and then escaped out through a cliff. But all of us are together and intact."

"Then where are you?" The tone of her voice said that she was going to come find them if he didn't give a good answer.

"It's a longer story than I can tell right now, but we're near Erlinda. We might need to stay here for a bit." He looked toward the town itself and frowned.

Carabella was silent long enough that Jenna wondered if the wand had stopped. "But you're all fine. You *are* fine?"

"Yes. Did you go to the cave-in in the canyon?"

"Yes, we were coming into the valley when the sound of it rocked through everything. Then I was told you'd all gone there. You can't blame me for fearing the worst. We're working on expanding the Zalin shelter into a safe place for more people. I need to go back, but I couldn't until I knew how you were."

"We're fine. Can you notify the royals? And have them set up guards at the mouth of that canyon—no one goes in." He glanced over to where Crell and Edgar were now talking to others into their wands. With a lot less noise. "I think the others are being informed now."

"When will you be back?" Her voice was still loud, but she sounded more at ease than when she first responded.

"I'm not sure. Erlinda has been completely taken over, and I fear we might need to be here." He gave Jenna an odd look that was focused on where she had the cuari book in her vest pocket. "We'll keep in touch as we can."

Carabella said her goodbyes and ended the call.

Jenna nudged her horse closer to him. "You think we're supposed to be here? Considering everything that led to us being here, it seems more chance than anything else."

"Ah, most prophecies have difficult circumstances. I think once we get settled, you should take a look at a certain tome." He nodded as if that explained everything as he put the taran wand away.

Crell and Edgar finished their conversations and joined Ghortin and Jenna.

"I reached Garlan," Crell said, "he told me what I overheard Carabella yelling about—the collapse of that tunnel in the canyon was heard throughout. He's calling back most of his guards from the canyon but leaving a few there in case something finds a way through."

Edgar nodded. "I reached Rachael. She wasn't as hysterical as your mother, but there was a strong tone of relief that all of us were fine. She reiterated that she's getting too old for this. But she is glad that we're well. She, Tor Ranshal, and Wilty will dig deep into the archives to see if there's anything about that weird world cavern. She'd never heard of it before."

Tireli walked over once all three taran wands were put away. "If you want to follow us, you might want to get off your horses. Higher profiles are easier to spot by the soldiers on the city walls. Some of my people are already heading back with those odd birds. What are they?"

"No idea. But you might want to have one of our

magic users go over them before you cook them." Storm swung off his horse as the rest followed.

Jenna hoped that Ghortin could do some magic for food and supplies, although it wasn't healthy long term. Those dinohawks were nasty enough that eating them didn't sound appealing.

"Good point. There's a storehouse hidden in the forest somewhere. The mayor was in charge of it, but then she and her cabinet died before they shared where it was," Tireli said as they walked. "Maybe it can be found by stronger magic."

Ghortin nodded, but he continued to look out across the beach. "What do you know of the kraken attacks?"

Tireli's laugh was kept low but was real. "The sea monsters? They don't exist."

Jenna shared a look with Storm. Yes, that attack had been further out to sea, but something should have been visible from land, even at beach level.

But Ghortin nodded. "Ah, we weren't sure. That's good to know." He saw Jenna's expression and shook his head.

"Whatever Captain Talia or her brother have said, they aren't real." Tireli smiled. "Just what we need on top of everything else would be monsters coming from the sea."

Talia and Diath remained quiet. Jenna followed suit; it would be dealt with later. Or maybe the creatures were actually too far out to see from the beach. There was a lighthouse in the distance but if Erlinda had fallen there might not have been anyone up there.

Tireli chatted with Diath as they made their way through the dunes. The city walls of Erlinda were far enough away that details couldn't be seen, but close enough to make her nervous.

"We're almost there." One of Tireli's people, a derawri woman, came up along the other side of Jenna's horse as they walked.

"That's good. Knowing what's been happening, makes me feel exposed out here."

"Don't worry, we'll be safe." The woman smiled but her eyes were sad.

"How many people did you lose?" Jenna kept her voice low enough that if the woman wanted to ignore her, she could.

"Ten close friends. My entire unit died trying to get people out of the city. We're not even certain why they took Erlinda," her voice was rough.

"Isn't it a strategic sea town?" Things seemed desolate out here, but as the furthermost north coast Traanafaeren city, it would be a good foothold.

"It is, but they started destroying the docks a few days ago and appear to be building a massive sea wall. Why take a place for sea access, then block it?"

Jenna shrugged. Maybe *some* people had seen the krakens and their work.

Tireli stopped in front of what looked like an abandoned barn. "We only have three low-level mages, but they keep this working." He smiled and went inside, then vanished. The barn was in such shape that it could be seen through. But nothing appeared. More of his people followed and also disappeared.

Then Ghortin and Storm vanished as they went through the door.

CHAPTER THIRTY-FOUR

EDGAR HESITATED AND THEN FOLLOWED them. "We might as well go in." Crell led her horse over to Jenna. "Unless you're sensing anything wrong?"

Jenna paused, but nothing jumped out. Typhonel or the elementals might have noticed something, but they still weren't responding. "Nothing." She smiled at the Erlindan derawri who'd walked up with her and the three of them walked inside the barn.

That it was strongly cloaked was a given, but the place inside was imposing compared to the exterior. Aside from the obvious lack of supplies. Beds were made of hay and grass, and a big fire in the center was their only place to prepare food.

She was impressed with the level of magic it took to hide everything inside here—and the smoke from that fire.

"We need to find where the mayor hid supplies." Tireli motioned around the large space. "We're safe here, but we won't last for long if we can't get food. And winter will be here soon enough to cause added concern."

"You could go to Irundail." Edgar left his horse in the makeshift stable and then looked around. "Or go to the Zalin shelter, a lot of your people are safe there. And they have supplies."

"I know, and that will be our last option. I want to make sure that we're here to help anyone else who escaped. Plus, this sounds odd, but I have a weird feeling that if we leave, we won't be able to get this close again." His shrug indicated he wasn't sure why he felt that way, but he did.

Ghortin looked around the massive structure. "You could have some seer in your ancestry. Many spells linger here, and not all of them are the ones your mages are maintaining. Our enemies would know people were out here and are hoping to force you out before even tighter control of this area comes into play."

"How long have they been building the seawall?" Jenna figured that knowing what the enemy was doing would help with figuring out why they were doing it. And finding a way to stop them. She hadn't had a chance to look at the cuari book yet, but once Ghortin mentioned it, she had an itchy feeling that there was something in it about this place or the ocean.

And that they needed to rescue Erlinda.

"Since yesterday. They were bringing in more troops on ships the entire time up to that. Ships would dock and unload troops that marched to the south. A few stayed in Erlinda, but not many. Then suddenly ships stopped coming and the people who took Erlinda moved most of their forces to wall building and dock destroying." Tireli turned to Talia and Diath. "We saved some ships before they began burning everything. Including that one of yours. They're hidden in the Noxan Cove, only three, but it's something."

Diath grinned. "Thank you. With any luck, we can do something with them. But Noxan is close to the Khelaran border. Have there been problems from the north?"

"No." An older kelar who sat near the fire got to her feet as she spoke. "The Khelarans have done nothing good or ill during this. Our first intel indicated that they had led the attack, but we don't believe that is the case now." She smiled to all of them, then gave a short bow to Storm. "I am Altheria, and I am pleased to meet all of you, especially Prince Corin."

Storm's jaw twitched but he nodded in return. "I am pleased to meet you as well, Altheria. Please, all of you, call me Storm."

They went around introducing everyone to Tireli's people except Talia and Diath as they were already known.

Altheria paused at Keanin's name and stepped closer to him. "Are you from Khelaran?"

"My parents were. They fell in the Markare and the Traanafaeren royal family took me in as a baby." Keanin ofttimes seemed uncomfortable discussing his family, but he appeared relaxed around Altheria.

"Might I know their names? There is something familiar of you." Altheria laughed. "And as this is the first time I've seen Prince Co- *Storm* in person; I doubt that I have met you before."

Keanin shrugged. "Flouth and Lasissa Plantarie. They were academic scholars investigating the Markare. Their entire party was killed, but my mother lived long enough to get me to the Traanafaeren royals in Irundail before she died. She is buried there."

That was news to Jenna. Keanin never seemed fond of Irundail, nor had he ever spoken of his mother's grave.

"Those names do tickle my memories, but I can't grab them." Altheria smiled. "I'm not as old as Mastermage Ghortin, but I count over a thousand years. Many of them were in Khelaran. I am pleased to meet you, son of Plantarie." She gave Keanin a long look that ended in a smile.

Jenna watched them. Although Altheria implied that she didn't know Keanin's parents, she seemed to know something that she wasn't sharing.

The relief on Keanin's face when Altheria stopped her questions pointed out that he might not want to know. At least not now.

Jenna was turning to stable her horse when she caught

a concerned look pass between Storm and Edgar. They knew something as well, and it also wasn't something they were going to share at this point.

She'd have to wait until she could get Storm alone to find out. She understood that not everything should be shared with everyone, especially their new allies, but if it was something that could endanger Keanin, she needed to know. He was like her brother from a different world.

The rest of their people moved their horses into the stables. There was plenty of room as Tireli's group seemed to only have a dozen horses. They had truly fled with nothing.

Jenna went to Ghortin as he settled his horse. "How are we going to help when no one has supplies? I can see if there's anything in *that* book, but unless these people are willing to leave, they will be starved out before they can do anything. Us too." She folded her arms tightly and glared at Ghortin. "No mage food." When she and Ghortin were caught on the road while traveling to Lithunane for the ball a year ago, he'd created food out of nothing for them along with tents and bedding. She'd pondered it when thinking of that or eating those dinohawks, but long-term mage food would be worse than nothing. And she now had a feeling this might be a long-term situation.

She wouldn't mind the magic-created bedding, but while the food had seemed filling at the time, by the time they got into Lithunane the next day, she found she was starving. Mage food could suffice for a short time, mostly because it fooled the brain and stomach into thinking there was nutrition involved. But that spell only held for about eight to ten hours and could cause a backlash worse than the initial hunger.

Ghortin hadn't explained any of that at the time.

"I wasn't thinking of that." He gave a haughty sniff. "I can make bedding for everyone here, and it will last for a few days. But food is another issue. We need to find the storehouse the mayor left."

"My rangers and I were discussing that very thing." Crell came over. "I wouldn't be surprised if Erlinda had a storage set up centuries ago. Many outlying towns do."

"Do you think you can find it? There's still a few hours before nightfall, and I don't think I'm alone in hoping for something else to eat other than those birds." Jenna shuddered. Up close they looked even worse than they had outside. Long greasy dark brown feathers might have nothing to do with the interior of the vicious-looking thing, but she still would rather not find out.

"With my rangers?" Crell grinned. "Aye, shouldn't be a problem. Do you want to come with us?"

Jenna nearly said yes, then thought about the cuari book as well as whatever had prompted the odd look between Storm and Edgar. It was gone too fast to be certain, but it seemed to be extremely serious. "I'd better stay here. I need to work on some magic issues." She patted the vest pocket that had the cuari book.

"Ah, good idea. I'll see if Talia and Diath are up for a jaunt. Nothing against Tireli's people, but if they've been looking for it since they had to flee the city, they might be biased about where it's not." Crell gave Ghortin and Jenna a tight nod, then went to pull her rangers together.

"I'll make up a story about you needing to work on your magic lessons for Tireli and his people." Ghortin looked around the extremely open barn. "It might be best for you to stay in the stables though. We don't have time to verify that all of these people are who and what they appear to be."

"That'll work. There's a nook past that stack of hay. Another thing though, did you notice Storm and Edgar?"

He frowned. "That look between them about Keanin and what Altheria said? I did. I never deeply searched Keanin's family history. His life was already too tragic for that and Rachael said that she knew his parents had been researchers. But I have a feeling your fiancé might be hiding a secret about Keanin."

Jenna grinned at his term. She was wearing the simple engagement ring that Storm gave her, but so much happened lately, that she'd nearly forgotten about the real engagement. "I do believe you are right."

Tireli and his people were working on cooking a meal of the birds and a pile of sad-looking vegetables. The invaders had done a serious job on destroying anything that might help any people hiding from them. Crell, her rangers, Talia, Keanin, and Diath were heading out on their patrol. This would be probably the best chance to talk to Storm and Edgar without interruption. Or Keanin.

The two were off to one side and were sharpening blades with small stones. They looked up when Jenna and Ghortin stopped in front of them.

"And to what do we owe this pleasure?" Edgar kept sharpening his blade and nodded as one of Tireli's people passed them.

Ghortin moved closer with Jenna right behind. "We think there is something that you two know about Keanin. Something that Altheria might have an inkling of as well." As he spoke his right hand moved slightly and a spell not unlike the one Dantil had used in the Irundail Castle covered all four of them. It was subtle enough to avoid detection by anyone not specifically looking for it. But would keep their voices from being heard by others outside of the bubble.

Providing Ghortin kept his voice down.

The same look of concern as before appeared on both of their faces and Jenna was glad that Keanin had gone with Talia and the rest. Hiding whatever this is from him wouldn't be easy.

Storm ran his fingers through his hair. "I take it we're cloaked?" He kept his voice low. At Ghortin's nod, he continued. "When we were in Erlinda before, we found out that the enemy was looking for *two* royals. Two princes. Myself and one from Khelaran who'd been lost as a baby from a distant family line. One that they were laughing about the Traanafaeren royals being too stupid to know they raised."

"We couldn't find out anything else from them. But I felt the truth." Edgar shrugged. "My gran was a hearth witch and passed some of it down. Strong emotional truths, that the speaker believes so thoroughly to be true that they would never question it, resonate with me sometimes. Those words did this time."

"Keanin is a Khelaran prince? How could they have misplaced him? Doesn't that mean one of his parents was a royal as well?" Jenna wasn't certain what she'd been expecting, but this was definitely not it.

Storm had told her that growing up together, everyone in the palace said that Keanin seemed far more like a royal than Storm did. But this was crazy.

"That's what it appears." Storm resumed sharpening his blade.

"There was a second royal line of Khelaran. But it was destroyed over three hundred years ago," Ghortin said as he watched Altheria chop vegetables in the kitchen area. "Maybe they'd managed to hide and were not all destroyed. And someone finally found them."

"You think the death of his parents and the rest of the researchers in the Markare wasn't random," Edgar said.

"With this new information, I do. And I'd say his mother was the royal and one gifted with Powerful magic to have escaped the attack and make it to Irundail."

Jenna looked around. This wasn't the place to reveal this to Keanin. Aside from him being a bigger target than they thought, it wouldn't help anything. He might be of royal blood, but his family had been out of power for over three hundred years. Then another thought hit her.

"Was what happened to him in Shettler's Point because of that?"

Keanin was attacked on a magic level and his essence, and Power, went into several demonspawn women. When he, Storm, and Edgar fled Khelaran, they'd been chasing the few extremely pregnant survivors who'd gotten on a ship.

And lost them on the ocean.

It spoke a lot of Talia's influence on him, that Keanin had shoved aside the search for them for now.

All three men looked grim, but Ghortin finally answered. "I don't think that could be excluded. If these people who were looking for you in Erlinda knew about him, others might as well. Keanin's Power is growing, and he hasn't reached his peak. A Powerful mage with royal blood could prove extremely valuable to the wrong people."

CHAPTER THIRTY-FIVE

ALL FOUR REMAINED SILENT.
Finally, Jenna spoke. "We have to tell him. We can only defend him so much, and if he is aware, he can take more precautions."

Storm gave a grim laugh. "Keanin isn't the same man he was a few months ago. He's swung from overly cautious to bloodthirsty and reckless. I'm not certain that knowing his ancestry is going to help."

"I agree. Keanin's Power has grown on levels unheard of in such a short time," Ghortin said. "I think the attack on him not only created whatever those demonspawn were trying to make but triggered something deep inside him. He's not coming from a stable place and knowing this could make things worse."

"I'm with Jenna." Edgar put down his knife. "The price on Keanin's head is higher than we thought. He's going to need to be aware of the threats against him."

The discussion went back and forth with good points being brought up on both sides, but no resolution. Everyone stuck to their opinions when Ghortin finally released the silence spell, Tireli's people were starting to notice, and they broke up.

Storm and Edgar continued sharpening their weapons but were clearly listening in on the Erlindan fighters around them. Ghortin went to Altheria and joined in prepping the vegetables. Knowing him, he'd probably find out what she suspected about Keanin before the stew was done.

Jenna went to the nook she'd spotted and pulled out the cuari book. She felt odd being so secretive. Only a handful of people in this world would even know what the book was, and fewer could open it. But there was no way to know if Tireli's people were all who they claimed to be. Any of them could be demonspawn.

This book had more history than she'd originally thought, but she figured that might be what they needed. The rumors, however slim, of a second portal in the ocean, or on an island, were concerning.

It took a few minutes to find anything in the cuari book that seemed to be tied into Erlinda, but it didn't refer to it by that name. The section she found spoke of a small village near a cove, that was long fought over by the newer races due to a powerful item there.

These books were supposed to be from the time of the old cuari—before humans, derawri, or kelar came around. Jenna reread the passage; she was tired and might have misread.

Nope. Still said it was fought over. But it seemed to be changing the words as she read. Now it said, *the people fought over it*, not the newer races. Having Rachael or Tor Ranshal here would have been extremely helpful. Ghortin might be able to help, but his ability to read the shifting cuari books was still inconsistent. A peek around her hay bale wall indicated he was still working on getting information about Keanin from Altheria.

With a sigh, she continued reading. Although she did send a mental request to the book in her hands to stop changing things.

The description of the village, and the ocean that faced it, was detailed. But, she'd only seen part of Erlinda when they came in and even a great description was useless if she couldn't compare it. It might be Erlinda, or anywhere up the coast.

Then she found the huge Dark Cliffs of Obsidian

marked in the book which helped lend the village mag-ical Power. There might be more places like that, she'd have to find out, but it sounded like what surrounded Irundail and what they'd come through to get here.

She had more hope now as she kept reading. But, aside from words like 'protectors of life' and 'needed to save the world', she couldn't find out why anyone, in this case, the cuari, would have been fighting over this. Unless they were all pointing to an underwater portal.

Those words were important, but with nothing to hang on them, they weren't helpful. Judging by the number of cuari fighting, this event took place before the full-scale attack on the deities and the decimation of most of the cuari.

If the main portal was so well known, why was this one barely mentioned? And where was it?

With a sigh, she closed the book and dropped her head down into her hands. The feeling of needing to do some-thing important here was clashing with the cuari book's inability to tell her what it was.

"That bad, eh?" Ghortin kept his voice low but still made her fall off her bale of hay when he spoke.

"Yes. There's something here about a battle, portal, and a lot of cuari. At least I assume it is referring to Erlinda, but no idea what, why, or if this is even the correct spot." She rubbed the back of her neck. "I'm getting the feeling that something has to happen soon though."

"Might I?" Ghortin held his hand out for the book.

"Knock yourself out. I didn't see enough of outside to know if this is even the right place." She gave him the book and stretched back into the hay. "I'm wiped out, but at the same time jumpy."

Ghortin slowly turned the pages as he read. "When did both start?"

He sounded so much like a doctor back home that Jenna laughed. "As soon as I read that section. And it changed some of the words. Only once, but still." She dropped her voice and told him what had changed.

"You're certain?" He looked up, then shook his head. "Of course, you are. Once the taran wands have recharged I'll try reaching out to Rachael." He dropped back into the book. "This description does sound like Erlinda. I haven't been here in a long time, but some features stay the same. I never heard of Erlinda being a place of any type of focus though. Its importance is normally because of the proximity to Khelaran."

"Who founded the town? You and your friends created Irundail and Traanafaeren as a country—how did Erlinda get started?"

He shut the book but kept his thumb in place where he'd been reading. "It seemed to grow. Like people were drawn to Irundail when we first set it up, sea-going adventurers were drawn to this area. It didn't even have a name for the first few years. But they settled in, built the town, and traded with Irundail. Erlind was the name of the first official mayor."

"When was the Zalin shelter built?" She knew that Carabella was well aware of the shelter but it hadn't been in any book she'd read.

"About the same time. It was good to have a safe place outside of Irundail for travelers. Didn't get used much as Traanafaeren became larger and there were more coastal towns."

A shiver hit her. "Could that hidden supply area inside the shelter caves that Carabella mentioned be connected to that weird world cavern we fled from?" They seemed close to each other and some magic had kept the supplies cave in the back of the Zalin shelter hidden for centuries.

Ghortin had already gone back to the page he'd been reading. "What? No." He scowled. "It could be. Too many things have been crowding together and I missed that." He reached into his vest for the taran wand, then swore under his breath. "It won't be ready yet, none of them will be. Hopefully, Carabella hasn't opened a path to that cavern world."

"Does she have enough magic to do that?" Even though she'd thought of it before he did, Jenna knew that Carabella's borrowed magic from Meith had serious limitations.

"She might. Zalin's storage was created to be accessible by any magic user who knew of it. It hadn't been used in centuries, but in the past, yes. Her current abilities could open the shelter's storage."

"But there's no record of that weird cavern connected with the shelter? Maybe it's sealed off." Judging by Ghortin's reaction, she figured he hadn't heard of the cavern world before, but they hadn't time to talk about it at the time.

"No. Three thousand years old and I should have heard about something like that. There might not be a link through to the shelter. But there's no way to know until I can use a wand again." He shook his head. "More troublesome events and things are appearing, but I'm not seeing the connections. That could be fatal for all of us."

"Did you ask Altheria about the hidden cavern? If she's lived here long enough, there could be rumors or myths about the place. Erlindan forces got through there at some point. And it seems they went through regularly for a while. At least judging by the bodies." She'd been trying to ignore the weird dagger at her side, but it was interesting that none of Tireli's people even asked her about it. Diath had said it was definitely old Erlindan.

Ghortin sighed. "My student has surpassed me. I'm afraid I was focusing more on what Altheria might know about Keanin. She was cagy and I fear unless we're completely ready to bring her into our confidence, she won't fully share what she knows about that lost Khelaran royal line. But she could know rumors of a cavern world and be willing to speak about them." He handed the cuari book back. "Keep reading until Crell and the folks with her come back. I'll go back to Altheria and find out more of what she knows." He marched back toward the fire.

The cuari book didn't shift anymore, but knowing that this was the area it was speaking about made the information in it make more sense—sort of. The original cuari had fought here long ago, but it wasn't against their kind or any deities. A strange word, one that seemed to consist of letters piled on top of each other shifted and solidified before her eyes.

She kept her swearing low as the word showed itself. The cuari fought demonspawn. Ones who came through whatever portal had been out here long before the one in the Markare was created. She closed the book and got up to grab Ghortin when the ground shook and the two guards at the door yelled.

"We're under attack!" One of the guards yelled and they stepped outside the doorway with swords drawn.

Storm and Edgar were at the entrance before the yell ended. Ghortin, Altheria, and the rest of Tireli's people were armed and running up as well.

Jenna started to grab her sword, then felt an odd magic pressure building outside of the building. She left her sword and pushed her way to the front of the defenders.

"Let her through!" Ghortin bellowed. He had pulled up at least two spells, and although her magic felt different than what Jenna was used to, Altheria was ready magically as well.

The pressure from outside was growing and Jenna knew that if it wasn't stopped it would destroy them. Even though she wasn't certain what it was. She stepped past the guards and froze.

The outside looked calm. But it was as if a storm was coming right at her and invisibly pushing a deadly energy toward the building.

Jenna called up a shield spell, increased it as much as she could, and wrapped it around the building.

Hopefully, Crell and the others weren't caught up in whatever this was, but she couldn't spare magic right now to search for them.

There was still no sign of actual attackers.

She kept her shield up and watched the area around them, but leaned toward the closest guard. "What did you see?"

"It was stupid. I thought I saw attacking hordes. But they vanished."

Ghortin came to her other side. "They might not have. Jenna, hold onto that shield. Everyone else, including the guards, stays in this building until I yell otherwise. Make sure the injured are protected. Altheria? Would you like to assist me?"

The kelar woman's grin was close to Carabella's when she was ready for a fight. She hadn't taken the attack on Erlinda well. "I'm ready. You lead." Her hands were curved around invisible spells.

Jenna felt her Power and she might be able to give Ghortin a run for his money. It was a good thing she was on their side.

Ghortin pulled in a different spell, one Jenna had never felt before. Altheria nodded and switched the spells she was holding for new ones.

"That's an old spell you're pulling in," she said without looking away from the space before them.

"It's an old one we're facing," Ghortin said. "Jenna, whatever happens, don't drop your shield. The rest of you, stay inside. Yes, that means you two."

Jenna glanced over to see Storm and Edgar scowl in unison and drop back behind her shield.

A moment later, Jenna buckled as her shield took a

massive invisible hit. She reinforced it as much as she could and managed to keep from dropping to her knees. But another hit that hard and she and the shield would collapse.

CHAPTER THIRTY-SIX

GHORTIN AND ALTHERIA STRUCK OUT with spells at an unassuming grassy dune at the same time. The pressure that had been building gave a screech like metal being twisted and then sounded like shattered glass.

An instant later, forty screaming invaders appeared over the dune. From the amount of noise they were making, they'd been doing it for a while and hadn't realized that the spell hiding them was gone.

Ghortin and Altheria staggered a bit, and Jenna yelled for Storm, Edgar, and the rest to come out. That Ghortin simply stepped aside, taking Altheria with him, spoke volumes of how much those spells to reveal the attackers cost them.

Jenna adjusted her hold on the shield spell and was standing out of the way when a wave of fury hit her. At first, she looked around, wondering if the anger itself could be a spell. Then she realized it came from inside her.

Fury and Power slammed into her. Something about the people running toward them made either Typhonel or the mysterious former Protector in her body, furious.

She'd guess it was Typhonel, as she hadn't felt anything from the echo for nearly a year. But Typhonel's incident didn't happen here and he'd never reacted like this.

Without a thought, her right hand raised and blasted a swath through the attackers. They screamed and changed form.

"Demonspawn!" Storm yelled as he engaged two of the unchanged attackers.

There was a chance that not all of them were demonspawn, but two more passes with whatever spell her right hand was casting revealed that they were all demonspawn.

And the spell did more than simply reveal them. Demonspawn were fast and deadly, but these appeared to be injured and dying.

Whoever had sent that spell through her wasn't done. There wasn't the same energy as before, but the fury was still there. But when it tried to force her to run closer to the fighting she was able to pull back and stay in place.

There were enough fighters already out there—especially considering the condition of the demonspawn. She couldn't leave the injured or Ghortin and Altheria behind. Neither had collapsed, but they didn't look good.

"You did your job, but I'm not leaving." Even though she kept her voice low, and it was gritted out through her clenched teeth, Ghortin still looked back at her.

"Who are you speaking to?"

"No idea. But they were behind that spell revealing the demonspawn. And they're being pushy." Now that she had a moment, she realized that it didn't feel like the echo or Typhonel. But disturbingly like a bit of both of them had found a friend. Or something else. There was an odd warmth coming from the cuari book in her pocket. She didn't think it had the ability to do what just happened, but those books were as unpredictable as the cuari themselves.

The battle continued and even though Storm and the rest were originally outnumbered, it didn't stay that way long.

However, one of the demonspawn did make it past the others and charged Jenna. She wasn't about to drop the shield spell surrounding the building, and she didn't have her sword. But she did have that weird dagger.

She grabbed it and faced the demonspawn. The monster came to a halt. It still had elements of the human male it was disguised as, but also the odd disjointed appearance of a demonspawn.

He screeched and lumbered forward, but he reminded her of a zombie movie extra. He stopped again, but he was now close enough that she didn't have to release the shield spell to lunge forward.

Dagger against long sword-like arms should have been a stupid idea, but she got in and stabbed the demonspawn, then backed out of its way before it could do more than collapse.

She took a few more steps back, but it didn't do much more than fold in on itself. Even the green blood on the dagger dried and flaked off. "Handy, but ew. Ghortin? How are you two?" She remained facing forward in case any more demonspawn came up, but the more she looked the more they appeared to be badly made-up zombies. Who were losing their battles quickly.

"We'll be fine. That spell was trickier than I thought. But how did you destroy them?"

One by one the demonspawn collapsed. Whether or not someone was fighting them. "I have no idea."

She staggered as she felt her energy start to flow toward the sea, like a wave, but she held on to the shield spell. The pressure from before was fading along with the demonspawn, but that didn't mean they were through this.

Crell, Keanin, and the rest came running over a hill as her knees buckled.

"Good timing. I'm not feeling so good." She stumbled as Storm grabbed her.

"I have you; we should get back inside. Crell and the others can do recon."

Jenna smiled up at him. That was possibly the first time she'd heard him back down from looking for more demonspawn. "I look that bad?"

"No, just, pale. I think—"

His words were cut off as he was torn away from her and flung against the building.

Everyone else was also shoved back and Jenna forced herself to stand.

A dark space appeared ahead of her. Man-shaped, but impossible to tell anything more than that.

The only thing she'd seen like that had been Sacaranz when he'd attacked the ball back in Lithunane.

She drew in as much Power as she could. None of her friends were standing, but they all appeared to be alive and conscious. They simply couldn't move.

"We have been searching for you." The eerie whispery voice sounded like it came from the thing in front of her, but it also felt as if it was surrounding her. And trying hard to be creepy.

"Nice trick with the special effects. But I'm not scared." She was impressed that even though this person was terrifying, she didn't sound frightened. The past year of practice had helped.

And, while that overwhelming anger and Power from before had vanished, she was more than a little pissed off. Anger was useful.

"You were meant to be with us. Sacaranz brought you here for a reason." The being didn't move forward and appeared translucent.

At least she now knew she wasn't facing Sacaranz, that was a plus. She folded her arms and tried to appear bored. "I was brought here by accident when your Master was screwing things up. But, I've figured out that this is right where I need to be." She released a wind spell that didn't affect the image at all.

Yep. Whatever or whoever was facing her wasn't really here. That didn't mean that he couldn't still hurt her or her friends, but it did make her feel a bit better.

Honestly, she was stalling to see if Ghortin could push

back the spell pinning him down. His dark eyes were furious, but he couldn't even speak.

"You will complete the circle for us. This world will die. The world you came from and the rest will die. But the new kingdom will arise from it. Come now and we will spare your friends." A dark and misty arm reached out and Jenna felt a tug on her heart. The hand turned toward Storm and a lightning strike shot at him.

Jenna pulled her shield forward and blocked the strike. "Oh, hell no. You don't get any of them. Not to mention, keeping them alive for what? You told me that the big plan was to destroy all the known worlds. That *will* kill them, you know." She felt stronger. "Sacaranz needs to get a better class of minion. You're just not that smart." She waited until the one facing her sent another strike, this time at Ghortin. Then she grabbed the lightning from the spell, increased it, and fired it back at the sender.

The dark, misty, and not as scary as he was originally, being burst apart in slow motion. "You can't do this!" The screech sounded like multiple voices as it hung in the air, slowly dissipating.

"I think I did. My friends and I tell Sacaranz to go to hell." Another flow of Power fed her and she hit the form once more.

The yell increased, and then the thing vanished.

Jenna ran to Storm first, but he was already getting to his feet. "Thank you."

"You're okay, right?" Lying about injuries was a risk with him but she couldn't see any wounds.

"A bit stiff, but yes."

He went with her to help the others. One of the rangers had landed badly on her arm, and one of Tireli's people had broken his leg when he collapsed. But aside from bruises, everyone else was fine.

Even Ghortin and Altheria didn't look exhausted anymore.

"We'll talk about what happened later, but you did well." Ghortin peered into her eyes as if they could give away how she did what she did. Then nodded. "Later."

"We should get back in the building. There are strange creatures out at night." Tireli checked on his people, then looked around until he saw Crell. "Did you find anything?"

She grinned and ducked behind a dune and came back with a large bag of supplies. So did everyone who had gone with her. "Aye, we did. And I agree about the building. We heard strange sounds in the woods as we came back. The storage location is secure for now."

Ghortin and Storm stayed back with Jenna as she let everyone else go inside. Her shield felt like it was holding, and while the building did have its own spells, they were mostly to keep things hidden. Hers would keep things out.

"We can alternate holding the spell overnight," Ghortin said softly. "While your recent actions were impressive, I don't want to push them too far."

"I still look bad, don't I?" Jenna grinned at him and Storm. "You two are extremely obvious. I feel a lot better than I did before, but I agree, the shield needs to stay up overnight and more than one of us should do it."

Tireli was the last one beside the three of them who was out. "Thank you. Whatever you did, you saved us. And your people found the storage when we couldn't. There might not be as many of you as I'd hoped, but I think we got the help we needed." He clasped arms with each of them and then went inside.

Ghortin followed him and Storm dropped his arm around Jenna's shoulders. "You're certain you're okay? I don't know magic, but you were doing some different things from what I could see."

"I'm fine. And this wasn't the first time weird magic has gone through me." When she'd first arrived here, she and Storm had faced a pack of extremely determined ertin outside of Ghortin's cottage. She'd had mystical help at the time in chasing them off to their deaths—and saving Storm.

"You think that your echo is back?" He walked toward the nook she'd been reading in.

"I'm not sure. But something was involved. Did you see any demonspawn fall apart like that when you were in Craelyn?" She originally believed it was whatever spell had gone through her—but looking back she wasn't sure.

"No. At least not before Edgar and Keanin were done with them. But these looked different." He motioned for her to sit and she gave in.

"Zombies." When he raised an eyebrow, she continued. "You might have another word for them. Dead things that come back to life. They were falling apart even as they fought."

"You had zombies in your world?"

"Not real ones, only for entertainment." His eyebrow vanished up under his hair band. "It's not as weird as it sounds. Honest. But something was destroying them. And it wasn't us."

Ghortin came over with two bowls of stew and some thick bread. "The bread's still shaking loose the storage spell but, it'll be fine in a short while." He came back a moment later with his meal and took over a large bale of hay. "But, it might have been us, destroying the demon-spawn."

"And we didn't notice? You and Altheria looked pretty much out and I didn't do it." The stew was better than expected and the bread tasted as if it had just come out of the oven. Whatever spells were on that storage building, she needed to learn them.

"No, but it might have been tied to the spell you uncloaked them with. I've been speaking to Edgar and Keanin about the way they uncovered and destroyed the demonspawn they faced in Craelyn. This sounds like an extension of that."

"Which would be great if I knew what I did." She went over what happened and how little she had actually been involved. "At least up until Sacaranz's representative appeared. That was me." She shrugged. "With some help. But before you ask I have no idea if the echo was back, if *he* was back, or if something else popped in." It felt weird enough speaking Sacaranz's name out loud, but without Carabella, the term wouldn't hurt anyone. She had no idea if any of Tireli's people had a background in ancient deities—but this wasn't the time to find out.

Typhonel's name could remain unspoken.

A ruckus came from the back of the building then Tireli called to them. "Help! The dead are rising!"

CHAPTER THIRTY-SEVEN

———◆———

ALL THREE PUT THEIR FOOD down, got to their feet, and ran to the back of the building.

"What? Make sense man." Ghortin reached Tireli first.

The healers who'd been helping the injured drew swords and stood between the two beings trying to stumble to their feet and the living patients.

"These two were seriously injured before we found you and passed away during the fight out front. I didn't want to risk going out at night to bury them so we wrapped them and stored them back here until morning." Tireli raised his sword as he led them forward. "They almost choked one of my people before we realized what was going on. What kind of magic is this?"

Ghortin looked to Jenna but she shrugged. "Like I said, they weren't real…where I came from. Is this connected to those demonspawn?"

"I don't think so." Altheria joined them. "I've never heard of the dead returning."

"Something caused this to happen." Keanin, Talia, and Edgar were also on what was becoming the front line. "We can blast them apart and sort it out later." Keanin's face was grim and he looked ready to be the one doing the blasting. With or without help.

"No." Jenna narrowed her eyes as she watched the zombies. They weren't very impressive and wouldn't have even made extra status in a cheap zombie movie. In the time they'd been standing here, the two had groaned and managed to look gross, but they hadn't gotten close to the patients.

Which had given the healers time to move them out of the way. In moments, Jenna, Storm, and the rest were facing the two zombies directly.

"Stop. Please." The words were broken, but the terror on the face of the closest one was horrible to see.

"They're still aware. Whatever brought them back, left them in there." Now Jenna was the one calling up spells to end their suffering.

"Let. Us. Go." The second one's voice was little more than a whisper.

"Are they alive? They died. I saw them." If Tireli grasped his sword any tighter he was going to snap the hilt.

"This is some foul magic from the ones who attacked us." Altheria held her hand up in a spell but seemed at odds about using it.

"My shield should have stopped anything from coming in." Jenna knew her magic could sometimes be off, but she would have noticed if a spell made its way in.

"Unless one of us brought it in." Altheria's voice was low, but she moved back so she could watch the zombies and the rest of their people.

"You think one of us is a traitor?" Tireli's focus was on his deceased teammates, but now he also looked around the building.

"It might not have been deliberate." Ghortin released a subtle calming spell as he spoke.

Jenna thought that was a good idea; the people behind them were now watching each other warily.

"If I were trying to destabilize a group, this would be a way to do it." Edgar moved so he could watch everyone. "Make your enemies doubt each other."

Jenna closed her eyes and thought of the zombie demon-spawn who had attacked her. She watched his movements in her mind. "Damn it. That last zombie touched three people when he came for me. He appeared to be moving slowly, but he still had some speed. Going for me was a distraction." She opened her eyes and sent a cleansing spell at the three Erlindans who'd been touched. All three froze as her spell hit, then passed out. "They'll be fine. But we have to let those two go in peace."

The zombies were now standing still, but the pain in both sets of eyes was brutal.

"Release."

Altheria stepped forward. "I'll do it. They know me." She held her hands up as she stepped forward. She didn't touch either one, but a spell flowed from her and they collapsed. She turned to Jenna with a grim nod. "You were right, they were still in there until I released them. We have to find the ones behind this and destroy them."

"That's the plan." Ghortin waved his hand and two shimmering shields appeared over the bodies. "I think getting them outside would be best."

Tireli still looked ready to be ill, but nodded. "There are enough magic users to get graves dug swiftly."

Ghortin raised the bodies and followed Tireli, Keanin, and two other magic users out.

Jenna felt the shield let them out but mentally tightened it after they passed through.

"Will these three be okay?" A derawri woman pointed to the three who'd brought in the zombie contact.

"They should be. Altheria? Do you have a way to double-check what I did?" Jenna didn't think this was the time to publicly admit that she had no idea what she was doing with this.

"I felt the spell on them, once we knew what to look for." Altheria walked over and dropped down to each one. "They are clear. And to be certain, I'll search all of us." The look she gave Jenna indicated she'd like her to be first, but she wouldn't push it.

Jenna stepped forward. She had connected with the zombie when she stabbed him, after all. Altheria nodded and raised her hands over Jenna.

"You're clear." She smiled, but there was an odd look in her eyes. Jenna might be clear of carrying the zombie spell, but something about her concerned Altheria. She'd have Ghortin talk to her when he came back.

Soon everyone, even those who had remained inside the building during the attack, were cleared. Altheria gave Jenna a crash course on the scanning spell so she could verify that Altheria was clear.

Ghortin looked grim as he and the rest came back after burying the two zombie victims.

"Should we expect another attack like that? The ones we've faced from the people attacking Erlinda were far more straightforward." Tireli appeared to be under control now. Zombies would disturb anyone and it sounded like he'd been running hard with this group for a while.

"I'd guess that this attack wasn't from Erlinda," Crell said as she joined them. "We passed relatively close to the city as we searched, and aside from work on the sea wall, Erlinda appeared to be locked down."

"Which would make sense, unless zombies have shown up before?" Edgar turned to Tireli. The rest of his people were busy sorting the supplies they'd brought in.

Jenna wondered if the Erlindans should stay here after she and the others from Irundail did whatever they needed to do and left. Providing that they couldn't reclaim Erlinda before that. While she felt that there was something they needed to do, the feeling that it was to save the town was becoming less focused. And Tireli's plan of relying on the hiding spells locked into this place was probably not going to work anymore.

"No. I've never heard of them and I'm older than everyone here aside from Ghortin." Altheria spoke up from where she was checking on the remaining injured.

None of them appeared close to dying but she was making sure they stayed that way.

"*I* haven't heard of them." Ghortin paced a bit, caught himself at the lack of space, and stopped. "But was it intended? Why would you sacrifice your demonspawn fighters like that?"

"You wouldn't. Unless something impacted the demonspawn that wasn't involved with whoever is controlling them." Edgar was walking along the walls slowly, looking for breaches but he came back now. "A lot is going on here, and we have no idea what's behind it." He got some stew and settled in to eat. He looked up as everyone watched him. "Those things out front were deadly, and what happened to your friends was horrific. But if we don't eat, we'll be too weak to fight back."

Slowly everyone gathered food and sat in small groups.

Jenna, Storm, Ghortin, and Crell gathered in a corner. Keanin stayed with Talia and Diath, and Edgar took his food and roamed around speaking to Tireli's people.

After a few minutes, Altheria came over. "Do you mind if I join you?" She spoke to Ghortin but kept glancing at Jenna.

"By all means. Thank you for scanning everyone." Ghortin smiled but the look in his eyes pointed out that he hadn't missed the way she kept looking at Jenna.

Jenna felt it was like Altheria wanted to say something but was afraid to do so.

"You might as well ask." Jenna sat aside her now empty bowl. "Otherwise Ghortin will keep staring at you."

Altheria laughed. "He does have an intense look, doesn't he?"

"I am right here."

Storm and Crell laughed. "And you do have a certain look."

"Fine." He sat back and folded his arms. "Ask my apprentice anything."

"Your apprentice? That's an interesting tidbit." Altheria's smile faded. "I'll be blunt, I believe that Jenna is our rescuer. Oh, not from the current attack, although that would be helpful as well. But the one that will save us from the horror that has been poised to destroy the world for a long time."

Jenna gave a slight tilt of her head but kept watching Altheria. "Ghortin? This is your call." There was no way she was going to sort out who could be told what unless it was a life-or-death situation. This entire thing was becoming more confusing by the day.

"So, it is." He put down his empty stew bowl and launched the silence bubble around them. Crell and Storm didn't react, they wouldn't have felt the spell. But Jenna was surprised that he hadn't asked Altheria's permission first.

Altheria's eyes slightly widened, but she didn't look like she disputed the need for the shield of silence. "I see. Thank you for taking me into your confidence. Is that why you're here? To stop the attack? I'll be honest, the old tales spoke of armies and creatures of myth supporting the rescuer."

Jenna laughed when Ghortin nodded for her to speak. "Not at all. Us being here was a complete accident." She briefly filled in the story of them being trapped on the other side of the mountain and having to break through. The hidden cavern world wasn't relevant to this story— she hoped—and if it turned out to be so, they could fill Altheria in.

"But, I am trying to save the world." That sounded insane to say out loud, but Ghortin nodded so she kept going. The short version of being from another world, Guardians, Protectors, and Sacaranz took far less time than she thought it would. Before each new segment, she'd glance to Ghortin. He watched Altheria but kept nodding.

Storm and Crell were visibly getting concerned and both rested their hands on their weapons.

Altheria finally spoke. "I have heard of these Guardians. I believed they were who was coming to rescue the world. I grew up in Craelyn, or rather, in a small village right next to the capital. The ruckus of the day was the forming of a new kingdom—Traanafaeren as it came to be known. As soon as I was old enough, I traveled to the south. But as a child, there were tales that our entire world, not just Khelaran, would come under a devastating attack. Not well-known tales, only one old man who insisted he knew what was going to happen. He was mostly crazy but he told a good story. He claimed that our world was in danger and that a rescuer from a far and distant place would be the only one to save us." She shrugged. "Or doom us. He wasn't certain which side it would fall. I believed he meant the person would come from this new country and so I took off to find them. I never thought it would be a thousand years before it happened."

"Was that man related to the royals? To the lost line?" Even though a thousand years ago, Keanin's family wouldn't have been lost at the time, Jenna felt there was something there. The story was little more than a bit of whimsy from a teenager a thousand years ago. But something rang true. Not long before that time, Ghortin, Carabella, and their companions had fought a monster in the Markare that had come from the portal. Repercussions of it were felt everywhere.

Altheria wasn't the only person drawn to the new land even if they weren't sure why.

Altheria glanced over at Keanin, who was across the building and lost in a tale that Diath was sharing. Then she nodded. "I didn't realize it at the time, but he was. I went back to Craelyn to look for him when the other royal line was lost, but he was gone. You know, don't you?" She looked at Keanin again.

Jenna, Ghortin, and Storm nodded—Crell turned to where Keanin sat and tilted her head in question.

"I take it something to do with Keanin is woven into this story?" She relaxed but didn't move her hand far from her sword.

Altheria nodded. "Yes, or so I believe. And I think your friends do as well."

Storm nodded and briefly told of the thugs in Erlinda looking for the other prince—and the indications it was Keanin.

"It also would explain his magical ability," Ghortin finally said. "The lost royal line was filled with Powerful magic users. The impact of the slaughter in the Markare as a baby repressed that in him. But he is still building his abilities. I doubt that the current royal Khelaran family would stand aside for him to take their place, but Keanin is going to change the world."

"I believe you are right. I have some seer in my family, and when I saw him it was as if the earth shook." Altheria kept watching Keanin.

"It sort of did. Are there always this many earthquakes here?" Although they'd started in the canyon in Irundail, Jenna didn't know if the continuation of them was indicative of something larger.

"Not normally. But I do believe that is something with you, not him. His royal standing might not even make a difference, although it does reflect on what he will become. It's you, Jenna, who is causing changes here. You'll either save Erlinda or be the death of it." Altheria was extremely calm for someone who was talking about the place she'd probably called home for a few hundred years.

"That's comforting," Storm said.

Crell shook her head. "But not surprising."

Jenna smiled. "I felt it when we arrived, something was pulling me here—I'm just not sure what." She took a chance, Ghortin could cut her off if he wanted to. "Do you know of a passage to a hidden cavern? A hidden world that Erlindans went to long ago?"

Instead of answering immediately, Altheria looked around the rest of them. "Yes. It was long ago, and even though I did live here at the time, I first thought it was nothing. Small bands of heavily armored and armed adventurers claimed to have found a way to mountains of gold and gems. A few came back with a handful of treasures. They all restocked supplies, gathered more companions, and left again."

She gave a sad smile. "At that point, the village elders, of which I was one, tried to stop more from leaving. They wouldn't listen. After a year of no one returning, I, and three other magic users went up the mountain. The one you came down. We went inside a short way, but all we heard were the sounds of animals fighting. Then we saw the bodies. We raced back out and closed the passageway." She leaned forward and stayed silent for a moment. It might have happened hundreds of years ago, but she still felt the pain. "I'd hoped that some of them survived. But I never believed it was a separate world."

"Then this is from them, I found it in the tunnel on the way out." Jenna held out the dagger. "It's decided to stay with me for now, but maybe it would be happier with you." Granted, Diath claimed that since she was the first to touch it, she might be stuck with it for now. But, Altheria was a magic user and a local.

Altheria leaned forward to look at it but kept her hands at her sides. She shook her head and pulled away. "Those daggers were myths even before I came here. The adventures who left Erlinda wouldn't have had anything like that unless they found it along the way. But no, I don't want it."

"People were going there for a while." Storm watched the dagger, but when it didn't do anything, he looked to Altheria. "Is it going to be a problem for Jenna? No one else can touch it."

"Can you get rid of it?"

Jenna shook her head at her behavior. "I hadn't tried. Which probably says something itself." Ghortin hadn't expanded her education into magical relics that much—there weren't many around from what she understood, and none of the known ones did what they were supposed to. She sat the dagger down on the ground between them. And found she couldn't release it. "Seriously?" She tried again, then took off the sheath, put the dagger in the sheath, and again tried to set it down. Nope.

"I can leave it in the sheath when it's on my belt, but not otherwise?"

Altheria winced. "Well, that does indicate that it very well might be one of the Jarila daggers. Until they complete their task, they stay with whoever found them." She shrugged. "Or until you pass on. I am sorry."

"I've heard of those." Crell didn't make a move for the dagger in Jenna's hand but did point to it. "But the Jarila daggers are supposed to be a trio—as in they only work as a trio. Don't they? Shouldn't this one be dormant without its friends?"

"Possibly. As I said, they were naught but rumors by the time I came down here. But, if the other two are still here, perhaps they are close enough to make it react."

"Or the other two were in that cavern world and they don't need to be near each other to react," Storm said. "To the best of your knowledge, is this a danger for Jenna?"

Jenna smiled. He'd not liked the lack of response the first time he asked the question.

"I wish I could answer that for certain. But they were never said to be dangerous to their holders."

"That didn't stop the prior carrier from being killed," Crell said.

"That might have been because its powers were limited." Ghortin frowned as he studied the dagger and sheath. He also caught himself twice reaching for it. "I'm thinking that this one made its way to that cavern, an exceedingly long time ago, without its mates. But the other two are somewhere near Erlinda." He ran his fingers through his beard. "Not to mention that the obsidian rock we went through does hinder magic. One of the many reasons my companions and I created Irundail in the middle of it."

"Seriously, I need to know what to do with it." There was a lot more, like could it help her fight. Jenna wasn't sure what caused her change in abilities nor the flood of anger that hit her when those demonspawn attacked. If it was this thing, then priority needed to be given to getting rid of it. Power was good, but not when she didn't have control over it.

"There's something else, isn't there?" Altheria was observant.

Jenna sighed. "Yes. Something or someone was helping me when those demonspawn attacked. I have no idea where that demonspawn exposure spell came from. But there was a lot of anger behind it." She looked to Ghortin. "It wasn't like anything I'd felt before." Yes, they were bringing Altheria into their circle quickly, but Typhonel and the mindslave echo didn't need to be brought up right now. Not to mention, she was beginning to think that they weren't involved in this case.

"Edgar and Keanin cast spells against the disguises of the demonspawn when we were in Craelyn. Could you have somehow tied into that?" Storm asked.

Ghortin turned his thinking scowl toward Jenna. "You and Keanin do seem to have an odd magical connection when you two aren't separated by hundreds of miles. We should check with him if what you did was similar."

"Not to mention, although he's keeping it mostly hidden, Keanin still has a lot of anger about the demon-spawn." Storm looked over to his friend.

Jenna did as well. Keanin appeared relaxed as he, Talia, and Diath sat around sharing stories with two of the Erlindans.

"I don't think he did something deliberately; he might not have even been involved." Jenna didn't want to take away his current relaxed happiness. He'd been through a lot and regardless of what was going to happen here, he was going to have a hard time once they went to the Markare.

Jenna had been frustrated while in Irundail that they had to wait to attack the portal in the Markare. It had to be brought back and opened by the other side before it could be destroyed. But once that happened, they had to move quickly to destroy it. Keanin was as well, but it was a desperate fear combined with needing to destroy the portal completely.

Maybe there was something here that could help all of them.

Edgar walked over to them and waited at the edge of Ghortin's bubble until Ghortin raised it to let him in.

"It's a good thing that Keanin is relaxing and not watching you all. I could feel your stares from the other side of the room and they weren't directed at me." Edgar smiled at Altheria and flashed a bit of his courtly knight persona her way. "I am pleased to have you helping us, Altheria."

"As I am pleased to be part of such an august grouping. I do wish we knew more about what you are all here for. And how Keanin is involved." A line formed between her brows as she briefly glanced at Keanin and then back. "His magic is quite odd. Even knowing his background."

"It is, and getting more so. I don't have time to mea

sure it or work on further training." Ghortin repeated the same look and turn back that Altheria had.

The rest of the discussion broke up when Ghortin and Altheria discussed magic elements of far more things and people than simply Keanin. Jenna's eyes were starting to glaze over when he finally released the rest from the shield but kept it over him and Altheria as they continued their discussion.

The other four drifted toward the front of the building.

"Along with much-needed food and spelled water jugs, there were supplies," Crell said as they reached one of the drop-off spots. "We brought back enough to make tonight not miserable. Although, if we're going to be on the road for long, we'll need to find our own."

"Where was the storage? Is there going to be enough for a long siege?" Edgar took out a bunch of thick blankets and handed them around. "I don't think the Erlindans should stay here though. Jenna can't leave her shield spell, and even if all of those demonspawn are gone, someone knows where this place is."

Jenna set up a rough bed with two blankets. "That was my thought as well. When I realized where we were, I had a strong urge that saving Erlinda was important." She shrugged. "I still think we ended up here for a reason, but not sure it's the town we're supposed to save now." There was a chance that the rumored second portal was somewhere here and that could be what was nagging at her.

The discussion broke down to what Crell and her group had seen. The secret storage place was well hidden but surprisingly close to the city walls. "It was impressive. Keanin and Diath felt the layers of spells on it before we found it. Keanin was the one who found it though. Diath doubted that he have could done so had he been on his own."

"I'm glad you found it, but having it be that hard-to-find sort of seems to be defeating the purpose." Jenna sat on her rough bed. She'd reinforced her shield spell on the building for the night, but Tireli's people were still standing guard inside the door.

"It does, but I have a feeling that no one, even the former mayor, expected this to happen. They didn't have the time they'd believed they would." Storm set up a similar bed near hers.

The discussion continued but Jenna felt an odd sleepiness overtake her. As she was falling over, she saw the surprised looks on her friends' faces, then she was back on the chaotic plane.

CHAPTER THIRTY-EIGHT

"DAMN IT!" THE SLEEPINESS VANISHED and Jenna rolled to her feet and glared around the far too-familiar jungle. "Meith? Did you do this?"

There was no response but a distant howling. It sounded more like a howl of loss rather than aggression—or so she told herself. "Meith? Come on, you're the only one up here that I know." Or so she hoped. There were still gaps in the times that neither she nor Meith had pulled her up here.

She might have done it this time—if so, it hadn't been intended.

The jungle appeared normal, or what she thought of as normal, but at the same time it had that faded and tattered look. She'd noticed that on a few of her previous visits but wasn't certain what it meant. It appeared to be getting worse.

"Jenna?" It was Meith's voice but it was like the slowly fading howls—wispy and seeming to come from all around her.

"Meith, where are you?" She moved forward slowly. She still wasn't certain how space went up here and didn't want to go wandering around too far looking for him. "Did you bring me up here?"

"We lost. We all lost." Still faint sounding, but less Meith-like.

Jenna stopped walking and folded her arms as she glared at the fading jungle around her. Sacaranz had tried to trick her before by pretending to be Meith. Granted, he'd done it in Irundail's castle, but she didn't have a reason to believe he couldn't do it up here.

"Who lost? What was lost? Come to me." In the castle, Sacaranz had maintained a transparent image of Meith, but it had felt wrong. If he did it again, she might be able to catch him.

"We died. Earth died. All the worlds died."

"And why am I here if everything died?" She dropped her arms and hit the dagger's sheath on her sword belt. Her sword wasn't here, but it was. Sometimes when she was here, her body stayed in the real world—sometimes it came along. Judging by the solid sheath at her side, that happened this time.

She winced. Explaining that she sometimes vanished wasn't going to go over well with their new friends. Hopefully, Storm and the others could cover for her if any of the Erlindans noticed.

"Jenna? Why are you here? It's not a good idea right now." *That* sounded more like Meith—slightly annoyed at being disturbed from whatever he was doing.

"I have no idea." She spun and smiled as he came out of the jungle. "But I think someone was pretending to be you again."

As soon as Meith appeared, the weird voice pretending to be a grieving Meith, and the wolf or dog howls, vanished.

His frown deepened. "That is unacceptable and I'm still trying to get assistance stopping him. In the castle again?"

"No, we're on the road, but he was pretending to be you up here." She was fairly certain that this was the correct Meith. However, not only could Sacaranz have stepped up his copy, but Meith ofttimes didn't want to know specific details since time appeared to move differently for both of them. Keeping the particulars of where she was back in the normal world would probably be the best idea when possible.

She'd once seen a version of him after everything had collapsed. It still haunted her nightmares.

"Ah, and you brought a friend." Meith took two steps back from her as he watched the sheath like it was a venomous snake. "*That* shouldn't be here." The calmness in his voice was at odds with the terror in his face.

"You know what it is? Was it from before?" There could be a chance that he knew of relics that came about after he and the cuari were banished. But he looked too familiar with it.

"There were cuari who made things that they shouldn't. Long before the time of the final battle. That thing, and two more like it, were those." He shook his head but wouldn't come closer. He folded his arms and glared at the sheath. "They were supposed to have been destroyed."

"They can't be. They aren't done yet." This voice was softer than Meith's and entered the area before a tall cuari woman came in. She was close to Carabella in height and build but had blond hair and dark brown eyes.

"Xalie? I haven't seen you in a long time." Meith's demeanor perked up but he still didn't move closer to Jenna and her dagger. Or to the cuari woman.

"I have been in contemplation." She gave a regal nod to Jenna. "I have been watching you for a long time. Even before you were you and before you came here. I am Xalie, as Meith said. I was one of the cuari who fought to save the deities but chose to return here."

"I thought the one hundred were the ones who fought to help. Are you saying there were only ninety-nine in the world before they were taken?" She was trying to get more things sorted out, not find new weirdness in what they thought they knew.

Xalie's laugh was deep but sincere. "You don't trust me, as is right. No, I did help defend the deities in the final battle, but afterward I realized what they were going to do to our minds. My mind is the most important thing in my existence. I stepped aside when the one hundred were called and they took another cuari who had fought for them in my place. I came here to have time to contemplate."

Jenna had wondered about there being an even one hundred cuari who'd fought to help the gods and goddesses. It seemed an oddly convenient number. "There were more than one hundred."

"Yes. That was another thing I disagreed with. I fought to save the deities, and so did many others, but instead of letting all of us live our lives alongside the new races, they took the ones they wanted, made them their puppets, and shoved everyone else into limbo up here." She smiled. "I can feel your anger at their actions. There was no reason for Carabella or any of them to be removed from their memories."

"Wow. No one knows this. I mean no one." Jenna dropped to sit on a rock.

"You refer to the Guardians?" Xalie smiled at Meith when he frowned at the term. "Meith, you might not feel comfortable here. I am not judging your lack of action eons ago, but some things might be better if you don't know at this time."

"I feel responsible for Jenna…but you're right. There are things I shouldn't know. I will be back." Meith nodded to them and left.

The bush he passed through lost a dozen leaves even though he barely touched it.

"Why is the chaotic plane fading? It used to appear bright and vibrant, but most times that I've been here as of late it looks like it's all dying."

Xalie came closer and another rock appeared next to Jenna's. "It *is* dying. I don't want to go into it, what you've seen wouldn't be any better for me than it would be for Meith, although I might handle it better than he would. But the plane is dying. The battle in the world below is pulling out the essence of this place and it will be the first to fall. It will destroy the captured cuari after all the land is gone, then those like Meith. Then the ones like me." She shrugged as she adjusted herself to sit on the new rock.

"But we're not facing massive battles yet. I thought that once war began the fighting would be brutal and swift." She had not been looking forward to that, fighting was still difficult for her. But she wanted this to be over.

"Not all battles are fought that way. The beings you are facing are still regaining their strength and doing small strikes to gather more Power and destabilize the lands they will destroy." Xalie's face was calm, but her fists were clenched in her lap. "You have to free the trapped cuari, some of us might be able to return then as well. Together we will face the final fight and the destruction of the portals."

Jenna dropped her head. "So, there were two?" She'd felt that in her gut but was hoping she was wrong.

"There still are. The first one vanished in the ocean during a battle long, long ago. I led our people in drowning it and destroying the demonspawn who'd come through. We foolishly believed that it was destroyed at that time."

"It's not, right? But how can we find it if it's at the bottom of the ocean? Can't it stay down there? Demonspawn can't survive that, can they?"

"Easy, child. You have the gifts to do what needs to be done. You will need help but have faith it will be there. And I believe that dagger came to you at this time for a purpose." She sighed. "As for what those monstrosities can or cannot survive? Even I'm not certain. Thousands of years ago, the demonspawn made their first incursion to your new world. But they wouldn't have survived coming through a portal at the bottom of the ocean."

"But they have changed." Jenna saw it on Xalie's face even though she didn't say it. Sea-going demonspawn wasn't what she needed right now. "We ran into some demonspawn, rather they ran into us. They seemed to be dead and reanimated."

Xalie's face stilled. "Are you certain?"

"Yes? As much as I can be. In my former world, we made up stories about zombies—dead creatures coming back to life. These looked like that. And they were carrying a spell to reanimate more dead."

Xalie got to her feet and stomped around. Again, reminding Jenna of Carabella. It was debatable if there were any truly calm cuari. "They are crossing the lines. The deities cannot let this happen. I need to speak to them." She stopped marching about, closed her eyes, and sent out a spell.

Jenna jumped as Typhonel answered. In her head

"*Yes, child?*" His voice was stronger than the last time he'd visited. She'd find out later where he'd vanished. They could have used his help a lot in the past day.

"*I didn't call you, Xalie did*," Jenna said mentally and felt Typhonel look at the cuari woman. She also felt his surprise.

"I remember you. You kept to yourself and thought about the worlds. How did you find me?" This time he spoke out of Jenna's mouth.

If Typhonel was surprised, Xalie looked ready to jump out of her skin.

"I feel what you are. But how?" Xalie got over her shock and came forward to place one hand on either side of Jenna's head. "I did not see you. In all my time looking at this, I never saw you. The lost god hiding in plain sight all along."

"I didn't know who I was until a short time ago, but yes, I am what remains of Typhonel."

A muted conversation that Jenna could only feel the

edges of took place between the two. That it was mostly inside her head made it that much more disturbing.

Finally, Xalie stepped back with a smile. "This is a hopeful thing. Typhonel was a just god and didn't deserve what happened to him. He believes that he can bring me back to the world below."

"He can bring the cuari back? We need them to close that portal in the Markare." Jenna was startled when her voice was out loud. He needed to warn her when he switched who was in control.

"*I can only bring her back at this point. And she will be limited in abilities until we stop the spell that is capturing the cuari. It might not recognize her, but we shouldn't take that chance.*"

"Better than nothing." Jenna smiled at Xalie. "Sorry, talking to that voice in my head." She turned her voice inward. "*But where were you? A lot has happened.*"

"*I don't know. We were in Irundail, then I felt Xalie calling.*"

Jenna shoved that worry aside. Having a god on their side, even one only in her head, was good. But only if she could reach him when she needed him.

Xalie scowled as she stared at a rock in front of her. "I think we need to leave now. I have left a message for Meith."

Jenna shrugged. "I have no idea how to get back. With or without you." She waited but there was no response from Typhonel.

Suddenly the world dropped out from under her and she found herself in the midst of yelling and fighting.

She thought she'd jumped time again, but then she recognized the building of Tireli's people.

The walls were engulfed by fire.

CHAPTER THIRTY-NINE

———◆———

"JENNA! GRAB YOUR SWORD!" IF Storm was surprised at her sudden appearance he didn't show it. Everyone else around them was so busy fighting that they didn't appear to notice her arrival.

Jenna grabbed her sword and pulled up a spell. She didn't see Xalie, but she could be anywhere. Or Typhonel hadn't been able to bring her through. A quick mental yell in her head indicated that he wasn't there or couldn't respond.

The only good thing was that the ones they were facing weren't demonspawn. Some lingering aspect of the disclose spell she'd cast left her with the ability to tell. She'd ask Ghortin about it later. But that could be extremely handy if it lasted.

Ghortin was using his staff and sword to keep the enemy at bay, but the fighters weren't having a problem getting in.

Jenna felt the tattered remains of her shield spell that protected the building as she ran forward. A burly kelar raised his sword to block her. She reached for magic, but there was an odd dampening. Which explained the destroyed shield spell and why Ghortin, Keanin, and the other magic users weren't using magic.

She blocked the attacker with her sword, spun, and stabbed him with her dagger.

That she didn't recall pulling out of its sheath—it was suddenly in her hand. She made a mental note to sort things out with that dagger one way or another.

She stepped aside as the attacker dropped his sword, clutched his side, and collapsed.

"We need to push them back out; we can't use magic in here!" Keanin got close enough to her to add, "Glad you came back." He turned and engaged two more attackers.

Jenna sent another test spell to the burning walls, but nothing happened. Aside from a massive stab of pain between her eyes. The bulk of the attackers were still between her and the doorway, but Keanin was right. Something connected to this place was blocking magic inside of her and the other magic users. She needed to get out of the building.

"Cover me!" she yelled to Keanin and Storm and then raced for the door. The attackers hadn't counted on that—or maybe they'd believed that the Erlindans would die rather than run. But that was their issue, not hers.

A bolt of lightning cut across her midsection as she crossed the threshold.

Or they weren't worried about anyone leaving because they had their own spell to disable people on their way out.

The pain wore off as she forced her way through and ran out of the building. There were no attackers out here, but she sent a spell to dampen the flames. It didn't do much but caused the fire to sputter a bit.

The damage was done, this hideout was gone, but hopefully, she could keep the place from collapsing until they could get everyone out.

"Let me help." Xalie appeared next to her and a stream of magic joined Jenna's in subduing the flames.

"Thank you." Jenna turned to the cuari as the flames vanished. "Um, you don't look solid." The fighting was still going on inside, but the building should stand for a bit longer.

Xalie was mostly there. Jenna could feel her as well as

see her. However, she could also see the dark shapes of the dunes around them through her body.

"Yes. There was a bit of a problem getting me here. There's a spell blocker on that edifice that you were in. Since *he* is tied to you, and *he* was bringing me down, that broke the connection." She scowled at the building. "I also can't enter there."

"Can you tell what the spell is? I felt it hit me as I ran out, but it didn't seem familiar. And *he* hasn't come back." Jenna agreed with her about not speaking Typhonel's name out loud. But she was still mentally trying to reach him. Hearing her voice echo around her head wasn't comforting. What if she could only reach him now on the disintegrating chaotic plane?

"I cannot. But it has been thousands of years since I've been around the magic of others. And unless it is cuari or demonspawn in origin, I most likely won't understand it." She gave a fierce smile. "Yet. Fear not, I am a quick learner."

Jenna approached the doorway. The inside didn't look good and there were still more attackers than defenders. She cast a low-level spell, one that would stay with her, and put her hand through the doorway.

She thought she found a way to push the magic-blocking spell back. Then a shock, larger than the one she'd felt on the way out, slammed into her and threw her backward. Luckily, she landed on one of the dunes and not a rock. But it still hurt.

"I felt that." Xalie drifted over to her. "For a moment you disrupted the spell. Unfortunately, not enough to stop it and it fought back. Do you have mirror spells at your disposal?"

That was an odd way to put it, and Jenna first shook her off. Then swore and grabbed the cuari book out of her vest. "No, but this does. Providing I can find the spell. Things seem to move around in here." She kept the book closed. "I'm not sure if this will affect you though." Carabella could be around the cuari books, but she didn't know what they were and she couldn't be told anything inside of them. Jenna had no idea what rules might pertain to a cuari like Xalie.

Xalie laughed. "Never fear. Even though I fought on the side of the deities, my memories remain intact. What the one hundred can't be exposed to will not affect me."

Jenna nodded. That would be handy, especially if Xalie was going to remain bodiless.

It took a few minutes, during which neither side in the fight appeared to gain a lead, but she found the spell. It would reflect the magic-blocking spell upon itself and cancel it. A spell mirror.

"You have another problem." Xalie pointed behind Jenna. Pre-dawn was coming over the ocean. But so were torches, which indicated more fighters coming from Erlinda.

"We must be a bigger threat than whatever they're building that sea wall against. Or at least we are right now." Jenna took one more look at the spell, then put the book away. "Can you appear to those people who are running here? Make them think that you're some sort of ghost?" The new people weren't that close, but those lights were moving as if they were jogging.

"I can try." Xalie drifted away as Jenna ran back to the building. "*You can call me like this if you need.*" That part was disturbingly like Typhonel's mental speech and only in Jenna's mind. As handy as mental communication was, she hoped that it only lasted while Xalie was in this in-between state.

The spell had seemed simple while reading it, but there was a subtlety that made executing it difficult. Her first two attempts resulted in more stinging attacks on her hands and arms as the other spell fought back.

Jenna took a deep breath and slid her spell through

the open doorway. She was flung back again, but this time there were no lightning strikes and she felt the magic-blocking spell vanish. She rolled to her feet and ran for the doorway. "Use magic!" Yelling it wasn't the best idea, everyone would hear. But there was no other way to let Ghortin, Keanin, and the rest of the magic users know. Not to mention, she was guessing that the attackers didn't have a lot of magic users in their midst, or they wouldn't have blocked their own people with that dampening spell.

Keanin responded first and flashed an evil grin as he blasted two of the attackers apart. Ghortin was more understated and three attackers near him collapsed with a wave of his hand. Soon, the attackers were dead, unconscious, or had managed to escape out the burnt walls.

Jenna remained at the entrance, but there was no way she could catch them and they avoided coming her way.

She raced to Storm once the building was clear.

"More enemy fighters are coming from Erlinda. Ignore any weird ghost person you might see out there though." There wasn't time to explain about Xalie but she didn't want them wasting time dealing with her. This might be their best chance to reduce the number of defenders of Erlinda.

He didn't ask, but grabbed some fighters and ran out. Ghortin ran up to her.

"Where are they going? We have to get everyone and everything out of here." He looked winded but uninjured.

Jenna told him about the new wave of fighters. "But you're right, we need to get everyone and everything out of here. I put out that fire, but I have a feeling that it might have been too late." The beams above them groaned as if to reiterate that statement.

Looking at it closer, she was surprised that anything was still standing. "Where's Tireli?"

Ghortin ran his hands through his hair. "Where's any-one? Those people broke through your shield when everyone was sound asleep." He nodded toward the back. "But I think he's back there." He pointed to where a portion of the building had collapsed.

Three Erlindans were moving wood away from a col-lapsed section.

"Damn it, are there people under there? We need to clear this building." Ghortin waved his hand and the wood began to fly away. Two bodies were underneath.

"Tireli?" A woman ran forward and grabbed his broken body. "We need a healer! They're barely alive!"

The second form was a human woman.

Ghortin lifted them, but only enough to get them clear. "We do need a healer, but I'm afraid of jostling them. Both are near death." He kept his voice low so only Jenna heard it.

"Can't you get them out?" The woman who'd run to Tireli pulled on Ghortin's arm.

"We need healers. Moving them is too risky." To accent Ghortin's words, the wooden beams above them groaned.

"They're all outside." Another Erlindan came back but then moved supplies out once he realized there was nothing else he could do.

"*Xalie? We need help.*" Jenna had no idea what Xalie could or couldn't do, but right now she was the only option. The advantage of Xalie possibly scaring the new attackers would vanish once Storm and his fighters caught up to them.

Xalie appeared and looked around. That no one else, even Ghortin, seemed to see her was disturbing. "What do you need? Oh, they are dying. That was uncommon in my time." She floated to Tireli and put her hand over his forehead. It went right through it as she tried to touch him. "That won't work. Come here." She didn't look away from the dying man as she waved Jenna over.

"We'll have to do this together. At least until a certain deity makes me solid again. Hold your hand on his forehead like this. I'll warn you; it's going to feel odd."

"Jenna? What are you doing?" Ghortin came forward.

"It's okay, I have help." Jenna knew he'd assume Typhonel, but there wasn't time to explain. Xalie didn't pause but as soon as Jenna's hand touched Tireli's forehead, the cuari woman cast her spell.

It didn't feel odd, it was as if an electrical jolt shot down from Jenna's shoulder and into Tireli's head. Just when Jenna felt like she couldn't hold it any longer, it stopped and Tireli slowly opened his eyes.

"Her too." Xalie had already moved over to the human woman and they repeated the maneuver as the walls collapsed.

Ghortin shouted a spell that kept the shattered and burnt beams from falling on them, but Jenna could tell he was fighting to hold them up.

"They're stable, help us carry them out!" Jenna grabbed Tireli's shoulders and the woman who'd initially run to him grabbed his feet. Not the best way, but she could sense he wasn't dying anymore, and Ghortin couldn't hold up the entire building for long.

Two more people picked up the fallen woman. With Ghortin pushing them from behind, and the collapsing building following him to reinforce things, they made it outside.

A group of Tireli's people stood guard a few feet from the building. The injured from their prior fights were resting on the dunes. Horses, piles of food, supplies, and belongings sat off to the other side.

The sun was up now and the view would be lovely, aside from the current situation.

There was no sign of fighting near them, but it could be heard.

"We should get the injured and supplies somewhere

safe," one of the guards said right before the building behind them collapsed with a roar.

"I agree. And thank you, but I can stand now." Tireli didn't try to twitch out of their hold but looked ready to. The formerly injured woman appeared recovered as she got to her feet.

Jenna and the other woman set Tireli down and he quickly got up.

"Thank you for saving us, and for what your people are now doing." He looked around. "I'm not sure where to go now."

One of Crell's rangers was standing on guard as well. "I can lead you to the storage shelter. It's messy inside, but there's plenty of room for everything and everyone." He nodded to the horses standing calmly past the rest.

Ghortin might not have been the one who spelled the animals this time, but they were too docile for all the stuff that was going on around them.

"Let's do it." Ghortin turned to Tireli. "Unless you suddenly have a better plan? I can do a sweep for spies, but I think getting away from here while the fight is still going is the best option."

Tireli bent over and grabbed a pile of supplies to load on the horses. "Not at all."

Soon all the horses were loaded with either non-walking injured or supplies. Xalie had vanished after she healed Tireli and the woman, and Jenna hoped that no one would ask her to heal the rest of the injured.

The questioning looks from Ghortin were enough to deal with. He might have thought it was a new trick from Typhonel, but he appeared to be rethinking that.

The sounds from the fighting seemed to be quieting down and Jenna couldn't see any more fighters coming out of Erlinda. She wanted to go help her friends, but Ghortin was the only major magic user here and these people wouldn't be able to go fast.

She would need to keep them safe, while Ghortin made sure no one saw them.

A ranger took the lead as the group finished gathering things. He first led them away from the fighting and Erlinda. Jenna's life had become such that she immediately suspected him. That was until she recalled who he worked with. Crell would never have anyone questionable in her inner circle.

Not to mention that the move was sound as they couldn't go directly to the storage spot.

"Don't worry about the others, I left a spell for Keanin. He'll know where to take them." Unlike everyone else, Ghortin wasn't leading a horse or two, but his hands were busy sending his spells around them as he diffused their passage and searched out watchers.

"Thanks. I was more worried about getting there unseen. And a bunch of other things." She flashed him a smile and then went back to her own spell watch.

A massive yell came from where the fighting had been. It sounded like a good one for whichever side yelled it. Then people were running through the dunes being chased by Storm, Keanin, Crell, and the rest of their fighters.

The attackers kept running down the beach but didn't run toward Erlinda.

CHAPTER FORTY

———◆———

"DO THEY HAVE A SHIP hidden out there that I'm missing?" Jenna watched as the crowd ran away from the city walls and toward the ocean.

"Not that I…oh." Ghortin came to a halt as a massive bluish head and tentacles rose out of the water. The water was deeper there than it appeared, as a thing that size shouldn't be able to be that close to shore.

Storm and his people stopped running and it sounded as if they were trying to call the enemy back.

Without pausing, the remaining attackers ran into the water.

Jenna watched as the dozen or so people were grabbed by tentacles and dragged under the water. They didn't even appear to be fighting back and most dropped their weapons on the beach. "What just happened?"

"I have no idea. But we need to keep moving." Ghortin increased the level of his spells as the entire group jogged. Not everyone had seen what happened, but a feeling of fear seemed to be affecting them all.

The ranger took a few more twists onto different trails, then doubled back into a thick wood and slowed to a walk. He paused in front of a solid appearing cliff face, tapped a series of knocks on a tree, and then stepped back.

The rocks of the cliff moved with a magic that was strong enough to most likely be felt by non-magic users. Mage lights flickered within the cavernous hole as the ranger motioned for everyone to get inside.

Jenna and Ghortin went in with the ranger.

"That is extremely impressive." Ghortin nodded in admiration as he entered.

Jenna could tell he was mentally trying to reconstruct the layers of spells involved.

The ranger knocked on a rock embedded near the door, also in a specific series, and then the wall shut. "Now that Kcanin found out how to open it, that is. But yes, it is impressive." He paused. "What happened out on that beach?"

Jenna looked to Ghortin who shrugged.

"I'll tell everyone when we're unpacked and set. The injured will need a safe place to recover."

Tireli was already doing that and by the time the injured, the horses, and the supplies were sorted, the rock wall at the entrance started to move again.

Jenna and most of the remaining fighters ran over in case it wasn't their people.

The ranger had his bow out and was ready to shoot the first thing through.

Storm raised his hands as he stood at the entrance. "It's only us." He'd seen the ranger first, then everyone else. "We have three injured."

"I'm fine." Edgar was a bit behind Storm and leaning oddly. His left arm was also hanging uselessly from his shoulder.

"Not right now you're not." Jenna ran forward to help him. She couldn't tell if Edgar's odd stance was from the pain he was in because of his arm or some other injury. And as one of the few people more stubborn than Storm, she wasn't going to trust anything he said about what hurt.

He pulled back, but Keanin moved to his other side and blocked his escape.

"You can come with me and be treated, or Keanin will

help you." Jenna kept her smile hidden as Keanin looked ready to reach for Edgar's injured arm.

"I've always wanted to be a healer." Keanin's grin was evil.

"Fine." Edgar rarely sulked, but he was doing it now. His face was also about ten shades lighter than normal as he let Jenna lead him to the group of injured in the back.

"It's my arm—"

"And that's why you look ready to collapse." Jenna gently helped him onto a cot. There was something else wrong. She'd seen Edgar take worse injuries than this and not look half as bad as he did right now. "Is there a healer free?"

Another of Crell's rangers came over. "Yup. What have we here? Shattered shoulder?"

"He got smacked by some guy with a club. Then kept fighting with his other hand." Talia was standing by another injured person but came over. "Too stubborn to stand down."

"I could still—" Edgar screamed once then collapsed as the healer touched his injured arm.

"It's worse than we thought." The man pulled back Edgar's shirt as gently as he could but Edgar remained unconscious. Oozing green pus coated the underside of his arm and side. "We have to get this off, but I need a shield around us."

Jenna was about to ask what it was. It looked far too much like demonspawn blood, but the healer clearly thought it was something else.

Possibly something worse.

"I have a spell around us now." Ghortin pushed the rest of the people back but stayed with Jenna, the healer, Edgar, and Keanin.

"Keanin, you don't need to be there," Jenna said.

"He's my friend and I need to do something. I have magic for a reason."

Talia hadn't moved fast enough to get under Ghortin's shield but she stayed close by. Along with Storm.

"Who saw what attacked him?" The healer asked as he continued removing Edgar's jacket and shirt.

"I did." Talia was the only one to raise her hand. "Things got a little close in the fighting but he was fighting the big guy. Didn't look completely human or kelar and he was twice Edgar's size. That being said, they were evenly matched until that club came down." She paused and tilted her head. "It wasn't a normal club. Damn it, I can see it now, but didn't at the time. Something from the club wrapped around Edgar's arm, and then Keanin blasted the big guy apart with a spell."

Keanin watched as Edgar's shirt was removed with a growing frown. "I don't rem…wait. Yes. I was fighting two others and heard you scream. I sent a spell to help."

Now Talia scowled. "I didn't scream." She shook her head. "Yes, I did. Something out there was messing with what we saw."

"Let's see what we have. Distance from the event and the blocking of this shelter should recover those memories." Ghortin called Crell over to the outer edge of the shield and told her to pass the information along. And have someone make notes of what happened.

Edgar's shirt was now gone, and the odd green goo with it. But his entire injured arm, from shoulder to fingertips had turned greenish gray. Marks on the underside of his arm looked like small, jagged bite marks.

"What got him?" Jenna was terrified for her friend. And that they'd all been out there facing whatever the thing was that did this. And not even known it.

Xalie appeared and hovered over Edgar, even fainter than before. From the lack of reactions, again, no one else saw her. "He was attacked by a naglefish. A creature that died out from this world before Ghortin was born.

It invaded hosts and then used them to destroy others. Many good cuari died before they were stopped."

"You have to help him," Jenna kept her voice low; she realized it looked like she was speaking to no one, but she didn't care. "Do whatever we did saving the others."

"Jenna? Is something wrong?" Keanin didn't move from Edgar but turned her way.

"No. I might be able to help him. Give me a minute." Jenna nodded. "I might appear to be talking to myself—I'm only sorting something out."

"*Maybe we should talk this way.*" Xalie's voice was stronger in her head. "*Quickly.*"

"*Are you leaving us? You can't. Whatever that naglefish did to him, it's killing him. You have to stop it.*"

"*I don't know that I can. I thought that my odd appearance down here was due to the spell on that building as I was being brought down. I now believe that something, or someone, is blocking me. I will be forced back to the chaotic plane soon.*"

"*No.*" Jenna clenched her fists. "*You have to save him.*" She had no idea what this fish thing was supposed to do, but Edgar was moaning and twitching. And the gray-green color appeared to be seeping from his shoulder into his torso.

"*You need to take him outside. Ghortin's shield might not be enough to protect everyone if he explodes.*"

Judging by the looks facing her, Jenna knew she looked a bit mad having this fight inside herself. She didn't care. Edgar was slipping away before her eyes. While she knew there was a good chance that she would lose friends in this fight—she wasn't ready to start now.

"Increase the shield on us please." Speaking out loud felt odd, but Ghortin nodded and the shield became opaque.

"*Do what we did before. I'll touch him and you save him.*"

Before Xalie could respond, the healer yelled and was

flung back against the shield by Edgar. Even though he remained unconscious.

"*You have to do it now!*" Jenna frantically went through any spells she knew that would help, but couldn't find anything.

"*I can't. The kind of healing he would need would be far more invasive.*"

Jenna grabbed on a silent pause. "*There's a 'but' there, I felt it.*"

"*It's a big one. And it could destroy me as well as your friend. But, in my current non-corporeal state, I might be able to take him over. Not fully, and hopefully long enough to save him. However, it could fail and kill both of us. Not to mention nagle-fish work on creating as much bloodshed as possible. We could still explode and kill everyone in here.*"

Jenna looked at Edgar's face. He was a dear friend. "*If there's a chance? For both of you?*"

Xalie watched Edgar carefully, then gave a tight nod. "*I'll still need you to act as the conduit. Move everyone back as much as possible, they must not touch him until he and I have joined completely.*"

Jenna stood next to Edgar and motioned around. "Everyone needs to stay back. As far back as you can go, even everyone outside of the bubble."

Ghortin looked seriously concerned and didn't move.

"I can't explain, this might be the only way to save him…and everyone. You have to trust me." Jenna put as much sincerity into her words as she could. As much as she wasn't a fan of people being able to speak to her in her head, she wished that she and Ghortin could still do so. She was asking a lot from him.

He watched her for a moment and then stepped back. "Move back, everyone."

Xalie lowered herself so she was touching Edgar—or would be if she could physically touch anything. "*Touch his forehead. And you might want to hang onto the cot with your other hand. Oh, and tell the ones in this bubble to not come forward no matter what happens."*

Jenna held her palm over Edgar's forehead, but paused and turned to Ghortin and the others. "No matter what you see, do not come closer. And don't try to stop me."

Ghortin nodded, but his eyes were narrow. He trusted her but was going to get answers about all of this soon.

Jenna touched Edgar's forehead and jumped back. Pain, terror, and horror were all slamming from him into her. She hadn't been able to see the minds of Tireli or the other Erlindan that they'd healed, but she was seeing and feeling everything from Edgar.

She gripped the cot harder as Xalie put her hand over hers. Edgar bucked and screamed as Xalie continued going into his head. But he didn't try to move Jenna's hand. It was as if Edgar knew what was happening and was fighting to help them save him.

He didn't use it often but he was a magic user and might sense some of what they were trying to do.

"I am here with him. Step back to the others and let's see if this saves him or dooms us all."

Jenna quickly moved back against the spell bubble. Xalie still spoke in her head, but Edgar's lips were also moving. If this worked, there was going to be a lot of explaining going on.

Ghortin turned to her briefly before looking back at Edgar. "Something went inside him," he kept his voice lower than she'd probably ever heard.

"Yes. They're trying to save him." As she watched, Edgar's thrashing grew weaker and the healer moved forward. "No. We have to let this run its course. It was a one-time spell that I can't repeat." Stretching reality a bit. But like healing Tireli, she couldn't repeat this without Xalie.

Edgar clenched his jaw and his fists were so tight that they looked more like pale stones. But he didn't get up.

The first sign that something was happening was that his arm began to return to normal. Edgar had dark skin naturally but his arm, torso, and face were a pale, grayish green. They were now coming back to normal.

"What kind of spell did you use?" Keanin was obviously fighting not to run forward toward his friend, but he had one hand ready to spell blast anything that needed it.

"It's complicated." Jenna gave a slight nod. "And I had help." She trusted that her friends would think it was Typhonel and not some cuari whom they had no idea existed, who was fighting to save Edgar.

Keanin was about to ask more but shut his mouth and returned to watching Edgar fight for his life.

Even though she knew it had only been a few minutes, this felt like it was dragging on. Edgar was now sweating profusely and seemed to be muttering spells under his breath.

Jenna hoped that she was the only one who caught that the voice didn't sound completely like Edgar. She also shoved back the fears that were now arising. What did she really know about Xalie? Meith knew her but hadn't seen her in a long time. What if this was another attempt from Sacaranz?

Ghortin took her hand. "I don't know what is going on specifically. But you did the right thing. I couldn't have saved him in time."

Jenna squeezed his hand. "Thank you."

Edgar gave another yell, one also not sounding completely like him, and then collapsed.

"*Are you in there with him?*" Jenna had no idea if Xalie could hear her now even if she was inside of Edgar's mind.

"*I am. I'm not sure how long…*" The words drifted away as Edgar became completely still.

CHAPTER FORTY-ONE

KEANIN TOOK A STEP FORWARD but waited for Jenna to respond. "Is he okay now?"

"I think so? I'm sorry to be so clueless, but this was new to me as well." Jenna, Ghortin, and Keanin all approached Edgar.

Right as he gave a soft snore.

Storm laughed from the other side of the spell bubble. "I heard that. He's asleep. He'll be fine when he wakes up, right?"

Jenna put her hand on Edgar's forehead. It was cool and his color looked good the vicious bite marks on his arm had vanished. "I think so." She nodded to the healer and he ran over and checked Edgar's vitals.

The healer smiled as he looked under Edgar's eyelids and checked his pulse once more. "He's asleep. I'd say you chased out whatever was attacking him."

"Can you drop the spell bubble?" Storm was so close to it that Jenna was surprised the spell hadn't pushed him back.

Ghortin nodded and the bubble fell.

"What did that thing do to him? It messed up all of our memories as well. How can we defend against whatever it was?" Talia joined Keanin but looked like she wanted to go hurt something.

Jenna didn't blame her, but she was going to have to be creative in her answer. "It's called a naglefish. From my studies, they were destroyed thousands of years ago. They were from the sea but could take over land dwellers and create havoc through them. Apparently, they can also disrupt memories of those around them." She hoped that Xalie was inside Edgar still. They needed to find out everything she knew about those things. And so much more.

Altheria swore and pushed her way forward. "Those were nothing more than myths. Like the kraken."

"Which, unless none of you saw what happened on that beach, are not myths." Storm shook his head. "Those invaders raced into the ocean after they saw the kraken appear. They ran for it as if it would save them."

"Most likely the kraken has some magic." Ghortin held up his hands. "And I agree that Edgar appears to be recovering, but I will put a light spell protection on him just in case. Don't worry, if any healer needs to help him, they can. But there are too many unknowns to leave him open. And we need to discuss this away from the injured."

Altheria nodded. "We do."

Ghortin led Jenna, Keanin, Crell, Talia, Tireli, Altheria, and Storm to a slightly closed-off room but held off going inside. Whoever created this place had added areas for privacy.

"This wasn't originally created as a simple storage area." Jenna touched the rock wall. There was so much magic flowing through it that it felt alive. And it was old magic.

"I agree." Storm nodded to the area behind them. "It reminds me of Ghortin's cave—it's a place to hide when all the other options are gone."

Tireli moved more healers into the back treatment areas. He then had some of his people sort into guard teams before he joined Ghortin and the rest. "I overheard that. I couldn't answer one way or another. I was a guard, but unless they let higher-ranking ones know about it, no one told us about this until a week ago." He looked to Talia.

"I knew there was something in place in case of a massive attack, but I wasn't high up enough to know what or where." Talia looked around the walls. "Diath might be able to tell us something about how this was made. Or at least how long ago."

Ghortin nodded.

Her brother was chatting with some of the Erlindans when Talia waved him over.

Diath nodded before they finished explaining what they needed him to do. "I felt it when we came in. Old, old stone magic. I'll start in the back and work my way forward." He left quickly.

They all went inside the room and Ghortin closed the door.

"Now, what happened to Edgar? What was that thing? Is it connected to the kraken?" Storm ignored Keanin's attempt to defend the kraken.

Jeanna didn't blame him. No matter what Keanin had felt about the kraken he and the others freed, they all saw the kraken kill the attackers fleeing the beach. Granted, they'd been enemies of their group, but she doubted the huge sea monster knew that or cared.

The discussion then dove into what was known of naglefish—not much and, as Jenna couldn't get a response from Xalie, she couldn't answer most questions.

"It was believed that the naglefish worked with the kraken," Altheria said. "Or rather, that was what was said in the stories. By the time Erlinda as we know it, came about they were nothing but myths told to scare children from going into the water before they were ready."

"I know little of them." Judging by the scowl on his face, Ghortin's admission was hard. "But Carabella was more of a sea wanderer in the past. Or so I heard. When she vanished, tales of her going up and down the coast were passed along to me."

Talia gave a small smile. "Not that I doubt Keanin, but

he told me that your mother hid from you for a few hundred years?"

"A thousand." Ghortin sighed. "And yes, she has an odd sense of humor. I'll try and reach her later. I don't even know what time of day it is right now."

"Early afternoon judging by when we came in. My teams will scout and report back." Tireli frowned. "I'm not happy about sending anyone out there so soon, but I don't want surprises."

Talia and Keanin shared a look but she spoke. "Keanin and I can set up followers. They're spells that can warn us of visitors."

Tireli narrowed his eyes. "That we can see in here?"

Keanin shook his head. "No, the spells on the rock protect us, but they also block us from seeing outside. But if we line up the follower spells we should be able to tell when they've been triggered. I'd feel it if I stay close enough to the door."

They broke down into discussions as to whether sending out scouts or counting on the follower spells was the best approach. And they left the room. Ghortin waved Jenna off to another small alcove as people disbursed. Storm looked over but when Ghortin shook his head, he stayed with Keanin and Talia.

Ghortin's voice and face were neutral once they were alone. "That wasn't Typhonel who helped you, was it? He might have heard of the naglefish if they were as far back as I believe. But I don't believe he is the one inside Edgar."

Jenna let out a long breath. Xalie hadn't said she couldn't tell anyone. Besides, if Typhonel had sent them back as planned, Xalie would have been visible to everyone. Oh.

"What? I know that look."

"I realized that we might have had an issue with Carabella and the other three cuari once we all rejoined—due to my new friend. She's called Xalie. I met her when I was pulled up to the chaotic plane." Keeping her words low, she gave a brief outline of the true cuari and deity situation.

"There were more than one hundred? And the others have all of their memories? And one of them is inside Edgar?" Ghortin fought to keep his voice down but it wasn't his natural setting and this was big news.

"Yes. And my reaction right now was that I made the connection that the one hundred, like Carabella, can't be introduced to someone like Xalie."

"Oh, dear yes. And once we figure out how to get Carabella's compatriots free, how do we keep the others from leaving the chaotic plane?"

Jenna leaned forward. "Should we? I know, Carabella and the rest could face conflicts if the rest of the non-one-hundred cuari appeared. But we might need them."

"How could we include them in this, if it means perhaps injuring or even killing the one hundred? I doubt that even Rachael or Tor Ranshal would know what that meeting would cause." He patted where his taran wand was and looked around. "Do you see any place even more secure? I'm sure eventually they'll all know we have some far-speaking device. But with the topic matter, I need solitude and the large room didn't seal well."

Jenna looked around. The more she looked, the more smaller spaces she found. It was a place to ride out the end of the world. "Maybe that storage closest?"

"Good spotting. I'll need you to come along in case there are questions. But first, is that cuari inside Edgar still?"

"I think so? There was no way for her to save him like she saved Tireli and the woman. She could speak to me in my head for a bit, but I haven't heard anything since Edgar fell asleep."

Ghortin tugged on his beard. "She might have done what she needed to do then gone back to the chaotic plane. Let's go find out what Rachael and Tor Ranshal know."

It took a few minutes for the wand to connect, and even then Rachael's voice was fainter than usual although Jenna had her head pressed next to Ghortin's.

Ghortin gave a brief explanation of what had happened, including the demonspawn zombies, naglefish, and then a more detailed one about the cuari situation.

Rachael asked a few questions about the attack but stayed silent as the naglefish, kraken, and the truth about the cuari came about.

"This is all new to me. There could be information in those two destroyed cuari books. Tor Ranshal and I have been trying to put them back together, but it is extremely slow going. Why create the Guardians and the Protectors if they were functioning on incomplete information?" There was an anger in her voice that Jenna rarely heard.

Not that she blamed her. Jenna was new to this entire thing and the fact that the ones who were supposed to keep the world from ending hadn't been given thorough information was pissing her off as well. She could only imagine what Rachael and Tor Ranshal were feeling.

"That's what I was thinking. Jenna's mental friend has vanished since he sent Jenna and the cuari back down here."

Jenna held out her hand for the taran wand and gave more information about what they thought Xalie was currently doing. And the state of the chaotic plane.

"Hopefully, this unknown. and previously believed non-existent cuari, is doing what she said. The healing of Edgar is a good sign, but I still have many concerns. The fading of the chaotic plane is not a good sign. Tor Ranshal is in the library with Wilty and the destroyed books, but he did more studies on the plane itself. Nothing should be able to wear it down like that." She was silent for a few moments, then came back. "For now, use your judgment in dealing with Xalie. And work on all magic users with you building up their ability to cast the demonspawn disclosure spell. It will work with the naglefish if there are more, as well as demonspawn. But you must find a way to destroy that underwater portal."

Ghortin shared a look with Jenna. "It's at the bottom of the ocean. Any ideas on how to do that?"

"Jenna, look in the book you have. Near the back. Have you noticed anything odd about that book recently?"

"I think it's jumping things around. And that never happened before." There were plenty of pages and sections in the different books of the cuari that she couldn't open. But either she was losing things, or the pages in this one were changing places. Perhaps even creating new sections, but she had no way to prove it.

"That reconfirms that you need to destroy the ocean portal. The book you have is unique among the original three. It is adapting to the presence of the portal. We believed that all of the three would do so once we were ready to destroy the one in the Markare, but to be honest, information about the ocean portal was not solid. That book should help you."

Ghortin took the taran wand back and tried to ask more questions, but the connection became worse.

Finally, Rachael got tired of the breaking up. "The place you're in is blocking the taran wands, but don't go out of it until you're ready to destroy that portal. I'll contact you if Tor Ranshal or I find anything. Stay safe." Rachael's voice vanished.

"I'm not happy that we'll be attacking a hidden underwater portal without any real information." Ghortin put the wand away. "Your friend knew of it?"

"Yes, it seemed that it was built before the one in the Markare. They'd thought they'd destroyed it by sinking it deep in the ocean." Jenna wanted more information as well. She understood that Rachael was trying to piece things together, but unless there was a spell to give everyone with them gills and a way to blow up the portal, she had no idea what they could do. "Could getting the trapped cuari free help us destroy the underwater portal?"

"I don't know. They will be needed to destroy the one in the Markare. But, as there was little information about this portal at all, who knows?" Ghortin ran his fingers through his hair. "One would think that the defense of all the known worlds would have better instructions."

CHAPTER FORTY-TWO

JENNA HAD NO RESPONSE ASIDE from extreme agreement. As the Protector, it fell on her to save everything—or at least be the driving force behind it.

But it felt like she'd been tasked with building an ornate life-sized castle out of over-cooked pasta.

"So, we stay here and hide but at the same time find out how to destroy a portal at the bottom of the ocean, with kraken and naglefish on the loose, as well as who-ever is controlling Erlinda. Which might include zombie demonspawn." She tried to keep her tone light, but the weight of the truth of it all derailed that.

"I believe you summed it up precisely." Ghortin sighed. "I feel we're attacking a mountain with a soup ladle."

They came out of the small room and saw that Tireli and Keanin were still in debate over what to do for the approaching evening. Talia stood back, watching them with her arms folded. As his Captain, she could order Tireli to follow their lead. But something was holding her back.

"What do you think about that?" Ghortin pointed his chin toward the polite argument.

"Part of me thinks we need to have guards out there. But the other part believes in the strength of this place. We're safe here if the doors stay closed. And if Keanin and Talia can rig something to give warning without risking anyone?" She shook her head. "Enough good people are going to die in the upcoming weeks, I don't think it's worth the risk to lose more now."

"Well put. I will remind them of that. I agree on protection, but Tireli's people have been through a rough week and need some rest. We could use it as well."

Jenna looked over toward the injured. Edgar was visible as most of the healers and patients were avoiding him. "I want to check on Edgar and see if she's still there. If she is, we'll have to tell him when he wakes up, but I'm not sure who else should be told beyond our immediate group." She had nothing against Crell's rangers or Tireli and his people. But this was a weird situation for anyone.

"Agreed." Ghortin puffed up his chest and stomped toward Tireli and Keanin's discussion.

Jenna mentally reached out to Xalie, but there was no response. Judging from a few snorts, Edgar was still asleep and that could be the reason she wasn't responding. Hopefully. She pulled up a chair next to Edgar and gently took his formerly injured hand. It felt right; color, muscle tone, everything felt normal.

What she wanted to do, would be to wake him up and check on him and Xalie. But even before she came to this world with magic, she knew that sleep was an excellent healer.

It did make things more difficult when she needed an awake patient at the moment, however.

"Jenna? I feel your presence, but not much more. Your friend is recovering."

Jenna fought to keep from jumping or reacting as Xalie's faint voice spoke in her head. Apparently, she was still there and could communicate even if Edgar was asleep.

He was going to like this situation even less. Unless Xalie could leave before he woke up.

"How are you doing? I've told Ghortin about you. We also told the Guardians."

"I won't lie, I've been better. Not to mention that a few thousand years in contemplation of the Universe does make one a

bit weak. I don't think I can leave your friend at this time. Or anytime in the near future. He is still incredibly frail."

"*He will be okay, right?*" Jenna felt the trickle of uncertainty in Xalie's mental voice.

There was a much longer pause before Xalie came back. "*I don't know. And, if you've been around Carabella much, you'll know how much cuari hate to admit that. Sleep will help, but beyond that, I have no idea.*"

Her voice faded toward the end and Jenna couldn't call her back. With a heavy sigh, Jenna rubbed Edgar's arm and put more blankets on him.

She walked into Storm as she turned away.

"I was going to ask how he was. But that look isn't good." Storm kissed her forehead and they left the area.

Jenna gave him an incredibly brief update of who was healing Edgar—from the inside. She also told him what Xalie said. "I'm worried for both of them. And that we have to find a way to destroy that portal at the bottom of the ocean. Not that I want it, but I thought there would be more plain fighting." She currently felt like she was standing on a wide beach at low tide and a massive wave was coming toward her and her friends. She rubbed her arms as a chill hit her.

"I don't like this either. Are you sure you're okay?" The concern in his blue eyes brought her back.

"Yes. No. And not a clue. I wish we knew more about getting that portal out of the ocean. Or even finding where it is down there."

Keanin, having won the battle of whether people were going out or not, waved to her and Storm as he and Talia set up cots near the door. Ghortin had gone after a few mages in the corner.

"We've got the followers out there, but I will need to remain near the door for the night. What are you two looking worried about?"

Jenna and Storm pulled up cots as well and Jenna told Keanin and Talia about their issue with the portal in the ocean. It was too open right here to tell them about Xalie yet.

Talia nodded. "My ship, well, technically mine and Diath's ship, is in a harbor with two others. We could triangulate the location of the portal if you have a way to track it."

"That's a great idea about the tracking part. But no idea how to avoid being spotted by the people who took over Erlinda and those kraken." Jenna also had no idea how to track the portal, let alone triangulate that. She dropped her face into her hands. It felt like there was something out of reach that would help. Not with the kraken or the potential demonspawn hordes, but targeting the portal.

"Anything in your book?" Storm asked softly.

She shook her head, then swore, and took it out of her vest. "I'm definitely far too tired. I didn't think of that. Rachael said that this book is changing because of the proximity to the portal. There might not be any information *in* it, but we might be able to use it to help us pinpoint the portal." She sighed. "That will still be at the bottom of the ocean and could be guarded by a group of hungry kraken."

"I know none of you believe me, but I think I can work things out with the kraken." Keanin held up his hands. "They aren't the monsters everyone thinks they are. The one I freed was kept prisoner by those pirates for years. It wanted freedom."

"We did see one eat those people." Talia took Keanin's hand. "Granted, they weren't our people, and some of them might have been demonspawn, but it did use magic to make them run into the ocean."

"We don't know what its intentions were. But it did remove some of our enemies," Keanin added stubbornly. "I think that if we can get the three ships, have mages on each one connected to Jenna and her book, we can find the portal. Once there, we can destroy it."

Keanin sounded so calm and confident that Jenna had to take a closer look to make sure it was him. "We first need to speak to Ghortin. That's some heavy magic, Keanin. And we have no idea what we're doing." Jenna looked around. Ghortin had moved over to Crell and Tireli in a serious conversation.

Tireli wasn't happy about not sending patrol groups out, but this might be something else.

Storm looked over as well and got to his feet. "I'll go and get them. Crell looks ready to start punching Tireli and that won't be good."

Jenna took a few moments to ready her cot. It might be a basic travel cot, but right now it looked like the most beautiful thing in the world. She agreed they needed to work through things tonight, the sooner they could gather the ships and get this plan going the sooner they could go onto the next disaster. She dropped to her cot and sighed.

Talia came to her. "What's wrong?"

"Everything?" Jenna laughed. "Life has been getting far messier than I'd like. It started when I came to this world." No one else was near them aside from Keanin, but she kept her voice low. "I love the people who have come into my life because of it, but it feels like we're in constant danger. Okay, we *are* in constant danger. It gets old and tiring."

"I can only imagine. But this isn't how this world normally is. When this is over, you'll see. I promise to show you some beautiful and peaceful places." Talia took Jenna's hand. "Keanin is lucky to have you in his life. And so am I." Her smile lifted Jenna's spirits. She was glad Keanin fell for someone like Talia. Even if together they sometimes made Jenna nervous.

Ghortin and Crell, with Storm trailing behind, came to

their corner. Storm found some chairs and brought them along but seemed to be trying to stay out of whatever Ghortin and Crell were discussing.

"I don't think we can take that chance," Crell said as she stood by one of the chairs once Storm placed them. She sat only when Ghortin did so.

"But we may not have a choice. We can't be everywhere, you know."

"Trouble?" Keanin looked at Storm first, but he shrugged.

"I have a feeling that there's something wrong with some of Tireli's people." Crell gave Talia a nod. "I know you know Tireli, but how many of the others did you know?"

"Not many, to be honest. I knew of some of them, like Altheria, but there are only two other guards in that group besides Tireli. What do you suspect has happened?" Talia had only met Crell a few days ago, but there was complete trust on her face. If Crell suspected something, she'd look into it without question.

"It's more a feeling than anything direct. Although finding this place wasn't as hard as Tireli indicated. Getting into it was, but with magic users, his people should have at least found this. It shouldn't have taken them a week."

Keanin scowled. "I'd been so caught up in opening it, I hadn't thought of that. But she's right. This wasn't that hard to find. But it took a healthy level of magic to open it."

"I'm not a magic user, so I sensed nothing," Talia said. "What else?"

Ghortin laughed and smiled at Keanin. "I like her, direct and to the point." His smile dropped. "Crell fears that we may be best working on our own."

"It's more complicated than that, but sort of. I believe someone was pushing those attackers to run into the water. Keanin's kraken friend might have been involved as well, but they looked like they had no control over their actions."

"You think someone in here might be a demonspawn?" Keanin's voice was low and he scanned the room.

"I didn't say that," Crell said. "But there is something off about some of the people with Tireli. How easy would it be to slip into a group on the run? Talia is an Erlindan captain and even she doesn't know everyone here."

"Maybe one of his magic users is influencing them for the other side. But what would be the point of hiding this place? A place that the attackers shouldn't even know about?" Jenna agreed with the ease of slipping a spy into a group of fleeing and desperate people. But she didn't see how knowing where this place was would help the enemy.

Unless the plan had been to destroy it.

"We believed there were already insiders when the first attacks came as our group fled. There was no way to find out who though." Talia glanced back at Tireli who was holding his own meeting with a few of his people and Diath.

"Can we pull off our plan without using them?" Storm followed the direction of Talia's look.

"What plan?" Ghortin was slipping into his thoughts but shook himself. "Making plans without me?"

Jenna grinned. "You were busy. But an idea has been proposed about finding the portal." She motioned to Keanin. "You tell him."

"It's your book."

"It's your idea."

"Children, one of you tell me now." Ghortin folded his arms and split his glare between the two of them.

Jenna gave Keanin her best smile. He sighed and then shared the plan with Ghortin.

"That could work. I can create a connection between Jenna, myself, and Keanin. Put one of us on each ship and we follow Jenna's book. But how are we going to avoid the kraken? Or even the Erlinda invaders? They might be focused on building that sea wall, and I assume whatever their reason was for taking over Erlinda. But we can't assume they don't have access to any ships."

"I can take care of the kraken; I know I can communicate with them." Keanin was no longer waiting for others to accept it—it would happen.

Talia gave a slow nod. "I don't want to deplete fighters to run the ships, especially if we're not bringing Tireli's people, but Diath, Crell, and I, plus one or two of her rangers, could do recon on the town. If they do still have ships, they'd be to the south. If we have a low-level magic user who can make fire, besides Diath, and a bunch of arrows, we can make sure they can't go out."

"That's an idea. However, I'm still not hearing how you plan to go down to the portal and destroy it. I believe it needs to be seen to be completely destroyed. Even if we could create magical explosives of some sort, I wouldn't want to take the chance—we need to see it be destroyed." Ghortin looked around the group. "Unless someone has a spell for becoming a fish that I don't know of?"

"Nothing that I know of or that is in the book." Jenna frowned. "Or at least it wasn't there the last time I looked, who knows what's in there now." These books were already difficult to sort, and having one that changed was worse. She put her hand over her mouth as a yawn escaped. "Sorry. I'll get right on checking the book."

"You'll get to sleep. I doubt you got much wherever you went," Crell spoke first, but Storm and Ghortin looked ready to say the same.

Jenna shook them all off. "It's still early and if we want to get this done soon, we need to find out what our options are."

"Soon, not today." Ghortin rose to his feet and stomped over to her. "And you are exhausted. I think that healing Edgar took far more out of you than you know."

"I'm fine. Seriously." That yawn happened too fast for her to block it.

Storm leaned over and rubbed her arm. "You look worn through. Do I have to say royal command?" The look in his eyes said he wouldn't. Probably.

Royal command was a way in which all mages in Traanafaeren were connected to the royal family. If so commanded, any mage, even one like Ghortin, had to follow their order.

Jenna had only felt it once. The battle during the ball in Lithunane. She'd wanted to leave a seriously injured Storm safe behind a table while she crept toward the fighting. He'd used royal command to force her to bring him along with her even though he could barely walk.

It wasn't only because he was stubborn and thought he could still fight—it turned out he wanted to ensure that she was transported to Irundail with him when the rescue spell for the royal family was triggered. He had to be touching her or she would have been left behind.

Even though it was for a good cause, she hated the feeling of that royal command.

"No, I'm good, no command needed. I'll go to sleep." She looked around. Most likely the others would keep talking and Keanin couldn't move far from the door in order to pick up on anything from the followers. Even as tired as she was, sleeping in the middle of a planning committee was going to be impossible.

"Don't worry, you won't miss much." Ghortin smiled. "Crawl under that nice blanket and think sleeping thoughts. You won't hear a thing."

Storm gave her a quick kiss and stepped away from her

cot. A moment later a silence spell bubble, one that even dimmed the light, flowed over her.

A few more serious yawns, most likely encouraged by Ghortin's spell bubble, and she was out.

Chapter Forty-Three

Jenna awoke in a strange place. At first, she thought it might be another twisted version of the chaotic plane. But it was completely lifeless and the sun hung low in the sky but only gave a little light. There was no sun that she knew of on the chaotic plane; it seemed to have an invisible light source.

The ground was covered in gray dust and rubble. "Meith? Are you here?" Her voice echoed oddly in the dusty air. She walked forward slowly. Most likely this was a dream of some sort but there was enough dust on the ground to hide tripping dangers if it wasn't.

A dim light, different from the faint sun, appeared ahead of her and grew as she walked forward. She was on top of a hill. Fires burned below her, but she recognized the decimated skyline.

Los Angeles.

"This isn't funny. Whoever brought me into this dream, take me back." Again, her words felt as if they were echoing off the silence itself. "Okay, so what did this? How can I stop it? If you're not going to be helpful, knock it off."

The last time she'd seen an alternative Los Angeles, it was falling prey to attackers from other worlds. This destruction was the aftereffect of Earth being on the wrong side of that battle. If she focused, she saw downed jets littering the land. Also burnt.

She didn't need to see this. She already knew that if they failed to destroy the portal in the Markare, her former world, and all the rest of the worlds beyond it would also fall.

So why would someone want her to see this? It could be simply a nightmare, but it felt far more real than that.

"Okay, I've seen this now. You destroyed my world. What are you expecting from me?" She found a large lump of flat metal, dusted it off, and sat. She'd thought that her prior visits to her world being under siege had something to do with someone on the chaotic plane. Now she wasn't so sure.

"You don't understand. This is what we need you to provide. You weren't pulled into that Jhilax body by accident. Sacaranz didn't know he was only a tool. He still is. But we can give you this world, safe and intact. If you leave the portals alone. There is more at stake for everything than you know. Although this is what would feed us." A translucent massive hand waved toward the remains below them. "This is what we will give you. You can bring your loved ones, they will be changed to fit your world, but they will be with you." The image before her changed so dramatically that the sudden brightness hurt her eyes. Los Angeles, as seen from the Griffith Observatory, sprawled out before her. Cars and people went about their business. She felt a pang of sorrow at the place she no longer called home, but it vanished quickly.

"Who are you?" She hadn't missed the dismissive way the voice spoke of Sacaranz. And the words of her being chosen, and not simply an accident pulled out of her former world by Sacaranz, rang true as well. She assumed that the word Jhilax meant mindslave as that was what fit.

"We are beyond your concerns. Your confusion and loss is clouding your mind. Return to sleep. You have one day to decide."

"No. You need to tell me more." Jenna ran to the edge of the hill. "Tell me now. I can't do what you—" The rest of her words were swallowed and she woke up in the dark. Again.

She rolled out of her cot, wondering if whoever was messing with her was still doing so. Her eyes adapted and she saw small, mostly dimmed mage lights hovering above. She checked where the spell bubble had been with her hand first, but there was nothing. She'd probably been asleep for a few hours. Long enough for everyone else to drift off.

Checking on Storm, Keanin, and Talia showed they were all alive and sleeping soundly. From the sounds filling the cavern, almost everyone was.

Aside from Ghortin. She saw him in the small room near the entrance. Mostly hidden by the walls around him, he had the door cracked and the heavier glows within indicated that he might be reading.

Jenna patted her vest pocket but her cuari book was still in place. She knocked softly and heard a soft muffled noise that sounded like swear words.

Ghortin stuck his head out, looked around the darkened cavern, then pulled her inside and shut the door.

He also turned up the mage lights. He'd pulled in a cot and a box for a nightstand. The book he had was old and familiar. He hadn't said he'd brought his cuari book along.

"I thought you couldn't recall enough of that book to read it?" Jenna looked at the gray book of the cuari. When she'd first come to this world, Ghortin had been working on sorting out this cuari book. At the time, he didn't know the backstory of the cuari or what the book truly pertained to. When he was returned to his body after having it stolen by Sacaranz, he couldn't even open it.

He was even more upset about that when he was told what the book was and the true nature of the cuari.

"Yes, well." Even in the mage lights, Jenna saw his face

darken in a blush. "Rachael and I were discussing it in Irundail. She suggested that the book simply didn't know who I was. My body did go through some adventures, after all. So, I've been carrying it with me for the past week. Didn't open until this evening though."

"That's great. Why do you look like you're embarrassed? Isn't this a good thing?"

"It is. I still don't recall it, but we're getting along much better now." He smiled, then let it fade. "Fine. *I* apparently set the lock on this book. I'm the one who made it so that I couldn't open it. And I should have noticed my signature on the lock immediately, but didn't."

"Things happen. Look, you said yourself that you still don't recall any of it. How could you think that you would have spelled it?"

"My spell lock had my mark on it. But never mind that now, we're back together. Although, shouldn't you still be asleep?" He switched his annoyance from himself to her.

"I was. Then I had a weird nightmare that I don't think was all in my head." She explained everything to him. "The voice said that it was a Jhilax body that I'd been put into. And that they did it, not Sacaranz."

Ghortin's frown got deeper the further into the story that she got. But he waved his hand at the term. "Do you mean Jhil*ax*?" His emphasis on the last bit was more like the voice's, than hers.

"Yes. It means mindslave, right?"

"Sort of. The term is older than the mindslaves. Qhazborh didn't begin calling for those sacrifices until a thousand years ago or so. But the concept was around long ago. Did the being who spoke to you say who they were?"

"No…wait." Jenna hadn't heard it at the time, but echoes of the voice were bouncing around her head. "I think it was Qhazborh. Or the deities on the side of evil who are creating that single persona." She rubbed her arms as a freezing feeling crept through her. "It was them, wasn't it? In my head. They have the ability to do what they said." She looked around. "Mind if I sit on your cot? I don't feel so good."

Ghortin motioned her over. "I haven't heard of deities popping up in dreams. Aside from those who visit their dedicated followers." He narrowed his eyes, a thing he'd started doing when he didn't have room to pace. "I wonder if Tor Ranshal could bring the taran wand to Dantil. His group knows more about all the gods and goddesses than probably anyone else alive today." He looked over at Jenna. "But, in the morning. And, if you can't fall back asleep, I can make a potion for you. Might be a good idea anyway to keep unwanted visitors out of your head. We won't be going after the portal tomorrow, but there will be a lot of preparation work taking place before then. We need you rested." He spoke a few soft words and a clear glass appeared in his hand.

"No swirling colors?" Jenna didn't reach for it. Rachael had demonstrated that potions didn't have to be nasty, but Jenna wasn't certain that she completely trusted Ghortin on this.

"Now, now. I was trying to make a point at that time. This is simply to help you sleep and to keep interlopers out of your head."

He didn't sound as sure about the second line as he did the first, but Jenna would take it. She took the glass and downed it. It tasted like a glass of water. Then she tried to get to her feet and her knees buckled.

"I do need to get back to my cot, you know." She didn't feel that tired, but an odd numbness moved through her body.

"That's how we know it worked. Not a fret, I can help get you back." Ghortin lifted her off her feet.

Her eyes slammed shut the moment her head hit the pillow.

Whatever Ghortin put in that drink, it knocked her out. Not only did she not have any weird dreams, but from the sounds around her when she finally did wake up—everyone else had been awake for a while.

The smell of breakfast beckoned to her, along with the fact that everyone, even Keanin, was near the back where a kitchen was created.

She smoothed her hair as best she could—she'd deal with it better after food. They had discovered a large bathroom and shower area, but she was starving and needed to eat before anything else.

Storm grinned and patted at a place next to him. One that already had a plate piled high sitting there. "Ghortin mentioned that you'd be a bit late. I got you this. Tea as well."

Jenna noticed that most folks looked like they'd already showered. Her stomach let loose a huge rumble as she sat—she'd made the right choice.

Keanin was on her other side and leaned in. "He also said that you'd had a magic-fueled adventure last night and would be starving." The question lingered in his golden eyes.

"He was right, I guess." She inhaled a piece of toast. "I hadn't thought about it pulling at my magic, but I'm feeling it now." The drain was probably also from the amount of magic she'd used in general yesterday. "But I have a feeling he'll want me to wait until we're all together to talk about it."

Keanin sighed and sat back. "I figured that might be the case."

Discussion around her was mostly light and Talia and Tireli were comparing guard stories with the rest of the former Erlindan guards adding in.

"Is Edgar still asleep?" Once the edge was off her hunger, she realized he was missing.

"Yes, although I think Ghortin might have helped with

that," Crell said from the other side of Storm. "The healers said he was starting to wake up about an hour ago. Ghortin went over to see and Edgar dropped back to sleep. Ghortin said he wasn't ready yet."

The wording caught Jenna's ear. "That Edgar wasn't ready or that Ghortin wasn't?" Since Ghortin was the only one who knew about Xalie, it could be him.

"I'd originally thought he meant Edgar." Crell tilted her head to look at Ghortin down at the end of the table in conversation with Altheria and Diath. "But he had an odd look on his face as he said it."

"It's hard to tell what he's thinking sometimes." Jenna glanced at Ghortin but he gave no indication that he noticed. He might have sensed something or just wanted Edgar to remain unconscious until Jenna was able to help.

The rest of breakfast went quickly and seemed to be void of any intense conversations. Jenna knew the rest of the day would be spent in planning.

People began getting up and taking their dishes when Jenna finally caught Ghortin's eye.

He'd been smiling but it turned to a worried frown when he looked her way. Something was very wrong.

Chapter Forty-Four

—◆—

"THAT'S NOT A GOOD LOOK." Keanin remained next to her as Storm and the others left. He turned toward Ghortin. "Neither is that one. By the way, Ghortin told me to stay with you, that he had tasks for us after breakfast."

"He has something on his mind, that's for sure." Jenna guessed that there was something wrong with Edgar, but she'd wait until they had more privacy to bring it up. Ghortin went back to whatever he was talking about with Altheria. Diath had already left to join a group near the weapons.

Crell stopped by, grabbed Jenna and Keanin's plates, and tilted her head toward Ghortin. "His mageness would like you two to wait for him in his room."

"Thank you." Jenna turned to Keanin. "We'd better not keep him waiting."

"But he's still sitting there." Keanin might still have some lingering magic discussion fears, judging by the way he hesitated.

"Yup. And he'll be annoyed if we don't beat him there. Come on, you can bring your tea with you." Jenna got to her feet. Ghortin still wasn't looking their way, but she had a feeling he knew she'd gotten up.

Keanin kept his cup of tea but got to his feet before she'd taken two steps. "You know what he wants to talk to us about." It wasn't a question.

"I have a good idea. And it is something that should be spoken of in private."

Keanin continued to sip his tea, but he clearly had more questions. That was one thing that remained constant with this new Keanin, always nosy. Even when he wasn't certain that he wanted to know—he *wanted* to know.

Of course, the old Keanin would have found out the information, and then run back somewhere safe to wait it out.

Like under a pile of covers in his locked bedroom.

This new Keanin was more likely thinking of charging into a fight first, then finding out what the problem was.

Jenna hoped he would end up somewhere in the middle.

Ghortin, Altheria, and three chairs floating in the air followed them into Ghortin's annexed room.

Ghortin triggered the mage lights, shut the door, and motioned to the chairs that had now landed. "Please take a seat. The four of us are the strongest magic users in this group and I need all of us to have the same information before we head forth into battle tomorrow. I was hoping we might have a day or two beyond that before tackling everything, but I now feel that we're limited in time."

Jenna smiled at Altheria. She agreed that having the strongest mages aware of what was going on was important—but they'd just met Altheria.

"I know, I know." Ghortin waved his hand between Keanin and Jenna at their unspoken questions. "But I trust Altheria. And I believe we'll need her. I've already told her of the cuari and our situation—the real situation. But, I wanted Jenna to tell you about Edgar and what happened to her last night."

Jenna lifted her eyebrow at that but Ghortin gave a reassuring nod. Trusting someone new wasn't high on her great idea list. But, she did trust Ghortin. She made the tale of Xalie as brief as possible—pointing out that there were cuari like her who were not part of the captured one hundred—was unknown to them as well until yesterday.

"There's a disembodied cuari inside of Edgar? Is that a good idea?" Keanin asked.

"That would have probably been the only way to save him if the tales of the naglefish were true," Altheria answered before anyone else. "Although not something that would have been thought possible unless one could find one of the one hundred." She turned toward Ghortin. "I know your mother is one, but they can be extremely capricious."

Ghortin gave a barking laugh at the understatement then nodded for Jenna to respond.

"That was what Xalie said. She was hoping she could simply heal him and then leave, but it seemed like it was an ongoing fight to save him." Jenna turned to Ghortin. "Is that why you helped him remain unconscious?"

Ghortin nodded. "He was waking up, but as I'm not sure who was going to wake up, I thought it better to wait for you. Plus, once he is aware, I doubt he's going to be happy with his mental companion."

"I agree with him on that." Jenna laughed at the look on Ghortin's face. Then turned to Altheria. "I doubt he told you about when his body was kidnapped and I got to have Ghortin in my head for a month or so. It was *interesting*." Jenna put a heavy emphasis on the final word. If Ghortin wanted Altheria to be involved completely— it would be completely.

There wasn't much more to say about Edgar and Xalie, at least not until they knew what was going on and who was going to wake up. Jenna had tried to mentally reach Xalie since she woke up, but there was no response. Ghortin wanted to wait until everyone else was sorted into their tasks for tomorrow and busy working on them before trying to wake up Edgar.

Altheria looked around Ghortin's room. "Since we're not certain who will be waking up, nor that everyone else should know, maybe we should bring him in here before waking him? Or them?"

"Excellent point. Yes, we can say it's for the safety of everyone. Unknown repercussions of naglefish poisoning and the whatnot." Ghortin nodded.

Jenna figured most people wouldn't ask, but Ghortin always wanted to have a cover story at the ready.

"Now, what happened last night that left Jenna in a serious magic-fueled hunger even though I know she didn't go anywhere?" Keanin gave her his best glare but softened it with a smile.

Jenna ran her hand through her hair—which reminded her that before they brought in Edgar and woke him and Xalie up, she wanted a shower. It was one thing to rough it on the road, she'd gotten fairly good at that. But it was a completely different situation when there was a magically powered shower nearby. "You know I've had visions and trips to the chaotic plane." Keanin nodded and a nod from Altheria pointed out that Ghortin had filled her in on that as well. "Last night I went to my former world and it wasn't pretty." She filled them in on the important parts and watched as Altheria's face grew pale.

"They showed you a future seeing and it was from Qhazborh?" Even though Altheria had been told about the groups of deities making up each of the three religious names, using one per group was still easier.

"I guess that's what it was. They said the image they showed me would fuel them when it became reality, but they were willing to leave that world alone and bring over everyone I cared about from this world if I stopped trying to close the portals."

"They don't know you very well, do they?" Keanin said with a small grin.

"No, they don't. And the fact that they offered me my

old world to save instead of this one, reiterates that this world and the portals are key to everything. The images they made me live through would only happen if this place fell. And I don't think we're planning on letting that happen." Jenna still felt sick about the images she'd walked through. But the part of her that insisted they would never become real was keeping her calm. For now.

There were a few more minutes of discussion before Ghortin finally got to his feet. "They are sending scouts out to investigate the area around Erlinda. Storm and Talia are leading one group and Tireli and Crell are the second. I wanted to wait until we were ready to attack to leave this place. But we need more information about the town, the ocean, and those ships before we can launch."

"I should go with them." Keanin was on his feet the moment Ghortin said what the teams were that were going out.

"No, you're needed here. You all *can* come with me to send magic scans out as we open that door, however. Then we'll bring Edgar back to this room." Ghortin opened the door and held it for them to go out.

A group was gathering at the door, all dressed in dark clothing. Storm, Talia, and Crell must have borrowed what they wore, as the clothing they had was limited to what they'd been wearing.

Keanin nodded at the clothing. "There was a supply of clothing in the back areas too. Not fancy and most from any time in the past hundred years, but it would be good to have options before we get back to Irundail."

"That's for sure. I'll hunt some down before I get my shower." Jenna turned to Ghortin. "I'll make it fast, but I'll be much happier if I shower before we work on Edgar. Besides, you're not ready to bring him in yet." Most of the people were up front, but there were still many milling around in the back. Even though she figured that Ghortin would keep Edgar in his slumbering state while he moved him, there was always the chance that something would go wrong.

Ghortin folded his arms. "Fine. We should take positions in front of our two groups and check things out before they leave. I'm glad that your follower spells didn't trigger anything during the night, Keanin. But there could still be other magics floating about."

"Not a problem. I'll pull them back as our people go out." He was already on his way to Talia, and Jenna followed over to Storm.

"Off on adventures?" They'd put some plant darkening on their faces, which worked aside from the fact that Storm's blue eyes appeared luminescent. Hopefully, a pair of floating bright blue eyes in the deep woods wouldn't be suspicious.

He engulfed her in a hug. "Yup. I understand you have some adventures of your own going on here. And already had some?" Storm was getting better at not being overprotective, but there was still concern in his voice.

Jenna stretched up for a quick kiss. "We can sort things out when you get back. Take care."

"I will. I love you."

"I love you too." Those words still got her each time she spoke them. "Crell looks ready to jump out and leave now. Better do our check."

Jenna, Keanin, Altheria, and Ghortin all stepped out the door. They hadn't planned who would take which section, but they covered the woods in front of them. It was a simple magic searching spell that was only useful in unpopulated areas.

Or rather, areas that shouldn't be populated.

Jenna felt a slight tug, just as she was pulling back her spell. She sent it back out, but even after covering all of the area in front of her, she didn't feel it again.

"Something?" Ghortin was next to her and peered out both magically and visually into the woods.

"I don't know. I felt a brief pull over there. But then it was gone." She stared at the area the tug had come from, but there wasn't any movement.

Ghortin also stared at the section she pointed to. "It could have been a fluke or a mage escaping Erlinda. Our people are going toward town, not away from it. But I'll warn Diath and the other mage they have with them."

Final instructions were confirmed, there were five people in each team and each had a mage. The plan was to circle the town—better done at night, but this would give them a clearer idea of what they were facing during the day. Neither group was to move far out of the protection of the woods until they traveled out of view from the Erlinda walls and rejoined at the cove with the ships.

Jenna watched them until they faded from view and Ghortin forced her to close the massive door.

"They will be fine." His look was gentle and she knew he meant Storm more than anyone else.

"I know, but I don't like us splitting up." She raised her hand to stop what he was going to say. "I also know that it sounds like I'm being more protective than Storm. But I can't shake the feeling that we'll need everyone when we take down that portal in the Markare." A part of her wanted them to be on their way to do it now. Waiting for the right time was difficult. On the other hand, she also wasn't certain that she felt ready.

And the growing feeling that she was going to have to lose someone she loved to destroy that thing made her sick to her stomach.

"Listen to your feelings. More than most you have unique tides pulling at you. But don't let them control your emotions." Ghortin tilted his head. "I believe you wanted to take a shower before we tackle the Edgar situation?"

"Thanks. Are you going to contact Rachael and have her take the wand to Dantil? Qhazborh taking direct action like my dream is disturbing." More like terrifying, but disturbing work.

Ghortin patted his vest pocket. "That was next on my list. Altheria will work on moving more people to other parts of the shelter so we can relocate Edgar without notice."

"I already took a shower," Keanin said as he came over to them. "What should I do?" He'd stayed near the door until the groups were out of sight as well.

"I think you should go sit by your friend, Edgar. Don't break the sleep spell, but being there might give him comfort."

Keanin shrugged and walked back toward the healing area. Jenna followed him to get some fresh clothes and towels.

"How are you really holding up?" He got out before she could ask him the same thing.

"As well as can be expected. That nightmare last night was more about trying to get into my head than any real offer of a deal. I have no doubt that Earth would still be destroyed if they won, regardless of what they agreed to. Just maybe after everywhere else." She bundled the clothing and towels close and leaned forward. "How are you doing?"

"Ah, sister of my heart. You always see right through me." He took a deep breath, then exhaled slowly. "I'm holding on. Talia taught me some deep breathing tricks when we were going to Craelyn, they seem to help." He gave her a tight hug and then went to Edgar.

Jenna's shower was quick and uneventful. And she worked on forcing the images of her nightmare out of her head. They kept transposing themselves over images from this world—just without the advanced technology.

She wasn't letting Qhazborh or Sacaranz take up room in her head unless it was finding a way to destroy them.

Ghortin had the door to his room shut, most likely

discussing things with Rachael or Dantil. Jenna raised her hand to knock, then stopped. She knew that there were some things they felt better about her not knowing right now. She didn't always agree, but at the moment she had enough on her plate. Altheria was in a low discussion with one of the healers over a female patient. Keanin was speaking to a sound asleep Edgar. From his wild hand gestures, Keanin was regaling the unconscious man with some elaborate tale.

"Has he joined in?" Jenna asked as she came over.

"No, but I could tell he was terribly impressed with my story." Keanin lowered his voice. "Or maybe *she* was."

Ghortin came out of his room and headed their way. He didn't look happy but she knew him well enough that whatever got him in such a state, he wasn't sharing until he'd processed it further.

Altheria ended her conversation with the healer and joined them. "I told Salin the healer that we would be taking Edgar to Ghortin's room for safety. She agreed and would tell everyone to stay clear of your room. She did point out that it was a storage closet and there were larger rooms in the back."

"I know, but this one suits me. And I prefer to be near the door." Ghortin walked around Edgar slowly, then muttered a spell and Edgar rose off the cot. "Now, if Altheria will lead and Jenna and Keanin walk on either side, I will maintain the spell from the back."

Jenna knew he wasn't concerned about his levitation spell, but he kept a close eye on Edgar as they moved forward.

"You're afraid there might be someone else in there?" Jenna kept her voice down as they quickly walked to the room.

"There might be. I am even more concerned about it since I spoke to Rachael and Dantil. Especially Dantil. We have underestimated the collected knowledge of the helaermages—badly. He pointed out that the dream that attacked you shouldn't have been able to get inside this shielded shelter."

Which meant that others could have been under attack also. Jenna tried to reach Xalie and then grabbed one of Edgar's hands. She wasn't certain what she could do if something else was in there with them, but she felt better touching him.

They got into the room without incident and Edgar gently drifted down to the cot.

Ghortin not only shut the door, he put a few layers of magical shields and locks on it. No one was getting in, or out, without his approval.

Jenna had a bad feeling that it might be more on the side of something getting out than anyone getting in.

Chapter Forty-Five

"I NEED TO TOUCH HIM TO release the spell. Jenna, stay near me. Keanin and Altheria, stay near the door. If there is someone other than Edgar or the cuari inside him, they cannot be allowed to leave this room." Ghortin waited until everyone took their positions before approaching Edgar.

"What do you want me to do?" Jenna asked. Edgar appeared to simply be sleeping.

"Be ready if anything goes wrong." Ghortin focused on Edgar in such a way that Jenna figured he wouldn't be able to clarify that.

She pulled up the freeze spell. She would be safe, but the other three would be frozen if she needed to use it against Edgar. But it was the best way she knew of stopping Edgar if he or Xalie weren't the ones inside him right now.

Ghortin repeated his wakening spell twice before Edgar's right hand twitched and he moved as if coming out of a deep sleep.

Jenna tried calling out to Xalie again, but although she seemed nearby, there was no response.

Edgar groaned and rubbed his injured arm. Jenna moved closer as he opened his eyes.

"How are you feeling?" What she wanted to ask was *who* was waking up—but better to start with basics. If this was Edgar he might not be aware that Xalie was with him.

Or Xalie could have vanished during the night. She

felt that it was important for her to come here, but since she hadn't made it fully down she might have ended up being drawn back to the chaotic plane.

"Like a herd of horses ran over me. Repeatedly. With brick-filled wagons behind each one." He squinted his eyes open and then dropped his left hand over them. "And I might have been drinking heavily. The last I recall was chasing those demonspawn monsters into the ocean. Everything else is a blur." He sounded like Edgar.

She turned to Ghortin, but he shrugged. And didn't release the spells he was holding ready.

Jenna held the hand that wasn't covering his eyes. "You nearly died. You were attacked by a sea monster and almost didn't make it. Is it too bright for you?"

"Yes. It's painful."

Ghortin dimmed the mage lights.

And Edgar glowed.

"I don't think that's good." Jenna didn't release Edgar's hand, but neither he nor Xalie should be glowing.

"He was attacked by a night visitor. I fought it off, but part of it remained. I'm not strong enough to save him from it."

Jenna sighed in relief at Xalie's voice—not that she couldn't stop whatever was after Edgar, but that she was still there.

"What do you need me to do?" Jenna saw the concern on the faces of the other three, but there wasn't time to confer about it.

"Shut us down. I see a gotha spell in your mind. A freezing spell. Shut us down now!"

Xalie's words hit her hard with a feeling of truth. Edgar was now tossing, turning, and glowing but his eyes were closed and his fists were clenched. He had enough magic ability that if he were being taken over, he could cause serious damage. With or without access to Xalie's abilities.

"I'm sorry." Jenna got out before releasing the freezing

spell. Ghortin, Keanin, and Altheria looked shocked as they froze, but Edgar fought through it.

Jenna couldn't cast that spell again for a few hours, but she could try to trap it with him and hope that would make it strong enough to stop what was happening. She created a spell bubble, sloppier than Ghortin's but when she slammed it over Edgar and the cot, he stopped moving.

And a layer of ice formed on the inside of the bubble.

There was a reversal spell for the freeze spell. But she hadn't tried it yet since it was constructed more as a blast like the original spell was. She'd end up releasing Edgar as well as the others if she cast it. She had no illusions about the strength of her spell bubble, she knew it wouldn't hold against a concentrated attack.

She stood next to Ghortin and took a deep breath. If she could focus the reversal spell on him only it might work. He could have another idea on how to resolve this without exposing Edgar.

Or letting whatever was in him finish its task. Before she'd released the freeze spell, she'd seen the wards that Ghortin put up around the door flare as if they'd been magically tested.

She focused on reversing the freeze spell, but not releasing it from her mind as she grabbed Ghortin's arm with her hands.

"—are you doing?!" He'd been in mid yell, at least he'd intended to be, when her freeze spell stopped him.

Jenna caught him as he stumbled forward a step. He'd probably also been running forward at the time. "Sorry. Xalie said that Edgar was attacked last night and that spell was the only way to stop it."

Ghortin looked around, noticing that Keanin and Altheria were still frozen. Then he took in the frost-encased spell bubble around Edgar. "Interesting. I've not seen this spell be reversed like this. I assume that you added the bubble as whatever is inside Edgar fought through the freeze spell?" Even in a deadly situation, Ghortin's love of knowledge was strong.

"He was fighting through. Xalie was worried about whatever attacked him last night." She shrugged. "As for the reversal spell change? It was a shot in the dark."

"Your unorthodox way of using magic has helped us once again. Can you wake the other two the same way? We will need to get to the bottom of whatever is attempting to control Edgar, but I think we need all four of us to do it."

Jenna repeated her focused release on Keanin first and then Altheria. She quickly told them what happened while Ghortin marched around the frozen spell bubble glaring at it.

Jenna knew he was working through something. She hoped it was going to be enough to save Edgar. And Xalie. There was no idea what would happen to her if Edgar died, but it wouldn't be good.

Ghortin looked up at them. "Jenna, stand near his head. I'll take his feet, Keanin take his left side, and Altheria his right. I have no idea what will happen, but I've reinforced the protections in this room. When Jenna drops her spell bubble everyone needs to put up their personal shields, but stay connected. Keep yourselves protected." He rubbed his hands together, then nodded to Jenna.

Jenna dropped the spell bubble and threw up her shield.

Edgar didn't move and she thought that maybe her freeze spell was holding. Then his eyes opened. His arms were covered in frost, but he was waking up and fighting through the spell.

Ghortin grinned from his place at Edgar's feet. "Whom do we have the honor of addressing?"

"You can't fight us. We will win. We have always won and will do so again. Stop going after the portals and we will save your people."

It was an odd voice, made up of many and strangely robotic to Jenna's ears. But it was covering the same core points of Qhazborh when they'd taken her on her nighttime adventure.

"Now, that's where you are horribly mistaken. You have no idea who you're up against. You have already failed; you just don't know it." Ghortin lashed out with a spell that cracked through Jenna's freeze spell.

"*Tell him to keep doing it. You have to help him!*" Xalie's voice was stronger.

"Help Ghortin! But don't drop your shields." Jenna trusted Xalie, but going in shieldless would be madness. Jenna took Keanin and Altheria's hand and both of them grabbed Ghortin's. A wave of power flowed through the room.

"You cannot do this. This is our timmmmeeee." The last word stretched out in a wail and Edgar's body arched up painfully then crashed down.

"You have no ground to stand on." It was Xalie's voice but coming through Edgar. It was out loud and Jenna felt the powerful spell behind it. "Go now." The force of power coming from Edgar-Xalie not only expelled whatever was inside Edgar, but slammed Jenna, Ghortin, Keanin, and Altheria back against the walls.

Then the mage lights extinguished.

"Hello? Who's out there?" It was Edgar but Jenna had never heard him sound that exhausted. "Keanin? Jenna?"

Ghortin raised more mage lights and revealed a confused and pale Edgar sitting up on his cot.

"I'm glad to see you all. I had some weird dreams and feel awful."

Ghortin didn't get to his feet, but gave a small smile and waved his hand. A clear drink appeared near Edgar. "This will help, and they weren't all dreams. Drink it all and we'll explain afterward." He looked at the other three. "How are all of you feeling?"

"My aches ache. Is Edgar clear now?" Jenna also responded from her seat on the floor. She was dizzy, exhausted, and a bit sick to her stomach. Getting to her feet right now wasn't going to happen.

"Am I *clear*? Of what?" Edgar paused drinking but resumed at Ghortin's glare.

Ghortin waved some of the mage lights closer to Edgar and they slowly circled him. "It's a long tale, but yes, I believe so."

"Everything hurts, but I seem to be intact." Keanin got to his feet and then sat back down. "Nope, too much effort right now."

Altheria shook her head. "I've been living a quiet and uneventful life for decades. This is a bit more excitement than I'd like. But never fear, I'll see this through to the end. The war or myself. Whichever comes first. As long as we don't have to get up anytime soon."

"I'm assuming that with the level of magic in this room, something bad happened?" Edgar finished his drink and the glass vanished. Like everyone else, he remained seated.

"It did indeed. Jenna? Can you sense anything?" Ghortin's pointed look was asking if she could reach Xalie.

Jenna shrugged and mentally called out for Xalie. She was hoping for a ghost-like form or even better her to have found a way to solidify.

"I am here. The damage to your friend from the naglefish is still lingering. Nothing should be able to use it to take him over again, but he is still in danger."

Edgar didn't jump off the cot, but his entire body tensed. "What the hell was that?"

Jenna winced. She hoped that by speaking this way he might not notice. "It's a long story."

"I heard a woman in my head. A strange woman who said that your friend is still in danger." Edgar was one of the most balanced people Jenna had met in this world or her old one. But he didn't look it now. "Why am I hearing her? Why aren't they?" He clutched the edge of the cot *but used his chin to indicate the other three.*

"I am sorry you found out this way. I am called Xalie and I am a friend of Jenna's. It's complicated, but I am a cuari." By the looks on all three faces, this time Ghortin, Keanin, and Altheria all appeared to have heard her in their heads.

"How did she get in my head?"

"She saved your life." Ghortin got to his feet and came over to the cot. "You were dying after being attacked by a naglefish, an ancient and deadly foe. One supposedly destroyed by the cuari before their battle with the deities. Xalie is not one of the one hundred, and her being down here is a long tale that won't answer anything." He put both hands on Edgar's shoulders. "None of us could save you. She was our only chance. You were dying."

"He's still dying. I could slow it and throw out the recent attacker. But unless I regain my full strength I can't completely heal him."

"You can't see inside my mind? My thoughts or memories?" Edgar was still tense, but he sounded a bit more like himself.

Jenna got to her feet and went to him.

"I can't see anything you do not want me to see. Except, I can see your health. I can read your body and am constantly adjusting to keep it working. The strand of poison from that naglefish is no longer as strong as it was. But it is still deadly if left alone," she paused, *"but I believe in free will above everything else. If you want me to leave, I will do so."*

Edgar looked at Jenna and she nodded. "She's even more determined than Carabella. And she means it. She will leave you even if it means both of your deaths."

"Both? She's only alive through me?"

"Not really, but I've never been incorporeal before. I've also been living on the chaotic plane for a few thousand years. I was growing weaker before I stepped in to save you. However, this is up to you. It is your body."

Edgar took a deep breath, then nodded. "Okay. I have an invisible cuari in my head. Might help keep us out of trouble, right?" His stomach rumbled loudly. "I'm not sure about her, but I'm starving."

Keanin helped Altheria up and Ghortin released the seals on the door.

Edgar took a deep breath, jumped off the cot, and folded to the floor.

Jenna helped him up and made him lean on her with her arm around his waist and his around her shoulder.

"I'm not responsible if Storm gets mad and starts accusing me of trying to flirt with his fiancée." Edgar's laugh was good to hear.

"You're safe, he's out stalking Erlinda with Talia and others." Keanin had seemed okay when they'd left—mostly—but now the Edgar drama was over he was looking toward the doors so often he tripped on their way back to the food area.

"If I am no longer needed, I would like to prepare for tomorrow." Altheria nodded to Edgar. "I'm glad that you have come back."

At Ghortin's nod, she left.

Jenna led Edgar to a bench and Keanin and Ghortin brought over a mass of food. Most of it was cold, but Edgar dove in anyway. He was only a few inches taller than Jenna but he could put away a lot of food under normal circumstances.

Right now, he looked ready to keep eating until he hit the table. He waved a free hand as he swallowed. "So, she can't hear me unless I want her to? Like now, I'm talking out loud, can she hear me?"

Ghortin and Jenna shared a look then shrugged.

"I don't think so. If her transfer is similar to when I had to seek Jenna's head, I wasn't aware of things unless I was called. Mostly. I'm not sure if this case is the same, but I'd guess so."

Jenna waited for Xalie to say something but didn't call her. Nothing. "I think she's not hearing you unless you call her. Or I do."

Edgar nodded thoughtfully and kept shoving more food in. "She could be a tactical advantage in our upcoming fights. You said there were more of them up on the chaotic plane? I know we need to get Carabella's friends out, but wouldn't the others be helpful too? How'd she get down here anyway?"

"I'll let Jenna explain. I have some things to go over with Keanin." Ghortin reached out to grab Keanin as he started to walk away. "Call us if anything odd happens." With a nod, he led Keanin away.

Edgar kept his laugh low. "The look on Keanin's face just now was the first time I'd seen him look like the old Keanin in a long time. Now, about this cuari situation." He returned to eating as Jenna gave him an abbreviated version of what had happened. Then she told him about her nightmare and that she suspected the attack on him had been the same people.

"I thought something else had gone on. Couldn't tell much, I was still asleep, but there was an evil presence in my head. If you and she can keep that from ever happening again, she can stay."

"I can't guarantee anything, and I think she'd say the same. But we know what they can do now, and that's the first step in stopping—" Jenna's words were cut off as the entire cavern shook.

CHAPTER FORTY-SIX

———◆———

"WHAT WAS THAT?" JENNA ALMOST fell off the bench and Edgar hung onto the table. There was an electric charge in the air that dissipated quickly.

Armed defenders ran for the door, but it was still closed. Keanin and Ghortin checked on she and Edgar and then they ran to the front as well.

After admonishing Jenna to stay in the back with Edgar.

"We should be helping." Edgar looked ready to run, but hadn't gotten off the bench yet.

Jenna knew there was more than only Ghortin's command keeping him in place. "Can you walk unassisted?" She wasn't trying to throw it in his face, but Storm, Keanin, and Edgar shared an unreasonable stubbornness.

"Probably not." That was clearly hard for him to say. "I'm glad to be alive, and don't even mind sharing my head, but I need to get back into the fight soon." Life as a spymaster and knight didn't leave a lot of downtime, and he liked things that way from what Jenna could tell.

"Eat more." Jenna shoved another platter of food in front of him. "There's nothing to do until the scout teams get back."

"And that quake we just had? While I don't recall walking into this place, it appears solid. I think it would take a lot to get it to move like that." He worked his way through the food but kept looking at the people gathering near the door.

"I agree. But this place is old and tough. I doubt that

Ghortin will let anyone out yet. It was risky enough sending the scouting teams." Jenna shoved aside the tendril of worry about Storm and her friends.

Edgar noticed her face anyway and gave a comforting smile. "Any groups being led by Storm, Crell, and Talia will be safe—mark my words."

A second rattle shook the floor, far lighter than the first, but it still made the hairs on her arms rise. The outer door opened and although she couldn't see well because of the dense woods outside, there couldn't have been more than a few people who went out.

And Ghortin seemed to be holding onto Keanin until the door shut again. Then Ghortin moved on to a discussion with two of the older Erlindans.

"If you promise not to move from this bench, I can run up and see if they know anything."

"I promise. I'll stay right here and keep eating. You can even tell Xalie to keep me here."

Jenna shrugged. She wasn't sure if Xalie could do that, but hopefully, if *he* thought she could, he'd stay in place. There was still an odd and edgy feeling in the air and finding out what to expect could be important. Not to mention her concern for the teams outside.

Jenna ran up to the door as Ghortin finished talking to the Erlindans. Keanin was standing near the door with his arms crossed but hadn't forced his way out. His grim look didn't bode well for anyone who tried to stop him again if there was a third earthquake, though.

"What was that?" Jenna watched Keanin as she spoke to Ghortin.

"A mage quake. Ancient magic that vanished eons ago. Yet, like other things, seems to have come back into existence here." He shook his head. "Had we known that Erlinda was more than a sleepy fishing town…I will need to speak to Carabella about this. Even though we weren't speaking when she was roaming around the coast, she would have gotten word to me if there was something dangerous about the area." He was mostly muttering to himself.

"That's a good idea. But how dangerous was it and how do we stop it? And are the others okay?"

Ghortin gave a small smile. "You held out longer than I expected on asking that last question. I have no idea, but they're people I'd bet on to survive almost anything. And I'd say that we're safe in here as well. Two of Tireli's scouts left to see if there was any damage nearby. Mage quakes are usually focused on something. They can go deep underground and be used to weaken towns. If something was being attacked, I doubt it was this shelter."

"Could someone have used it against Erlinda?" She had no idea who else out there might be on their side, but it would be good to gain allies. Especially ones with tricky old magic.

"It could be? I have no idea who though. As I said, that is ancient magic. One that neither myself nor Carabella even have access to. *No one* should have the ability to use it." He folded his arms and frowned at the door.

A pounding on the door brought Keanin to attention. Ghortin as well, as he took hold of Keanin again as the door opened.

Jenna didn't grab Keanin, but she stayed near him.

Two Erlindans came inside. They had not gone with Storm or Tireli, so she guessed they were the ones just sent out. They came to Ghortin.

"It seems fine out here. But there appears to be downed trees closer to Erlinda."

"Talia and the others might be in danger. Or injured." Keanin could easily open the door, but he was holding back. Probably because Ghortin was glaring at him.

"I don't think so." Altheria joined them with her head tilted as if listening to something. "Those came from the ocean. The echoes are coming from deep in the ocean."

"The portal?" Jenna asked.

"No idea. But I've become in tune with the water over the decades. Even through these walls I feel that's where the disruption came from. I doubt that any of our people were in the ocean."

"No, but they were checking the ships." Keanin wasn't frantic, but he was fully armed and looked ready to charge the door if he had to.

Ghortin folded his arms and pinned Keanin with a low-level glare. "They didn't leave long enough ago for that yet. Checking on the ships and sorting out the odds of us being able to use them was the last item on their agenda. Need I remind you that those two groups are well trained in this type of activity? Every person we send out is another risk that our attack tomorrow will be compromised."

Keanin tried to glare back, then surrendered with a sigh. "Fine. Back to our training?"

Ghortin grinned. "Indeed. Altheria? Will you stay up here in case of any problems?"

Jenna knew Ghortin was more concerned about Keanin going out than anything else. Once they'd identified the location and there were no more rumbles, he'd lost his concern about the mage quakes. For now.

From the small smile on her face, Altheria realized it as well. "Of course."

"And you, who's guarding Edgar?" Ghortin had already taken Keanin's arm but spun to Jenna.

"He promised to stay put. But once he finishes eating, he's going to want to be filled in on the plan." She glanced over where he was still eating and watching them. "Unless he can't move, it's going to be impossible to leave him behind tomorrow."

"You're probably right." Ghortin frowned. "It's what we get for having so many stubborn people in our group. Go fill him in on anything that might have been skipped, and then both of you need to get a nap. Neither of you had a good evening, and I fear that when our scouts get back, we'll have to plan our next move quickly."

Jenna nodded, then rejoined Edgar, and filled him in on the mage quakes. He'd never heard of them before.

"I feel better. I could do something besides resting." Edgar pushed away his empty plate.

"You might not feel it, but our visitors from last night took a lot out of each of us, even if our experiences were different. You don't recall any weird dreams?"

"Not that stand out. Honestly, everything after the beach is vague and dreamlike. I know I spoke to people, and now I'm beginning to recall coming here, but that's about all." He looked around at the increased activity. "I know we need to rest and wait right now, but what is the plan so far?"

"We're going to try to locate the underwater portal with my cuari book. Then somehow use mages on the three ships to find its location." Jenna sighed. The more she said it, the less she thought it would work.

"And?" Edgar asked when she didn't continue.

"And, that's as much as they came up with so far." She glanced over to Keanin and Ghortin in a far corner blocking out magic spells. "I'm thinking that's one of the things Ghortin is working on with Keanin. But unless it's the ability to grow gills, I don't see how we can get down to the portal. From what I've studied, the spell bubbles can't hold up well in water."

"They don't. Tried it once as a kid. Utter failure." Edgar gave a massive yawn—one that he unsuccessfully fought. "Don't tell Ghortin he was right. He's too smug already. But I need to find a place to rest. There's a lot of activity going on right now and as tired as I am, I need quiet."

Ghortin was good at tracking multiple things and although he was still watching Keanin demonstrate a spell, a cot flew to his room.

"I think he's suggesting his closet." Jenna got to her feet as a yawn hit her. "Can you walk?"

Edgar got up slowly but stood on his own. "Much better than before. Shall we nap, m'lady?" he gave a courtly bow. Edgar was a knight, but it rarely made an appearance.

Jenna's nap was short and blissfully uneventful. Although she was confused as to where she was in the first few moments after waking. Edgar snoring loudly in the cot next to hers made it even more bewildering.

Then her brain kicked in and the low-level mage lights helped her see the room.

There was no way to tell how long they'd been asleep, but she figured if it had been too long, or something had happened, Ghortin would have gotten them.

She debated letting Edgar rest while she checked on things, but he seemed to be tossing a lot and she didn't know if leaving him alone was a great idea.

Reaching out to Xalie didn't bring a response, so she switched to trying for Typhonel. He'd been thrown through the portal in the Markare, but as this one was supposedly shut down before that happened, he might have some insight.

Like Xalie, no response.

"Never a disembodied person around when you need one," Jenna spoke softly, but Edgar jerked awake and sat up.

He was also reaching for a weapon that fortunately wasn't on him right now. "What's happened?"

"You woke up from a nap." Jenna slid off her cot but on the side away from him. She didn't believe he was compromised again, but better to be safe. Even without magic or weapons, Edgar was a skilled fighter.

"I…oh." He let out a long breath and ran his fingers through his hair. "I remember now. The lights are so dim that I couldn't sort things out." The mage lights flared brightly, then settled down to a normal illumination level. All without any discernible spell being cast.

"You're good, I didn't even feel the spell." He hopped off the cot.

"That didn't come from me."

"I didn't cast a…spell. But I thought it. Is it from the cuari? Xalie?"

Jenna shrugged. "Not a clue. Try reaching her." She was tempted to try so again herself, but if those two were going to be together for a while, they needed to speak to each other.

Edgar closed his eyes. Then came back. "She's faint, but said she didn't do anything. I asked her what it meant, and she said to keep track of how many times it happened. That's not helpful."

"No, we can ask Ghortin. But that's the type of answer he gives when he doesn't have a better one." Jenna opened the door to far more noise than she'd expected. People were running everywhere, and the door to the outside was open.

Edgar grabbed one of the Erlindans as there was no way to see any of their friends. "What's happened?"

"The scouts were attacked; they're coming back but we're going to meet them." The woman pulled free and ran to the door.

Edgar went after her but Jenna stopped him. "We should get weapons first. And I'd be careful about anything you think about. At least until whatever's going on is sorted."

He nodded and followed her to get their weapons. Hers were at her prior cot and his were tucked under the one he'd been on in the healing ward.

They were running to the door when another mage quake happened. This one was strong enough to knock them off their feet and cause pieces of the roof to drift down.

Chapter Forty-Seven

"EVERYONE SEEK SHELTER OR GET out!" That was Ghortin from somewhere in the front.

Jenna and Edgar shared a look, there wasn't much back here but cots. They got to their feet and raced for the entrance.

Ghortin and Altheria were the last out, but it seemed as if the shaking had finally stopped.

And the shelter was still in place.

Jenna looked toward a group coming their way through the trees and ran when she saw Storm in the mob. Keanin was already hugging Talia.

Storm looked roughed up a bit but was helping one of Tireli's men and didn't appear too injured himself.

"What happened?" Jenna slipped her shoulder under the injured man's other side to give more support. His left leg was dragging and he appeared to have been hit in the head.

"We were on our way back after checking on the boats when a group of soldiers from Erlinda charged us. They were blaming us for the earthquakes and appeared more interested in capturing us alive than killing us."

"That's good, I guess." She adjusted her grip on the injured man as he faded in and out of consciousness.

"Depends on their reason." Storm didn't look happy.

"My theory is that they were looking for whoever was trying to blow up their seawall." Crell came up along Jenna's other side. "They were kind of upset out about it."

They got to the shelter and at Ghortin's nod continued in.

Jenna glanced back after they got inside and noticed that Ghortin and Altheria were standing on either side of the door and were scanning everyone who came in. It was slowing bringing the injured in, but an excellent precaution. If Jenna never had to see another zombie demonspawn in her life, she'd be eternally grateful.

"Everyone is upset about it here too," Jenna said to Crell as she and Storm took their injured man to the healers. They'd all remained with the patients who couldn't be moved and had already set up more cots. "But did it take out a lot of the seawall?" She stepped out from under the man's arm as a healer took her place and another took over for Storm.

"Not enough from what I could see." Storm allowed a healer to bully him to a nearby cot. That he didn't even complain was a major move forward. He'd been known to fight back even when he was barely conscious. "The quakes did seem to come from the ocean though. Or under it. The wall is intact but they will need to do some repairs."

Crell remained with them. "And none of the ones who attacked us changed into demonspawn or zombies." Her look was grim. "But they all fought to the death."

Edgar drifted back to them as he helped one of the Erlinda fighters. She didn't appear to be that injured but did seem to be enjoying the attention from him.

Storm looked down at the rocks and dust coating the floor. "It hit that hard out here? And no one knows who is behind it?" He kept his arm steady while the healer finished closing a slice wound and then hopped off the table.

Jenna filled him on the quakes. "I lived through a lot of earthquakes back in my old hometown. These weren't like them at all, aside from the ground shaking. There's an odd residue in the air when they hit. But it doesn't last long." She tried to think of the term, but this last one was as if she'd gotten an electric shock. She didn't know how to translate electricity into magic. "Like a lightning strike happened nearby."

Edgar joined them after escorting the injured woman to the healers. "She says that, but I didn't feel it. It's been a weird day though."

"I felt it a little, but until Jenna mentioned it, I wouldn't have thought anything about it." The lines on Keanin's face relaxed as he and Talia came over.

"Diath took a blow to his head, but he was already complaining, so I think he'll be fine." Talia looked back toward the door as the final people came in—and were still being scanned. "Good idea, but I don't know that any of us were separated for any time."

Storm frowned. "None of us saw Edgar attacked before—or at least recalled it. If they wanted to replace someone in our group then a fight would be the time."

Ghortin and Altheria walked into the shelter with Tireli. The three were in a serious discussion, one that Ghortin appeared to be winning and Tireli wasn't happy about. Altheria stayed in between the two men but didn't look to be taking sides.

"I know you'll have to repeat it later, but when Ghortin gets that look he's not giving up soon." Jenna turned back to Storm. "What did you find?"

Storm glanced over her head, then nodded, and led them all to the tables and benches near the kitchen. "I agree about Ghortin. I've seen him argue for hours when he's that set on something. Whatever it is, Tireli should just surrender." He turned toward Talia. "It's your town."

Talia gave a grim smile. "Aye. And it will be again. We made it to the north end, and Tireli and his group went to the south. Crell can fill you in on that part. The town is sealed off well. Too well. They only took over a week ago but some fortifications they have should have taken years to put up. And they have serious weapons. They weren't up along the edge, but it looked as if there were several catapults up top. We never had anything like that."

"Same to the south, although until Tireli started swearing about them, I had no idea those were all new." Crell shook her head. "But while they look imposing, they don't feel that way. My people have a way with stone and when I touched one of the fortifications, they felt oddly weak."

"An illusion spell? If they don't have enough people to defend Erlinda, that would be my guess." Jenna looked around. "Not to mention that while I'm grateful you didn't face more demonspawn, I think the fact that no more attacked you is telling."

"That they probably don't have any more here. Which should make getting back Erlinda easier, but I was hoping to destroy more of them." Keanin's voice was light, but his jaw clenched.

Jenna knew the odds of the missing shipload of pregnant demonspawn women being in Erlinda were slim, but Keanin was holding on to that limited chance. And until then, he was making it his duty to kill as many demonspawn as he could find.

Even only knowing part of what had happened to him, Jenna didn't begrudge him a bit.

"I don't know if we can get it back at this time if there's a chance those fortifications are real." Jenna originally thought that getting the town freed was her goal here. But more and more she realized they might not have time. Destroying the portal could bring the invaders of Erlinda to such high alert that they couldn't free the town. And they needed to destroy that portal. She didn't miss that Qhazborh said to leave the portals alone. Plural.

"If we free Erlinda, you don't have to worry about them when we go after the portal," Talia said.

"But we might not be able to free it with this group," Tireli added as he, Ghortin, and Altheria joined them. "I think there are more people inside the town walls than we knew. The foundations might be part or all illusion, but I saw a fair amount of people marching around on them. I don't believe they're fake, not to mention it would be pointless to create that illusion. Few people would be able to get as close as we did."

"Then why did they send so few against us? They wouldn't have known that we were all who was out there." Talia put up her hand. "I agree with Storm that they were trying to injure and capture us, not kill. But that should have meant more people, not less. They only had a few more fighters than we did."

Crell caught Ghortin and Altheria up on the oddness of the town walls. "But Diath and the other magic user didn't feel any magic coming from them. I know that something was wrong with those stones."

"We kept the higher-level mages here in case someone found this place, but that might have been an error." Ghortin tugged on his beard. "What was discovered about the ships?"

Talia nodded. "All three remain hidden and appear unmolested and secure. Diath and I checked them all personally. And we were attacked far enough from their hiding place that I don't think the invaders tracked us there." She paused. "But they did seem to be pushing us toward the water. At least initially."

"No kraken?" Keanin asked.

"Nope, but those quakes disturbed the fighters against us," Crell added. "That's when they started trying to capture us. Badly, I might add. And if they had magic users, they didn't cast any spells."

"I don't believe that they intended to capture us initially," Tireli said. "Even with our scouting, I think we're missing something. We might want to wait a day or two before we move."

"*You can't wait.*"

With all the voices popping around in her head, Jenna would have thought she'd gotten used to it. Nope. She jumped at Typhonel's mental comment, then closed her eyes.

"*Why? What happened to you? Can you fix Xalie once she saves Edgar? What do you know about this portal?*" She knew she looked odd when she was speaking to someone in her head, but Typhonel could be the piece they needed to destroy that thing out in the ocean.

"*I can't explain, but something is trying to block me. I don't know about the cuari, I will have to see how we are later. Whatever is trying to stop me interfered with her arrival. I know of the sea portal only in passing, I wouldn't have information on how to destroy it—it was by different builders than the one I was thrown through. Most of the deities didn't pay attention to what that group of cuari was doing until it was too late.*"

Not as helpful as she'd hoped, but Jenna was glad he was back even just for a while. A thought hit her. "*What about the evil deities? Did they fight the cuari?*" It struck her that the group behind Qhazborh was duplicitous about most things. She had a difficult time believing that they would assist the other gods and goddesses.

"*They didn't at first, but then when I was lost, they joined to close the portal in the Markare. At least I feel they did.*" Typhonel sounded confused. But he had been killed right before then, so it was interesting that he knew anything.

"*Was there a Protector for you to go into?*" She'd never asked him about how his spirit, or consciousness, got back to this side when his body was destroyed.

"*No. I…I'm not sure what happened during those first years. But I know there had to have been three corners of Power to close the portal. We'd already been planning on how to destroy it before I was lost.*"

Jenna felt a touch on her arm and opened her eyes.

Ghortin was in front of her. "Typhonel?"

"Yes." She closed her eyes again. This information could be vital. Mostly for the destroying of the Markare portal, but there could be something to help with this one. Even if it was constructed differently. *"How were you going to destroy it? Why didn't it work?"*

"The Power of all the deities would have been combined into a single strand of energy and blast the portal apart. From what we understood there was no way it would fail. We waited too long, however, hoping that the cuari would change without us engaging. When they threw me into the portal, the deities finally acted but it was too late. They couldn't destroy it. I must go for now, but I will be back." The last sentence was as if he was a bit of smoke that floated away.

At least this time he warned her that he'd be gone. Jenna let his words sink in. Logically, she knew that the deities, and then later Ghortin, Carabella, and their adventuring crew, were unable to destroy the portal in the Markare—they could only close it. However, hearing it from someone who was there when the portal was functioning, and the fact that what the deities had planned was supposedly foolproof, made her feel small and insignificant.

They had failed.

Maybe if the mindslave whose body she'd taken over had survived, they might have a chance. The Protectors had knowledge that was passed between them through generations. None of which Jenna had available to her. When Sacaranz and the followers of Qhazborh created the mindslave, they'd destroyed the generations of memories and instructions in that woman's mind. With Rachael's help and the books of the cuari, Jenna was playing catch up.

But it wasn't going to be enough.

Even if some of that knowledge had subconsciously

been from Typhonel, there was no way that she could destroy what a bunch of gods and goddesses, as well as a group of powerful mages, couldn't destroy.

They were doomed and she felt it in her soul.

She opened her eyes and wiped a tear that she didn't realize she'd shed. Then tried to force a smile when she saw not that only Ghortin, but everyone else who'd been talking about plans was now staring at her.

Storm came and held her tight. He didn't ask what was wrong, just held her.

Ghortin waited until she and Storm stepped apart. "Child? What happened?"

"I made a realization that I don't want to say out loud right now. But Typhonel was here, he's gone now, but he said he didn't have any ideas about destroying this portal." A lump in her throat stopped her words. She couldn't tell them that she knew she couldn't destroy the portals and they might as well go find a cozy place to ride out the end of the world. Worlds. "I'll be fine. He did say that the ocean portal was made differently than the Markare one."

"That's not that helpful," Keanin said before Ghortin could.

"It's a little bit. At least this way we'll know that whatever we come up with to blast this one, won't destroy the one in the desert." Storm gave a smile that only looked a little forced. Even though Jenna didn't say what made her cry, Storm knew it had to be something big. "It will save time when we're trying to shut down the one in the Markare." He kept his arm around her shoulders. He wouldn't pry, but he would support her.

"Altheria and Edgar have come up with a plan." Ghortin beamed at the two of them like a proud father.

"You resolved it while I was in my head? For less than five minutes?" Jenna knew they'd been talking but this seemed sudden.

"Yes, actually. Well, myself, Edgar, and Xalie sorted it out." Altheria shrugged.

"And are you going to share it? Are we rescuing Erlinda or destroying the portal? Tomorrow? A few days from now?"

"She's fine." Storm kissed the top of her head. He and Ghortin used to say she asked more questions than anyone they knew.

"Well?" She looked around.

"Both. Tomorrow." Altheria and Edgar grinned. Even the rest looked more positive than before.

"*That* is not useful. How?"

"We have to move tomorrow for both because of what happened today. They know we're out here somewhere and they will be able to find us eventually," Storm said.

"You'll be on the one belonging to Talia and Diath. Keanin and I will be on the other two ships," Ghortin said. "Hopefully, your mental friend can help, but if he can't, that's okay, we will have enough magical strength to blow that portal to bits."

Keanin's grin was seriously huge. "And I'm going to call in my friend. The kraken." He added that with far too much enthusiasm.

CHAPTER FORTY-EIGHT

JENNA LOOKED AROUND, BUT NO one, even Storm and Ghortin tried to dissuade him. "You're going to call him up like a pet dog?" She'd only seen part of that monster, but that was enough. The thing's head alone was huge.

"I know it sounds improbable, but he will come to me." That level of confidence was only found in madmen and fools. Usually, Keanin was neither, but this might be an exception.

Jenna felt the weight of her discussion with Typhonel, and the ensuing depression, begin to fade. It lingered though. Deep inside she still felt that she couldn't find a way to destroy the Markare portal, but the sorrow was more distant now.

"So, we split up on the ships, I use the cuari book to find the portal, we converge over it, and you three will tie into it along with me. We'll create a blast point and Keanin and his kraken will what, ride down to make sure it destroys it? I'm still lost." While working through this issue was a good distraction, everything felt too tenuous for this to be happening tomorrow.

"It'll make sense, I promise." Keanin's grin was getting more extreme.

"Okay. So, the town?" Maybe focusing on something else would help. She felt the concern about the Markare portal creeping back into her mind.

"Storm, Tireli, myself, my rangers, and most everyone else aside from the healers and injured will be liberating Erlinda." Crell looked as giddy as Keanin. "Talia will be captaining your ship. We have others selected for the other two. But the rest of us, get to charge an illusion."

"Seriously? I was in my head for five minutes. How did you come up with all this?" Jenna carefully looked from person to person, but they all appeared extremely confident.

Ghortin didn't have a grin but he did look smug. "One of Crell's rangers chipped off a piece of the wall and brought it back. I was studying it while you and your friend were discussing events. It was more like ten minutes, by the way. However, I was able to determine that it was real stone. With a magic overlay that made it ten times as easy to get in place. That thing would have crumbled completely in about two weeks. Which means, that they only needed the town for a short period. It also means that a few spells carried by low-level magic users could destroy the walls. I'd say the magic quakes were to bring the sea walls down, but the beings casting them were too far out to sea." He gave Keanin a look—they believed the kraken were behind it.

Jenna ran her hand through her hair. A move more often done by Storm and Ghortin, but it felt appropriate. "I still don't get all the details, but I'm thinking you'll fill me in."

They discussed and debated strategies all through a meal that was an early dinner or late lunch. Jenna barely noticed what she ate. Even though the others had seemed confident, they were still examining other options.

But it kept coming back to destroying the portal, freeing Erlinda, and then heading back to Irundail.

Until the Markare portal reappeared and they had to race to destroy it. Jenna twitched and shoved that thought to the back of her mind. They couldn't enter the Markare until the portal came back, but once it did, they had little time to get their troops there to destroy it.

"What's wrong?" Storm stayed seated next to her.

"Nothing, just a few random and unrelated thoughts." She hated lying but the feeling that there was no way for her to destroy the Markare portal when the time came was still strong. "Although, if they don't have a lot of fighters inside the city walls, where are they? I still think the demonspawn turning into zombies wasn't deliberate. So where are the rest of Sacaranz and Qhazborh's forces?"

"That's an excellent question and one Xalie has asked as well." Edgar was adapting to his mental companion far quicker than Jenna had. With any of them. "Unfortunately, we have no idea, and won't until we can get inside the town."

Tireli remained mostly quiet, aside from a few strategy items that he and Talia conferred about. Talia was conflicted as she wanted to be in both places at the same time. But she'd given Tireli information that might help if things went wrong in the attack on the town. "I don't know that we have time to sort that out," he said. "I'm sorry that you'll face more battles, but right now I need to focus on saving Erlinda. We also should assume that many of the captured townsfolk may be alive and are being held."

The rest of the discussion went into alternatives they might have to enact for each event.

But it seemed that destroying the portal was going to end up being completed, or not, by Keanin's kraken friend. He felt he could control the kraken to escort the destructive Power generated by the cuari book and the three mages to the portal.

That he couldn't say exactly how he could do it tied up Jenna's stomach.

———

Jenna didn't feel any better the next morning. She'd wanted something to happen, but this didn't feel right.

Or it could be the guilt she had that all this would be for naught when she failed to destroy the Markare portal and the world ended horribly anyway.

She mentally reached out for Typhonel, but wasn't surprised when he failed to respond.

"Child? I don't mean to pry, but I can feel your distress. It's far more than the battles that will be faced today," Xalie's voice was soft. If Jenna told her to leave her head, she would.

"It's nothing." Jenna sighed, she needed to tell someone and she couldn't handle more guilt if she told Storm or Ghortin. *"It is something, but please don't tell Edgar or the others. I won't be able to destroy the portal in the Markare. I realized it yesterday. I don't have the ability or training."*

"But you didn't feel this before? The task has not changed."

"No. I think I was great at lying to myself." That was another hard thing to swallow.

"I feel something has changed within you. But I cannot pinpoint it. Yet. Do not give up hope and don't try to reach Typhonel until I have spoken to you. You need to focus on the task of today—many a mage has failed because they doubted themselves. You cannot have doubt."

Jenna took a deep breath and shoved the fear and hopelessness aside. For now. *"Thank you. I will try. No, I will do it."*

"Be well." Then Xalie vanished from her mind.

Jenna got up off her cot and joined the controlled chaos of preparing for battle. Or battles. She would have liked to have more people on the three ships in case the Erlindan attackers came out on the water. But she also wanted more people with Storm and the rest taking back the city. Even with all the debates yesterday, she still wasn't sure she agreed with doing both at the same time.

People around her were still gathering their things when she was finished and ready to go.

She returned to her cot and pulled out the cuari book. Like before, things had shifted around. Something about

Erlinda, the underwater portal, or the ocean was still impacting it.

A quick check revealed a pair of spells she'd never seen before. She read through them but they were too complex to memorize in this short of time. She mentally told the book not to lose them.

"Anything new?" Ghortin joined her and peered at the book.

"Two new spells." She held the page open for him but he didn't try to touch it.

"Those are good. And old. My book is still trying to help me recall it, or so I believe." He jumped as the taran wand buzzed in his vest pocket. "I'll never get used to that." He answered hello with a grin that faded as he heard the person on the other side. "Is there any contact with Carabella or anyone inside?" The increased frown told her the answer was no. "She's next to me, you can warn her yourself." He held out the wand. "The Zalin shelter was attacked an hour ago and their entrance is completely blocked by a landslide. Carabella isn't responding to calls on her wand."

Jenna took the wand. "Hello?"

"Thank goodness," Rachael's voice held more concern than Jenna had ever heard before. "Ghortin told you about Zalin. Prince Justlantin has a troop going to dig them out. But I have a horrible feeling that whoever did it is heading your way. And they are specifically after you." Her tone was grim but also calm. "You have to leave."

"I can't. We need to close the portal here and free Erlinda. You don't know what attacked the shelter?" Jenna wasn't used to Rachael panicking, but the fear in her voice was strong.

"No. I wanted to go with the troop, but I was out-voted. They have mages going, so hopefully they can pick up on something. I'm using a borrowed wand, one of

Edgar's extras, so mine won't be depleted. I had a feeling you wouldn't leave, but please be careful, don't listen to your fears, and contact me if you need to." She paused and it sounded as if she was speaking to someone out of range of the wand. "Dantil and a group of the helaermages are going to the shelter. I need to speak to him before they leave. Take care of each other." The call ended before Jenna could say goodbye.

"That wasn't helpful." She told Ghortin what Rachael said and handed Ghortin back his taran wand. "And now this will have to recharge."

"We can get Edgar's wand until then if we need it." He shook his head. "I don't like this. The Zalin shelter should have been impossible to pull down—we made it to last and the main cave was already in place when we came. I'd like to send you somewhere safe, but I doubt we have that option."

Jenna looked around to make sure she had everything. This shelter would be sealed from the outside once they left. There were still a few injured who couldn't be moved and they and their healers would remain. Providing they won, Tireli and his people would come get them.

Once outside and the shelter sealed, they split up into their groups.

Jenna hugged Storm tightly. "I understand the reason behind being separated, you're the best at what you do. But I hate fighting apart from each other."

He looked down into her eyes. "I do as well. Sometimes a sword can do what magic can't. Don't forget that." He gave her a long kiss, then went to sort his troops. He and Tireli were again splitting the group and hitting the town from both sides. They then marched toward Erlinda.

All of those going to the ships stayed in the forest. The idea was that they'd travel perpendicular to the ocean until they had to cut over to the cove. Timing-wise,

Storm and Tireli would have begun their assault by the time they got on the ships.

Hopefully.

Talia led the way, with Ghortin following close behind. He also had his nose buried in his cuari book.

Jenna was trying to stay focused on their task and left her cuari book in her pocket for now. She felt as if she was hanging on by a thread. One bit of weirdness from that book and she might lose it.

Rachael had backed down when she told Jenna to leave, but there was still a feeling of wanting her to do so. Combined with the other negative things going on, Jenna felt as if someone had painted a massive bullseye on her.

Chapter Forty-Nine

<hr>

THEY CAME OUT OF THE woods near a beach and Talia led them behind a pair of dunes. Based on the lack of people coming their way, it didn't look like they'd been seen by anyone in town. The dunes helped reinforce it would stay that way.

Ghortin put away his book and took his staff free of the strap across his back. He still wore a sword, but he'd decided the staff was handy. From what she'd seen this wasn't the first time he'd used it, as he was proficient.

Talia slowed the group down and held up a fist to pause. The people who were on each ship separated into their groups, but they would still go out to the water together.

Keanin was the only one who didn't seem concerned at all.

Jenna hoped that his belief in the kraken being able to support them was valid. The gathered Power of the Ghortin, Keanin, and herself, along with anything else the cuari books had to offer, might reach the portal and destroy it. But there was no way to be sure.

The ocean appeared calm and the waves hitting the beach were low. Under other circumstances, it would be a nice day for a picnic on the sand. A tug at her heart reminded her those days were probably gone for good.

Talia paused behind the last dune before the cove. If there were any watchers on the town walls, they'd see them going to the ships, even at this distance. Talia had strongly encouraged everyone to run to their ship.

Each ship had a mage; either Jenna, Ghortin, or Keanin. Each had a captain. Then there were three experienced sailors on each to help get them out to sea and defend if necessary.

Jenna felt if they fell under attack there wouldn't be anywhere near enough defenders. She understood that the Erlindans wanted to free their town, but this weakened both tasks.

And fed into her general funk.

Talia dropped her fist and everyone ran to the ships. At first, things went smoothly, then a volley of arrows came as all three ships set sail out of the cove.

"Support the sails!" Keanin had shown the other magic users how to use magic to fill the sails.

It was an odd feeling, but Jenna pushed the sails as hard as she could. Talia finally turned and waved her off as they quickly passed the other ships—even the one Keanin was on.

"That's fine, Jenna. Let the others catch up." Talia didn't laugh but there was a small smile as Keanin's ship came closer to them.

Ghortin, looking more than a little annoyed, was last. "I didn't know it was a race."

Jenna shrugged. She couldn't explain why she pushed as hard as she did, but her fear of failing was spiking her adrenaline. Great. Depressed and over-wired. She took a deep breath and shook out her shoulders. Yep, they were tense.

The shapes on the shore were small, but Talia had a far-seeing glass aimed at them. "I'm not certain they were from the people in the town." She handed the glass to one of the Erlindans. "Jhal, do you recognize their clothing?" She looked at the other two ships. "Did anyone pick up an arrow? I doubt we did at the speed we were going." She flashed Jenna a smile.

"We have one on the stern. Might take me a while to

get it," A short ranger on Keanin's ship said as she looked down at something close to the waterline.

Jhal handed the far-seeing glass back to Talia. "They look like Craelyns. Heavily armed Craelyns."

Jenna caught that he mentioned people from the capital city of Khelaran specifically and not just Khelarans. There was a bit of a snarl in his voice as well.

"Damn it. They might be trying to take advantage of the situation." Talia focused back on the beach.

Nothing was clear at this distance, but even Jenna could tell that the people remained on the beach. "Have you had trouble with them?" As far as she knew the two countries mostly ignored each other aside from regular commerce traffic.

"Not usually. We trade regularly and ship traffic was normal until a few weeks ago. But these ships carry the Traanafaeren flag, why else would they have attacked us?"

"Not sure, but they're starting a fire." Jhal had brought out a second far-seeing glass. "A nice big bonfire. They're settling in, we're not landing there when this is done."

The other two ships were close enough to have their captains pull out their glasses and look for themselves.

"He's right. Plus, more troops are coming in from the north beach." A woman with short red hair swore as she handed the glass to another and went back to watching the open ocean.

The sails on the ships were filling on their own now, but still not quickly.

"What are they doing? Or rather, why? And where will we land?" Jenna wanted to boost the sails, but not until everyone had finished looking at the people on the beach. Then something she'd heard hit her. "Wouldn't they have needed a ship to get there?"

"Excellent point. They would have and there's no way they could have docked near the town. They came in from the north."

"There's a lot of debris off Dead Man's Cove." A man from Ghortin's ship called out as he looked to the north toward a larger cove. "The hull looks Khelaran."

Talia swore as she turned to look. "We need to do what must be done and then head south." She raised her voice. The ships were still close. "Keanin, if that Khelaran ship was destroyed by your kraken friends, we might not be able to trust them."

"Not all of them are my friends, only the one I rescued. But I recall Hon mentioning Dead Man's Cove and how dangerous it was when we left Erlinda before." Keanin was holding on to the kraken being on their side for all he was worth.

"Not our worry now." Talia turned back to Jenna. "Can you push us gently a bit faster? Then I guess, get out that book."

Jenna took the hint and slowly filled the sails. It was interesting that now that there was more direct danger, she felt like she had increased control.

Maybe the threats in her mind messed her up, but the ones in person were fine. Great.

The three ships got out far enough that the shore was nothing but a beige strip, with the town of Erlinda being a much darker chunk. Jenna thought of Storm, Edgar, Crell, and the rest. Hopefully, the town walls would fall as they expected.

Once Talia said she could stop filling the sails, she pulled out her book of the cuari. If the flipping of pages was any indication, they were near the portal. The pages actually weren't flipping that much, but their content was.

Aside from the two spells that Jenna had asked to stay put.

She sent a mental thank you to the book. No idea what it heard or understood, but it had kept those two in place for her.

"Okay, we need to find the portal." She whispered it,

but the book stopped changing pages immediately and then tugged in her hands. Not enough to fly out of her grasp, but it got the point across.

"We need to go left!"

"All ships, to the port side!" Talia called as she moved the vessel.

The ships spread out from each other but all moved in the same direction.

Jenna hung onto the cuari book as it pulled. She had no idea how it was doing this, but she also wasn't sure she wanted to know.

"Ship coming this way! Fast off the starboard side!" Keanin's ship was closer to the open ocean and it was one of his people who called out.

"What in the hell is that?" Talia had her glass out and a steady stream of swearing came from her. "It's massive."

Ghortin commandeered a far-seeing glass from the captain of his ship. Swearing came from him too. "It's carrying the Strann flag and has more gun ports than all three of these ships. We can't face it."

The ship was still a distance away but even from here it looked huge. Size-wise it looked to Jenna like a large cruise ship. Although she'd never seen one with that many cannons…or any cannons for that matter.

"Keep going to port," Talia yelled to the other two captains. "Jenna, I need you to get us moving."

Jenna called up the wind spell, but it didn't come as quickly as before. Something was fighting it. She turned back to look at the ship following them.

It felt as if that ship was slowing them.

"They have mages and are trying to keep us from escaping," Jenna yelled as the wind came up—trying to push them back instead of forward.

Ghortin's response spell was powerful and reduced the wind pushing against them. Jenna and Keanin got their ships moving forward and Ghortin followed them. He was running two spells so his ship being behind the other two wasn't surprising.

"We're going to have to face them," Jenna yelled to Talia. They couldn't keep up this speed, and that ship was still gaining.

"We can't. Even the three of us would be outgunned. And I'd say they have some serious mages over there too." Nonetheless, Talia yelled commands for all three ships to ready their weapons.

They continued to push their sails, but even at this distance, it was clear that the larger ship continued to gain on them. Only a bit slower.

"Separate!" Talia yelled to the other captains.

The attacking ship could only go after one at a time and there was a chance the other two could escape.

Ghortin sent another spell at the Strann ship, but Jenna watched as it was deflected and disbursed.

Keanin closed his eyes and held out his arms as the captain of his ship pulled away from them.

Nothing happened and Jenna wasn't sure what spell he was casting.

Then a massive kraken head appeared but it was closer to her ship, not Keanin's.

She wasn't an expert on giant, octopus-type monsters, but it looked pissed. And hungry.

CHAPTER FIFTY

"KEANIN? YOUR FRIEND IS HERE!" Jenna augmented her voice with a spell, but even then she wasn't certain he heard her.

Then he spun around and tilted his head—then shook it violently. "That's not the one I know! Get away from it."

Jenna looked to Talia, but the thing was only two ship lengths away and the Strann ship continued to close the distance between them.

They didn't have a lot of options.

"Keep going." Jenna ran to the back of the ship and reached out to the creature coming after them with a freeze spell. Either it simply didn't work over water or that thing repelled it. It wasn't swimming fast, but it was still coming for them.

"Turn around, we have to help them!" Keanin and Ghortin's yells echoed across the water.

The Strann ship was slowing down, probably waiting to see if the kraken would do their work for them, but it remained on course.

Jenna pulled out her cuari book, the two spells that she'd saved weren't for fighting off a single attacker, but there were others.

The book opened to a communication spell. "Great, but I don't think this is the time." She tried flipping pages, but it kept going to that one. "This behavior better stop when we're up against the other portal—or I'll throw you in it!" The books hadn't shown signs of being sentient until now, and this wasn't a great time for it.

She read the communication spell three times before she cast it, by then the kraken was close enough to see its alarmingly intelligent eyes.

It let out an odd watery roar. "Why you on water?"

"Oh…I understand you." Jenna was glad the spell worked but still wasn't sure it would stop that thing from smashing Talia's ship to splinters.

"Understand. You evil." The voice translated even deeper than the roar.

"No! No, we're not." She pointed toward Keanin's ship. "My friend over there saved one of your kind a while ago. Those behind you are evil." She took a chance. "The portal below is evil; we're trying to destroy it." If that portal was active, it could be messing up any sea-life in the area. Providing the kraken were native and hadn't come to this world through the portal.

The pause from the creature made her think she'd made a serious mistake.

"You destroy ring of death? Promise?" The kraken closed in and visually blocked her from seeing anything past it.

Jenna raised her hands to Talia and the others who'd drawn bows and arrows. "Don't. Please don't fire. It's on our side." That was a stretch, but she doubted the arrows could hurt it.

"Yes, we need to stop that ship and then destroy the ring of death." That thing could call the portal whatever it wanted as long as it didn't destroy them.

The kraken submerged.

That could mean it was leaving them alone. Or that it was planning on coming up from underneath the ship as it ripped it apart.

"We have to kill it if it comes back up," one of the

Erlindans on the ship shouted. But the shaking in his hands showed he realized that wasn't an option.

"Can you use magic against it? How are you speaking to it?" Talia was calm, but she didn't lower her bow.

Jenna didn't turn from where the kraken had gone underwater. "I don't think any spells I could use would stop it. I already tried one of the strongest I know and it didn't do anything. As for understanding, *that* I could do with magic. I don't know that it wants to destroy us." That was a massive guess based solely on the way it referred to the portal as the ring of death.

"I hope you're right. Unfortunately, that Strann ship is picking up speed again." Talia put down her bow and stayed the course, but they wouldn't be able to get away.

The Strann ship's captain must have decided that if the kraken wouldn't destroy them, it would.

"It's coming alongside and looks to be preparing cannons." The crew member with a far-seeing glass shouted.

Talia turned toward the front. "Wave our other two ships off, they can't help us and will be destroyed."

Another crew member waved a red and black flag. Keanin's and Ghortin's ships slowed and came to a stop. Jenna wished she could speak to Ghortin in her mind now. They needed to get further away.

The ship shifted under her feet and she pulled up a spell that's sole purpose was to shove something away. Whether it would work on the kraken or not was another issue.

The kraken came back to the surface without attacking their ship. Another monstrous head appeared behind it.

"We help. You destroy death ring." The first one roared. The second one added something, but while she understood the first one, the second sounded like a muted roar. Like her friends not being able to understand the one she spelled, she couldn't understand its friend.

"Great. How?"

"Come." The kraken raised a tentacle and pointed in the general direction of the Strann ship.

"You want this ship to follow you?" She wasn't sure what good it would do. The Strann ship seriously outgunned them and they obviously had powerful mages onboard.

"No. You. Come with."

"I can't swim like you can." But she removed her sword and handed Talia her cuari book. The dagger wouldn't be left behind, but she secured it in a pocket in her vest. The cuari book was becoming tricky, but she doubted it was waterproof. "Guard this."

"Are you seriously thinking of going with that thing? Are you crazy?" Talia looked ready to grab Jenna and tie her up. But she gingerly took the cuari book and put it into a pouch on her waist.

"Might be. But as soon as we do whatever we're about to do, you need to get this ship out of here."

Talia opened her mouth to say something but was cut off by another roar.

"Go now." The kraken reached over the ship with a tentacle and then wrapped it around Jenna's waist.

"Trust me and it. Please." She tried not to squirm, but the tentacle was even slimier than she expected.

Talia motioned for her people to lower their bows. "I hope you're right. Storm will never forgive me if something happens to you. Keanin either."

Jenna barely heard the last part as the kraken swam toward the Strann ship. Still holding her above the water.

Or mostly above, she was going to be soaked by the time she got there. What exactly the kraken felt her part was going to be in this, she had no idea. It must have faith in her magic even though the freeze spell had failed against them. She had no weapons and two kraken.

The Strann ship fired cannons as they approached and the kraken muttered something and submerged.

Jenna shut her eyes and held her breath as she was pulled under. Then she opened her eyes. An iridescent case flowed around her. She was still soaking, but she couldn't feel the water now. Not a bubble really, it was only about an inch from her skin.

The kraken dove deep and she doubted she could hold her breath long enough for it to surface. Taking a chance, she opened her mouth. And could breathe.

Another pair of kraken joined the first two. Their roars underwater were far gentler than on the surface and weren't roars at all. Lovely, but she still wasn't certain what they wanted her for.

Cannonballs dropped from above, but the kraken easily swatted them aside. The one holding her came up behind the Strann ship, but none of the kraken were trying to destroy it. Judging by their size, and the fact that there were four of them—that would have been the easiest way to get this done.

But the kraken all remained a safe distance away, aside from the one holding her. That one sped close to the back of the ship and dropped her on the deck.

"Magic. Need your magic. Ours not work. Break shield, we finish."

Jenna stumbled to the deck. That would have been good to know.

The Strann crew ran for her with swords and she hit the first group with a stun spell, then grabbed the closest sword for herself.

There were more crew racing toward her. Her only chance was to break the shield protecting this ship and leave those kraken to destroy it.

She gave a yell and fought the next ones coming at her with sword and magic. Her next spells were oddly dimmed—the effect of the shielding spell on the ship.

However, there was a current of magic. When she cast her recent spell, she felt the pull. The shielding spell was anchored somewhere near the back. There was nothing there at first, then a flicker revealed a tall pole that was the focus of the spell protecting the ship.

Fighting two more crew, she darted back and struck the pole that was welded to the back of the ship with a shield breaker spell as magically powerful as she could send. She wasn't sure if she hit it at first, then tentacles began appearing over the railing and the Strann ship tried to go further out into the open ocean.

Jenna continued to fight the Strann people who ran to her, but there were fewer with many going overboard and more being plucked off by kraken tentacles. Why they thought going into deeper water would help against massive sea monsters, she had no idea.

Even though the shield protection was gone, the ship must have had further reinforcements as the kraken were pulling on it, but it was still intact. And still moving.

"The masts! Grab the masts!" She wasn't sure if there were more Strann ships nearby, they shouldn't have any at all, being a landlocked country, but they needed to destroy this one.

Four tentacles came over the side but were met with swords and magic.

Jenna ran over and fought back to allow the kraken to do their work.

One of the Strann people remained off to the side and appeared to be muttering spells. She ran toward him and sent a few of her own.

They bounced off.

With him still spell casting and enough defenders keeping the kraken from the masts or ripping apart the ship, there was a chance the Strann ship would survive long enough for any reinforcements to arrive.

Torn between the two fronts, Jenna brought her shield breaker spell up, packaged it with a freeze spell, and ran toward the mage.

The kraken continued to keep trying to reach the masts.

Then Jenna noticed that Talia was within firing range and that the other two ships of theirs had turned back and were racing for them.

Which might help, if they could slow this ship and get that mage to drop his spells.

Jenna jumped to attack the mage with her sword as she finished concocting the spell bundle.

Her borrowed sword made it through his spell and she sliced him across the mid-section before jumping back.

He wasn't armed but began calling up a nasty-sounding spell. The moment he tried to send it, she sent her magic concoction at him, and dove to the side.

It worked, sort of. The mage's shield fell, but he appeared to be fighting back against the freeze spell.

Ghortin had claimed that when cast, no one could defend against the freeze spell. But this man was freezing, busting through, then freezing again. Each time he came back a bit stronger.

Not unlike when Edgar was possessed.

The deck rocked as Talia's ship came alongside and fired cannons.

Jenna had no idea why this ship hadn't fired back. Then she saw cannons being flung in the air and into the ocean. The kraken didn't like them and were making certain they couldn't be used.

The masts were also torn out and flung into the water as the last spells protecting the ship fell.

Ghortin and Keanin's ships were now within firing range and both mages were shouting spells.

The Strann mage she'd cut snarled at them then turned to her. "This isn't over. You'll fail. Everyone in this world will fall and die."

She didn't think it was a spell, but pure depression and hopelessness slammed into her and dropped her to her knees. She couldn't breathe. She couldn't think. He was right, she needed to give up now. Everything was pointless.

Then a tentacle smacked her.

She'd fallen to the deck and was in a fetal position. And the mage she'd frozen was slowly making his way to her.

The tentacle raised for another strike. "Fight!" That roar was a serious bellow and it told her which of the kraken was smacking her around.

She pushed herself up, grabbed her stolen sword, and jumped for the mage. Whether she survived or not, this man wasn't going to. Whoever he was, he was too powerful to be left alive.

She drove her sword into his partially frozen body and saw him grimace in pain. Then he vanished.

"No!" She swung with her sword in case he'd somehow gone invisible, but there was nothing there. Either he'd spelled himself free, or someone he was working for did.

The ship continued to rock as the kraken, Talia, and the captain on Keanin's ship all worked to destroy it.

The Strann crew dove overboard to avoid the attacking tentacles but judging by the way the water churned around the ship, they weren't getting far.

The ship cracked in half and began to sink.

CHAPTER FIFTY-ONE

"JENNA! JUMP TO THIS SIDE!" Talia had her ship close, but Jenna knew she couldn't jump that far. Then a tentacle grabbed her and deposited her on the deck of Talia's ship.

A kraken head appeared. "Destroy death ring." Then it went back to ripping apart the Strann ship.

"We need to get away from here immediately," Talia yelled to the other two ships, then turned to help Jenna to her feet. "I'm glad you were right, but this area is going to be a mess for a while." She also handed her the cuari book. "It fared better than you did. Sorry that you're drenched."

Jenna looked at her clothing, it hadn't fared well. She buckled on her sword belt and added the dagger back to it. She held up the sword she'd taken from the Strann ship. "We have another spare though."

Talia smiled. "Good, can always use more weapons." She barked a few more orders and the three ships moved further out to sea.

Jenna wrung what she could out of her clothes, and flipped open the cuari book. It didn't even fuss with changing pages this time, just immediately tugged them to the right.

"Right this time!"

"All ships starboard!" Talia yelled then turned back to Jenna. "Any idea how far out we're going? Kraken might not be the only danger out here."

Jenna shrugged. "It is only telling me a direction." She

glanced back where the kraken were still destroying the Strann ship. It was as if they were taking pleasure in it, as they could have sunk it the moment she took out the shield and the mage. Hopefully, her kraken friend would come join them. Or at least respond if she called. They were still in the same situation—they should be able to focus the cuari spell book to hit the portal, but there was already a lot of water beneath them.

Keanin waved at them from his ship. "Jenna! You bonded with one!" He was far too happy about it. But they had shared an odd connection about magically related items in the past. Maybe this was just one more.

"Not sure if I'd say bonded, more like we agreed to help each other. But those kraken aren't mindless killing machines, they're smart."

He smiled and nodded.

Jenna looked back at the distant ship collapsing behind them. That mage shouldn't have been able to fight her freeze spell like that or almost destroy her by hitting her with crippling fear and self-doubt.

And he shouldn't have been able to vanish right in front of her.

But the kraken had somehow realized what that mage had used to get in her head. And it had disrupted it. Too bad she didn't think there was a way to make the kraken land-worthy. And small enough to fit in her pocket.

More things to talk to Ghortin, Rachael, and Tor Ranshal about.

They followed the odd pulling of the cuari book without kraken escorts. Finally, the book settled and stopped pulling. It returned to flipping page content, however.

"I think we should stop." Jenna didn't look up as she called out. There might be a reason for the order of the pages changing, but as of now, she couldn't sort it out.

Talia called for the other two ships to move into position as her crew dropped anchor.

It took some maneuvering to get the other two ships into position, they needed to be a specific distance from Talia's ship and all facing the center of the water in front of them. Each time Talia attempted to change direction to help the other two out, Jenna's book got cranky.

After a half hour, they were in position. At least as far as Jenna could tell.

The cuari book remained on the calling spell page, the one that should create the explosive power needed for the portal—and join everything she, Ghortin, and Keanin could throw at it.

"How are we going to know if it works?" Talia asked. "I don't think we want to stay out here longer than needed—there might be more Strann ships and we've no idea what the Khelarans were doing."

Jenna glanced toward the shore, but it was little more than a thin line. However, Talia made good points. Not to mention the sooner they made it back to shore, the quicker they could help Storm and the rest.

Providing there was a safe place to land the ships.

"Try calling the kraken," Ghortin shouted.

Keanin appeared to be trying to do that from the bow of his ship. As before, his eyes were closed and he was muttering words.

Jenna kept her eyes open but tried calling the kraken she'd dealt with. She had no idea if they had names, or even what gender it was. She hoped that since it had wanted that portal destroyed as well, it might answer her.

She was about to give up and tell the others that they'd have to cast the spell without it when the creature appeared off to the side of the ship.

Then a second one rose out of the water next to Keanin's ship, and a third, lighter and larger one appeared next to Ghortin.

"We take. You magic."

"You can take our magic to the portal?"

"No. We take you. You take magic."

"Oh." That odd protection that had helped her breathe under the water. Neither Keanin nor Ghortin were going to like this.

"It says we need to go to the portal to directly focus the magic that will destroy it. But I need the book to set the spell. I'll set it, you two add to it so we're linked magically, then jump in the water near your kraken."

Even Keanin was startled at that and he'd been cooing at his kraken friend.

"We can't swim to the bottom of the ocean. Have you seen how far out we are?" Ghortin marched to the railing of his ship. "I don't have a spell that would protect us. It's impossible. Why can't they simply confirm when we destroy it?"

"That might have been our plan, but I don't think the kraken agree."

The kraken near her bobbed its head in an almost human move. "Agreed. You miss and death ring stays."

"What did it say?"

"That the odds of us missing from up here were too good. We need to go down there." She briefly explained about the protection she'd received when the kraken went after the Strann ship. "Depth didn't appear to bother the protection, and I didn't feel any change in pressure." She now wished she'd paid more attention, but at the time not dying or panicking was her main goal.

"I don't know." Ghortin paced along the railing.

"We don't have a choice. What if we leave this portal, manage to destroy the one in the Markare, and then whoever is trying to come through finds a way to come out of this one? The kraken calls it the ring of death. I think they have a reason for that." Jenna took a deep breath and shoved aside the idea of any underwater, but not from this world, monsters who could destroy the kraken.

"I hope you're right." Ghortin took off his cloak, and outer vest, and left his sword and cuari book on the deck. He kept his staff.

Keanin got ready as well. Although he seemed excited about the adventure. From the muttering coming from Talia, she certainly wasn't.

"For good or ill, let's do this." Ghortin stood like an avenging deity with his staff in one hand and a spell ready in the other.

Keanin had his hands at the ready for spells.

Jenna gave the cuari book one final glance, then gathered the spell in her mind. "I have no idea how long this will take," she told Talia. "But hold these positions as long as you can."

She didn't feel as hopeless as she did about the Markare portal, but Jenna knew there was a chance none of them were coming back from this. But if those voices that she had faced wanted her to leave the portals alone, that was the last thing she was going to do.

She took her sword belt off, but felt an odd tingle from the dagger. She left the sword, but kept the belt and the dagger. A warming feeling replaced the tingling. If it wanted to get soaked again, more power to it.

At Talia's nod, Jenna cast the spell that would target the portal's unique properties and destroy it. Once she felt it solidify, she shared it with Keanin and Ghortin. Most spells didn't leave a presence, but this one had an odd glow that changed color slightly from each mage. Then the three lines crossed to each other and vanished into the water.

"Water, now!" The kraken bellowed and Jenna jumped into the ocean. She was glad that she hadn't dried off yet.

Keanin followed without hesitation, and then Ghortin begrudgingly jumped in.

The kraken she was talking to swam to her and held

out a tentacle. It didn't grab her but motioned for her to come to it. Then it gently circled her waist.

The same happened with the other two, although Ghortin batted at the tentacle before giving in.

"You'll be able to breathe, but you might want to hold on to the tentacle," Jenna yelled before being pulled under. Even knowing that she would be able to breathe, she found herself holding her breath.

The kraken dove quickly but the other two were close enough that she saw their faces clearly. Keanin was laughing. Ghortin appeared to be holding his breath and had his eyes closed.

She figured he'd have to release his breath eventually.

The water grew murkier, but that didn't slow down the kraken. She had an appreciation for their speed now. She wasn't sure of the distance, but she'd bet they could go from Khelaran to the far southern tip of Traanafaeren in less than an hour.

The water cleared, but it was too dark to see far because of the depth. Then Ghortin started glowing. Rather, he'd cast a mage light spell, then he released another to go ahead of them.

Jenna hadn't thought of that. She hadn't known if a spell could cross the membrane that was protecting them—obviously, it could.

She and Keanin repeated Ghortin's spell as the kraken continued going deeper.

They were in some sort of a sea trench. Part of her wondered if they had those odd-looking deep-sea creatures that were found in the extreme deep back on Earth. Then she laughed to herself as she held on to the tentacle that was pulling her. A kraken was definitely an odd creature.

She'd seen drawings of the portal in the Markare, but as there was nothing around it, there was no way for her to comprehend the size.

If the huge pile of rocks that their streams of magic and the kraken were heading toward was the portal, it was as long as a football field. It was also probably twenty feet in width.

Jenna swore under her breath. How could any magic destroy something this big? And the Markare one was larger? The feeling of being doomed only hit her briefly, mostly because she was faced with the massiveness of what they were trying to do here and now.

Their magic was traveling ahead of the kraken but now slowed. Even though she was part of her magic, she didn't feel like the combined force was part of her.

The three kraken hovered over the massive portal and released their people. Jenna had a moment of panic as she was afraid the spell that was allowing them to breathe would go as well, but it held.

Feeling oddly weighted, Jenna dropped to the top of the portal along with Keanin and Ghortin. Their spell crackled around them and the kraken pulled back.

"Now what?" Jenna had to yell to be heard but Ghortin nodded.

"We aim the spell. Here, I'd guess. You need to tie into the spell, not only your part. Then we release it." Ghortin sounded like he did this regularly.

"Now? I feel the spell, but it needs an anchor." Keanin held out his hands, palms facing the portal below them.

"I agree on needing the anchor, but maybe it needs all three of us to be prepared. Jenna? Are you ready?"

Jenna swore. She didn't feel the magic. Not hers nor theirs. There was nothing there. They were going to fail and die down here.

Then she took a deep breath. Whatever had taken root in her mind, it was insidious and branching out. Not this time. She focused back on the magic and felt the full spell. And some tugging from her dagger in its sheath. "I'm ready. The dagger seems interested though." It was an odd term to use, but felt accurate. It was physically pulling toward the portal.

"Take it out and hold it as far from you as you can, pointing toward the portal," Ghortin said. "Maybe that will help."

Jenna wasn't happy with him saying maybe in this case, but she did it. The dagger was almost purring now.

On Ghortin's count, she and Keanin released their spells. Still wound together, they were pulled into the dagger, then a single beam slammed into the stone under their feet. At first, it appeared that nothing had happened. Then an electrical crackling spread out from the center to the edges. A kraken took each end and one wrapped its tentacles around the top where they stood.

"Come. All come." It was her kraken and it motioned for her and the other two to come to it. It spared a tentacle and grabbed all three together as Jenna sheathed her dagger.

Then all three kraken pulled as the combined spell ripped into the stone portal.

"Now!" Her kraken yelled as it ripped apart the center of the portal, then pushed off and shot for the surface.

The other two kraken had done the same with the sides.

The portal was exploding through magic and force and even though that wouldn't be how the one in the Markare would be destroyed, it was still fascinating to see.

They bobbed to the surface as a series of explosions followed them up. Her kraken dropped the three of them on Talia's ship.

"Go quick. Thank you." Then it dove back into the water.

"You heard the kraken—set sail!" Jenna knew the others couldn't understand the creature but it was pretty emphatic in its roar.

Talia barked orders to the other two captains and then turned to Jenna. "Where to?"

"South? Sorry, not sure where else to go." The Strann ship was destroyed, but there could be more. Not to mention those hostile Khelarans on the beach. The other two ships followed as Talia led them south of Erlinda.

They came a little closer to shore, but still far enough away that it was hard to see what was happening in the town.

"I'm sure they're okay." Ghortin came up behind her far more silent than a dripping wet man with a staff should have been able to.

"I hope so. I can't shake this feeling of doom." She hadn't brought it up before, almost as if she shouldn't. But it came out automatically this time.

"About them?"

"About everything." She shook her head as a feeling of not wanting to share overwhelmed her. People were counting on her, she couldn't tell them that she couldn't do it. "I'm sure it's nothing."

CHAPTER FIFTY-TWO

DIFFUSED EXPLOSIONS FADED AS THEY sailed away, but the waves continued to spread out in massive circles behind them.

"I take it the portal is destroyed?" Talia stayed near Keanin but there was no doubt who was the captain of this ship.

"As far as I know." Jenna glanced behind them. "I don't think the kraken would have let us go if it wasn't destroyed." There was no sign of the giant things, but they were definitely okay in her book now. She patted her dagger. Being stuck with it wasn't so bad now either.

"There's a smaller cove that's not far from Erlinda, but will allow for easy escape if we fall under attack." Talia waved to a stretch of land to the south. "We can dock there, leave enough crew to move the ships if needed, then see how the town fares." Even though Talia had made it known she was staying with Keanin and the rest until this war was over for good, the concern in her voice concerning Erlinda was clear. It was still her home.

"Smoke! There's a fire in the city!" Talia's lookout continued watching through the far-seeing glass.

"Damn it, we need to get there now." Talia turned toward the cove, then waved to the three magic users. "Can you fill the sails on all three ships even though you're all on this one?"

Ghortin paused, and then he nodded. "We should be able to. Might want to move a little bit closer and on either side of us." He moved closer to the ship he'd been on, Keanin took the other side, and Jenna stayed in the middle.

The sails filled and the ships picked up speed.

"The fire doesn't seem to be spreading." Along with earthquakes, Jenna was well-versed in fires. While there was a fair amount of smoke, it was confined to one area and went up into the blue sky in a thick column.

"Edgar, Altheria, and a few other magic users are in the two groups—they could be containing it." Ghortin continued his wind spell but nodded toward the town. "That's hopefully a good sign though."

As they approached the cove, there was a thin line of people running away to the north. If they were the attackers, Jenna hoped the Khelarans were still camped out there.

She really didn't want it to be Storm and her friends. Storm wouldn't abandon a fight unless things had gone horrifically wrong.

They got the ships into the cove. There better not be any defenders in that tower or along the walls or they'd spot the ships immediately.

Ghortin, Keanin, and Jenna took the lead, with Talia and three of the crew from the ships with them.

There weren't enough left with either the departing group or those staying on the ship to be a serious force. But they need to save their ships and five of them could move them if needed. It could be argued that Jenna, Keanin, and Ghortin were formidable enough to balance things on their end in the town.

"Is there a drying spell or something?" Jenna held out her waterlogged arm as the approached Erlinda. "If anything, just to keep our sound down if there is any sneaking involved. We make too much noise like this."

"I can try," Ghortin spoke a few words, and an odd wind came from the ground, circled the three mages, and then vanished. "That's a bit better. I don't want to do more until we know what we're up against. Making noise might be less problematic than draining our magic. We've all been using a lot."

Jenna nodded. Her clothing now felt like it had come out of a dryer a bit too soon.

The tower appeared abandoned and the shattered door leading up indicated that it hadn't been by choice.

The walls surrounding the town were in an odd state of decay.

"Are they foaming?" Jenna tried to keep her voice down in case anyone was still out here, but the beach leading to town appeared abandoned. There was an odd mixture of gray, green, and brown foam dripping down the walls. And they were now less than ten feet high.

"Looks like. I wouldn't have thought the spells would work like that, but it's getting the job done, albeit slower than expected." Ghortin stopped and scowled toward the water. "They might not have built them to last, but we don't want our new friends attacking the town now that the walls are down."

"True, but might be best to make sure our side won." Talia waved her sword toward the entrance to the town. It appeared to have been roughly barricaded before, but now had no one or anything blocking it beyond a pile of rubble. "If our side didn't win, I like the idea of those kraken taking the town."

"Let's see what's happened then." Ghortin used his staff to help him get through the dunes and led the way in.

Talia was behind him and in front of Keanin and Jenna with the rest following. Ghortin could blast anything that attacked, and Talia would know if they were friend or foe.

The damage was extensive, but it was impossible to determine as they walked by if it was from the initial attack, or from their people. It was also troublingly quiet. The slowly melting sea wall made a disturbing dripping sound.

There were faint yells to the north, but nothing near here. Jenna had a flash of concern for Storm, Edgar, and Crell, but shoved that aside. Those were three of the best fighters she knew. And Edgar was a mage with the mental support of a cuari. They had to be okay.

Jenna moved further away from the sea walls as she heard muffled sounds. They were so faint that even their footsteps and the gloopy sounds from the sea walls first hid them. "Hold on, I heard something down this street." It was a narrow road, but looked like it led to larger buildings. "What's down this way?"

The captain from Keanin's ship was closest to her and looked down the road. "It's taken some damage, but this was the warehouse district. Supplies, factories, nothing to help us right now."

"But what's that sound?" Jenna held up her hand for everyone to be quiet for a few moments. "Those are voices."

Talia tilted her head and then ran toward the faint sounds.

Jenna thought it sounded like people asking for help but it could be a trap. But, if those voices were prisoners, they needed to be freed.

It might have only been a week, but Erlinda had fallen hard. Many buildings were damaged and in danger of collapsing.

The structure they ran to was intact with chains running through a pair of wide door handles. No guards were visible.

Talia raised her hand to slow down, then finally raised her clenched fist for everyone to stop. Jenna might not see any guards, but Talia wasn't taking chances.

Satisfied that the rest would wait, Talia moved forward. Keanin took a step to follow, but then held off.

Jenna smiled. He was learning.

Talia crouched behind a crumbled wall near the doors.

She might not have magic, but she was good at what she did. After a few minutes, she waved everyone to her.

"People are yelling for help, but I can't be completely sure they're our people."

Keanin tried to listen but then shrugged. "But do you think Tireli and the rest would take the people who attacked their town prisoners?"

"Good point. I know I wouldn't." She looked at the chains. "Could you?" She wiggled her fingers at Keanin.

He gave one of his trademark fancy bows, then sent a spell at the chains. They took a moment to break but then slid off.

Talia moved forward, but Jenna stopped her. "It might be better to have Keanin and me go first, blast anything that might not be on our side. Ghortin can keep an eye on us."

Ghortin opened his mouth to argue, then shrugged.

Talia nodded but remained close to the doors.

Keanin and Jenna each took hold of a door handle, cast blast spells, and flung the doors open.

A single spell shot out, mid-height to catch more victims, but Keanin and Jenna destroyed it before it got two feet toward them.

The warehouse was dark, so Ghortin sent in mage lights. There were probably over a hundred people inside, all Erlindans based on their clothing. They stayed near the back and at first, Jenna thought they were afraid, but then she realized they were all chained. Long thin chains, but they were limited to the back of the warehouse.

"We have to free them!" One of Talia's people ran forward, but she held out a hand to stop him.

"There could be more magic traps on those chains. We want to rescue them, not bring this entire place down."

"Jenna and I can check." Keanin and Jenna went forward.

The people looked upset, but also ready to fight. Some wore the remains of armor, but none had weapons.

"Thank you. We heard fighting earlier but they didn't come closer and no one heard us." A tall man was closest and held out his chained hands. "They didn't kill us, even made this place homelike. But we were to be offered to the sea beasts once they were done with Erlinda. They liked reminding us of that. And the mages with us when we were captured were taken somewhere else."

Jenna reached for his chains, then pulled back. A low current indicated there was magic within the chain. Not a lot, but it could be connected to something bad. The attackers might not care if their offerings to the kraken were alive or dead.

"But why build the sea wall to keep them out if this was their plan?" She gently took the chain and found a spell to disconnect it. It would take time to get them all removed.

"The sea monsters were after the attackers," a woman said as Jenna removed the spell from her chains. The chains themselves dropped off once the magic was removed. "They had some plan to offer us when they were done doing whatever they were doing. To appease the monsters."

Jenna and Keanin continued working on the chains, but it was slow work. They needed to get out of here and take down the rest of the attackers. And find their friends.

Two of Talia's people came forward. "We're low-level magic users, not strong enough for the enemy to care about. We can keep working on the spell to release them."

Talia nodded. "Good. Once you get them free lead everyone out of town." She pointed to a few of the fighters in the captured group who appeared ready to argue. "Once free, your job is to find weapons and move these people to safety—and keep an ear out for others who might be trapped."

They still didn't hear fighting as they left the building, but the town was long. The smoke was focused on the northern end.

"I still don't smell a fire though," Jenna kept her voice low as they slowly made their way further into the town. "Nor hear anything." She was glad they found that group, but this town would have held many more.

A twinge of fear hit her, they hadn't heard anything more about Carabella and the rest trapped in the Zalin shelter either. One disaster at a time.

The sound of fighting finally reached them. No more groups of prisoners, but they couldn't check all the likely places for them. With luck, they'd defeat the attackers and reclaim the entire town.

Or they might not be able to get anyone out.

Jenna stayed up front with Talia and Keanin. Ghortin was bringing up the rear by choice. He was still the strongest magic user they had.

The smoke was toward the back of the town, away from the ocean, but still was contained in an odd column. Something was burning, but nothing they could figure out until they could get there.

The fighting was taking place close enough to the northern entrance to the town that they saw the beach. And a group of soldiers waiting on that beach. All were heavily armed, but even the archers weren't firing on the fighting people inside the town. Or crossing into the town itself.

"Those are Khelarans, right? What are they doing?" Jenna asked Talia as they jogged closer to the fighting. Aside from Storm, Crell, Edgar, and the people she knew, figuring out which side was which was going to be hard.

Which might be why the Khelarans were waiting for the two sides to finish.

Talia said what Jenna was thinking. Good to know

that they would be facing another fight once they got through this one.

"They seem well balanced; I have a feeling that the invaders had less than we thought and our people found reinforcements." A tall woman who'd been part of Tireli's crew said as she used one of the far-seeing glasses to watch the fights.

"Could make sense. If they were saving their prisoners for something else, they'd want to keep most of the fighters together." Talia studied the buildings around them for any help, or more attackers.

"I see Storm!" Jenna didn't have one of the far-seeing glasses, but she'd recognize that hair anyplace. He was fighting three attackers and whirling so easily as he pushed each one back that it took her breath away.

Until a fourth came racing up and took a swing at his head with a club. Storm ducked but still took a hard hit to his shoulder that caused him to lose the second smaller blade he was fighting with.

"Oh, that's not happening. Sorry, everyone." Jenna pulled her sword free of the scabbard, then took out the dagger as well, and ran over the piles of stone debris. Storm was swinging up as all four attackers charged him when she struck one. A blur appeared from the left, Altheria. She took down a second one with a bow to Jenna.

Storm didn't seem to be able to move the arm that got clubbed, but he was still trying to fight the remaining two attackers off.

"Men." Jenna met Altheria's eyes as they ran to get the last two.

Storm might be stubborn, but he was smart enough to realize when he should pull back. He let Jenna and Altheria finish off the remaining attackers.

"Thank you, there are still more down that alley." He was barely holding his sword with his good arm.

"Not for you. Go back to the southern entrance and look for a group heading to the ships." Altheria's voice reminded Jenna of Crell right now. The don't-even-think-about-it tone.

Storm shook her off. "We found more fighters for our side, but we'll still be out-numbered when the Khelarans come in here. And something beyond the spells our people used is shattering the sea wall."

Jenna hadn't noticed, but at some point during the run over, the sea wall began collapsing faster. Where it had been sloughing off slowly, entire chunks were now being ripped off.

She wasn't surprised when she saw tentacles tearing them off. "It's the kraken. They're on our side." She hoped she was right. They might have only worked with them to get the portal taken out.

"Nice to know Keanin's not the only one to make friends with them. But I can't leave, we have to finish this fight before they get through."

Jenna wanted to grab and shake him but given the paleness that was taking over his face, she didn't think that was a great idea. "Go, we can take care of this, but you need to catch up to the others." She hated sending him away but a cold feeling in her gut told her they needed to finish this fight now. And he was in no condition to join them.

"I can still—"

"Die? Yes, you could. And be a distraction for Jenna and your friends who love you." Altheria's tone was wise counselor, but she'd picked up Storm's second blade and had her arms crossed. "You need to leave."

Storm didn't blush, but he gave a sharp nod. "Agreed. Stay safe." He gave Jenna a quick kiss on her head and slipped out of the fighting. He was already near the edge of the battle, so it looked like he'd be fine, then a massive human rounded to attack him. The attacker took four arrows to the back before Storm could even turn around.

"Hon!" Talia yelled as a new crew came running in from the back road into town. Eighty or so swordspeople and archers, and from the crackling spells flying around, mages as well. They quickly engaged the enemy. Although the Khelarans weren't attacking inside the town, they also wouldn't let anyone leave and the Erlindan attackers were forced back to fight the new forces.

The retreating invaders tried running toward the direction Jenna and her people had come in, but she didn't know how much better that way was going to work.

Carabella was leading her own attack force from that side.

The attackers continued to hide, but they were up against people who knew Erlinda—even in its distressed shape—far too well.

Meanwhile, the sea wall was still being pulled down.

Jenna ran to Carabella. "I thought you were all trapped in that shelter?"

"We were. And I have a feeling it was whoever those people are working with who did it. Long story, but we made a new exit." She tilted her head as she glared at the attackers then turned toward the sea wall. "Is that a kraken taking apart that badly made wall?" She didn't sound concerned, only curious.

"More than one probably." Jenna smiled. "They're tentatively on our side."

The fighting continued, but the attackers' numbers were winnowed down quickly.

"What are we going to do with them?" Talia pointed her sword to the Khelarans blocking the north. None of them had entered Erlinda, but they also hadn't lowered their weapons.

CHAPTER FIFTY-THREE

"I TAKE IT THAT THEY AREN'T on our side?" Carabella grinned and raised her sword toward the Khelarans.

Jenna hadn't noticed her use any magic, which was for the best. That didn't mean that things couldn't change. Especially if Carabella got caught up in the fight and forgot.

"It doesn't seem like it, they fired arrows as we took the ships out." Ghortin waved off the questions Carabella was going to ask. "Long story, we'll explain later. However, they haven't tried to do anything else beyond stopping people from escaping that direction."

"Who lit the fhalon fire?" Carabella turned to the single column of smoke near the northern edge of town.

"Damn, I didn't recognize it," Ghortin swore and stomped over to the part of town that it came from. "Come on Jenna and Keanin, this will be a learning experience. Talia, I trust you can keep the Khelarans out and your people in?"

She nodded and the three of them walked off.

Carabella gave a blood curdling yell and charged a group of attackers. She might have recognized the fire, but she wasn't that interested in it.

"What's a fhalon fire?" Jenna hadn't heard of that one and aside from lining the sky with smoke, she really had no idea why it was there.

"It's an old magic. Designed to draw in people who want to put it out, and given enough time, it can sway the weak-minded to a cause not their own. Honestly, of all the old spells that keep popping up as of late—I don't know why someone did this one." He grinned. "But as neither of you has seen one of these before, it will make a great learning experience."

Keanin kept turning back toward the fighting. It was dying down as the attackers were overwhelmed by Carabella's troops. "They're still fighting. And those Khelarans could attack at any moment. Maybe this isn't the time for a lesson."

Ghortin was a few steps ahead of them but stopped. "It's always a time for a lesson. Not to mention, Carabella, Talia, and the rest have things well taken care of. I need you two to work together on more spells before we face the Markare." His brows lowered. "I have an odd feeling we'll be needing it. And a third." He held up his hands. "Don't ask, I have no idea who or where this came from. But my hunches are usually accurate." With a tight nod he turned and marched down a narrow road toward the fire.

Keanin gave a sigh and one final look toward the fighting, then followed.

Jenna trailed a bit behind them, something Ghortin said reminded her of something else. But it wasn't coming to mind yet.

The fhalon fire was disturbing in more ways than one. Although the column of flame and smoke was crackling along, it wasn't branching out to the structures next to it. Nor to the thirty or so heavily armed people gathered around it but not moving.

"Are they Khelarans?" Jenna didn't recognize the armor, but it did look a bit like what the Khelarans outside were wearing. She kept her voice low, but there was no reaction from them as Ghortin approached.

Keanin scowled as he walked to the nearest one and poked him in the shoulder. "Yes. But they're completely frozen." He waved one hand in front of the Khelaran man's open-eyed stare—but there was no response.

"That might be why the rest of their people are waiting outside. This group came in and were spelled." Ghortin slowly walked around the stunned Khelarans. "They are all still alive, but there's no way to know if they came here as friend or foe."

Jenna looked away from the fire. "Should we be standing here? Won't that spelled fire grab us too?"

Ghortin continued his walk around. "I put a protection spell over us as we approached, but a fhalon spell would have to be far stronger than this to catch any self-respecting mage. There's not a strong magic user in this group."

"Let's shut this thing down and get back to fighting." Keanin stopped looking back in the direction of the remaining fighting, but he held tight to the hilt of his sword.

"This might appear simplistic, and as I said, it most likely couldn't affect magic users of our level, but make no mistake, this is a dangerous spell if used correctly. Whoever cast it failed to complete it or these people would have been fighting us. Regardless of which side they were actually on."

Jenna thought of the non-magic user fighters they had in Irundail and coming up from the remains of Lithunane. "How far can this spell go? How many people can it hit?"

"As large as the mage who casts it wants it. As I said, it's not the most Powerful of spells, but if used properly, it could change the tide of a battle." He peered closer at the fire and smoke. Then at the guards circling it. "This one was set, then forgotten. Or the one who set it was killed before they could take control of the Khelarans. It's been running longer than would have been needed to influence these people."

"I get it, this spell is bad, and Jenna and I need practice.

Can we get on with it?" Keanin leaned closer to one of the Khelarans. "Do we want to release thirty armed fighters here though? We have no idea whose side they're on."

"Excellent point." Ghortin rubbed his hands together and gave a huge grin. "How would you two handle this?"

Jenna and Keanin shared a look and a shrug.

"Find the spell to release them? Which neither of us currently knows," Keanin said.

Jenna nodded. "Add a confusion spell so they are free, but will obey our commands to politely walk out the northern gate without fighting us? Hopefully, the rest of the Khelarans will back off when their friends are returned." She knew it was a long shot, but no one seemed to know which side the Khelarans were on.

"Jenna had the better answer. I know you're growing in Power, Keanin, but even you might be hard-pressed to fight off this many. Not to mention, if they aren't our enemies, we don't want to have to fight them. We need as many people on our side as possible." Ghortin's grin grew wider. "And both of you already have been trained in a spell that would work quite nicely in this case."

Jenna turned to Keanin but he seemed lost as well.

"The shield spell." Ghortin's grin dropped and he shook his head with a sigh. "If it is used to suppress the spell for the fire, it will put it out. It will work better with three, so let's spread out. When you send the shield spell make sure it encases the fire and smoke completely. Our spells need to overlap to extinguish the entire thing— and as Jenna pointed out adding a low-level confusion spell should leave them conscious but pliable enough to walk them to their friends."

He looked expectantly at them.

Jenna shrugged, pulled in the shield spell, a simple confusion spell, and aimed them at half of the column of fire.

Keanin did the same, then Ghortin. With each taking

half, they had significant overlap and the fire was completely enclosed.

The fire was extinguishing and the Khelarans were slowly coming back to consciousness when a yell came from behind Jenna. "Release our people!" Followed by the sound of a lot of metal on stone clanking.

Jenna and her friends might have believed the Khelarans were going to remain outside the north gate, but apparently, no one told the Khelarans.

"Hold the spell." Ghortin dropped his spell and Keanin and Jenna spread their spells thinner to make sure they still had a seal around the fire.

Jenna kept her eyes on the smoke and fire—and the still partially transfixed Khelarans. Keanin looked like he was contemplating turning around and fighting the ones behind them.

"Don't. Keep focusing on the spells," she pitched her voice low but judging by the frown on his face, Keanin heard her.

Ghortin moved past Jenna with his hand raised. His other hand was clutching his staff and it seemed to her he was limping—or trying to appear as if he was. "Now, easy, my friends. We didn't cast this spell. We're freeing them. Erlinda was overtaken a week ago by enemies of Traanafaeren. Your people got trapped."

"How do we know that you're not the attackers? King Philia sent us specifically to help Traanafaeren after the destruction of Lithunane. Yet our ships were set upon and only ours made it here before it was destroyed. Three of my people died and their bodies were thrown out to us when we tried to cross into the city. The rest are standing here."

The voice sounded like a big man, but Jenna wasn't going to turn around to look. The fire and smoke were condensing into a thin stream, but so far the Khelarans around it hadn't moved much.

Things could go bad extremely quickly if the mind-muddling confusion spells didn't hold. The kelar talking to Ghortin sounded like he was looking for a reason to start bashing people.

"I am Ghortin, Mastermage Ghortin. With me are two of our most Powerful mages who are trying to save your people. I don't know what I can say to make you believe me." He was good. Ghortin added a combination of strength with a twinge of old man to his voice.

"Free them and we'll see."

"That's what we're trying to do, in case you hadn't noticed. It's hard when a mess of armed people are at our backs," Keanin didn't yell, but he raised his voice. He also glanced toward the speaker before turning back to the fhalon fire.

"I know you." The kelar man stepped forward. Judging by the crunching sounds behind Jenna. "You were in the palace in Craelyn."

His voice didn't sound any more hostile than he already was, but he also didn't sound friendly.

"I was. We saved your king and your kingdom. Or did you miss that part?" Keanin's voice was so challenging that Jenna had to glance over to make sure it was him.

"You uncovered the demonspawn." Less hostility, but still wary.

"My friends and I uncovered them and killed many."

"Stand down. These are allies." There was a clanking as the soldiers who surrounded them relaxed.

The last of the fhalon fire extinguished itself and the thirty Khelarans who'd been held trapped blinked as one and collapsed.

Ghortin and a tall, broad kelar in heavy armor ran forward.

"How long were they here?" Ghortin checked the pulses and eyes of three of the fallen. "They're simply unconscious."

"They came in a week ago and the fire started right after."

Jenna and Keanin checked the ones around them. Jenna's were all asleep. Exhaustion was clear on their faces.

"They're going to need help to recover, they were trapped in their bodies." Carabella's voice startled Jenna. She was too good at creeping up on people. Or she'd been hiding during the entire event. "The town has been retaken. The kraken are finishing up destroying the sea wall and haven't eaten anyone." She marched up to the kelar leader and held out her hand. "I'm Carabella, nice to meet you."

The rough kelar shook her hand and then grew pale. "Carabella the *cuari?*"

Normally it was clear that Carabella was a cuari, but she'd taken to wearing a bandana over her ears and dressed like everyone else. Her cat-like eyes were a give-away, but you had to be close to notice them.

"The one and only." She winced at her flip words—she was the only cuari right now. "Your friends are suffering from extreme exhaustion and the aftereffects of that spell. Even though they were controlled by that wretched fhalon fire, they remained conscious. With no food or water for a week. They will need to come with us to Irundail to recover fully." She folded her arms as if she expected the collapsed soldiers to be carried away on her words.

"We came to help Traanafaeren, but we're not even sure if any of our other ships survived. I don't know that going to Irundail is a sound idea." The kelar had gotten over his brief concern about who Carabella was. "We need to go back."

"You came to help and now you're going to run away?" Carabella was a few inches taller than the kelar and tilted her head so she could really look down at him. "How is that helping?"

Keanin got to his feet after checking the last of the collapsed Khelarans. "And how are you going to get them back to Khelaran, walk? The Erlindan ships have been mostly stolen or scuttled and they can't spare the few they saved."

"Now, now. We shouldn't be fighting with each other." Ghortin stepped between the three. "King Philia obviously is on our side if he sent troops down."

That was a leap in Jenna's mind—he could have been sending them down to take advantage of Traanafaeren's weakened state. But they had to trust someone at some point.

And the kelar guard had sounded genuinely appreciative for what Keanin and the others had done to save his kingdom.

"We will go with you. Once we speak to whoever is in charge of this town. Our ships might come back, they were chased, but we didn't see them destroyed." He was a large man with short salt and pepper hair and a scarred face. "I am Captain Niat."

They quickly introduced themselves, but the rest of the Khelaran troop stayed silent.

"Maybe we should acquire wagons to transport our new friends?" Carabella came to Jenna and Keanin as Ghortin and the kelar guard worked things out.

Keanin continued to watch the kelars with a frown. "I'll stay here. In case there are any hidden attackers." The way he added that last part indicated that he didn't trust the Khelarans.

Jenna wondered how that might change—or not—when he found out that he was a Khelaran royal.

With all the other issues they were facing, particularly Keanin, she hoped they wouldn't have to tell him until long after all of this was over.

CHAPTER FIFTY-FOUR

GROUPS OF ERLINDANS FROM THE Zalin shelter were slowly moving through the town, freeing pockets of trapped citizens and hunting down the straggling invaders.

Carabella and Jenna recruited Diath and two of his friends to help them find enough wagons and carriages to move thirty unconscious kelars as well as their own injured.

Soon the Khelarans were loaded up and horses were found for the guards. Storm fought being added to the injured group and continued to say he was fine.

Aside from being unable to lift his damaged arm.

They compromised; he took his place alongside the driver of one of the wagons.

Aside from some of the fighters from the Zalin shelter, most of the Erlindans were staying to reclaim and repair their town. However, judging by the large pack she had strapped to her horse as she rode up, Altheria was going to Irundail.

"I have a strong feeling that, as much as I would love to help rebuild my town, I don't have that luxury." She lifted her face to the trees for a few moments, then looked back. "The final battle is coming and my place is with the defenders."

Tireli was already talking to the new mayor—he'd been the second to the former mayor before she was killed. They would rebuild the town, and send word via a far speaker of any ships spotted. They would also send troops if needed. They hadn't been told exactly what was going on in the Markare, but Tireli knew it was something big.

They were also going to ignore the kraken and hope they returned the favor. Once the hastily constructed sea walls were destroyed, the kraken had returned to the deep sea.

Keanin tried to call the one he knew back as he realized maybe the kraken could track the ship of demonspawn mothers. But they didn't respond, and Ghortin finally forced him to get on his horse.

Jenna noticed that Edgar was staying far in the back of the line. Most likely because of Carabella riding in the front with Altheria. They had no way to know if Carabella would be able to sense Xalie or not. But if she did, it wouldn't be good.

The ride out was peaceful but slow. Even though they had successfully destroyed the portal under the water, a wave of insecurity flowed over Jenna. It wasn't as strong as the other times, but it felt like it was going to pounce on her at any moment.

With a nod to Keanin and Talia, Jenna dropped back to Edgar.

He looked like his old self and grinned when she rode back to him.

"To what do I owe this honor?"

"Checking how you're feeling. You were fighting hard for someone who was close to death a day ago."

He laughed. "You sound exactly like Healer Maggie. But I feel much better than would be expected. Possibly due to my *friend*."

"That's good, and thank you for staying back here. I'd like to talk to her, if I could."

He tilted his head. "I thought you could speak to her already?"

"Yes, but it seems odd to be calling out for someone who's living in my friend's head." She shrugged. That was why she rode back—not to mention speaking to someone in her head tended to cause questions. If it wasn't an emergency, she felt it was better to come to the source.

"Understood. This way it looks like we're talking."

"Hello Jenna, what's wrong?" Xalie's voice was stronger this time.

"I was wondering if you've sorted out how we can get the rest of the one hundred cuari free? I have a feeling the Markare portal will be opening soon, but we need them to fight for us to have a chance of destroying it."

"Sadly, I have not. I don't think that Typhonel's way will work, unless you want them all disembodied like myself. But I am working on it."

"Thank you."

Jenna returned to talking to Edgar about the fight and his ideas on the Strann ships.

"I wish I knew how they got those things over land." He pulled out a knife and stone and sharpened the blade. "From what you've said, the ship that you and the kraken destroyed was massive. What's the point? The final battle isn't going to be at sea."

"That's what I think we need to figure out. Is there anything else along the coast to the south?" Jenna had been to the southern tip of Traanafaeren with Storm when she first arrived here. It was a rocky point that ended at the sea. There was no sign of any lands in the distance, but that didn't mean there wasn't something there.

"Only very far away. When I was a child, I was fascinated with the sea and what mysteries could be out there. But no Traanafaeren ships ever came back from being sent to the south, or across the ocean. And none have ever come to us."

The massive cruise ship size of the Strann ship stuck with Jenna. Most of the ships she'd seen in this world were far smaller. "Maybe that's why that one was so large. We had ships that big back home that could travel far distances. Damn it, what if they did get other ships past Erlinda? If they were far enough out to sea, they might not even be spotted as they passed."

"And if any were coming back, especially from the south, they wouldn't be noticed either. Lithunane was the primary shipping connection for Traanafaeren. With it gone and the remaining people down there fighting for their lives…"

"It would be easy to bring in huge amounts of enemy troops ashore without notice. Damn it, Tigan and his people are still down there, or were. But they wouldn't be looking to the ocean. Most likely any surviving Lithunane guards wouldn't either." Jenna had come to talk to Xalie about the cuari, but this was possibly bigger. "Can you reach Tigan with your taran wand? We need to warn them." The deathsworn would never drop their guard, but they needed to know what might be happening.

Edgar had the wand out before she finished speaking.

"Tigan? I can barely hear you. This is Edgar." His face grew grim as he listened. "Get everyone out and head north. They're coming from the coast and the ones you destroyed sound more like a scout troop than a full attack, but the rest will be coming. Did you find any more Lithunane guards? Good, get them out too. Lithunane will be reclaimed, but not now." He listened again then nodded to Jenna. "We're preparing, so come north." Then he ended the call.

"They're already under attack." It wasn't a question.

Edgar nodded as he put away his wand. "A small group of Strann soldiers hit them yesterday. And not only Strann. Tigan said he'd never seen the armor or markings of the people with them. There was nothing on the bodies to indicate where they were from."

"We need to get to Irundail immediately." She looked around as the line of wagons and horses wound its way up a long mountain road. "Is there any faster way?"

"Not unless Ghortin has one. I wouldn't recommend whatever spell you used to get here on your way back from Strann though."

"The slip spell." Jenna shuddered. "Not in my lifetime if I can help it. What's at the top of this road?"

"The Zalin shelter, or what's left of it. I'd still like to know who or what tried to trap them there. They were mostly refugees."

"And a certain cuari." Jenna watched the top as they rode up. "What if whoever was grabbing the cuari decided to trap Carabella since they couldn't get her?"

Edgar laughed. "Xalie said the same thing. She also said she might be able to pick up on something when we get up there."

Jenna was glad that Edgar and his mental companion were getting along well. Ghortin had confided in her that it might be a long time before Edgar was completely healed from the naglefish attack, but he wasn't going to tell him yet. Maggie and Dantil would have much better ideas on how to heal him—and maybe a way to get Xalie into her own body on this plane.

They continued riding in silence until they got to the top. Jenna let out a whistle, it was clear the damage was extensive even though she'd never seen it before. It didn't even look like there had ever been an opening there.

"Magic, I presume?" Jenna asked as she looked around the mess.

Ghortin and Carabella were locked in a debate at the front of the line. She finally got off her horse and marched to the side of the hill and an almost hidden indentation.

Edgar nodded. "That would have been the only way. I'm surprised the entire mountain didn't collapse." He frowned. "Xalie wants me to move closer and go inside the cave. But I'm not sure how to do it with Carabella stomping around."

Jenna got off her horse. "I'll distract Carabella, you take

your guest inside. But she needs to do whatever she's going to do quickly. Carabella can tell when something's up."

"Will do. Keep her away as long as you can." He tilted his head. "She said you might want to have one of those words that will cause Carabella to pass out handy. Just in case. That might be the better option if she starts to notice Xalie."

"Hopefully it won't come to that, but I'm ready." She walked over to Carabella as Ghortin went to go look at the collapsed hillside. Jenna slowly drew Carabella away as she asked about the Zalin shelter and if it could be related to the world cavern they'd found.

Edgar darted into the opening that Carabella and the mages with her had forced open, without Carabella appearing to notice.

The idea of the two locations being somehow connected was fascinating to the cuari as she'd never even heard rumors of anything like the cavern world.

Then mid-sentence, she froze and grabbed Jenna's arm. "Something…is…wrong." She dropped to her knees and clutched her head.

Edgar wasn't in sight, so the odds of her sensing Xalie were slim, but Jenna held the word 'dakair' in her mind. If anything worse happened to Carabella, Jenna would knock her out.

A sudden wave of air pressure slammed Jenna down to Carabella and knocked over a few people standing nearest to the hole Edgar had gone in.

Jenna waved to Crell and pulled her a few feet away. "Can you watch Carabella? If she gets worse, say 'dakair'." Normally Carabella's hearing would be good enough to hear her, but the fact that she continued to stay on the ground clutching her head said she was still impacted by whatever came out of that cave.

Crell nodded and ran back to Carabella.

Jenna ran to the hole and sent up a mage light. Another pair of them were far further inside so she went that way.

Edgar stood near the lights with his sword up as he faced three men.

Three cuari who appeared to be pulling up spells.

Chapter Fifty-Five

"STAND BACK, FOUL SPAWN OF evil! You can't beat us! We will defend the deities!" The closest cuari had a long gray beard and combined with the old-fashioned robe he wore, reminded Jenna of Gandalf.

Minus the tall pointy hat.

Edgar took a few steps backward and lowered his sword. "I'm not going to fight you."

"Then die where you stand, aberration!" The cuari raised his hand to release a spell and an annoyingly familiar spell bubble came directly for him.

"Dakair!" Jenna wasn't sure why this cuari thought he was still fighting for the gods and goddesses, nor whether the word from the past would knock him out before the magic seeking spell bubble could take him. But it was the best she could do.

All three cuari's eyes went wide, then they collapsed and the forming spell bubble vanished.

"Xalie says she knows them. They were part of the one hundred," Edgar said as he stepped further back.

"How did they get here? And why did they think they were in the past?" Jenna went to check them. All three were breathing, but unconscious. They'd have headaches when they woke up thanks to her using that word, but at least they weren't dragged back to the chaotic plane.

Even in the dim light, Jenna saw Edgar's frown. "*That* she doesn't know. She didn't know they'd all been trapped up on the chaotic plane until recently, so her information is limited."

"We have to get them out of here. Not sure how they were freed, but maybe they'll have information when they wake up."

"When who wakes up?" Carabella asked as she and Crell came inside. "Is that Vala? And Mariword? And Trisil? How are they here? Why are they unconscious? And what is hurting my head so badly?" Although she was standing, she didn't look happy about it.

Edgar continued backing away. "No answers, they appeared and then collapsed. I'll get help." He ran out of the cave.

Carabella scowled as he departed. "Is something going on with him? Edgar's never been nervous around me before."

"I think it's his recovery." Jenna nodded to the fallen cuari. "Are they friends of yours?"

"Eh, we don't socialize much anymore. But Vala and Mariword are good people." She pointed to the one who'd tried to fight them. "Trisil is a powerful cuari but also an extreme pain in the ass."

Ghortin, Keanin, Talia, and a dozen more people came in at that point.

Ghortin made a few laps around the fallen cuari before nodding at something he saw. "We can add them to one of the wagons of injured. But it would be best if we move quickly. No matter how they got here, we don't want them waking until we get to Irundail."

"Which is a full day's ride from here." Talia helped Keanin gently pick up one of the cuari and carried him out.

"I know. I will have to speed things up for the wagon they'll be in. I'll need the rest of you to stay at normal speed to keep the risk down." Ghortin waited until the other two cuari were carried out as well.

"Not another slip spell." Jenna followed him out.

"No, a spell far more dangerous." Ghortin pulled her aside as the three cuari were loaded into the wagon Storm and a slight derawri drove. "But, I assume the reason that the three cuari are unconscious is because they were made so by a word?"

"Yes. They thought we were aberrations and they needed to get back to fighting to save the gods and goddesses. I had to do something." She hoped when they woke up they'd have snapped back to the current time—or at least the time they were captured in. If not, it was going to be tricky containing them. Not to mention, according to the cuari books, they would need the full strength of the one hundred to be on this plane in order to destroy the portal in the Markare—that wouldn't work if they were stuck in the before time.

"You did the right thing. Also, I believe Carabella's collapse was more due to how those three got down here than a reaction to Edgar's mental companion, but we should continue to keep them apart. The spell that I am going to cast is dangerous on many levels. And there's a good chance that I might pass out when finished. Probably an excellent chance. But we can't risk those three waking up and getting taken again. The shields around Irundail will help protect them from any spell bubbles, but if I do pass out, get them to the helaermages immediately. Dantil can defend them."

Jenna took a few moments to process that. That he was going to use a spell that could incapacitate him was terrifying. Then she nodded. "Fine, I'll drag all of you to the helaermages. Warn me before you collapse."

"I might not be able to, but I'll try. I'm going to ride with Storm in case they wake up while we're traveling. We'll tie our horses to the back, along with Storm's. I don't think we can fit you in the wagon, but I'll need you when we get there. And to be caught in the spell, your horse will need to be connected to the wagon."

He dropped into his thoughts as he replaced the derawri who rode with Storm.

Jenna tied their horses to the back of the wagon but stayed off hers long enough to let Keanin and Crell know what they were doing. And to tell them to inform Carabella once they left. Ghortin didn't say anything, but it might be best not to have to argue with the headstrong cuari about this.

She'd just settled into her saddle when the world around them slowed down.

Even though she knew what was going to happen in theory, it was extremely unnerving as they passed the troops and her friends at an increased speed. It felt as if the horses were traveling like normal, but they were soon out of sight of the Zalin shelter. Irundail was far in the distance as they came over a steep rise, but at their pace, it wouldn't be long before they got there.

Ghortin swayed in his seat twice and Jenna wished there had been room for her up there. Luckily Storm was able to stabilize him with his good hand, since the spell was moving the wagon, he wasn't giving any direction to the horses.

The Khelarans in the wagon were still unconscious, but the three cuari were starting to twitch. Her horse was magically keeping pace with the wagon, but she wasn't certain that she was close enough to help if they woke up.

There was no way to know what would happen if she tried to use a word to knock them out again. Too close time-wise could cause problems.

The gates to Irundail were visible when Ghortin slumped completely in his seat. He grabbed the back of the seat to pull himself up, but he still had difficulty sitting up.

The guards stood fast in front of the gates as Ghortin collapsed and the speed spell stopped.

Storm yelled to the guards that they had injured, including himself and Mastermage Ghortin. This time the guards quickly opened the door and four of them rode alongside as Storm raced for the castle.

Ghortin was hunched over but he hadn't bounced out of the wagon. Yet. Jenna would have liked to release her horse to run alongside him just in case, but there wasn't time to stop to do that. The three cuari were moving more and if they still thought they were in the past they could cause a lot of problems.

They reached the top tier of the mountain when Trisil sat up and looked around in confusion. Jenna held off shouting the word that would knock him out again, but she would if she had to.

"Get Dantil of the helaermages!" She yelled to one of their escorting guards as Storm pushed the horses toward the helaermage building.

The guard leaped off his horse and ran inside the helaermage building.

Storm bought the horses to a halt, right as Ghortin started to fall out of the wagon.

Jenna jumped off her horse and ran to him, but all she could do was slow his descent—he was easily twice her size.

"Is he okay?" Storm came over to her.

"He's breathing. And extremely heavy."

"What is happening? I know that man, unhand him immediately." Trisil was not only awake but annoyed, judging by the tone of his voice as he glared down at Jenna and Ghortin.

"We're helping him." Before Jenna could explain further, Dantil and a dozen brown garbed helaermages came running out. A fleet of magical gurneys followed tightly on their heels.

"Dantil? What's going on? How did we get to Irun

dail?" Trisil was still sitting in the wagon, but he sounded less belligerent.

And it wasn't lost on Jenna that he knew who Ghortin and Dantil were and wasn't talking about defending the deities. That was hopeful.

"There's been issues, deadly ones. Do not try to cast any magic and we need to get you all inside immediately." Dantil quickly got his people loading the cuari as well as Ghortin and the Khelarans on their gurneys.

Storm waved them off and joined Jenna. "I can see Maggie when things are secure." He didn't put his arm around her. Even his good arm looked to be causing discomfort, but they walked in together.

"What's wrong with Ghortin?" Storm kept his voice low as they followed the helaermages. "I've never seen him collapse over a spell like that."

"Whatever that spell was, it was dangerous. He warned me that this might happen, but he didn't have any other way to get the cuari here quickly. At least Trisil seems to know the timeline he's in this time."

"Dantil would like to speak to you both once he has secured the cuari. If you will follow me?" A tall helaermage cleric motioned for them to go down a short corridor and into an austere room. It was an office of sorts but had nothing visible beyond a basic desk and three chairs.

Once she and Storm were seated, the cleric bowed and left the room.

"Do you know how those three got down here? Confusion or not, if we can get the rest of them down we can go after the portal when it reappears." Storm was growing paler, and clearly was trying to distract her.

"We don't know. They were certain they were in the past when Edgar found them," she lowered her voice. "The *distant* past. But if you don't go to get some medical help immediately, I'll drag you over there myself."

"I'm fine." Even he didn't sound like he believed it.

"No, you're not," Dantil said as he came in and shut the door behind him. "That was noticeable when I first saw you. But I do have some questions first." He tilted his head and looked closer. "Or not. You're about to pass out." He was calm about it, but he waved a hand and a long cushion flew out of a closed cabinet and appeared on Storm's other side.

"I'm…" Storm's eyes rolled back and with Dantil's help, he slid to the cushion.

"He is such a stubborn man. I didn't need to speak to him, I believed it might be better for him to collapse in private." Dantil made a few adjustments to make Storm more comfortable, pausing over his injured shoulder, then turned to Jenna. "The three cuari appear to be fine. The other two awoke when we transferred them. They're a bit confused, but we can't find anything wrong with them. Where did they come from?"

Jenna filled him in on everything—including Xalie, even though she and Edgar weren't here yet.

"It's interesting that Typhonel was able to bring her down, but then she never became solid. It could have been the spell you mentioned, or something with him. Has *he* come back?"

Jenna shook her head. "Honestly, with trying to destroy the portal, deal with the kraken, and save Erlinda, I haven't tried lately." She closed her eyes. "*Typhonel? Can you hear me?*" She tried three times before opening her eyes with a shrug. "Nothing. Oh, and the elementals took off before we went into that cavern world. They haven't come back."

"That cavern world strongly intrigues me. But as long as nothing comes out of it, I fear that will have to be an indulgence for after this world has been saved." Dantil rubbed his chin. "As there's little information about the elementals and none about a god lurking in someone's consciousness, I can't address those issues. As for the larger problems, Rachael, Tor Ranshal, and Wilty have mostly been living in the library since you all left. We should speak to them." He looked down at Storm. "And get him to Healer Maggie. I could heal him beyond what I did to help his pain, but he prefers Maggie."

"He's going to be okay, right?" Jenna shook her head. It had been an exceedingly long day, but she had already forgotten about Ghortin. "And Ghortin?"

"Our prince will be fine with Maggie's help. Ghortin will also recover. Judging by my first look, he was already pushing himself too hard when he cast the spell to get you here so quickly. Give him a day of sleep and he'll be fine." Dantil gave a gentle smile. "And I can feel the waves of magical and physical exhaustion coming off you too. You won't be any good to anyone if you don't rest."

"I'll talk to Maggie right after she sees Storm. I promise." Jenna got to her feet with only a slight wobble. She didn't know if it was the effect of Dantil's words, or everything catching up to her, but fatigue was hitting hard.

"And I'll warn Rachael that I'm enforcing rest for a full day for all of you." He tilted his head at something he saw on Jenna's face. "Or should I keep you here and spell you as I've done to the cuari?"

She raised her hands and tried to look agreeable. "No need. I'm sure Maggie will make sure I rest. Storm too."

A cleric and magic gurney rolled into the office and he easily lifted Storm onto it.

Dantil nodded for them to head out. "I will be checking on all of you. And I'll make sure that Carabella and the rest who are coming in are all fully examined. Particularly Sir Edgar."

Jenna nodded and followed the cleric out. Like most of the helaermages, aside from Dantil, this one was silent as they made their way to the house of healing.

Not surprisingly, Maggie and two other healers were already outside the door of the House of Healing.

"There you two are. The rest are staying with the helaermages? Is everyone back?" As she spoke she nodded to the helaermage cleric and her people led Storm's gurney inside.

"Most of them won't arrive until tonight, and there are injured with them too," Jenna said, then explained about Ghortin's spell as Maggie escorted her in. Not that she had the energy to do so, but by the way Maggie was watching her, even if she'd felt better, she wasn't getting out until Maggie said so.

"Adventures. You all had some serious adventures I'm sure. But Dantil said you need to stay asleep after I've examined you. Corin as well."

The exam didn't take long, Maggie diagnosed exhaustion as well. "Corin's shoulder has been fixed and he is comfortably resting." Maggie nodded to the bed Jenna sat on. "I suggest you do the same."

The door shut behind her.

CHAPTER FIFTY-SIX

JENNA WOKE UP REFRESHED, RELAXED, and confused. She didn't even recall falling asleep, but she woke up in a warm, nondescript nightgown, in a nice nondescript cozy room.

For a few moments, she thought she was back in her old room in the vortex of Ghortin's cottage.

Then reality snapped back.

Back in Los Angeles, she'd hated being bored. Hence the reason she had added degrees like some people bought shoes. But right now, she would love for the chance to be bored.

The old curse of living in interesting times had been made real to her in ways she never wanted to experience again.

She flopped back on her pillow and thought about all that had happened since she came here. She knew this was her world now, but the untrustworthy promise of Qhazborh saving the people she loved from here and her old world wasn't enough to toss this place aside.

It was part of her, more so than simply her partially taking over another person's body. She knew that she was needed to save this world—all the worlds. But that feeling of impending failure continued to haunt her every time she thought of it. She counted some amazing people here as dear friends, they were family. None of them would ever back down from a fight. Now that was true even for Keanin.

She couldn't tell them that when the time came, she'd fail.

"Child? Are you crying?" Maggie stayed near the door but Jenna hadn't heard her open it.

Jenna wiped her face but knew it was already too late. Too bad this world didn't have psychologists. "It's been a rough year."

Maggie peered down at her, then shook her head, and sat on the edge of Jenna's bed. "It's more than that." The tone of her voice indicated she wasn't leaving until she got answers.

Maybe they did have psychologists here, they just didn't call them that.

"Please, you can't tell anyone else—*anyone*." Jenna waited until Maggie gave a short nod. "I don't think I can destroy the portal in the Markare when the time comes. All the people who have already died fighting, and all the ones who will die when I fail…they're on my shoulders." Saying it out loud felt good, but a voice in her head said that telling anyone else would make things worse.

Maggie grabbed her hands and gave a soft smile. "Do you think you are the only one with doubts? I can promise you that everyone you know, yes, even people like Corin, Crell, and Ghortin, doubt themselves every day. Especially in times like these."

"This is more than doubt, this is absolute clarity. I *will* fail us all." As Jenna said it, a trickle of something came into her mind. She worked hard for what she'd accomplished in her life—both here and back on Earth. Doubt was always there, but she moved past it before.

Even in life and death situations, she fought past. This was larger, but she'd known that for a long time. So why the crippling doubt now?

"How long have you felt this?" Maggie's words echoed Jenna's thoughts.

Jenna tried to think back. It now felt like she'd always

believed this. But some part of her mind said it wasn't. "I think it started while we were outside Erlinda." She rubbed her forehead as a blast of pain hit. "It's fighting back. But it began when I had that dream visit from Qhazborh." The stabbing pain in her head caused her to cry out and shut her eyes. Opening them brought huge painful black dots obscuring her vision. It was like the worst ocular migraine she'd ever had times ten.

"Easy, Jenna. Take deep breaths. You've been spelled. This is out of my purview though. I need to get Dantil."

Maggie still held onto Jenna's hands and there was no way Jenna was letting her go. It felt like her only link to reality was through their hands. Storms of pain, terror, and loss rampaged through her mind.

"Don't. Let. Go." Jenna's jaw was clenched so tightly she had to fight to get the words out. She kept her eyes closed but felt Maggie squeeze her hands.

"I won't." Maggie gave a soft whistle and Jenna felt tiny mouse feet and the tips of lowered wings on top of her hand—a scree. "Tell Dantil we have an emergency." The feet left as the scree flew off to complete its task.

"Can't hold on." Jenna got those words out, but the tide of fear, terror, darkness, and depression was swallowing her. She could will herself to die. To end this pain. To stop the sorrow.

"Jenna!" That was Storm's voice, not Dantil's. But she felt Maggie give over one of her hands to him. "Come back, don't leave me."

Jenna wanted to open her eyes to see him once more, but it was impossible. The pain was too much.

"Let me go."

"Never. You do not get to leave us, to leave *me*. I love you, don't give up." There were tears in his voice but also a fierce resolve.

Jenna reached out to that and found the pain subsiding a little.

"Jenna!" That was Dantil. He didn't take her hand but put a cooling palm on her forehead. Either his hands were unnaturally cold, or she was burning up. "You cannot leave. We can save you, but not if you give up. Fight the darkness in your mind. It's a spell from Qhazborh, because they know you will destroy them. They are afraid of *you*."

Jenna tried to push back against the wave of sorrow and fear. Storm and Maggie squeezed her hands to send support. Then Dantil put his hands on her head and began chanting in a strange language.

She couldn't understand his words, or the ones that responded to him from inside her mind, but Dantil's words gave her the possibility of a way out.

"*This one is mine.*" That sentence was clear and creepy. But it also gave her a sense of hope. There was the tiniest spark of fear in it.

"*I belong to no one, you bad Tim Curry impersonator,*" Jenna shouted inside her head.

"*You need to die. It's the only way to save those you love.*" The voice was softer now, but the trickle of fear in it remained.

"*She needs to stay here to save them. And destroy you,*" Dantil said.

"*You cannot destroy the deities. The balance will be destroyed. DOL will not stand for it.*"

DOL was the group of deities that the helaermages followed. The entities who maintained the balance between Irissanta and Qhazborh.

Jenna heard Dantil's laugh in her head.

"*DOL was who told us what needed to be done. Your path was doomed centuries ago. Now leave her or be destroyed in this moment.*"

Jenna wasn't sure what Dantil could do against all the deities of Qhazborh from inside her head, but she shoved aside the last feelings of depression and fear and lent her strength to him.

Maggie wasn't a magic user, but her force of will, along with that of Storm, also joined in.

"*This fight is not over.*" Qhazborh made a final push against Jenna, trying to drag her into despair.

Jenna and the three with her shoved him back.

There was a weird feeling as if a strong wind rushed through her soul—then was gone.

"Jenna?" If Storm clutched her hand any tighter she might need another healing.

She opened her eyes. Still crying, but happy tears this time. "I'm here. The spell is gone. I'm still freaked out about what we're facing, but I think I can deal with it now."

Dantil stepped out of the way and Storm rushed forward to give her a massive kiss. "I thought I was going to lose you."

"You were." Jenna nodded to Maggie and Dantil. "Thank you all for saving me."

Maggie stepped back and wiped aside a few tears of her own. "This is well and good, but that took a lot out of two already drained patients. The rest of your massive party showed up from Erlinda a few hours ago and are all sleeping—whether willfully or not. The only exceptions were the uninjured Khelarans. They have been speaking with Prince Justlantin and Armsmaster Garlan for the last hour." She raised her hand when Storm and Jenna looked ready to get up and join them.

"No. Both of you are again, drained. Dantil? What is your view?"

There wasn't a pause. "They need to rest. Or I can make sure that you do so?" His smile wasn't quite friendly, but very sincere.

"We'll rest." Jenna turned to Storm. He got to his feet and looked ready to argue. "You don't want them knocking us out. Right now, everyone else is still asleep and your brother won't be ready to see you until he and Garlan have come to some sort of an agreement with the Khelarans."

He folded his arms. "Fine. But you have to promise me that if those feelings come back, you will tell me immediately. No more pushing me away."

"I promise." She gave a sincere smile. Hopefully, she hadn't just lied to him.

Maggie and Dantil shared a look, then she hustled him and Storm out of the room.

"I have no problem with you and your fiancé sharing a space, but I do need both of you to sleep." Maggie's smile nearly reached her eyes. She might not be a magic user, but she was still concerned about what Jenna went through. "I didn't force Carabella to sleep. She's with Rachael, Tor Ranshal, and Wilty in the library. Once I am certain that you and Storm are sleeping, I will go talk to them about what happened." A healer softly knocked on the door and handed a clear glass of water to Maggie. "Thank you." She turned to Jenna. "You can take this and sleep like you never have before. Or I can wait here until you fall asleep on your own. Thus, delaying my important task."

Jenna sat up again and took the glass. "I would have fallen asleep eventually, I'm exhausted." The rush of adrenaline she'd felt when shouting back at the intruder in her head fled as quickly as it came.

"I'm sure you would try. But this way I don't have to worry." Maggie smiled as Jenna finished the glass. "Good girl." She dimmed the lights and left.

———◆———

Jenna usually woke up with some recall of her dreams, even if was little more than a feeling. She woke up to nothing this time. She pushed herself up on her elbows and increased the lights to find herself facing the adorable yet odd face of a scree peering at her from a few inches away.

Scree were magical creatures that looked like a mouse combined with the wings of a bird. They were created eons ago and mostly worked as runners for people like Maggie. They could carry mimicry of the messages people gave them, but Jenna didn't know how much of what they repeated they actually understood. This one simply continued to stare at her.

"Hello?" She had run into them before on her first trip to Irundail, but then the creature had just repeated their message immediately. This one blinked, ruffled its wings, and continued to stare.

"Okay. I'm going to take a bath and change. You do whatever it is you're doing." Jenna gathered clothes and went to the bathroom. A warm and fragrant bath was already drawn—Maggie's people were good.

She'd bathed and changed when the scree flew over to her.

"Castle meeting. One hour. Library."

"Um, thank you? Why didn't you tell me that when I woke up?"

"One hour from *now.*" The scree nodded with enough awareness that Jenna was sure they were more than mindless automatons. It had held off telling her based on the way the command had been given and the time.

And that Jenna should have remained asleep about twenty minutes longer than she had.

"Thank you." She had no idea how to dismiss the scree, but once she opened the door it flew off.

The hall she was in was huge and lined with doors. Taking a chance, she walked in the direction the scree had flown out. She'd either find the exit or someone who could show her to the exit.

The scree knew the right way and soon Jenna recognized the front areas of the House of Healing. Storm, Edgar, and Keanin came down a wide adjacent hallway.

Keanin ran to her and scooped her up. "Storm told me what happened, but he's not told anyone else yet. Please, come to me if that ever happens again. I can't lose you any more than he can." He kept his voice low and spoke in her ear while he swirled her and then set her on her feet. "I'm so glad that you're okay."

Edgar and Storm joined them.

"I'm not going to spin you around, like someone, but *both* of us are very glad that you're okay. Xalie felt a disturbance while we were traveling but she couldn't tell what it was." Edgar dropped his voice as he said Xalie, but he didn't whisper.

Storm held her in a tight hug and then all of them walked out of the healer building and toward the castle.

"Anything happen after we left?" Jenna figured that Keanin and Edgar would need to fill the others in once they got to the castle, but she wanted the focus to move off her for a bit.

"Aside from a long ride with an annoyed cuari?" Keanin shook his head. "It was an extremely long trip. Carabella stomped and yelled when she found out what Ghortin had done. Their reunion won't be peaceful."

"Whose reunion?" Ghortin didn't run unless his life depended on it, but he was jogging as he came out of the House of Healing after them. "You could have waited for me, you know."

Storm laughed. "Carabella. Your mother is a bit upset with you. And the healer I spoke to said you were still sleeping and shouldn't be disturbed."

"Bah. I've been awake for hours. Or maybe a half hour. But I'm fine now. No lasting effects from that spell." He glared at Jenna and Keanin. "And no, I'm not teaching either of you it. Not even the name. Do not think about it."

Jenna shrugged. "Not a problem. I, for one, don't need to know something that wiped you out. But Carabella is going to want a full explanation."

"And she can wait until we meet with the others."

"Have you heard how the three cuari are?" Jenna felt less like the end of the world was coming, but having only four out of one hundred cuari needed to close that portal didn't make her feel much better.

Ghortin nodded. "I was on my way to visit them at Dantil's place when I saw you four escaping. The last I heard they were relaxing and mildly sedated. Dantil wants to find out how they got down here, but not trigger a slip into the past. Letting him work with them first is the most prudent idea."

The guards at the castle entrance bowed deeply as they came in. "Prince Justlantin asks that you join the others in the library."

"Excellent. Thank you." Ghortin grinned and marched down the hall.

The assistant pointed them toward the back and the room they'd met in before. The door was shut but there were raised voices heard—not a quiet discussion.

Ghortin knocked and then pushed open the door.

The yelling appeared to be mostly coming from Carabella. Rachael, Tor Ranshal, and Wilty were just the victims. Or bystanders. Carabella wasn't yelling at them but appeared to be directing her ire at everything in the room.

"Furthermore—" Carabella cut herself off as she spun when Ghortin and the rest came in. "Finally. Maggie wouldn't let me wake any of you up. What did you mean by taking off like that?" She stomped over to Ghortin and waved her finger in his face. "And you probably used a spell that even I won't speak out loud. What were you thinking?"

Ghortin folded his arms and waited until she finished.

"I was thinking that I needed to get those other cuari to safety as soon as possible. They were dangerously close to being retrieved by the forces that took them initially."

Jenna heard the slight pause in his voice—they couldn't tell Carabella about the word that knocked the three out, nor what Trisel had been yelling about.

Carabella caught it too and narrowed her eyes. "There's something else to it. Is it connected to that odd cuari disorder?"

"Yes, it is. The three are currently being watched and protected by the helaermages. I'm sure they'd like to see you when they are fully recovered."

"Hmm, we'll see. No idea how they got down here though. Why did they appear in the Zalin shelter?"

"Not a clue on either." Ghortin turned to the other three. "Have you found anything?"

Tor Ranshal's lean face was drawn. "Yes, the Markare portal has begun to reappear."

CHAPTER FIFTY-SEVEN

———◆———

JENNA FELT AS IF HIS words punched her in the gut. That was why Qhazborh pushed so hard to get her to back off or kill herself. She'd been waiting for this moment, but now that it was here, terror grabbed ahold of her.

"Why didn't someone come get us? We knew this was coming, but we're not ready." Ghortin also looked as if he'd been physically hit.

Tor Ranshal shook his head. "We were notified by a far-seer mage mere moments ago. That was what launched a certain cuari on a tirade."

"I thought she was upset about us leaving her after Erlinda?"

Carabella shook her head. "That too. I'm still mentally processing how we're going to destroy that thing without all of my people."

"Yes, we have to work on that." Ghortin stepped around her to join Tor Ranshal and Rachael. "What do we know? Has anything come through the portal yet?"

That was the issue. They needed the portal to be called back into existence before they could destroy it. But the opening was the sign that their time was short.

Storm and Edgar had long ago argued that troops should wait out there for the portal to be opened, and then they could destroy it.

Rachael and Tor Ranshal said the books of the cuari were clear about that, no magic users or troops could be near the portal when Qhazborh opened it. The timing between all the aspects was dicey at best and horrific at worst.

"Nothing that has been reported. It's not fully open according to the reports. But it's in progress." Rachael motioned for them all to take seats. "The far-seers are having a hard time focusing on anything in the Markare. The complications began yesterday."

"We only have four cuari, what do we do?" Jenna knew this final battle and the destruction of the portal was the cumulation of the Guardians and Protectors before her—but they weren't ready. "And how many troops do they have?" She wasn't a military strategist but the fact that there hadn't been massive attacks after the one on Lithunane, had given her hope that the other side wasn't ready either.

The attack on Erlinda was far smaller than the forces reported at Lithunane. And even the attacks on Irundail had relied on magic and guile.

The doors opened as Jenna spoke and Prince Justlantin, Garlan, and a dozen military advisors came in.

Prince Justlantin looked around the room. "That is something we need to discuss and the news isn't good."

Wilty was pouring over several books when they arrived, but he got up to make sure there were seats for everyone. The usually affable librarian looked tense as he counted the people and chairs. "Are there more coming?"

"Yes, the captain from the Khelarans is coming as well. He needed to gather documents from his pack first." Justlantin nodded to Jenna and the others. "I'm extremely glad that your adventures brought you back home."

"It wasn't as difficult as I would have believed, but we did have help." Ghortin briefly filled everyone in on the basics of their adventures and the help they received from the kraken.

"I believe you were drawn into the cavern world to stop you all, it was a trap. We will have to address it once this fight is done." Rachael nodded. "It was interesting that the kraken helped you though."

Edgar shook his head. "I can't believe I forgot this, but I did almost die, so the memory might not be what it was." He flashed a brilliant smile. Rachael, Tor Ranshal, and the rest close to them would be told of Xalie—aside from Carabella and the other three cuari. But right now, there were too many others who shouldn't know in this room. "I reached Tigan in the south as we were riding from the Zalin shelter. They were attacked far north of the remains of Lithunane by a scout group of Strann soldiers and unknown companions. They survived but were unable to find out who joined the Strann army as they were complete unknown in look and bearing. The scouts were killed but the rest of the forces went far south of he and his group. Tigan is bringing everyone north."

"He's not going to stay and fight?" Ghortin's tone pointed out that he was familiar with deathsworn behavior.

"He might have lied to me, but he knows the fight is up here." Edgar shrugged. "They found more of the missing Lithunane guards and were already escorting any stranded civilians they found up here."

"If that portal is already opening they won't get here in time." Storm nodded to a map that took over most of a large table.

The trip between the two points was a long one. Jenna had made the trip down from Irundail to Lithunane once—it was two weeks at a fast pace.

Tor Ranshal calmly nodded. His brief alarm when they first came in vanished. "While the news of the portal is shocking, I believe we have time." He picked up a loose piece of paper and then looked to Prince Justlantin, who nodded. "The pages of the two destroyed books have been fruitful even though we haven't been able to reassemble them completely."

Carabella got to her feet to go to him.

"No. Those pages are like the books. You can't see them." Ghortin blocked her.

"I thought perhaps a wee peek wouldn't hurt." She folded her arms and sat back down.

Jenna hid her smile. Considering how nosy Carabella was, the fact that she couldn't read the cuari books, use stronger magic, or know everything that was going on, and hadn't completely had a fit, was pretty amazing.

The captain of the Khelarans came in, escorted by a librarian assistant. He was quickly introduced to those who hadn't met him before as Captain Niat of the first royal regiment. A tall and stern kelar, his salt and pepper hair was cut short and he still didn't look like he smiled much.

"Thank you for allowing me to join you. And for rescuing our people who were trapped in Erlinda. We were tasked with examining the situation in your country, but our ship was destroyed once we got out of Khelaran waters. The other three ships with us were either lost or stranded elsewhere. While our initial task was to observe only, I sent communications to the King when we arrived here. He says that we are to offer our services in this time of need."

"Can he send more?" Storm asked.

"No. There is a chance that the dangers you saved us from might not have all left our country. Even sending us was a risk. But, myself and all of my company, over two hundred strong, will fight by your side."

Even though they'd clearly discussed this earlier, Prince Justlantin nodded at the pledge.

"Is there any other news?" Keanin asked. "Talia and Diath are gathering what Erlindan fighters came with us, but there won't be more than another hundred. Them plus the Khelarans won't be enough to destroy that thing."

Garlan looked up. "Crell found a mage who was able to track how some of her rangers were sent north, and half of the deathsworn were sent south. It's a little-known spell and a tricky one. The rangers were sent by the dead mage you found, but it is believed that he was initially trying to help. The deathsworn are another matter and she and the mage are trying sort it out."

"Can we get more of them down here?" Keanin leaned forward. "Not only the ones under her but more derawri deathsworn in general."

"Unknown." Garlan shook his head. "But there have been scout reports that Derawri is facing fighting all along the Strann border. Even if the spell is figured out and cast, they might not be willing to spare them."

"But if we lose and can't destroy that portal, fighting against Strann won't matter. Everyone will die." Keanin clenched his fists as he glared around the room. After refusing to go into the Markare for most of his life, he now wanted to charge in.

"I know, lad." Garlan was a gruff man, but the small smile he gave Keanin was gentle. "But it's hard to convince people to deplete their fighters on something they don't completely understand. They will defend their own first."

"That's why no more of my squads can come down. I understand a bit more of what we're facing," Niat said. "But I still would not deplete the protections of my homeland."

Keanin slid back into his chair. "Which is why there are these attacks. They have forces coming from an unknown land. How are we going to beat them?"

Rachael was the first one to respond to him, and there was a lot of sorrow on her tiny face. "We will go forward with what we have. But you need to be aware of the other information the far-seer gave us." She nodded to Tor Ranshal when he started to shake his head. "He needs to know. They all do."

Tor Ranshal's worry as he finally nodded scared Jenna.

"Keanin, you told us of a ship, one that escaped Craelyn over the ocean after your fight." There was no inflection in Rachael's voice.

Captain Niat leaned forward at Rachael's words and Keanin paled.

"They've been found?" Keanin's jaw tightened and Jenna debated running out and dragging Talia into the room before Rachael continued.

"They have. Five demonspawn women were spotted riding through the southern part of Traanafaeren and toward Shettler's Point less than a day ago."

"They're pregnant? How did anyone know they were demonspawn? They were still wearing disguises when we lost them." Aside from his paleness and the way his fists were now becoming stones, Keanin didn't seem that upset.

Or wouldn't to anyone who didn't know him.

Jenna wanted to run over and hold him, but that probably wouldn't be the best idea.

"They are showing their true selves, but the far-seer was able to see remnants of their disguises. They appear to be the ones who attacked you. But they aren't pregnant. However, ten adult kelar-hybrids are riding with them. They have your bearing."

Keanin's golden eyes were wide and his breathing came short and fast.

Jenna did go to him now. Talia would be better but they didn't have time. Keanin was slipping into shock.

"I'm sorry, Keanin, there was no easy way to tell you." Rachael didn't go to him, but she appeared ready to cry.

Jenna held him and rubbed his back. "What was taken

from you is horrific. But it was not your fault, nor who you are. Those creatures are not you."

His breath began to slow and sounded more normal. "There's no doubt of them?" He was hanging onto Jenna but directed his question to Rachael and Tor Ranshal.

Tor Ranshal shook his head. "No. The seer felt the connection. They are not kelar, they are demonspawn monsters. The seer felt nothing but darkness coming from them."

The Khelaran captain looked pale. "They attacked him to create worse monsters? I didn't know that was possible." He held up a hand. "I studied the demonspawn for years before we were attacked. There was no evidence of such abilities." He glanced at Keanin and narrowed his eyes. "There is something familiar about you. More than a brief sighting in Craelyn."

Keanin shrugged. "I'd been to Craelyn before with the Traanafaeren royal family. But it was long ago."

There was a soft knock at the door and Wilty opened it to reveal a concerned Altheria.

"I was working with Talia and Diath, but I think I need to be here." Her face was a combination of concern and confusion.

Ghortin nodded and quickly introduced everyone.

Altheria sat next to Keanin. "There's a tide pulling this world and something has given it teeth."

"That is an old proverb and few today would know it." Rachael nodded. "I would try to catch you up on events, but I believe you are here because you know some of them."

She looked to Storm and Jenna, then nodded. "I know that Keanin was attacked and that horrible event brought forth new enemies. A situation that could only have come by Powerful demonspawn attacking an equally Powerful royal mage." She said her words softly, but from their reactions, the entire room heard.

"But I'm not a royal by blood. I was adopted by the Traanafaeren royal family, but I don't share their blood."

Captain Niat paled as he looked between Keanin and Altheria. "The lost family. That's why you look familiar. There are paintings of your line deep in the Craelyn Castle."

Keanin barked out a laugh that died when he saw the looks around him. Not everyone in the room knew, but his friends did. "What do you mean? How can this be? And no one told me?"

Storm leaned across the table. "We weren't certain. Before we went to Craelyn we found out that the thugs in Erlinda were looking for two royals and laughed that the Traanafaerens didn't know who they'd raised. Altheria confirmed it. There was no good time to tell you."

Keanin wasn't hyperventilating but he didn't look good.

Jenna did slip out of the room at a run this time. One horrifically traumatic issue was bad, this was worse. She raced to the guards' training area and spotted Talia doing drills.

"Keanin needs you." That was all she needed to say and Talia left Diath running through things.

CHAPTER FIFTY-EIGHT

A LTHOUGH SHE DIDN'T ASK, JENNA gave Talia a summary of what had happened as they ran through the castle.

Talia went from furious to confused. "He's a royal?"

"Of a long dead line. The biggest issue was that since no one knew, nor knew what those demonspawn could do to him because of it, he's in a bad place." Jenna nodded to the library assistant as they raced by.

The back room was loud as she pushed open the door. Talia ran to Keanin and enfolded him in a hug even though he was in the middle of arguing with Altheria.

"They're trying to say that I'm a Khelaran royal, or whatever they'd call someone of a deposed family line." He looked to say more, but Talia shut his mouth with a kiss.

"You are still you." Talia pulled back but kept her hands on either side of his face. "Whoever your ancestors were, you're still you. Whatever was done to you, you remain you. We will get through this."

Keanin finally nodded and slumped down into his chair.

Jenna didn't blame him. Just one of those situations would have caused the old Keanin to hide in his room for weeks.

"This is egregious news." Prince Justlantin rose and bowed to Keanin. "I am so sorry what was done to you and that our lack of knowing who you really came from allowed this to happen. I can assure you that the King and Queen didn't know. None of us did. Your mother passed before she could say anything beyond asking my parents to save her child. But you remain a member of *this* family. No matter what."

Keanin looked at a loss. The horror that the attack on him by the demonspawn resulted in twisted offspring of a sort lingered in his eyes.

Jenna doubted he'd gotten far into thinking about the whole royal concept. She agreed with why the decision was made to hold off telling him of his royal connection, but this was possibly the worst time and place for it to be revealed.

Talia and Altheria stayed on either side of him. Altheria gave Talia a nod, then turned to face Prince Justlantin and the others.

"I am Altheria, Prince Justlantin. I have lived in Khelaran and Traanafaeren and pledge myself to support both royal households."

Justlantin nodded. "Thank you. We will need all the help we can get I fear."

Keanin's color was coming back as he got to his feet. Talia rose with him but kept one hand on his shoulder. "I would like to be excused. I have much to think about."

Ghortin narrowed his eyes. "You cannot go after them yet. And not alone."

Talia gripped Keanin's shoulder. There was no way she'd let him go alone—but she might go with only the two of them.

"If you go too soon, the other side wins," Rachael's voice was soft, but there was no doubt that everyone heard her. "Although it was unclear who was meant until now, you are mentioned in at least two of the books. You are crucial to demolishing the portal. Without you, just like without Jenna, we have no hope of destroying it."

Carabella answered before Keanin could. "We need to get the rest of my people out and we need to end this." She continued to watch the books and pages that Rachael kept in front of her.

"I won't go anywhere." Keanin nearly sounded truthful.

"You will try. And if I have to sit on you like I did when we were kids, so help me, I will." Storm watched Keanin carefully. They'd grown up as brothers and he knew even better than the others what Keanin might do.

"I won't let him either." Talia pushed him back into his chair. "I can't imagine what was done to you or what this news is doing to you. I will stand by your side through it all. But, I won't let you throw yourself away."

Jenna smiled at the determination in Talia's voice. She'd been afraid that the two would take off on their own. It was nice to be wrong sometimes.

"Fine." Keanin looked around the room. "Anyone else have horrible news they want to share?"

No one did and the discussion switched to trying to get more fighters to join them before they went into the Markare.

Ghortin, Carabella, Keanin, Altheria, Rachael, Tor Ranshal, and Jenna formed a smaller group to discuss freeing the trapped cuari. Storm and Talia moved to the larger group to help with the general strategy portion. After they gave serious warnings to Keanin.

"Have you been able to reach your friend? Does he know a way to bring down more of the cuari?" Tor Ranshal asked Jenna once they were settled.

Jenna startled. She immediately thought he was speaking of Xalie—she hadn't had a chance to tell them about her with Carabella right there. It took a moment to realize he was speaking of Meith. "I haven't, but I don't think he brought those three down."

"I think we need to speak to the cuari." Carabella glanced over to the larger group. "They'll be at it for a while."

"Agreed." Ghortin got to his feet and put his hand on Keanin's shoulder. "I won't make you come with us, but I don't want to have to point out, that if you leave before we're ready, I have painful ways of bringing you back."

Keanin got up to join Talia and Storm with a sigh. "I promise."

With that, they went to the helaermages.

There was no one else in the large room where the three cuari were resting aside from a pair of helaermage clerics. The three cuari might have been mildly sedated before, but they were sleeping now.

One of the clerics left to bring Dantil back at Ghortin's request.

"I'd like to be the one doing the questioning, at least at the start." Ghortin looked to Carabella as she approached the three. "If you don't mind. It might be best if you remained out of sight at first. I'm going to wake them one at a time, and you'll be a distraction for them."

She shrugged and stepped out of sight of a curtain that would have been used to separate the cots. "I'll let you start, but I do have my own questions. For now, I can listen for any lies in their voices."

Rachael and Tor Ranshal didn't hide but stayed near the door with Dantil.

Ghortin approached the first bed and softly spoke two short spells as he pulled up a chair next to Mariword's cot. The cuari woke up immediately but was restrained by the second spell Ghortin cast that kept him pinned to the cot. "Hello Mariword. What's the last thing you recall?"

Mariword scowled at being restrained but then shrugged. "The last thing was a spell bubble sucking the life out of me. Or so it felt. But whatever it was, I'm still alive." He looked to either side. "Trisil and Vala were taken as well? Not good. Someone has to stop whatever grabbed us."

Ghortin gave a sanitized version of the cuari being taken, aside from Carabella, how it was done, and that he and the others had found the three of them collapsed inside the Zalin shelter.

"We've been missing for months?" Mariword pursed his lips. "That is a lot to take in. Do you know where the others are being kept? Or how we got tossed into a cave down here? I have no memory of being held or arriving in a cave."

Ghortin didn't hesitate as he shook his head and lied. "Not yet, but I'm sure we'll track them down soon. I'd like to wake up Vala and Trisil before releasing you. Just to be cautious."

Mariword paused before nodding. It might have been whatever spell they'd been under when they arrived in the Zalin shelter, but he seemed far more relaxed than Trisil. Even spelled, Trisil's face was locked in a grimace.

Ghortin must have felt the same as he chose Vala to awaken next. Then went through the same story when Vala's last memories were of a spell bubble snapping over him as he was spellcasting his dinner.

So far, neither cuari had regained the lost memories from the battle with the deities—or coming back to this plane and thinking they were fighting to save the gods and goddesses. But Ghortin looked worried as he moved his chair over to Trisil.

Trisil appeared to be fighting Ghortin's spell and Jenna felt Ghortin increase the strength of it.

"Damn it! I'll beat you all! Stand still and fight!" That Trisil's yelling began before he opened his eyes was interesting, but Jenna moved closer to him in case she needed to spell him.

Or knock him and the other two out again.

"Shut up, Trisil. You were captured like the rest of us." Mariword shook his head at his fellow cuari. "Open your damn eyes."

Trisil looked even angrier once he opened them. Then he twisted around as best as he could, still being held on the cot by Ghortin's spell. "I know Ghortin and Dantil. And Tor Ranshal and the hedge witch Rachael." His thick gray brows lowered as he scowled at Jenna and Altheria. "Don't know you two. But I feel your Power."

Ghortin shook his head when Jenna opened her mouth to respond. Altheria simply smiled.

"This is my apprentice. Of course, she has Power." He told Trisil the same story he'd shared with the other two. "Now, what do you recall?"

"I was under attack in the Trojolian mountains. I go up to a cabin I have up there for retreats when things get too busy." Trisil already sounded calmer. "A small army of hoodlums found me and attacked. I fought back with sword and knife; I try not to use magic at my retreat. They had magic users with them somewhere but I couldn't find them in the crowd. I'd pulled up a massive destruct spell when they…" he paused and appeared confused. Then furious. "No, they stepped back. A spell bubble latched onto me. That was my last thought." He was livid. "They tricked me to call up that spell and fall into their trap!"

Ghortin nodded and said a single word. The spell keeping all three pinned to their cots vanished. "We still have no idea how you three ended up inside the Zalin shelter, but I believe you're all going to be fine."

Rachael came forward after a glance where Carabella waited behind the curtain. For one reason or another Carabella wanted to hear more before greeting her fellow cuari.

"Now I get to step in. Rather, Tor Ranshal, Dantil, and I. You've all been through a lot and your energies are drained. Not to mention that you're the first cuari to have escaped from wherever those spell bubbles took you." Rachael was tiny and looked like someone's favorite grandmother, but there was steel in those blue eyes.

"I'll help what I can, but my memories between being captured and here are thin." Trisil smiled. "I'd like to speak to Carabella when there's a chance."

"That we can do. She was wrapping up some things but should be here soon." Ghortin glanced back at the curtain, but Carabella still didn't come forward.

Jenna wasn't certain how Carabella could tell if they were lying, but if she could, that would be a great help. These three might or might not be able to assist in sorting out freeing the rest of the one hundred, but knowing if they were lying could determine if they were to be trusted or not.

Ghortin motioned for Jenna and Altheria to join him as he turned for the door. "We have a few other things to attend to but will be back. Rest well, gentlemen."

Altheria still hadn't introduced herself to the three but nodded to them as they left.

"When do we tell them about the impending war? How can we find how they escaped so we can free the rest?" Jenna asked as they left the helaermage building. She thought there would be more questioning. She knew there would be many battlefronts. But since closing the portal in the Markare was essential to saving this and other words, and the one hundred cuari were needed for that, she was focusing on those aspects.

"I'll wait until Rachael, Tor Ranshal, and Dantil give the word to tell them. And that Carabella feels they are being honest. They seem to be fine, but we have no idea what long-term effects those spell bubbles or being held on the chaotic plane did to them." Ghortin led them back to the castle. "As for how they escaped? That's a tricky one given the state of their minds when we first found them. They might not have escaped at all. In which case, it would be more of how do we find out who set them free and why. If they believed they were in the past they could have caused a lot of damage."

Jenna agreed with the annoyance in his voice. If the three cuari didn't get free on their own, then they were still stuck sorting out how to free the rest. And figuring out if those three were sent down here with their lost memories reinstated as an attack against their side. If that was the case, the attempt failed. But she could only imagine what could happen if more than three came down at once with the same mindset.

The three went back to the castle and Ghortin led them upstairs. "I don't want to interfere with Rachael, Carabella, and the others, nor do the military minds need us right now. But I think we need to make magical preparations."

"Should we get Keanin?" Jenna asked.

"At some point, but with all that happened earlier, I think his focusing on military aspects right now might be better. We need to research to make sure there's nothing else that his combination of royal and Powerful magic user could be used against us."

Altheria nodded as they went into his room. "And to find out how to destroy those demonspawn creatures out in the desert. If they are what I fear they are, their destruction needs to come quickly. And Keanin is in serious danger."

CHAPTER FIFTY-NINE

GHORTIN'S ROOM WAS HUGE AND had enough personal items in it that this had clearly been his home at one point. He went to a large table covered in books and pushed things aside.

"What do you believe they are? I assume you are referring to the monstrosities the demonspawn created by attacking Keanin?" Ghortin collected loose pages into a small mountain at the edge of the table and then motioned for them to sit.

"That they are the Neamhghlan, the unclean. Monsters told of so long ago in Khelaran, that few of us recall them." She nodded to Ghortin. "Not even you, from the look on your face. Great Power, royal blood, and a foul magic combine to create the horrors that will doom us all." She shrugged. "That's from the old tales. These demonspawn women were pregnant a short while ago, yet we're now facing ten adult Keanin copies? I'd say that's what we have. And I repeat, we need to destroy them *before* the final fight. They could be far worse if they get to the portal."

Jenna looked between the two. "How do we stop them then?"

"Two options, according to myth, which I do recall, but it took me a moment to mentally find it." Ghortin nodded to Altheria. "Kill the demonspawn who made them, or kill the father."

"We're not killing Keanin. Can't we directly kill the whatever they were called again?"

"Killing Keanin is obviously not an option." Ghortin got to his feet and paced. "And we can't let him know about that. He's become far more dramatic in the past month. I don't want ideas going into his head. As for a direct attack on the Neamhghlan, I'm not sure how. Keep in mind, these things were myths. Even demonspawn were little more than legends until a year ago."

"Could I destroy the demonspawn and their monster creations?" It would be hard to kill beings who looked like Keanin, but she had some odd abilities. And being the Protector should be good for something.

Ghortin narrowed his eyes and studied her. "You might be able to, as you are unique to this world. But we need more of our crew to help sort this out. Along with everything else."

"I fear our time is short," Altheria said.

"Agreed. And we need more allies. Any sign of my elementals?" Ghortin sat back in his chair.

"Nothing. They've haven't returned since we entered that weird world cavern." Jenna gave a brief explanation of them to Altheria. She found she had missed them the last few days. And they definitely needed more help.

"Do they look like that?" Altheria was the only one facing the door.

"Elementals?" Jenna turned as the entire door glowed. They were agitated as they swarmed over. Or more so than usual. Jenna held out her hand and a group came to her. More than the five, but maybe they traded off the position.

A clump also swarmed Ghortin but stayed out of his hair this time.

"Now, settle down. Where did you go?" Ghortin sounded stern but also happy at their return. He had created them after all.

"*Bad. Go.*"

Judging by the look of surprise on Altheria's face, she heard them as well as Jenna and Ghortin.

"We can't go looking for more bad things, we have too many already."

"*No. Bads. Attack home. We go.*"

"Someone attacked my cottage?" Ghortin jumped to his feet.

"*Our home too.*"

"Did you stop them?"

"*Yes, but still coming.*"

Altheria convinced some elementals to come to her hand. "They're fascinating. You made them through your vortex, right?"

Ghortin beamed. "I did. Not easy, by the way."

"You pulled them from the core of the vortex." She smiled as she watched them.

"So, he didn't create them?" Jenna ignored the wounded look that crossed Ghortin's face.

"I'll have you know that I did create them." A group of them buzzed around his head. "Okay, I encouraged them to develop corporeal forms within the vortex. But it was my idea." He shook his head as the elementals flew around the room. "Still not sure how they are surviving outside of the vortex. Or my cottage, for that matter."

Altheria laughed at something the elementals near her said. "They said they were bored. Nice lady let them out. And that you shouldn't have gone into the world cave. They fled when they sensed an attack on your cottage—images in their minds are blurred, but it seems that people were trying to burn it at the same time you were all heading into the cavern world." She tilted her head as she listened to them. "But they wouldn't have gone with you down there anyway. It's bad."

"How did you get all of that?" Jenna's envy was beat by now having a better way to communicate with them.

"It's a gift." Altheria smiled. "Different magic users have

different gifts. I can sometimes get into the minds of animals. But these beings are far more charming."

The elementals definitely understood her, as they all buzzed closer at her flattery. Aside from five that remained with Jenna.

"But my, our, cottage is safe, right?" The world was in danger, but Ghortin still looked ready to ride south immediately if his home was threatened.

Jenna smiled. She understood. When the world was on the brink of destruction, it was good to have something to mentally fall back on.

"They say yes. They left more of their kind to protect it. The horses traveled away with your friends." Altheria grinned. "These are the most amazing creatures."

"I'm glad you understand them better than me." Jenna's smile dropped. "But we're still not closer to figuring out how to stop those mutated demonspawn or get the rest of the one hundred down here."

"I took us away from the cuari because I want to speak to Xalie and Edgar first. Hopefully, Rachael and the rest can get useful hints from the three cuari as to how they escaped, but I have a feeling they won't. But, before I call Edgar to join us, I wanted you to see if you can reach your cuari friend on the chaotic plane."

"You have a cuari friend on the chaotic plane?" Altheria looked more intrigued than surprised.

"Yes," Jenna explained about Meith. "But I don't know how contacting him is going to help. He wasn't part of the one hundred, or even the others like Xalie."

"No, but he might be able to make more bracelets like he created for Carabella. I looked at hers and it's far beyond any magic I know." The annoyance in Ghortin's voice indicated how he felt about that.

"Good point. But I don't know that he can create more."

"That bracelet that Carabella wears allows her to use

limited magic without attracting the spell bubble and being captured, right?" Altheria asked and continued at their nods. "Could those bracelets be used to help break the spell holding the rest of the one hundred on the chaotic plane?"

Ghortin shook his head, then stopped. "I have no idea. Jenna? Can you find your friend?"

"It's not always that easy to reach him. But I can try."

At Ghortin's nod, Jenna closed her eyes and tried to will herself to the chaotic plane.

Nothing.

She took a few deep breaths, shook out her shoulders, and tried again, focusing on the chaotic plane more than Meith.

A moment later she was there. "Meith?" She kept her voice soft; it was so still up here that it felt odd to break the silence. Something she'd never noticed when she used to come here for magic. The plants and flowers were even more faded than before.

A soft warm wind blew through the area. That was hopeful and more like what it used to be.

"Meith?" She called out once more before a familiar form came walking out of the light-colored trees.

"This isn't normal." Meith scowled at the trees and plants. "Not at all."

"Do you know who I am?" Jenna knew the fading plants were upsetting and most likely a sign of something bad happening up here, but he had barely glanced at her when he came over. There were timeline issues with their visits before and sometimes he hadn't met her yet.

"Did you get hit in the head again, Jenna? Of course, I do. This is a weird vision." He went back to scowling at the plants.

"Yeah, they're too faded. But we've got a problem and need more bracelets." She explained about the three escaped cuari and the concern that they could be pulled back to the chaotic plane at any time. The request for bracelets for the rest of the cuari could be dealt with once she got these three.

"More?" Meith finished glaring at the plants and turned to her "I'm not certain that I should." He dropped his voice as he gave deeper scrutiny to the area surrounding them. "I've no idea how those three got free. It could be a trap."

"We've thought of that, but we don't have a choice— we need them. Giving them some level of protection could make a huge difference in what we're facing." She rubbed her arms as a chill wind blew through. She didn't feel like her body was up here, but that wind touched her soul. "Is my body actually here?" An odd thing to ask, but she needed to know if they had to move about.

"Ah, no it's not." Meith walked around her. "I didn't notice that at first. But I can fix that."

Jenna wasn't sure that being up here in her body was better, but before she could say anything, she could tell she was now inside her body.

Meith's eyes went wide as a discordant bellow came from behind them. "Stay close to me, but run!"

CHAPTER SIXTY

JENNA FOUGHT THE URGE TO look back. Judging by the volume of the sound, whatever was after them was huge and most likely deadly. She was already running as fast as she could, and terror might stop her if the thing behind them was as nasty appearing as it sounded.

Meith got ahead for a bit and then dropped back to her. "We must get out of this place."

Before Jenna could respond, Meith dove through a hole in a massive dark tree trunk, and she was pulled along behind him. It felt as if she'd fallen down a slide as she careened along at a steep angle. In complete darkness.

Then a light appeared at the bottom. Meith was gone, and she was flung out of the tunnel and landed in a clump of bushes.

"Sorry about that. I wasn't sure we were going to make it." Meith stomped over to the tunnel and it folded shut at his touch. "That should keep it out. Your unnatural field up there probably called to it."

Jenna picked herself out of the shrubbery, dusting herself to get rid of the leaves and twigs. "First off, how is that field mine? It's what I saw in my mind when I first came up to get Power—only my version was brighter and livelier. Secondly, what was following us?" She'd come across some nasty creatures during her time in this world, but never something that sounded like that.

"The place that I found you was not how the plane looks. Yes, it's mutable, but that wasn't normal. Even if it hadn't been fading. I'd say that you created it in your mind when you first came here, and it stayed." He shook his head. Something about that upset him, but he wasn't going to add more.

"As for what was hunting us? A fell beast. One unseen here before, but one that was once in the world."

"Does it have a name?" Jenna was fine with not turning to look at whatever screeched and slavered behind them while they ran for their lives. But she found that she wanted to know now that they were safe.

"A vaen." He began pacing. "Their shoulders are taller than your head, have heavily armored skin, and two huge horns. One on the top of their head curving up and another larger one right above their nose also curving up."

Jenna found a rock to sit on. "They sound like something we have in my former world, we called them rhinoceroses." She'd always liked seeing them at the large safari park. Massive, gentle beings who liked to eat apples.

"Were they brutal killers who gored and stomped their prey before tearing them apart and eating them?"

"No. Not at all." She pushed the happy memories of rhinos out of her thoughts. "What happened to the vaens? I've never heard anyone mention them." And if they were the size he claimed, they'd be pretty difficult to miss.

"They were thrown through the portal by my people before the battle with the deities." He gave a sad smile. "Before I met you I lived in a sort of fog, all of my people up here did. Some memories remained from my time before being here, but not many. I believe that your coming here shattered that. More thoughts, images, and events are coming back to me. And, I believe I've stabilized my timeline without seeing what is further ahead." He sat on a rock near her and held out something he'd taken from his pocket. "I agree that the cuari have a task to do. But it's not clear yet."

He held out three more cuari bracelets. Either he had them with him or made them on the spot.

"Thank you for these. The cuari are essential for destroying that portal, but unless you know where they're being kept up here, we have no way to find them or free them. And I think we're running out of time." She put the thin bracelets in her pocket. This would help, but not resolve getting the rest of the one hundred free.

"I wish I knew. Along with my memories returning, it appears that those of the rest of my kind on this plane have as well. But the deities, or some subset of them, continue to try to keep us away from each other. I rarely saw anyone else up here until the first time you arrived. You might be the clue to breaking the hold on all of us who are trapped here, including the remaining one hundred." He paused. "Or, you might be the one who destroys everything."

Jenna thought he was kidding. But Meith was somber, and the sorrow on his face indicated that he wasn't joking. "How can I be the one who destroys everything? I'm fighting to save it." She asked when the silence started becoming uncomfortable. Jenna felt that a statement like that shouldn't be left hanging there—but he looked ready to do so.

"There was a myth, one from the before times, when the other peoples were not even thought of in the world. It spoke of a being of immense Power, one who came from two worlds, and would destroy everything."

Jenna waited for more but he shut down again. "And? Why? Why would someone do that? Were they evil?"

He gave a sad smile. "No. The being was grieving so badly, at some unmentioned horrific loss, that they acted out. In fear, loss, and pain, the worlds were destroyed. The myth was from long before the battle with the deities."

Jenna let that drift down to her gut. Destroying things out of greed or control was something she knew she'd never do. It wasn't part of who she was. But out of grief? She forced herself to look at the memory of those two brief future events. One where she watched as Los Angeles fell under attack from beings that had no right to be on Earth. And the other where a frightened and beaten Crell appeared alone.

If Crell was in fact the only one left of the people Jenna knew and loved in this world, she could see grief causing her to lose her mind. A chill of terror went through her. She shook her head, just because she saw it happening didn't mean it would.

"Do you know of any way to stop that from occurring?" The sound of the vaen had terrified her. But not as much as the thought that she could destroy this world. And all the other worlds. She was fighting against that happening. The idea that she might be the cause was too horrible to think about.

"I don't." Meith gave a sad smile. "But, if you are the being of myth, then you need to save the world before it has a chance to cause you such loss. Easier said than done, I'm afraid."

Jenna pushed the dark thoughts far back into her mind. There was nothing she could do about them now, and being aware of them potentially happening might be enough to keep them from actually occurring. She hoped.

She reached into her pocket and pulled out the three bracelets. "This is a long shot, but could you create and give bracelets to the rest of the one hundred still trapped here? We need them to fight this war—and destroy the portal for good."

"I'm not sure if it's possible." The tone in his voice was sympathetic. "I now have an idea of where they are being held, but making the bracelets will be the least of my problems if I can't get to the cuari. Take those to the other three and I'll reach out to you when I've sorted this issue." He might be more willing to help her now that there was a chance she could destroy everything due to grief. And that she now knew it.

The destroyer and grief issues weren't good, but being willing to look into getting the bracelets to the rest of the one hundred was.

"Thank you."

"Don't thank me yet. I might not be able to do this. And I don't think the bracelets alone will be enough to release the rest of the one hundred from this plane. There will be more help needed."

"But it might give them and us a fighting chance." Jenna wasn't certain he heard her as she suddenly found herself back in Ghortin's room.

Lying on the floor with a surprised Ghortin, Altheria, and dozens of elementals peering down at her.

"How did I end up on the floor?" Jenna let them pull her to her feet as she felt extremely disoriented. Something that rarely happened coming back from the chaotic plane.

"You yelled, and then appeared here. The yell came through first, by the way." Ghortin made sure she was seated and then put a cup of tea in front of her.

A full tea service with food was now where the pile of papers previously sat. The mountain of papers had found a new home on the floor against the wall.

"Where did that come from?" She sipped her tea and nodded to the tea set.

"You've been gone nearly an hour and we needed sustenance." Ghortin slid tea sandwiches over to her, then finished off two himself.

"An hour? It was only a few minutes." She looked over as Altheria shook her head. "It wasn't?"

"No, Ghortin's correct. First, you were here but unresponsive, and then you vanished. We discussed what we could with the elementals, then got tea."

"Did the elementals have any ideas to help?" She got another pair of sandwiches. That hour trip had taken a lot out of her. Ignoring the fact that it still only felt like ten minutes tops.

"Sadly, no. But they did say they will help where they can. Or they said their version of it." Altheria shrugged.

Ghortin leaned forward. "Did you find your friend? Can he help?"

"Yes, I did. He gave me these for the other three." She handed him the three bracelets. "He isn't sure if he can create and get them to the remaining ninety-six trapped cuari. And even if he can, he doesn't think they'll be strong enough by themselves to free the cuari from the chaotic plane. Also, there seems to be a problem on the chaotic plane itself." She went over most of her encounter with the plane and Meith.

"And? There's something you're not telling us." Ghortin watched her closely.

Jenna finished her tea, poured some more, finished that, and then nodded. She didn't want to talk to anyone about her possibly being the one to destroy the worlds until she at least had a day or so to process it. Even Ghortin.

She sighed. They needed to know. "Meith spoke of a myth, one from before the other races." She explained the entire thing as emotionlessly as she could, but couldn't look at either Ghortin or Altheria while she spoke.

Even if she didn't believe it, telling people she cared about that she might be the one who annihilates everything was hard.

"Now, that might not be you at all," Altheria said with a forced smile.

"*You* think it is me." Not a question and Jenna saw the answer on her face before she heard it.

"It could be." Altheria sighed and held up her hands. "This is the time for truth above all. As I said, different magic users have different skills. I sensed a duality in you when we first met, but didn't know where it came from. Later, Ghortin told me about your mental passenger, so I believed it was them. But it might not have been."

"Or that Meith person could be completely wrong." Ghortin got to his feet. "It's good that we know what's been said, but I think we need to get the bracelets on those cuari now."

While Jenna spoke, the elementals slowly vanished. When Ghortin got up, the last of them went through the outer wall.

"Did they say anything before they left?" Jenna asked Altheria as they also got up.

"Only that they had things to do. They are charming but difficult to understand."

Jenna nodded at the understatement and they returned to the Helaermage House.

The three cuari were chatting with Carabella alone, but everyone seemed relaxed.

"Ghortin!" Carabella jumped to her feet. "Excellent timing. Rachael, Tor, and Dantil were called off to a meeting with Justlantin, but said that unless you had any objections, they felt these three could be released and join the battle preparations."

"As far as I know, they're fine. Jenna brought something for them." He held up the three bracelets.

"Jewelry? And we hardly know you." Mariword grinned at Jenna.

Carabella held up her wrist. "They're like mine. Remember that I told you I could access some of my older magic without risk? This is how."

Ghortin gave each one a bracelet and then stepped back.

Mariword and Vala slipped theirs on with smiles to Jenna. Trisil glared at his and kept watching it in his hand suspiciously.

Jenna was beginning to wonder if the man had any other facial setting.

"Are you certain these are okay? Who made them?"

"Trisil, stop being difficult. The worst issue is we get sucked back up to the chaotic plane. Which will probably happen anyway if we don't have protection." Vala shook his head at his companion.

"Put the damn thing on." Mariword looked at Jenna and Altheria. "There's a reason he is solitary."

"I question things." Trisil held up the bracelet and then looked at Carabella. "You can do older magic without being caught? Show me."

Carabella flung out her hand and trays from an earlier meal floated around the room. "Simplistic, but makes the point. You'll know if you try for a spell that is too new or too large. You get a wee shock from the bracelet."

Jenna hadn't realized the bracelet did that, but it made sense. Otherwise, it would be too easy to screw it up.

Mariword grinned, called out a word, then swore and rubbed his wrist. "Yup, it warns you." He then created a dozen mage lights and had them go around the room.

Trisil finally slid the bracelet on. "Feels fine. Now, Dantil said once you cleared us, we should relocate to the castle and see about helping to get the rest of our people free."

"And find out what we can do to destroy the portal." Mariword shot Trisil a look and shook his head. "They told us what we were up against."

"Come on, we can get you set up in the castle, and then bring you down to the rest of the group." Ghortin held open the door. "We have a source working on helping the rest of your people—trust me."

CHAPTER SIXTY-ONE

A DAY LATER, THE CUARI WERE settled and involved in the plans—as best as they could be. Edgar worked hard to avoid all four of them, and moving people around so that Xalie could provide input without the cuari being involved was tricky at best.

Even though the portal was now reappearing, it seemed as if a lot of things still needed to be taken care of before they could attack it. Move too slow and the other side would gain a solid foothold that would guarantee their winning the battle. Move too quickly and their troops could be decimated before the real battle began.

The timing had to be perfect.

Given that there were many moving parts—Tigan and the troops following him were still on their way, the demonspawn had left Shettler's Point in flames according to the far-seers, and things were still questionable about getting the rest of the one hundred cuari back— there was a constant state of fluctuation between rushing around and waiting.

After admonishing the elementals to keep an eye on Irundail but stay out of trouble, Jenna got ready to meet her friends for breakfast in the smaller royal dining room. The larger hall made her self-conscious. Granted, providing that they saved the world, she would be marrying into the royal family, but they still made her a bit nervous.

With the fate of this world and all the others weighing on her, she didn't need more stressors.

Not knowing if they would get the call to head off

today or not, also made getting dressed a longer process than it should be. She didn't feel comfortable walking around the castle fully armed and in travel clothes, but the incident of being trapped in the world cavern unprepared made her aware of what could happen at any time.

She finally settled on comfortable clothes that could be travel wear if needed and her dagger. The weird thing hadn't done anything since the destruction of the underwater portal, and she could take it off and leave it now. But it was still handy to have in case of emergencies. Even as a highly decorative, but normal, dagger.

The smaller dining room was down a long hall and Crell ran up as Jenna walked to it.

"Ready?" Crell was always in travel garb and usually armed, so it wasn't odd.

"No." Jenna laughed. "That's not going to change anything though. I doubt anyone is ready for a battle to save multiple worlds and planes of existence. Any word on the rest of your rangers or deathsworn?"

The rangers who had not been magically transported north a few weeks ago still hadn't arrived but they were reported to be within a day's ride of Irundail.

Not only would another eighty or so highly trained fighters come in handy, but they were important to Crell and the rangers who were already here.

The deathsworn were another problem. Tigan and his group had been sent to the south magically and against their will and were now traveling to Irundail. But getting the rest of Crell's company of deathsworn out of Derawri for the upcoming fight had become a political issue.

The Derawri kingdom was facing skirmishes from the Strann empire along their borders. Nothing too dramatic, but enough to make the Derawri queen want to keep her forces home. Although the deathsworn in Crell's company were technically pledged to her, they still had to answer to their queen. So far there was no indication that getting them south for any battle was going to happen.

Crell gave a long sigh. She often did that when trying to control her temper. "Nothing on my rangers, but I still have hope. I don't feel the same about my deathsworn. Queen Iltheria and her consort won't allow any fighters out—especially deathsworn. Unless I can go up there and convince her of the importance of what we're doing in person, she won't budge. Derawri hasn't been under serious threat for generations—she's too young and is panicking at Strann's actions."

Jenna hugged Crell's shoulders. "Maybe we'll be happier with food." She pushed open the door to find the room far fuller than she'd hoped. She immediately spotted Kaytine and Lilltkin—Storm's sisters. Not as scary as dealing with the queen or Prince Justlantin, but still— they were royals, future sisters-in-law, and Kaytine was a high-ranking cleric of the Irissanta religious order.

"I have it on good authority that neither of them bite." Crell stayed next to Jenna but had seen what made her stop.

"I know, it's just…difficult. I need to focus on what we need to do, but I'm also thinking about my life afterward—if we survive. They seem nice." She flashed both royals a smile as they glanced over. Most likely they felt her staring at them.

Storm waved from a half-empty table, then walked over to them. "Did you want to speak to my sisters?"

"Nope, nothing but chatting and thinking." Jenna hugged him. "Why are there so many people here?" She and Crell followed him over to his table. Only Keanin and Talia were there, but from the disturbed place settings there had been more.

"Fighters have been coming in from the smaller towns, so people are crowding in where they can," Storm said as he brought over food and tea for Jenna and Crell. "Also, a group of Lithunane guards split off from Tigan's group and escorted a large group of Lithunane survivors here. They got in late last night. Everyone is being checked out first, so they're staying on this level for now where they can be watched. Wilty has set up housing for them further back in the valley once they've been cleared."

"And some of us are enjoying a moment's reprieve." Talia grinned. "I'm grateful that so many fighters from Erlinda came, but getting them to work with the Khelarans has been difficult, to say the least. The longer I hide out here, the more I can delay dealing with it."

Keanin laughed. "She sent Diath, Hon, and Flini to go work with them instead."

"Only for this morning." Talia poured them more tea. "Yesterday was extremely busy."

"Are they going to be able to work together?" Jenna knew that having so many different sources of fighters could be problematic. But she'd take a few thousand more if she could. Armies wouldn't destroy the portal, but enough fighters could keep their enemies from it long enough for Jenna and Keanin to do so.

Talia shrugged. "I think they will. Eventually. The Khelarans are strict, but the Erlindans, even the official guards, not as much."

Kaytine and Lilltkin came over with cups of tea.

"Do you mind if we join you?" Kaytine's question was aimed at the group, but she was watching Jenna.

"By all means, please do." Jenna motioned to the empty seats.

Kaytine took the one on Jenna's other side, and Lilltkin sat next to her sister.

Jenna smiled and slowly resumed her breakfast.

"How are you feeling about what we face?" Kaytine's voice was soft, soothing, and hit the issue directly on.

Jenna swallowed her food. "Honestly? Terrified." Her

eyes went wide, she hadn't meant to say that at all—especially not to these two.

"That was sneaky, Kaytine." Storm shook his head at his older sister.

"I am sorry, I didn't honestly mean to push that. There's a certain deity influencing things." Kaytine didn't seem shocked or concerned that Irissanta, or the gods and goddesses behind that name, had worked through her. "But she does want to know if you're ready. *She* is."

Most people still didn't know that the three deities were actually made up of many gods and goddesses. Kaytine knew, but wouldn't speak of it in a group.

"I don't know if I ever could be ready for what we're facing. Or if most people could be." Jenna's honesty came out on its own this time. "But I'll do what I can. Is there any news?"

The Irissanta deities were working with the deities of DOL to help facilitate bringing the rest of the one hundred cuari to this plane. The interaction from the gods and goddesses had to be limited, at least for now. If they tipped things off to Qhazborh, they could make the situation worse.

Dantil had remained locked up with his people for over the past twenty-four hours, but nothing had been said yet. So far, the lack of details had done nothing to calm Jenna's fears.

"Possibly." Kaytine flicked her left hand and the sounds around them faded. Her silence spell was softer and more subtle than Ghortin's. "A connection with your friend on the chaotic plane has been made and he was able to create the bracelets. Once he can get them to the one hundred they will help bring them to this plane."

Storm frowned. "Then why do you seem upset?"

Jenna didn't think Kaytine appeared anything other than serene. But her brother would know better.

"Caught me. The bracelets will help, but we'll need

more assistance to free the cuari. Powerful assistance. By doing what they have already done, Irissanta and DOL are risking escalating the issues with Qhazborh—and they're not ready." She waved her hand at Storm. "I know that ending Qhazborh is one of the primary goals, but Irissanta is less sure of that than DOL. And their involvement will have to grow if we're to complete our task."

"A lot is riding on that. I hope you can get those cuari down and mentally intact. Or this is going to be a slaughter." Crell pushed her plate away.

"I'm going by the way." Lilltkin remained silent until now but jumped into the small gap in the discussion. She also had her arms folded and glared at her older brother. "It's not up for debate."

"I was wondering why you were here," Storm said. "We need defenses here when the troops leave. The mages staying behind can protect the valley to a point, but we need fighters too. I was counting on you being the captain of the fighters here."

Lilltkin leaned forward and narrowed her dark brown eyes. "Good play, Corin. You planned on me babysitting, not leading anything."

This came up before as well. Lilltkin was young and about the same as a twenty-year-old human. She wanted to fight for her people but her family was focused on keeping her safe.

"No, we do need people here. That's not a lie." He didn't lean forward, but his narrowed eyes matched hers in all but color.

"Are they always this stubborn?" Jenna asked before she caught herself. Both of them broke away from their stare-off to look at her. "Sorry, but the world is on the brink of destruction. This might not be the time."

"I like her." Kaytine burst out laughing and hugged Jenna. "Thank you, these two are the most difficult in a family of stubborn people. Corin, you know that you're not going to stop Lilltkin from going. Could you have been stopped at her age?"

Now Crell laughed. "He can't be stopped at his current age. But I agree. Lilltkin deserves the right to go with us and save the world. I would be honored to have her ride with my rangers." Crell had been the nanny for the royal family and still thought of them as her wards.

Lilltkin dropped her glare but also looked trapped. She couldn't turn down Crell without being rude, but even Jenna knew that Crell's rangers would make sure Lilltkin was protected as much as they could.

From the look on her lovely face, Lilltkin had planned on having her freedom.

But she rustled up a regal smile and gave a soft bow to Crell. "I would be honored to fight alongside them and you."

Storm sat back in his chair and made a show of surrendering.

Jenna could tell he was happy with the way things turned out, no matter what he was trying to project. The best situation would be to have his sister stay here. Having her under the watchful eyes of Crell and her rangers would be the second.

Judging by Lilltkin's sigh, she knew it as well.

The rest of the breakfast was mostly filled with local gossip. It was lighthearted and about people the rest of them knew. Jenna sat back, ate, and listened. It was so normal, a group of friends and family chatting about unimportant things. She could almost push back the horrors they were going to face far too soon.

They were starting to discuss an old teacher when Crell grabbed her pocket and removed her buzzing taran wand.

"Sorry, the real world beckons." She nodded to everyone, then left the room.

Talia also pushed herself away from the table. "I should

get going as well. My brother isn't as disciplined as I'd like. Leaving him, Hon, and Flini alone with the troop for too long could be bad." She kissed Keanin and left.

"I need to go as well, and make sure that my travel gear is ready." Lilltkin gave a glance to her brother. "In case something happens and we have to leave immediately." With a gracious smile to the remaining people, excluding Storm, Lilltkin left.

Keanin watched her go. "I feel like I should be rushing about preparing, but I don't have the heart for it right now." He gave a sad smile. He was still sorting out how best to destroy the demonspawn who had attacked him as well as the creatures which were the outcome of that attack. He'd been covering it with laughter during their gossip session, but it lingered in his eyes.

Keanin would be part of the group going to free the remaining one hundred cuari. His abilities were needed there. Then he, Jenna, and one, as yet unknown, third mage would be the ones to cast the spell to destroy the portal in the Markare. Once they freed the remaining one hundred and fought their way to the portal, anyway.

Ghortin had suggested that perhaps he was supposed to be the third, but after looking through the cuari books, Tor Ranshal and Rachael said it wasn't him. He had an important part, but he was not the third from the cuari books.

They were going to need that third to focus the spell against the portal. The continuing lack of finding them was another worry for Jenna.

The issue bothering Keanin was that the army going to the Markare might run into the demonspawn group before he could get there. It would depend on how difficult it was to get the cuari down to this plane and how long it took.

Keanin wanted to be the one who destroyed the demonspawn and their monsters.

"We have that meeting with Rachael and Tor Ranshal in another hour." Jenna flashed Keanin a smile. "I don't think anyone would object to us relaxing for a bit."

Jenna's last words were cut off by the sound of someone trying to raise the dead. Or at least it was the first time that Jenna heard anything that met that description.

CHAPTER SIXTY-TWO

EVERYONE JUMPED TO THEIR FEET and ran for the door. Storm and Kaytine were ahead of her so Jenna stuck with Keanin.

"What is that sound?" It wasn't as loud now, but it still made her ears hurt. People from other parts of the castle ran out as well, with everyone gathering on the front lawn.

"I think it was the new alarm system Garlan put in," Keanin said. "It is mage controlled but the response is automatic once it's triggered."

"Alarm for what?" Jenna looked around as they got outside, but there wasn't an attack that she could tell.

Edgar joined them from wherever he'd been. "What happened now? Xalie hates that sound by the way. Almost knocked both of us out." He looked paler than usual but seemed fine aside from that.

"As I was explaining to Jenna, I believe it's Garlan's alarm system to detect magical intrusion." Keanin moved closer to the edge of the lawn that looked out over the rest of the mountain and the entire valley. "If there was a magical intrusion, or even an attempt, there should be some sign." He pointed toward the back of the valley. "Like that."

A thin line of dark orange smoke rose in the distance. One that didn't waver at all with the wind.

"Someone magically broke into the valley? Why aren't we down there?" Jenna looked at the people standing around and calmly chatting. "And why did they all come out?" Alarms back in her home world made people leave buildings, but that was because they could be on fire.

There wasn't a logical reason to clear out the castle that she could tell.

"It's orange, so a non-threat intrusion." Keanin nodded, but kept turning toward the stables. Non-threat or not, he wanted to go down to the smoke.

Edgar watched the people around them. "As for the people milling about, this alarm is too new for anyone to realize what to do. Most likely as people saw others running out to assess the issue, they came along. I'd say that everyone in Irundail is waiting for the next disaster to happen."

"Agreed." Ghortin came to them as castle personnel moved everyone back inside. It was interesting that no one from either the Helaermage House or the House of Healing came out. They had to have heard the alarm as well. Jenna would be surprised if anyone in the entire valley didn't hear it. "Crell and her rangers are already heading down. Tigan spoke to her on the taran wands and said something was happening with the deathsworn in Derawri. She took off once the alarm went."

"She thinks it's her people who broke through to the valley? We have no idea who sent the other two groups. How can anyone breaching the valley protections be a good thing?" As it turned out, having the rangers up here had proven helpful, and Tigan and his group were able to coordinate the surviving Lithunane troops in the south—but even Ghortin had been concerned about the involuntary transfer of people from one end of the country to the other.

He didn't seem concerned now though.

"You know something." She focused a glare his way and Keanin echoed it.

"No, I have a hunch. Dantil said his people were narrowing in on the sources of both prior transfers." Ghortin nodded sagely as if that resolved everything.

"And?" Keanin might still want to go down the valley and see what was happening but his priority was now finding out the newest secret.

"Yes, and?" Jenna liked that Ghortin was calm about this, there was a lot to not be calm about right now. But this drawing things out wasn't fun.

Ghortin sighed at being denied extending his information. "*And* it is believed that in both cases they were prompted by an outside source. Or rather, sources. The mage in the first case was attacked and killed before he could finish but he was trying to save the rangers and did manage to get some out of harm's way. The same with the Derawri magic user who helped Tigan and some of his people go to Lithunane."

"Are you saying they did it with deity help?" Jenna kept her voice low even though no one was near them. She knew the deities behind DOL and Irissanta were going to work on overthrowing the ones who made up Qhazborh, but this seemed like a more direct interference than they were supposed to be doing at this point.

"We believe so. But if they did help again for a third transfer, it would be the last time. They have a larger task coming up."

"We're going down there, right?" Keanin was ready to sprint for the stables.

"Or we wait. Crell's taran wand is still recharging but I assume that she'll contact us once it is ready." Ghortin smiled to them. "And I believe you two have a meeting with Rachael and Tor Ranshal? I promise to keep everyone updated if anything unexpected happens."

Jenna noticed that he said unexpected, not interesting. Ghortin wasn't going to interrupt their meeting unless the castle came under attack.

Keanin sighed and gave one last look at the stables, and then the three of them went back into the castle.

Ghortin left them not far past the front hall and detoured to the library. Wilty and the four cuari were doing research nearly non-stop. It was interesting that none of them came out during the alarm, but they probably already knew what it was.

Rachael and Tor Ranshal commandeered a mid-sized room in their hunt to find the third mage for the portal destroying trio. Using information found in the cuari books and loose pages they were searching the higher magic users of Irundail for the third person.

In a little-known prophecy, three who worked as one would destroy the portal. Keanin and Jenna fit the requirements when Rachael magically scanned them. But they couldn't find the third. This meeting was supposed to use Jenna and Keanin to finalize the third person.

The room was spacious but only held Rachael, Tor Ranshal, and Edgar.

"I thought there would be more?" Jenna came in and took a seat when prompted by Rachael. There were three chairs placed in a triangle with Rachael and Tor Ranshal standing off to the side.

"You too, Keanin. Edgar take your seat as well." Rachael's smile was warm but there was a line of worry between her brows.

"There aren't more, because I believe we have run through everyone in Irundail with the ability to be the third. No offense to Edgar here, but it was believed that his magic wouldn't be strong enough to take the position." Tor Ranshal nodded to Rachael. "Until we realized his live-in cuari might be able to make up the difference."

"Ha, you just want me for my tagalong." Edgar folded his legs and leaned back in his chair. Then he tilted his head. "She says you might be right, by the way."

Rachael's smile was less stressed now. "Let's hope so. We're out of options. I am going to cast a spell in between your chairs, and the three of you will create a way to support the items in a tower form."

An image of a complicated tower of thousands of pieces came to Jenna's mind.

Rachael's grin as she sent the intricate image and spell didn't make Jenna happy. It might sound simple but it wasn't going to be.

The spell was made up of a few thousand baseball-sized magic balls that Rachael deposited in the middle of the chairs. They didn't want to stay in any shape and just rolled around the floor in uncontrolled chaos.

Keanin and Jenna worked well together and got some of them into formation. Edgar was struggling until Jenna heard Xalie mentally speak to all of them. "*All four of us have to work as one. I'm not a tagalong.*"

Edgar laughed and shook his head. "Still getting used to things." The load for the magical balls shifted now that four were working on it. Edgar on his own couldn't keep up, but with Xalie's assistance, he and she were creating and maintaining the structure with Jenna and Keanin.

Rachael clapped when the form was completed and a green glow came from the tall, elaborate tower. She waved her hand and it vanished. "Excellent. Edgar and Xalie, you have officially been recruited. It will be tricky, no matter what happens in the fighting around you, you all have to focus on getting to the portal. Once this is started, time will be short. Events must happen quickly. Any delays will cost us everything."

"You two aren't going?" Nothing was previously said about whether the Guardians were going or not.

"No, we're not. The risk would be too high and it's not clear that our being there would be advantageous." Rachael frowned. "We will have to steer things from here." The tone of her voice indicated that while she was adhering to what was passed down in the cuari books, she wasn't happy about it.

Tor Ranshal was better at hiding it, but he wasn't pleased either. The discussion broke down into passing along the skills and spells that would allow the portal to be destroyed.

Jenna was exhausted by the time they finished. The four of them repeated the same ten-minute block of layered spells until she felt certain there was no room in her head for anything else.

The portal had to be open when they cast the spell as the destruction had to start from the inside and move outward.

As long as no one stopped them, the portal would explode and be gone from existence.

Jenna figured those ten minutes were going to be the longest of her life.

Xalie was the one who convinced Rachael and Tor Ranshal that nothing more could be added. "*Everyone is pushing past fatigue.*" Again, the mental voice reached all of them.

Rachael and Tor Ranshal bowed.

"We cannot do more at this time." Rachael hugged each one. "You will accomplish this."

The three of them left and Jenna was surprised that it was late afternoon. And that there seemed to be more derawri outside of the castle than before.

"Are those the rest of Crell's deathsworn?" Jenna stopped and asked Edgar and Keanin. She'd only seen the entire group once, but they didn't look like the same ones who were with Tigan in the south.

"That's what it looks like." Edgar grinned and waved at one he knew. "These will be a huge help. I'm going to go check on them." He jogged toward the one he waved at.

"Are they setting up camp on the lawn? The castle is huge. There should be room for them all inside it and the other buildings." They were only going to be here for a few days at the most, but being inside would probably be nicer for them.

"Not for the deathsworn when they're out of their homeland." Keanin walked toward them. "They have an image to project, and feel that staying indoors ruins that. Honestly, Crell said that back home they live indoors and quite well."

As Jenna watched, fifty rough but sturdy tents appeared. "They're impressive. How do you feel about what we need to do?"

"Honestly? Terrified." He looked down at her and stopped walking. "But at the same time, it seems like this is why I'm alive. All that has happened to me has brought me to this place and this time. For the first time in my life, I have a purpose. What about you?"

Jenna looked out at the troops prepping. "I'm scared that I won't be able to do it. That it will be my fault that we fail." She nearly told him what she'd discovered about her possibly being the one who destroys it all, but she couldn't do it. Even though she felt that he'd understand. Telling Ghortin and Altheria had been hard enough.

Keanin turned her to him and tilted her face when she wouldn't look up. "Listen to me, sister of my heart, there is no way that you would ever give less than your absolute best. If we fail, it won't be because of you." He narrowed his eyes. "Now, smile, nod, and agree with me. I'm right."

Jenna laughed. "Okay, you're right. We all go down this path together, no matter where it leads."

"Much better. Let's go see how Crell is doing, shall we?" He slipped his arm through hers and they walked over.

"Is this all of them?" Jenna asked.

"A few were injured in prior weeks—Strann continues to cause problems on the border. But aside from the injured, yes, the rest of my troop is here," Crell said. "I feel better already, although once we resolve this issue I'll most likely be called to the Queen. I'm more a citizen of Traanafaeren than Derawri, and my commanding of these deathsworn has always been a difficult issue."

"Would she take them away from you?" Jenna had never had a long conversation with Crell about the deathsworn, just mostly stories of some of their adventures.

"I've tried to find a good way to turn over leadership in the past, but the title of Ki' is old and the queen is one for tradition. If she now finds a way to have this troop reassigned to another Ki' ,I would be grateful. It's not fair to them to not have their leader in the country most of the time."

"I never knew that you felt that way." Keanin laughed. "When I was a boy I thought it was wonderful that you had a group of fierce fighters you could call up at any time. I used to imagine having my own troop." He waved his hand. "Not to fight so much as to look out for me."

Crell hugged him. "You always had me. But I should get back to keeping an eye on things. It looks like the Khelarans are getting nosy and my people didn't have a good trip down here. They're a bit testy." She walked around the outside of the camp with a determined stride. Khelarans were taller than her, but she'd still get them to back down.

"I thought the Derawri and Khelarans got along?" It was hard thinking of them as separate as all the races intermingled in Traanafaeren.

Keanin sighed as Crell approached the lead Khelaran. It wasn't Captain Niat, but possibly one of his lieutenants. "They do, officially. Unofficially, both sides poke at each other from time to time. Nothing like what Strann is doing, but little things. It's good that she's heading that off."

Ghortin hurried over to them. Not running exactly,

more of a brisk, determined walk. Jenna didn't think she'd seen him run more than a few times.

"There you two are. Go pack, we have a way to get the cuari." He might not have been running but had been moving fast enough to leave him out of breath.

"We're leaving now?" Jenna knew things were fluid but the sun would be setting soon.

"No, tomorrow morning. The troops going to the Markare will leave and so will we. Dantil has made sure we can get the rest of the one hundred back with help from his *connections*. And then we go to war."

CHAPTER SIXTY-THREE

—◆—

THE NEXT DAY THE MORNING sun was just peeking out as Jenna walked through the crowded stable to get her horse ready.

And maintain a calm façade, which was a major battle right now.

They were charging forward into an uneven fight. The rest of Crell's rangers had arrived during the night. Adding them and the deathsworn helped with their numbers, but from Tigan's last report after his scouts followed their enemies out of Shettler's Point, even the over two thousand fighters he was bringing north into the desert weren't going to be enough to win this thing.

But as stated by Garlan and the rest of the military strategy planners, they weren't going to win this by might.

The goal was to hold off the enemy long enough for Jenna, Keanin, Edgar, and Xalie to destroy the portal. After Kaytine and a bunch of DOL and Irissanta clerics helped them rescue the rest of the one hundred.

Meith had sent Jenna a brief message that he'd made the bracelets, but might need help getting them to the trapped cuari—he told her to speak to Kaytine.

Kaytine smiled and said it would be done but didn't elaborate.

Then she and a few dozen clerics of Irissanta rode off with guards not long after dinner. Dantil was staying in Irundail, it was the base of the helaermages' Power, but his people were working on their end—which would be directed at helping destroy the portal.

After waiting for this to happen for so long, Jenna felt rushed and unsure.

"You've adjusted your stirrups five times in the last few minutes. Suddenly forget how tall you are?" Crell walked over with her own saddled horse trailing behind.

"Oops." Jenna verified that she hadn't messed up anything, then stepped back. "I was still trying to sort out how Keanin, Edgar, and I are going to destroy the portal if we can't get near it. We need more fighters." The current estimate of the enemy fighters was ten thousand with the unknown troops from the far south.

Even thinking of that number made Jenna ill.

Crell shrugged. "It's not the size that matters, it's the skill. My people are smaller than the humans and the kelar, yet we win more fights than they do. Mark my words, it's better to have a smaller well-trained force than a massive disjointed one."

Jenna sighed. She hadn't been attacked by the massive doom and depression spell that had hit her before, but she didn't feel great about their chances. "I hope you're right and that Dantil and Rachael are right about getting the cuari down to this plane. If we can't get them, it won't matter if we get through or not. I hate that everything is happening at once. Plus, we'll have those unknown fighters from the south. How can our forces prepare if they have no idea who or what these people are?"

Crell frowned. "Agreed. There was more concern in Tigan's voice than I've ever heard from him. And the fact that these unknown forces destroyed their own ships as they came ashore is extremely disturbing."

Jenna had only briefly heard about that. Last night the far-seers were able to verify that all the ships, aside from the two from Strann, that were docked in the south had self-destructed by heavy magics. One way or another, those fighters weren't going to be needing them.

"Everyone ready? My partner is." Edgar walked up leading his horse.

"As ready as possible, given the massive amount of unknown elements." Jenna looked around at the nearly empty stables. As they'd been talking, the troops had gone out to the grassy area in front of the castle.

The majority of them would be riding directly to the Markare and attack the troops already gathering and those coming up from Shettler's Point. Sacaranz was reported to be traveling from there with a small troop of demonspawn, including the ones who were believed to be Keanin's magically created offspring.

Tigan and the troops with him were marching into the Markare directly. The original plan of coming north to Irundail was dropped as the forces against them made their moves.

A smaller group, including Jenna, Keanin, Edgar, Ghortin, and Altheria and the cuari were going to a hidden temple of Irissanta a few hours south of Irundail. Where, in theory, they would have access to getting the rest of the one hundred cuari down.

The trapped cuari were becoming aware now according to Meith. He wouldn't clarify how he got inside the enclosure to give the remaining one hundred their bracelets, but the implication was that Kaytine sent some assistance from Irissanta.

Jenna was grateful that Storm's sister Kaytine had worked with the clerics to open the passage—or at least try to. Xalie was hoping that they could get more of the non-one hundred released as well. Until Tor Ranshal pointed out that it could seriously compromise the one hundred. Once they won this battle and the portal was destroyed, freeing the rest of the cuari should be much easier and have little risk. If they lost, nothing would matter. The worlds and the chaotic plane would be destroyed.

They were heading out when Jenna noticed a groom

readying two more saddled horses. She was surprised when Rachael, Tor Ranshal, and Prince Justlantin came into the stables—the first two wore travel clothes and had packs with them. Both also had swords.

"They're coming with us?" Jenna didn't doubt that they could fight, she'd seen it before. But it seemed odd to risk them like this. Especially since Tor Ranshal had never regained his magic.

Prince Justlantin finished his conversation with the other two and left to address the troops gathered outside of the castle.

"Yes, child, we're going." Rachael took the reins of her horse and walked over.

"This wasn't in the plans, you even said so yesterday."

Jenna focused on Tor Ranshal but she wasn't going to remind him of his lack of magic. Not all of their fighters were magic users, the majority weren't. But Tor Ranshal was used to being a Powerful magic user.

Tor Ranshal followed Rachael over. "The situation is shifting quickly and there were indications that the Guardians need to be in the center of things. I might not have magic anymore, but there is more that I can do."

Rachael gave a sad smile as she patted Jenna's arm. "This is where we are supposed to be."

Jenna wanted more answers, but she was cut off by a series of horns outside the stable.

"And that is our cue." Tor Ranshal led his horse out and the rest followed.

Jenna would have liked to find out the reason for the change, but seeing the grim lack of surprise on Ghortin's face as they came out of the stable indicated not everyone agreed with the change of plans even if they already knew of it. She'd have to find out the reasons later.

Prince Justlantin stood on a raised platform in front of the gathered troops with Storm and Armsmaster Garlan on their horses beside him.

Once the crowd fell to silence, Justlantin began, "I can't emphasize enough how much rides with all of you on this journey. Aside from that you are fighting for not only our kingdom, but our world and the other worlds that we will never see. Time is now of the essence, and there won't be time for long battles—this battle will be faster than anyone you've fought before. No matter what happens, you must keep racing for the final goal. Those of you in the companies riding directly into the Markare will need to hold the line until the rest of our forces, including the ones freeing the cuari, can join you. I won't lie. Many of you will fall in this battle. We could still fail. But we must try. I offered an option to stay here last night to the fighters going today. It gives me hope that no one took it." He looked around at the entire group. He had wanted to lead the troops, but it was strongly advised against it by everyone. Destroying his father and older brother had given the enemy strength. As the heir to the throne, he needed to remain safe.

"You have your orders and the well-wishes of everyone in this land and beyond. Protect each other and follow your captains. Prince Corin and Armsmaster Garlan will be leading the two main strike groups. On behalf of the royal family and everyone in Traanafaeren, I wish you good luck."

The look on his face and clenched jaw indicated that he still wanted to go. Jenna had only heard part of that debate. Kaytine had been adamant that Justlantin and their mother needed to remain here—and implied there was a higher force behind it. If she could have, she would have included Lilltkin but whatever had come down from Irissanta didn't include her, so she didn't have the leverage to enforce it.

If they managed to destroy the portal and come back, Irissanta felt it was crucial that the royal line of Traanafaeren survive.

The Markare group broke up as Garlan led the first teams down the mountain. Storm rode to Jenna then got off his horse.

"Logically, I fully know this separation is needed. But emotionally—"

Jenna reached up to pull his face down to hers and silenced him with a forceful kiss. "But emotionally it's terrifying. I know."

He looked down in concern and she waved him off.

"It's not that depression spell. Just good old-fashioned and fully justified concern. We went from moving slowly to speeding through and there are a lot of pieces to track."

"We will get through this." He held her close. "You need to get the cuari, and then Tigan and his army will be in the Markare, we win the battle, and destroy Qhazborh and the portal. Then come back home and live to a quiet and boring old age. Easy."

Jenna gave him another quick kiss. "I'm holding you to that. Easy. Quiet and boring."

Their moment was cut short as Edgar and Keanin came out of the back stable leading a huge herd of slightly spelled horses. They were for the cuari when they retrieved them, but keeping them under light spells would help keep them from spooking on the trip down. They nodded, then moved the horses to follow Ghortin, Altheria, and the rest of their smaller group as they made their way to the ramp down the mountain.

Jenna hugged Storm again. "I think that's my cue to leave. I love you, stay safe."

"I love you too. I don't think I can live without you." The intensity in his eyes as he studied her face hit her hard.

One more kiss and he ran to his horse to lead the final Markare group down.

Jenna mounted her horse and rode toward Ghortin. Carabella and the other three cuari were already on their way down. Ghortin might be the leader of this part, but that never stopped Carabella. She laughed as she raced the other three cuari to the floor of the valley.

Jenna watched Edgar and Keanin move the herd of horses to the side of the ramp. They were playing fast and loose with the potential problems that could happen if Carabella or any of the other cuari noticed Xalie and what she was. The best they could do was to keep them as separated by distance as possible.

Ghortin and Altheria followed, with Tor Ranshal and Rachael riding in front of Jenna, Keanin, and Edgar's herd of horses.

"It's not that I don't want either of you here," Jenna said as she rode up to Rachael and Tor Ranshal. "But I'm still not sure why you two are coming. You said that you could better serve the fight from Irundail. Is this worth the risk?"

"There were changes last night. Ones that require that the Guardians be on hand." Tor Ranshal was calm, but he looked older than he had yesterday.

"Not to be rude, but you don't have magic. Isn't it a pointless risk?"

Tor Ranshal smiled. "There are ways to fight even Powerful magics with wisdom and other skills." His smile fell. "We translated the final five pages from those two destroyed cuari books late last night. If the Guardians are not there at the final fight—this endeavor will fail." He patted his cloak and showed her the cuari books he carried. "The books, along with Rachael and I are needed to see this through in person."

Jenna turned to Rachael, but she nodded. "It will be what it will be. This is what all Guardians prepared for. But you must promise that no matter what happens to us, to *any of us*, that you, Keanin, and Edgar will destroy that portal. No matter who it is, no lives are worth losing that chance."

Jenna nodded and tried to ignore the chill in her soul. Nothing like terrifying promises before heading out to battle.

The trip down the levels to leave the mountain was uneventful and mostly silent, at least in the back. Jenna thought about riding closer to Keanin and Edgar, but her heart wasn't in it. She needed to sort the recent changes out.

When she'd first met Rachael, she'd claimed that she had hoped Jenna was a replacement Guardian. Rachael was almost two thousand years old—an old age even for the long-lived kelar—and she was ready to let go of this world.

She seemed healthy, but Jenna knew she was still ready to move on. Tor Ranshal had never expressed such comments, but he did keep things close. Glancing at these two, Jenna couldn't help but fear this was their last trip. And that they were fully aware of it.

Jenna didn't know what to do or say. She didn't think either would throw their lives away, but the fact that they found this information at the last minute and didn't fully share it was disturbing.

Once they got out of Irundail and on the road, Jenna might ride up to Ghortin and find out what he knew.

Storm and Garlan were already leading the bulk of the troops toward a road that would eventually lead to the Markare. The wave of riders crossing the countryside looked impressive—until she thought about what they were up against. Jenna quickly wiped a tear away. They had to survive this.

"It's okay to cry, you know. This is a dangerous time and nerves are fragile." Tor Ranshal rode a bit closer to her.

"I can't get past this terror." She gave him a brief smile. "No, it's not that depression spell again." She couldn't blame any of them for thinking that—but she felt the difference. "It's like we're missing something important. But I don't know what."

"We are as prepared as we can be. But there are many pieces in play and it's difficult to tell what will happen if one of them fails."

"The cuari."

"That's a big one, yes. But we have done what can be done at this point to get them back. That's all anyone can do. Now we must see it through."

Jenna shook her head with a sigh. "How do I become as calm and balanced as you and Rachael?"

"Live to be over a thousand, for a start." He grinned and they dropped back into silence.

Ghortin led them through rolling hills that Jenna hadn't seen the one time she came down this way. The valley that the clerics of Irissanta held down here was hidden and protected.

Altheria pulled off to the side and let Edgar and Keanin pass with the horses. She joined Jenna as Tor Ranshal and Rachael dropped further behind.

"How are you doing?" Altheria's face was comforting but didn't have that level of serenity that Rachael and Tor Ranshal had.

"As best as can be expected. Still not completely certain that I won't destroy everything, but cautiously optimistic about it."

A clump of elementals appeared and circled them.

"Hello friends." Altheria held out her hand and some settled there. Five came to Jenna.

"Good to see you. Aren't you supposed to be watching the Markare?"

"*Others watch. We guard.*"

"Thank you," Altheria said. "Maybe you could spread out and fly ahead as well?"

"*Yes.*" The ones with Altheria and Jenna stayed, but the rest of the group stretched out the length of the riders.

"How different do they sound to you? I mean, you were getting a lot more information out of them back in the castle. I only got what we just did, simple communications."

"When they are only speaking to me, I hear more nuances. More like their feelings than actual words. I even get it a bit when they communicate as they just did." She frowned at the elementals flowing through the horses ahead of them. "They are concerned for us. There is risk in getting the cuari back."

"But they won't tell us? The only risk I heard was that we might not be able to get them all free." Which would most likely doom the entire endeavor, but this sounded different.

"They don't seem to know." She shrugged. "Even with me, the communication isn't what we would hope. I'll warn Ghortin and the cuari if you can tell the others. We'll be at the valley of Irissanta soon."

At Jenna's nod, Altheria rode forward. Jenna dropped back, still with her silent elemental escorts, and told Tor Ranshal and Rachael.

Neither had sensed any threats but nodded in agreement to be wary.

Then Jenna rode up to Keanin and Edgar. Both immediately dropped their hands to the hilt of their swords at her words.

"It might not be a physical threat. Even Altheria couldn't get more out of the elementals, and these aren't talking."

"*Guard*," the five elementals with her said.

"Aside from that. Be wary and have access to some defensive spells. The clerics of Irissanta will protect the area the best they can, but there's still some serious magic up against us."

Ghortin slowed as he and Altheria spoke to the cuari. None of them appeared happy but at least they didn't do

anything drastic. Jenna knew that Carabella was probably not the same as all cuari, but so far at least Trisil had
shown to have her temperament. She'd seen him reacting
to shocks from his bracelet more than any of them as he
kept testing the limits.

"*Jenna? Are you there yet?*" A floating and ghost-like
form that sort of looked like Meith came alongside her
horse. Judging by the lack of reaction from her horse, or
any of the rest around her, no one else saw him.

"We're coming, but not there yet." She turned to Edgar
and Keanin as they gave her questioning looks. "Meith."

"Ah, tell him we're about fifteen minutes away. The
location is at the far end of the valley we're approaching,"
Edgar didn't look too upset about her speaking to invisible people, but he had one living with him.

"*Hurry. And be ready.*" Meith's voice was fainter that
time and so was he. He vanished before she could ask
him what was wrong. She didn't think this was the time
to follow him up to the chaotic plane—even if she could
get through.

"That's not good. He's worried about something but
didn't say what. Can you move this herd faster?"

Edgar nodded before Keanin did.

"Good, I'm going to ride up to Ghortin, we need to
pick up our pace." Jenna moved away from the herd and
caught up with the cuari and Ghortin. The four cuari
were bickering, but it sounded like Trisil was giving
unsolicited advice again.

"I was contacted by my *friend*. We need to move faster,
something's wrong."

Trisil opened his mouth, but Carabella spoke first.

"Don't even ask, Trisil. This entire operation depends
on us not knowing certain things. Who she's speaking to
is one of them and I won't let you mess things up."

He shut his mouth with a glare.

Ghortin swore and nudged his horse. "Everyone be on watch. This could go wrong quickly."

Jenna stayed up front and examined the trees around them carefully. This entire valley belonged to the Irissanta clerics but was a well-protected secret. That Meith and the elementals felt there was a danger here wasn't good.

Trisil might have been ready to demand answers, but he now rode off to the side of the group with one hand on his sword hilt. It was good that he wasn't going to rely on his limited magic and his moves indicated a background as a tracker.

Which probably came naturally if he was as solitary as he seemed.

The herd of horses was jogging along easily and Jenna felt Keanin put another spell of protection and calmness over the animals.

"There's a body." Trisil didn't ride to it but pointed at a cloaked form crumpled inside the tree line. "Might I check it?" There was a bit of snark in his voice, but at least he asked before acting.

Ghortin nodded and came to a stop.

Trisil jumped off his horse and came back with a scarf. "It was an Irissanta cleric, he was nearly cut in two. And stomped on."

"Stomped on?" Vela asked as he turned to look.

"Yes, by something massive. The ground is trampled." He got back on his horse, but kept the scarf.

"Vaens," Jenna said the word so softly that only Ghortin heard her.

"Those aren't real." But he didn't sound like he believed his own words.

"They are, or were. I can't explain how they are here, and I never saw them, but my friend told me of them after we were chased by them. On the plane." Since the vaens were from the prior time for the cuari, she didn't think mentioning their name again would be good.

"We need to keep moving." Altheria's eyes were wide. "Now. Move now!"

Ghortin didn't ask but nudged his horse, and soon all of them were running.

Jenna tried not to look, but there were at least ten brightly-clad bodies in the forest around them. Most were near downed trees. Which unfortunately supported her vaen theory.

The meeting area was distinctive by the tall arch before them. This area was normally cloaked but the clerics released that for this exchange.

They were nearly there when the ground began shaking and the horrific sounds she'd heard on the chaotic plane echoed around them.

CHAPTER SIXTY-FOUR

"RUN!" JENNA YELLED AS HER horse increased its speed without any nudging. It hadn't even turned back to look at what was chasing them. Jenna understood. She didn't look back either. The sound was the same as the vaen on the chaotic plane, but there was more than a single beast after them.

Meith appeared and floated in front of her horse and the elementals crowded around him. "Get through the arch. Set this spell as you cross. These can help." He waved at the elementals and vanished like a puff of smoke before she could ask anything.

But he'd left a spell in her mind.

She raced through the arch and released the spell. The elementals gathered around the arch and pulled the spell along with them.

Jenna stayed out of the way as Ghortin, Altheria, and the cuari, except for Trisil, raced through followed by the herd of horses and the rest.

"Trisil, get through the arch!" Jenna yelled as he looked ready to stand and fight. The vaen weren't in sight yet, but the ground was shaking more.

"I can stop them!" He'd turned his horse and was pulling up what sounded like a complicated spell. One which might zap him out of existence when he cast it.

"You stubborn idiot! Listen to Jenna, drop that spell, and get in here now!" Carabella rode back to the arch, but didn't cross it. "We need you with us!"

Trisil continued to look the way they'd come.

A group of elementals raced to him and poked his horse. The animal stopped listening to Trisil and let the elementals chase him under the arch.

Jenna slammed the spell shut and the elementals glowed golden yellow.

The vaen ran into view. Eight of them. From a distance they did remind Jenna of rhinos, until they opened their mouths to roar. Their teeth were sharp and plentiful; these were not plant eaters.

The leader didn't even slow as it raced for the arch. The elementals' glow changed to red and the charging vaen froze as waves of magic flowed over it, then its fried body was thrown into three of the ones following it. They stomped on it, but kept coming.

Two from the left charged the arch and faced the same result as the first. The remaining five snorted and pawed the ground but didn't come any closer.

"What are they?" Keanin looked fascinated and terrified at the same time.

Jenna shook her head. She still felt connected to the spell, but the way to cast it was fading quickly. "I can't say their name, but they shouldn't be here." She glanced back to the four cuari to make her point.

"That's not good," Edgar said. "We've increased the spell on the horses, but it won't last long with those things out there. Not to mention that we will need to leave eventually."

"Thank Irissanta you made it." Kaytine led a group of clerics out from a low structure that hadn't been visible until they got past the arch. "We were able to destroy the followers of Qhazborh who attacked us, but not those things."

Kaytine looked like the rest of her group, bloody and dirty from an intense fight. But she ran to Jenna and hugged her when she got off her horse.

"I'm sorry for your losses."

"Thank you. We will grieve when this battle has been won. Come this way, I believe we can still facilitate the release of the cuari."

Jenna, Altheria, and Ghortin were the three who would help the clerics and Meith send down the cuari. Hopefully.

"Are your people still strong enough?" Jenna had no idea how many they lost, but all the ones with Kaytine had clearly been in hard fighting.

Kaytine looked around her group and nodded. "We have all the strength we need." She led them into the building and motioned for the three of them to stand in the center. "We have a few resources that will help."

Before they'd left, Dantil told them that the deities would be involved this time, their eons of hiding were over. DOL was still stating that Qhazborh, or rather the gods and goddesses under that name, would be removed. DOL hadn't said how, however.

The room they were in was far larger than it looked from the outside and could easily fit a hundred or so cuari—once they got them down from the chaotic plane.

"What do we need to do?" Jenna knew there was some spell or something, but aside from saying that she, Ghortin, and Altheria, casting it, no further information had been passed along before Kaytine rode off last night.

"It's easier than you'd think." Kaytine grinned at Ghortin's doubtful look. "I promise." She was closest to Ghortin and motioned to him first as she stepped away from the center. "You stand here. Only stand, no spells right now. Don't even think them."

From the look on his face, he'd been already going through what spells might be needed.

"Altheria, you'll be here." A bit over from Ghortin, but not a full third away.

Jenna was a similar distance from Altheria. They were in an arc, but only covered half of the circle. "Don't we need to enclose it?" That was the expected theory. By creating a safe passage between this plane and the chaotic one, they could bring the remaining cuari here.

"Oh, it will be closed, never fear." Kaytine took up a position along the same arc as the others. Then two more beings appeared to finish the circle. They were vague and ghostly, and it was difficult to see their faces.

Rather, their faces kept changing.

"May I present; manifestations of Irissanta and DOL."

Kaytine seemed completely at ease with the deities, but Jenna wasn't sure she felt the same. As they settled into place, the Power flowing off them felt like it was going to knock over the entire building.

"But they can't interfere. It is forbidden." Altheria didn't move but she looked like she expected to be struck by lightning for being in the same room with them.

"We must not let what might happen occur. We will end this." The voices were even more disturbing than the switching faces and seemed to come from both beings.

"It will be okay, I promise you." The sincerity, compassion, and surety in Kaytine's voice was something Jenna wished she possessed.

Part of her wanted to run screaming out of this place, vaens or not.

Altheria looked to Ghortin and Jenna then nodded. "As it is willed."

Kaytine smiled. "You have not been forgotten, sister."

Altheria nodded back but didn't speak. That she had been a cleric of Irissanta at one point had never been brought up. At least not to Jenna. Ghortin didn't look surprised, however.

A cold wind went through the room and Kaytine shook her head. "You were not included. Don't even try."

The two deities reached up their hands and the wind stopped.

Jenna didn't hear a name but she felt Qhazborh's presence as it vanished.

"We have little time. Here is the spell, hold it close and honor it with your heart."

Jenna felt a spell come into her mind. No doubt it would vanish once they finished, like the others had.

This one was massive and seemed to fill her entire being. She tried to hold it, but it felt like it was engulfing her.

"Easy, child. It is your friend." The closest being waved their hand toward her.

Jenna took a deep breath and let the spell flow through her. Even though she was going to be the one casting it, she couldn't have told anyone what exactly it was.

The deities began chanting and Kaytine joined in. Then Altheria and Ghortin. Jenna was freaking out that she didn't know what to do, then the words flooded her mind. They were welcoming and filling.

The spell flowed around the chamber and then an energy filled the space.

A moment later a mass of cuari appeared before them and collapsed.

The urge to chant vanished and it did look like there could be ninety-six people on the ground before them. "Is that it?" Jenna hated to break the spell, but it felt like it was vanishing regardless of what she wanted. And the cuari on the ground still weren't moving.

"We must leave." Both groups of deities spoke at once, then vanished.

"Yes. And no." Kaytine ran to the closest cuari and looked them over. "They were supposed to be fully functional when they arrived. We can't hold this place for long and if they can't ride, we can't get them out. Something interfered with the process." She shook her head at the others. "Don't even say the name. Not here." She rocked back as the cuari she'd been examining blinked and sat up.

"Where am I?" The woman looked around, then reached for a spell. The wince and shaking out of the arm with the bracelet on it said it was going to be a powerful spell.

Kaytine smiled and helped the cuari up. "You are free and safe. We need your people."

One by one the cuari slowly woke up and Carabella and the other three came to help. The newly arrived cuari were confused, but at least they didn't think they were trapped in the past.

Once they were all on their feet, Kaytine addressed them and briefly explained what was needed.

And that they had to leave now.

"We're running to the Markare to destroy the portal? What madness is this?" A shorter cuari woman glared around the room.

"It's madness that will save or doom this world, Jarisa. Don't be so cranky. And they brought horses." That the words came from Trisil might have been funny under other circumstances.

All the cuari were asking questions until Carabella let out a loud whistle. "Folks, I was the only one of us not taken. You have questions, I get it. But right now, we need to destroy that portal and save the world. If we survive, you can ask all the questions you want." Then she nodded to Ghortin.

"As she says, we're out of time. Please go outside and quickly choose your horses. We're going to have to run our way out of here. Oh, and those bracelets will help you access your older magic, but don't try anything new or too strong. You'll get a warning shock and if you work through it you'll be taken. Or killed."

Jenna hadn't heard that last part before but he might have simply been trying to scare them.

They grumbled, but the cuari walked out of the building. Keanin was with the horses and Edgar had dropped out of sight. Staying clear of four cuari had been interesting to watch, hiding from a hundred was going to stretch even his spymaster abilities.

Each horse had weapons and a small pack, but nothing larger than what might be needed for a day. Either this was resolved quickly, or they'd all be dead.

Kaytine came out from a small building in the back, leading a saddled horse.

"You told Storm you'd stay here." Jenna had overheard that conversation. Then the rest of the clerics also brought out horses.

She shrugged. "The plans changed when we were attacked here. I ordered the island with our temple to be inaccessible to all until this is resolved. And our goddess wants us to be there."

There were about forty clerics armed and ready. The cuari were now on their horses as well. Their numbers weren't huge compared to what they were up against, but every fighter helped.

Jenna never thought of clerics as fighters, but judging by the weapons they had, they weren't strangers to battle. Dantil's helaermages remained in Irundail. They would supplement the remaining Irundail guards if anything came against them.

They rode toward the arch and the swarm of elementals still hovering around it. Edgar waved to Jenna from some trees and joined Tor Ranshal and Rachael. Jenna saw Rachael cast a simple spell and then nod to Edgar. Hopefully, she'd figured out something to keep Edgar's mental friend from being noticed by the cuari.

Jenna hoped that when they finished this the two could be separated.

"I don't see those creatures." Jenna stayed behind the arch but there was no sign of the vaens.

"*Gone.*" The elementals pulled away from the arch and clumps of them swarmed around the cuari and the clerics.

"Did you kill them?" Aside from the three burnt vaen bodies, there was no sign of them. But Jenna had seen how easily the elementals destroyed the ertin. Granted, the vaen were a lot larger, but Jenna wasn't sure it made a difference for the elementals. They could have chased them off and run them through.

"*No. Defend only. They run to desert.*"

Altheria rode up and frowned. "They can't go after those creatures."

"Are they afraid of them? Can they fight anything now?" Yes, having them defend would be good and they had killed three of the vaens. But there were still at least five more out there, not to mention she was hoping that the elementals could help with the fight.

"They're not afraid." Altheria held out her hand and tilted her head. The elementals buzzed around her and Jenna felt the edges of their communication.

Altheria sat back and shook her head. "They are currently limited in what they can do, but can't indicate why. They might be able to be more aggressive in the desert, but they might not. The only thing they say for sure is that they cannot attack those creatures." She'd dropped her voice but there were a lot of cuari milling around and they had excellent hearing.

Ghortin came over but kept watching the forest around the arch. "We need to get on the road, but we can't with five or more of those things out there. Not to mention that even I have no idea how they are even existing or how they got down here."

"I say we race out and hope they're gone." Keanin glanced back at the cuari. "I know you're being cautious, but the other four saw them and weren't affected. Maybe we just have to worry about them killing us."

Ghortin pulled on his beard. "I think their name might trigger something, but you are correct—none of them responded to their appearance." He waved Rachael and Tor Ranshal over. "Do either of you have a feeling about us charging forward? We need to get to the Markare."

"I don't sense anything. And I agree we need to move." Rachael leaned closer to Jenna. "Has your friend who is *not* from the chaotic plane been back?"

"No. He's not responding to me." Jenna had tried calling Typhonel last night and when they were on the road. Because of his inconsistent appearances, no plans had counted on him. But it would be handy to have him along on this. She gave one more try, then shook her head. Hopefully, he'd show up when they got to the portal. He'd been lurking in the heads of Protectors for generations in order to destroy this thing.

Ghortin walked his horse to the arch and faced the group. "We're running out of here to avoid some aggressive beings. Expect heavy fighting once we get into the desert. We have troops in place and on their way who will take on the bulk of it, but our goal is to get Jenna, Keanin, and Edgar to the portal. Don't engage in fighting unless it is to get those three through. May the Irissanta and DOL guard us." He nodded and turned back to the arch and his horse raced through.

CHAPTER SIXTY-FIVE

JENNA WAS RIGHT AFTER HIM. She'd never seen Ghortin show any kind of religious leanings in the past, but it felt right to include the gods and goddesses now.

Knocked down trees and torn earth indicated where the vaens had run, but there were no signs, or sounds, to indicate they were still around. She really hoped there was a high cliff for them to fall from not far from here.

It would be exciting to be in the front of the charge like this—if they weren't racing to fight to save the world.

The elementals stretched themselves out and flew around the entire group, but didn't do anything else. Jenna was grateful they'd been able to block the vaens from attacking them, but she wondered what made them back off from destroying the remaining beasts. One more aspect that couldn't be counted on.

They ran for about ten minutes before Ghortin began slowing down. They'd cleared Irissanta's valley and were trotting down a wide-open road.

Jenna didn't like riding through heavily forested areas, especially after seeing the bodies in the valley, but this felt too exposed. Like people miles away could see them.

She nudged her horse up to ride alongside Ghortin. "Isn't this dangerous? Anyone who knows where we're going can see us."

"True. I did release a light misdirection spell that's bouncing off the elementals. If someone gets too close, they'll detect us, but otherwise we should be able to cross unnoticed."

Jenna looked up at the elementals. She'd take his word for it about the spell, all she saw was a vague distortion around them. She glanced back but as they'd reached the open road, the riders spread out a bit. No one was close by. "What are our chances, seriously?" She'd never asked him that. Mostly because she was afraid of the answer.

"I won't lie. I don't think they're good. Even without facing the forces aligned against us, destroying that portal is a long shot. We have done all that we can to make it happen, however." He gave her a sad smile. "That's the best any of us can do. Now promise me that no matter that happens when we reach the Markare that you, Keanin, and Edgar will keep going. You and Edgar might have your hands full if Keanin sees the demonspawn offspring, however."

Keanin was chatting with Carabella and another cuari woman behind them. He looked up as Ghortin and Jenna glanced back at him. Jenna forced a smile and turned away.

"That's not going to be easy. All of Keanin's changes began with what they did to him." She and Keanin were close, but she doubted she could convince him to hold back. And she didn't know that any of them could magically stop him if it came to that.

"Agreed. With any luck, the creatures will have already been destroyed." Ghortin wouldn't look at her as he spoke.

His vest pocket buzzed and he pulled out the wand. "Ah, Mage Archion, what news?"

Jenna hadn't met Archion, but she'd heard the name. He was one of the high-ranking far-seeing mages. Hopefully he had something good to tell them.

From the growing frown on Ghortin's face, that wasn't coming.

"I see. You've warned Crell and Tigan? Good. I don't know that the deathsworn can get there before the conflict, but hopefully. Odd question, but there are five unnatural monsters roaming around. Have you seen them? Could you keep an eye out for them? Thank you." Ghortin put away the wand and glared at the surrounding open dirt and sand.

"And? Sorry, but I only heard part and it didn't sound good."

"It's not good. There are already a few thousand troops heading north in the Markare. They identified the mysterious ones who sailed up here from the distant south as Paunians because of the markings on their shields. The only reference to them are in ancient texts."

"Could the Strann empress offered them something to fight on her side against us? Like Traanafaeren? None of them might realize what will happen if Qhazborh, Sacaranz, and their followers win this fight. It also would explain burning their own ships after they landed." That bothered her. Why Strann was going through so much work to win a fight that would eventually destroy everything as they knew it.

Because they didn't realize that was Qhazborh's endgame. And they'd managed to find allies, most likely with Qhazborh's help, who also didn't realize it.

If Jenna's side lost this fight, it wouldn't be long before Strann and the Paunians did as well.

They didn't know it yet and the odds of them listening to anyone telling them that were nonexistent. Win or lose, they weren't getting Traanafaeren.

"That would be my guess. If they win, it won't take long for them to realize they've been tricked."

Jenna drifted back a bit as Ghortin went silent and appeared to be processing things in his head. There was nothing out here to distract her, so her mind made a beeline to worry about Storm and the rest of their friends.

They'd be in the Markare by now, or soon. While they were hopefully still further north than the troops coming from the south, there was no doubt they'd face fighting.

She nudged her horse back up to Ghortin. "But why didn't Strann forces come from the north as well? Why go through the hassle to build massive ships and haul them across entire countries to get into the ocean, when they could have just come across the land?" When they'd gone into Strann they'd crossed into it from Traanafaeren. But they'd only been a few days' ride from the Markare.

"That's a good question. I'd say it's due to the difficulty crossing into the Markare from Strann, and their border skirmishes with the Derawri are probably taking more troops than we believed. The far-seeing mages are watching for any movement from there anyway. We can't count on anything." He paused. "Speaking of which, anything from Typhonel?"

They were far enough ahead of the cuari that they shouldn't react to the name, but Jenna still turned to make sure. "Not a word. This is what he's been here for, shouldn't he show up to help the Protector do her job?"

"One would think, but Rachael wasn't certain how much he would be able to help. The cuari books only refer to him generally, nothing specific."

"Run!" The shout came from Edgar at the far back of the line. The elementals rose higher in the air and began zipping around.

Jenna turned and saw that the vaen had found them and had brought friends. Riders sending arcs of magic rode behind the beasts.

"Keep going!" Ghortin yelled at her as he pulled to the side.

"Why aren't you going?" Jenna knew they might have to split up, but this seemed too soon.

"You, Keanin, Edgar, Rachael, and Tor Ranshal have

to go ahead. Carabella and half of the cuari will ride to protect you as long as they can, but go!"

He might not have shared this backup plan with her, but Edgar, Keanin, Rachael, Tor Ranshal, and Carabella raced through the group with more cuari following. Tri-sil was at the end and he sent low-level magic spears at the riders after them. At least two fell before he turned back but if he also aimed at the five vaens, there was no impact.

Jenna swore under her breath and let her horse have its lead. It didn't need encouragement to get out of there.

Keanin and Edgar quickly caught up to her with Rachael, Tor Ranshal, and the cuari riding behind.

"We should stay and fight." She didn't want to face the vaens, but she, Keanin, Xalie, and Rachael were heavy magic users and could help.

"My companion says no," Edgar said. "She says our only chance is to get to the portal and destroy it—any-thing else might destroy us instead."

"I agree," Rachael added as she and Tor Ranshal rode closer. "Your purpose is not here."

"Damn it." Jenna crouched low on her horse as the vaens screamed behind them. She forced herself to not look back.

They kept running as long as it was safe for the horses. Because of the openness they were riding through, they saw that both groups had stayed to fight, but not the details.

Jenna patted the neck of her horse as they dropped to a trot. She wanted to go back and help the others, even though she knew why they couldn't.

"We keep going." Edgar took the lead. Whatever spell Rachael had placed on him must be still working as Car-abella and her cuari were close, but didn't seem to react to Xalie's presence.

Ghortin and the rest eventually faded completely from view and Carabella rode up to Jenna.

"He'll be fine. That son of mine is too stubborn to die and he won't let that happen to any of the others. Trust me." Carabella's smile was sincere and almost reached her eyes.

They kept to a trot for another hour with still no sign of Ghortin or the rest.

Edgar swore and pulled the taran wand out of his vest. "Ghortin?" The rest of the conversation was one-sided, but Edgar looked grim. "Thank you. Stay safe." He put his wand back.

"He says that the beasts escaped, and the fighters attacking them seem to be mostly trying to slow them down. Two clerics and three cuari have fallen so far. They'll catch up to us when they can. Oh, and he and Altheria spelled the taran wands. They won't need recharging, but they will probably be finished for good in a few hours. We won't have any way to communicate if this goes on longer than that."

Jenna shuddered. If this wasn't resolved by then, their side had lost and the wands wouldn't matter.

"Riders heading this way!" one of the cuari behind them shouted out.

A trail of dust indicated the direction of the new attackers—obviously, speed was more important than stealth.

"We keep going." Edgar's jaw clenched and his face looked like those words weren't his.

"*Keep going*," Typhonel's voice was faint but it echoed Xalie's.

Jenna was glad to finally hear him, faint or not. "*Where have you been? We're going to need help.*"

"*Qhazborh is blocking all deities. His avatar is ahead and must be destroyed. Ignore the ones coming toward you. I—*" his words cut off.

"*Typhonel? Are you there?*" Jenna called but there was no further response.

Keanin slowed as something about the approaching riders caught his attention. Jenna couldn't see anything beyond that there were riders and they were pushing their horses too hard.

"We have to keep going toward the portal," she said. If Typhonel and Xalie felt it, that was good enough for her. She still didn't like it.

"Something vile is coming our way." Keanin's face went pale and he pulled up a nasty feeling spell. "It's *them*." He kicked his horse to change direction to go after them, but the animal dropped its head and didn't move.

Rachael came next to him and put her hand on his arm. "You can't face them now. They were created to distract you. The powers behind them know that you are a key to destroying the portal. Listen to me, Keanin." Her voice was soft and if Jenna hadn't been next to them she wouldn't have heard her.

"I can't let them live." Keanin was shaking, but he wasn't trying to continue toward them.

"They won't. But we *have* to get to the portal before they do."

Jenna felt a spell flow over Keanin and his head briefly dropped.

"I will kill them all."

Rachael patted his shoulder. "You will. Not right now."

Jenna knew Rachael was a stronger magic user than most people realized, but she was still impressed at the subtle spell she'd put on Keanin.

He nodded then sent his horse trotting the way they'd been going.

Rachael came alongside Jenna as they rode. "I can't hold him for long. He'd break through a less subtle spell immediately, but this one works for now. He can't face them. Ever. It would destroy him. We weren't certain, but I feel it now."

"You said they were created to distract him from what he needed to do." Jenna kept her voice low but there was no one near the two of them as they rode.

"I lied." Rachael let out a sigh. "Those things were created for one purpose—to destroy Keanin. If that happens, we lose this fight."

Jenna watched as Edgar joined Keanin. She was impressed that Rachael's spell distracted him from his goal. But it was a matter of time before he shook it off.

"There's no other way we can protect him, is there?"

"Not unless the deities fully step in and destroy the aberrations. The demonspawn themselves were only able to get to this world because of Sacaranz and behind him, Qhazborh."

The land around them looked the same as it had for the past two hours, sandy dirt and a few rocks. In the distance ran a long mountain chain.

But even with the sameness, she swore she felt a chill in her soul when they crossed into the Markare. "We're here, aren't we?" She'd never been in the desert before, but some part of her recognized it and froze in terror. It was all she could do to not turn and race back out.

"Yes." Rachael reached out for her arm. "You need to stay calm. The essences of the Protectors who came before you are part of you—part of this. They will help you, but only if you stay calm and don't let their fear control you. Their terror is affecting you."

"Shouldn't someone have warned me of this?" Jenna focused on staying calm, but her heart was beating faster. "I *really* don't want to be here."

"Telling you earlier would have only made you more worried. Talk to them. Remind them this is why all of you are here. They can't reach you directly, but their emotions are flowing into you."

Jenna looked at her in doubt, then shrugged, this wouldn't be the strangest thing she'd done in the last year. *"I know you're frightened, and probably a few of you had bad things happen here—but it ends today. All that you lived and died for, ends today."*

There wasn't a verbal response, even in her head, but a slow-building wave of love and support flowed over her and the pressure to run away vanished.

"Thank you." Jenna turned to Rachael. "They aren't as upset now. Any chance they can help me destroy the portal?"

"Possibly, but they don't have any magic, it was all passed to you." Rachael's smile turned into a scream as an arrow missed Jenna's head by inches.

"We're under attack!" Edgar yelled as more arrows came their way.

"Elementals, can you block them?" Jenna yelled as all the mages cast shield spells. A riderless horse ran off into the desert, pointing out that not everyone had been covered.

"Protect."

Edgar, Jenna, and Keanin took the lead, with Rachael close behind.

"Paunians!" Tor Ranshal yelled from behind them. The attackers came into view. Tall and pale, they appeared to be kelar, but the markings on their faces made it difficult to tell. They held long bows and were far too good with them. The shield continued to protect Jenna and her companions but it appeared to be flickering.

Another group of attackers came from the other side. These weren't firing arrows but were pulling up spells.

"Followers of Qhazborh!" A cuari from the back shouted then raced his horse out of the protecting shields. He got a spell out and had stabbed one of the fighters when a familiar black-garbed being waved his hand from his horse and destroyed him.

"Ranz!" Keanin yelled this time. The Traanafaeren king, the man Keanin had viewed as a father, had been murdered by Sacaranz. Keanin charged toward the dark shape.

"I can't stop him this time." Rachael was feeding more spells into the shield but the enemy was coming close enough that it wouldn't matter anymore. And the elementals were winking out of existence as well.

Jenna and Edgar shared a look and raced after their friend. Jenna heard Rachael and Tor Ranshal yell after them but there was nothing they could do. Sacaranz wasn't getting Keanin if Jenna and Edgar could stop it.

Jenna glanced back as a roar was heard. The Paunians hit the line and mostly magicless fighting ensued. The cuari were using what magic they could but most of them were fighting with swords.

She saw more than a few struck down.

Keanin wouldn't stop and Jenna and Edgar raced alongside him. They'd nearly caught up to Sacaranz, he wasn't charging toward them but had come to a stop as his people attacked the line of cuari.

Jenna pulled out her dagger, magic alone couldn't kill him.

"Thank you for turning yourselves over. I promise, your deaths will be—"

Sacaranz's eyes went wide as Jenna threw her dagger, stabbing it into his chest before Keanin reached him.

Not a fatal shot, as he was still breathing, but Jenna kept moving forward and hit the dagger with the same magical force used to destroy the underwater portal. She felt the prior Protectors rally around her as they fed emotional energy through her and into the dagger.

"You can't—"

"We can." Jenna jumped off her horse as it got to Sacaranz.

She saw Keanin and Edgar fighting to keep the beings

with Sacaranz away from her, but she didn't care. He was the one who mindsacrificed the Protector whom Jenna had been shoved into in this world. He was the one who pulled her from Los Angeles and caused countless deaths.

She forced more magic and Power into him as she shoved the dagger further. "This is for everyone you've destroyed." She ducked away just before his body exploded.

Chapter Sixty-Six

—◆—

"JENNA! LOOK OUT!" KEANIN YELLED as a horse bore down on her.

She scrambled out of the way to find her horse standing nearby. Along with a clump of the remaining elementals.

"*Protect.*" They waited until she got back on her horse before returning to the battle.

The death of Sacaranz disbursed some of his people, but there were still too many fighters.

Jenna raced back into the fight; they couldn't win, but she wasn't going down easily.

A loud horn came from somewhere behind them and another group charged their way.

"What now?" Jenna yelled.

"It's the deathsworn! I can see their banner." Rachael also yelled, but it was in relief.

Jenna glanced over but the Paunian she was fighting commanded her attention. She'd take Rachael's word for it. There might be a banner over the quick-moving troops but she couldn't see what was on it.

Then the derawri came into view. On foot. Crell would have been proud as Tigan and his people turned the tide. The Paunians and Sacaranz's remaining followers they had been fighting were killed or raced off to the south.

Tigan was dirty and bloody as he jogged up to Jenna. "We are proud to have served." From his grin as he bowed, none of the blood on him was his own. "Thank you for saving some for us."

Rachael called everyone together, looking over the injured and saying a prayer over the dead. Then she turned to Tigan. "Your timing was welcome. But we still have to get these three to the portal." She looked around. "What happened to Ranz?" Because of the number of cuari surrounding her, she used the non-triggering nickname.

Edgar nodded toward Jenna. "She did. I saw him explode. Some of his followers escaped, but hopefully, they'll get lost in the desert."

"Good." Rachael and Keanin said at the same time.

"Are you okay?" Rachael asked Jenna but Keanin looked like he was about to.

"Right now, I have enough adrenaline to climb a mountain. Ask me when this is over." Jenna knew she should be freaked out by what she'd done, and she would be if they survived.

Carabella came forward and clasped Jenna's arm. "Thank you. I don't think I'm allowed to know who he really was, but that thing tried to take my son."

"You're welcome. How many were lost?" The dead cuari had vanished after Rachael's prayer.

Carabella's face was a combination of sorrow and confusion. "Fifteen. I honestly thought we couldn't die."

"Their sacrifices will never be forgotten." Tor Ranshal looked roughed up, but his sword was still out. "We need to keep moving."

Rachael nodded. "Edgar? Lead on."

Jenna looked around as they rode at a trot. "What happened to the elementals? They helped me not lose my horse or get trampled but then they vanished. I thought they'd come back to the group."

"Maybe they were called somewhere else," Carabella said as she rode alongside Jenna.

"I hope so. I'm sorry some of your people died."

"Thank you. When it was said my people were needed

to end this thing, I imagined a hundred, fully magic-using cuari simply destroying all that was in front of us. This wasn't what I thought would happen." She was silent for a moment. "But we will all give our lives to destroy that portal. Know that without a doubt."

"I think a scout or two might be in order as we get closer. Prince Corin and his forces should be making a stand not far from here," Tor Ranshal said.

Carabella nodded and waved to Mariword. "Let's show these young ones how scouting is done." With a nod to Jenna and the rest, the two cuari took off across the desert.

And came racing back less than five minutes later.

"We didn't see our people but there's a group behind us. And I don't believe it is Ghortin and his troop," Carabella said. If she was concerned that something got past Ghortin, she was fiercely not showing it.

"Stand and fight or run?" Keanin looked ready for either option. Most likely because he believed the ones behind them were the demonspawn.

"Running will tire your animals out." Tigan pulled out a far-seeing glass and looked behind them. "Standing is the better option."

"I agree for most of us." Tor Ranshal held up his hand. "Jenna, Keanin, and Edgar have to keep going. We can hold the enemy here, but if those three don't make it through, this is all for naught."

Tigan nodded and waved to a group of the deathsworn. "These will run with you and protect you as if you were our own."

Jenna opened her mouth to argue, she was leaving too many good people behind. If the demonspawn were behind them, there was a good chance that Ghortin, Altheria, Kaytine, and the rest were lost.

"No. You must do this. A warrior goes where they need to be. You three have a task that none of us can do," Tigan cut her off before she could argue. "My people know how to protect you. Let them do their job."

Jenna finally nodded and turned her horse back the way they'd been going. Edgar again took the lead and she, Keanin, and the deathsworn raced after him.

The deathsworn were impressive. Even at a full run they easily stayed with the horses.

Until they were suddenly surrounded by demonspawn.

Everyone skidded to a halt as a dozen demonspawn and a group of men who looked like distorted versions of Keanin suddenly appeared around them.

The horses reared, but Edgar, or most likely Xalie calmed them.

"We have been waiting for you." One of the Keanin clones grinned and stepped toward Keanin.

He was frozen, and his eyes were locked open in terror.

"That's what they did to him when they attacked him." Edgar raced forward knocking the closest copy to the ground. His horse stomped it into the ground.

The remaining copies and the demonspawn didn't even look at the fallen one but began chanting.

"They're calling their evil god to them!" Tigan ran through another clone. Again, none of the demonspawn looked like they even noticed.

Jenna felt the hair on the back of her neck rise. They were bringing Qhazborh to this plane.

"*Typhonel, they're cheating.*"

"*No, let it go.*" His voice was still faint.

"*Let what go? They're bringing in Qhazborh!*"

"*It needs to happen. I can't stay.*"

"*Typhonel?!*" Jenna yelled out in her mind, as a cold wind blasted through them.

The creature before them was similar to, but also different from the appearance of Irissanta and DOL. It was easily twenty feet tall and cloaked in black, but the face switched as the deities behind that name all showed themselves.

Unlike when the DOL and Irissanta had appeared, this being crackled with horrible and deadly energy.

"You believed that you could stop us? You? A nothing. A usurper of a true Protector. You aren't worthy to be alive." Qhazborh raised one hand and pointed it at her.

Jenna screamed as a bolt of energy flew into her and every nerve in her body felt like it exploded.

"Die now and take your worlds with you." Another bolt hit her. The demonspawn and clones were now fighting the deathsworn and her friends. Keanin had recovered and ran through two demonspawn and was spinning toward a clone when two beams of light appeared.

This time DOL and Irissanta were also twenty feet high.

"You have gone too far this time. You have done what cannot be undone." A lightning bolt ten times larger than what Qhazborh had hit her with slammed into the evil deities. Then a second one.

Jenna tumbled off her horse and fell to the ground. She had nothing left.

"You cannot remove me. The balance will be lost." Qhazborh tried to fight back, but the strikes against them were too much.

"The balance was destroyed long ago, and you broke the accord by repeated direct action on this plane." Irissanta took a step forward and put her hand on Qhazborh's heart. "Be gone."

Qhazborh exploded and the other two vanished.

The demonspawn collapsed and then turned to dust.

"At least they aren't zombies." Jenna laughed at her joke from her spot on the ground but she was sure no one else even heard it. The remaining Keanin clones appeared weak but they snarled as one and attacked.

One took an arrow to the throat and war cries were heard as more arrows flew.

Ghortin and Altheria led their group of cuari into the mess and quickly dispatched the remaining clones.

Jenna was glad her friends were still alive, but she still couldn't get to her feet. Her horse calmly remaining near her was the only thing that kept her from being trampled. There were still no elementals, but maybe they'd left instructions of some kind with her horse.

"Can you get to your feet?" Rachael got off her horse and ran to Jenna.

"I don't know. Whatever that thing did…it hurts." That was an understatement—there wasn't a part of her body that wasn't screaming in pain.

Rachael put her hand on Jenna's forehead and frowned. "Ghortin, when you're done having your moment, could you come here? Your apprentice needs you."

"Child, I am sorry." Ghortin was next to them in a moment. "Rachael, what do you need me to do?"

"That thing took too much of her energy. We need to replenish it, or she'll die before we can get to the portal. Are you able to assist?"

His look was grim, but he nodded.

"What? How are you two going to give me energy?" Jenna was alert enough that she didn't like the look on his face.

"I can help as well," Altheria said as she also got off her horse and joined them.

"We will all feed our energy to you. With three of us, the strain won't be too much for any of one person." Rachael's smile was too wide to be sincere. This was dangerous. "Before you protest, again, I have to remind you that if you or your two companions die before you destroy the portal, everything is lost."

Jenna nodded. "Fine, but only enough so I can destroy that thing. I can't lose any of you." She hoped that

Rachael recalled what Jenna could become if she lost too many people she cared about.

"Done." Rachael only said that word, repeated by Ghortin and Altheria and Jenna felt a rush of energy hit her.

She jumped to her feet. All three looked paler than before, but were trying to hide their fatigue. "Thank you, but it was too much."

"Not for what you three need to do." Ghortin adjusted his tunic. He was bloody, but intact and far better than she'd expected after facing the demonspawn.

She hugged him. "When I saw the demonspawn, I feared the worse."

"They fought us only to get around us and go after you. We held them as long as we could. Now, shall we destroy a portal?" He still looked tired, as did Rachael and Altheria, but they all got back on their horses.

Jenna got back on hers as well. "Let's do this."

Edgar again took the lead. The sounds of fighting were clear now so it wasn't hard to determine which way to go.

Within minutes they were on the rise of a hill, one that looked down over a plain with a massive stone ring taking up most of it.

Jenna took a few deep breaths. What she wouldn't give for a few dozen land dwelling kraken right now. The portal under the ocean had been huge, but this one looked to be a few city blocks long and easily five times as high as the deities who'd just left. How were three of them going to destroy something that big?

The fighters weren't that close to the portal itself, but five vaens were. They spread themselves out only a few feet in front of it. Right where Jenna and the others needed to be to cast their spell.

Tigan ran to Jenna. "I can take my people to remove

those things. Will you be safe with your remaining guards?" He nodded to the cuari and clerics behind them.

"Yes, but will you be safe? Those things are killers."

His grin was deadly. "So are we." He gave a deep bow, then he led his people through the fighting and toward the vaens. It seemed like he'd added more deathsworn as he ran, but Jenna didn't see Crell in the group.

Carabella rode up. "My people and I will escort you three once those monsters are gone. Be ready, there could be more enemies coming."

Jenna nodded and motioned for Edgar and Keanin to move closer to her. "As soon as it's clear, we let the cuari take us down there. Start saying the spell as soon as we're close enough."

"We're ready." Edgar's grin was calm.

Keanin looked a bit more on edge, but he gave a nod.

The deathsworn reached the vaens and a group of heavily armed Paunians who rose to defend the beasts.

The fighting was short but intense. Then there were only two vaens and a handful of Paunians all of whom ran off with the deathsworn fast behind them.

"Now!" Carabella yelled and took the lead as the cuari surrounded Keanin, Edgar, and Jenna and raced to the portal. The fighting was still fierce around them, but no one successfully stood against the cuari. The cuari might not have much magic right now, but they were still a force to be reckoned with.

Jenna tried to focus and not look around for her friends, but it was hard.

They got to the front with the cuari forming a wall behind them. All three jumped off their horses and began the spell as the sound of the fight pushed closer.

CHAPTER SIXTY-SEVEN

THEY COMPLETED THE SPELL, CAREFULLY ignoring the desperate fighting all around them.

But nothing happened.

The portal was still standing. The three looked at each other and ran through the spell again as the fighting behind them grew closer.

The portal was no closer to exploding than it had been when they got there. Jenna felt the spell, it was exactly how they'd practiced it—but the portal stood there silently mocking them.

"We need to do something to make it work!" Jenna yelled to Edgar and Keanin but they shrugged and began the spell again. The cuari guarding them were holding on, but many had fallen. And the fighting closing in on them from all sides.

"*Typhonel! We need help!*" Jenna put as much Power into her mental cry as possible. This was his purpose, he needed to be here. "*We can't destroy the portal.*"

"*I have found what is wrong. You must go through the portal and return me to my body.*"

That wasn't what she'd been hoping for. But she and the others continued to recite the spell that should destroy the portal, but nothing changed.

She'd been afraid of losing someone she loved, the greatest sacrifice. She hadn't realized that it would be herself.

"*Is there no other way?*" She continued repeating the spell words.

"No. I now know why the portal couldn't be destroyed before. My body and soul were split and that is holding the portal open. The passage will remain open as long as I remain separated."

"But you'll die too." Jenna looked around. Storm and many of her friends had been pushed closer to them, but they were still fighting for their lives. And to protect the three of them. The numbers of their enemies were reduced but still overwhelming. And there was always the chance that armies of horrific monsters could come through the portal if it wasn't destroyed fast enough. Her people weren't going to be able to hold on for long.

"My existence will be whole again and I will continue." There was enough sorrow in his voice that she figured out the same couldn't be said for her.

"What do I do?"

"Cast this spell to keep others away from you, then run into the portal. It will be destroyed."

Jenna felt the spell as he mentally sent it. It was strong and would help if anyone figured out what she was doing and tried to stop her. Then she jogged toward the area in the center of the portal. She'd been closer to the side when they cast their spells, but she needed to make sure no one could block her.

"Jenna? What are you doing?" Storm's fight had moved him even closer to her and after running through the Paunian he was fighting, he raced over to her.

"I have something to do. It's what was meant to happen." A strange calmness came over her—this was intended for the Protector since the beginning. The final act of protection.

Would have been nice if there had been a warning about it in those cuari books.

Her intention must have shown on her face as he turned to the portal, then back to her and grabbed her arms. "No!"

Jenna clutched Storm as he fought to hold her back.

She forced him to look down into her eyes. "I love you more than anyone I've loved before. You mean more to me than my own life. But I can't let you stop this. It's what needs to be done." She put her hand on his chest and sent the spell into him as she kissed him. "Typhonel is what's keeping the portal open. I have to take him back."

"Jenna, you can't—"

Jenna cut him off with another kiss, their last, and pushed his chest. Hard. The spell she'd sent into him sent his body flying over the rest of their people but would give him a soft landing. She'd be gone by the time he could run back to her.

Then she ran like mad and dove into the open portal.

The feeling of a slamming door as she cleared the portal told her that the spell they'd used to destroy it was now in play. They'd just needed this one final piece for it to work.

There was nothing where she was now. Light and sound flowed around her but were distant and vague.

Her body felt like it was being pulled apart slowly.

"Thank you." A force pulled itself away from her and appeared before her. Tall and severe, she somehow knew it was Typhonel. "I will now exist as I was meant to. But as I could not remain on the other side in my partial state, you cannot remain here."

She felt a shove, not unlike the one she'd hit Storm with, and then she was flung out of the portal and slammed into the sand on the other side. Hard.

A moment after she hit the ground, the huge portal exploded into a massive dust storm.

Storm fought his way through the sandstorm of portal particles as they whirled in a massive cyclone to reach her first.

"Jenna!" He slid to her, holding her so close to his chest that she couldn't respond.

Even when the air came back into her lungs.

She patted his back to get him to release her. "I'm here." She was laughing and crying as they held onto each other.

"I thought I'd lost you."

"You did. Typhonel left me and sent me back here." She felt okay but odd. A part of her was missing.

Fighting continued around them, but the followers of Qhazborh and Sacaranz were growing fewer. The remaining Paunians were fleeing in the distance, most being chased by some enthusiastic cuari. And there were two more dead vaen nearby.

Ghortin, Keanin, Edgar, and Crell all ran forward. They were battered and bruised, but alive.

Then Xalie stepped out from behind them. And she looked solid.

Jenna panicked as she looked where the cuari were finishing off the enemies from Strann. "How are you here? And should you be here?"

"Edgar has recovered enough to be on his own." Xalie grinned. "Typhonel pushed me into a full existence on this plane when you both vanished into the portal. In part because of the destruction of the deities known as Qhazborh. Their collapse destabilized the spells set upon the cuari. *All of the cuari.* The one hundred will have their real memories slowly returned to them. The rest of the cuari who were not following Sacaranz or Qhazborh will return here. You saved us."

Jenna smiled and looked around. The injured were being attended to, and the dead would be buried. But the world was safe. All of the worlds were safe. She leaned into Storm's arms. "I've had enough excitement for a dozen lifetimes. Let's go home and have a nice boring life."

Dear reader,

Thank you for joining me in the concluding adventure for The Books of the Cuari trilogy. Writing this third book has been a joy tinged with sadness—saying goodbye (for now ;)) to any characters is always hard. But more adventures might just pop up for our friends down the line!

Until then, check to see if any of my other series tickle your fancy. *https://marieandreas.com/books.html*.

The website also has a blog where I post ramblings of writing, my words, and sometimes character interviews!

If you want to keep up on the further adventures of any of my characters, make sure to visit my website and sign up for my mailing list. *http://marieandreas.com/index.html*

You can also sign up on Amazon to follow me and they will keep you updated on new releases. Marie Andreas Amazon

If you enjoyed this book, please spread the word! Positive reviews mean more than you know.

Thank you again—and keep reading!

Marie

ABOUT THE AUTHOR

MARIE IS A MULTI-AWARD-WINNING FANTASY and science fiction author with a serious reading addiction. If she wasn't writing about all the people in her head, she'd be lurking about coffee shops annoying total strangers with her stories. So really, writing is a way of saving the masses. She lives in the fantasyland known as Southern California and dreams of castles and forests.

She is a proud member of SFWA (Science Fiction and Fantasy Writers Association) and NINC (Novelists, Inc.).

When not saving the masses from coffee shop shenanigans, Marie likes to visit the UK and keeps hoping someone will give her a nice summer home in the Forest of Dean or Conwy, Wales.